Nightwood

Elana Gomel

Crystal Lake Publishing
www.CrystalLakePub.com

WELCOME
TO ANOTHER

CRYSTAL LAKE PUBLISHING
CREATION

Join today at www.crystallakepub.com & www.patreon.com/CLP

Dark Fantasy set in the Soviet Empire.

"...intensely creative, hard-hitting work..."
- Kirkus Reviews

"The place where all the victims died, the bloodlands, extends from central Poland to western Russia, through Ukraine, Belarus, and the Baltic States."

—Timothy Snyder, *Bloodlands*

Part One:

A Good Marriage

Suzie was lost once again.

Mitch Webster was not worried. He knew she would turn up soon enough, wandering into the living room or the kitchen with that gentle, dreamy expression on her face that he had learned to dread, the fat tomcat named Max following, rubbing against her legs in the hope of getting a treat. She would call him Patsy. Patsy the dachshund had been dead for six years.

Mitch got up from his kneeling position in front of the fireplace where he had been patiently stacking firewood, his lower back responding with a flare of pain. The aches that a body accumulated as it moved inexorably toward its final destination were getting worse. Well, every man had to die. But he was determined to go into the darkness with his mind intact, and so far, his resolution seemed to work. As for Suzie . . .

It was not Alzheimer's; the doctors said. They averted their eyes and spoke in smooth platitudes about "unspecified dementia" and "general decline". These were sneaky codes for their ignorance and helplessness. But Mitch knew what it was. The love of his life was leaving him.

A door banged and Suzie walked in, shedding twigs and needles from the disheveled bunch of branches she carried in her arms. Could she be so far gone as not to realize that green wood was useless for fire?

She looked animated, her eyes sparkling, and his heart leaped, as it always did when he saw her. Forty years of marriage, and the magic was still there.

"What is it, darling?" he asked gently.

"I found it, Mitch! I found it!"

"Found what, baby?"

"The tree!"

"What tree?"

She pouted and dumped the branches onto the floor in front of the fireplace. Max scuttled away, his tail indignantly lashing his rotund sides. Mitch sighed. He would have to clean up the mess later, after Suzie went to bed. She often grew upset when he corrected her household blunders. She threw a fit when he was too conspicuous about laundering the red-stained lace curtains she had put into the washer together with a velvet throw.

"The singing tree. The ash! Come on, Mitch, don't you remember?"

He had no idea what she was talking about, but then something stirred at the back of his mind. A fairy tale, wasn't it? A guest at one of the dinner parties from the time when they still had dinner parties . . . He saw an ash-tree, rare in the redwoods of Northern California. What did he say? Ash, a pale tree. Ash, a maiden tree. Ash . . . a witch-tree?

"I thought we cut it down a long time ago," he said uncertainly.

"No! It's still there! Bigger than before!"

"What about it?"

"It spoke to me!" Suzie cried triumphantly.

Mitch felt a chill worm its way down his back. What if Suzie's problem was getting worse? What if it was developing into psychotic delusions?

"Come on, Suzie!" he barked, desperate to force herself back into sanity. "Trees don't talk!"

"Really?" she sneered. "What about that?"

She picked up one of the branches and thrust it into Mitch's face. He drew away from the leaves that rustled loudly . . . too loudly.

He bent closer, listening. How could the leaves rustle at all when Suzie held the branch steady? And yet he could distinctly hear a soft susurrus, a humming overlapping sound.

He pulled back and stared at Suzie in horror. Was she infecting him with her madness? Was it his turn to succumb to the ravages of age that were devouring her mind? But she looked neither senile nor decrepit. The dusk erased her wrinkles, and the fire in the fireplace lent its glow to her cheeks and its luster to her eyes.

The voices rose from the greenwood like dripping sap, vague but overwhelming, shaping themselves into articulate words.

Song of youth
Music of rebirth
Ash will sing
Ash will sing for you

"What is this?" Mitch cried.

"The trees are speaking," Suzie explained patiently, as if talking to the toddlers that their middle-aged sons used to be.

"How is that possible?"

"They've always spoken, Mitch," Suzie said. "You know it. This is why we are here. Because they've always spoken to us. Trees are our friends."

Yes, indeed. This was why they were here, in that isolated house in the remote Santa Cruz Mountains. This was why they always rejected the subtle and not-so-subtle hints from the kids that they should move down to the Peninsula and look for a nice senior facility. Because this was the place. The place of magic. They worshipped in the Church in the Woods but in truth the woods themselves were their church.

Suzie let the branch drop and smiled at Mitch, blinding him with her suddenly resurrected beauty. The branch rustled at his feet. The rest of the tree limbs scattered on the floor took up the chant. The firs and redwoods outside amplified it to the point of the volume being almost too high, the meaning almost too clear . . .

Music of youth
Song of rebirth!
"They are giving us a chance, Mitch. A new lease on life."
Ash will sing
Ash will sing for you.

"The trees live long and put out new leaves every spring. The trees know the secret of rejuvenation."
Song of rebirth!
"Ash will sing for us, and we'll be young again. Just as we used to be, my love!"
Ash will sing!
"Yes," Mitch whispered. "Yes!"

The woods were magic, he had always known it. And if this magic wanted to reward him, give him back what the cruelty of time had taken away, why not?
Ash will sing for you!
"We'll be young again!"
Ash needs to be fed.

You'll feed Ash and he'll sing for you!

"What?" Mitch shook himself, surfacing momentarily from the enchantment that enveloped him like the memory of Suzie's smile on the day they met. "What does it mean?"

"Nothing comes for free, darling. We know that. You pay for what you want."

"Pay? How?"

"Ash is hungry. Ash will feed. Ash will sing for you."

Susie's hair, still long and full, swished about her shoulders, its silver turning back into gold.

"Trees need to be fed. The soil here is thin and bitter. They'll make us whole again if we give them what they want."

Song of youth

Song of rejuvenation.

"I'll bring tons of fertilizer if this is what they want!" Mitch cried.

"No, not chemical muck. Something else, something real."

"What's real, Suzie?"

"Blood."

Chapter 1:

Homecoming

There was a face in the cabin's window.

Ally blinked and it was gone. Just a spot of reflected light in the dirty glass. She twisted in the passenger seat, looking back at the ramshackle little hut made even smaller by the contrast with the impossibly tall trees that nodded over it.

"Somebody lives here?" she asked Carl.

"Nah! It's been abandoned . . . like, forever. I don't even know who it belongs to. The Websters may know."

Yes, the Websters. And the Singers. And the Murphys. And the gay couple whose names Carl had forgotten. And Mike and Laura, whose name he pronounced differently every time. And some families who were of no account because they rented their mansions on the mountain rather than owned them. All the people Ally had not met yet. All her future neighbors.

The Tesla navigated yet another hairpin bend in the road, which narrowed down to one lane. Ally gripped the edge of her seat, trying to convince herself she could drive. She had received her international driver's license from an outfit that would certify a blind man for an appropriate fee. Her Gucci bag slipped off her knees, the wallet flopping out. She quickly picked it up, reassured by its thickness. It held her license and her green card, along with her embarrassing and soon-not-to-be-needed passport.

Carl's hands were negligently caressing the wheel. Square hands lightly dusted with . . . freckles?

Age spots.

The view was breathtaking. The road was dappled in gold and green as the sun broke through the feathery branches of Douglas firs. Under their thin crowns, curlicues of shed bark created a mosaic of bronze, ocher, and pink. Occasionally, the bright strawberry-colored trunk of a madrone flashed by like a ruby set in jade.

Another hairpin—and she gasped. The redwoods started here, slender giants piercing the pale sky whose light caught in their furry paws. Their size felt like a personal insult, reducing her to the insignificance of a bug crawling in the grass.

She glanced to the right and was surprised how far down the slope she could see through the sparse undergrowth. The tree colossi let few rivals flourish around their majestic trunks. The moss-covered ground was dotted with giant mushrooms. She blinked and reality reasserted itself: they were actually boulders, sticking up from the powdery soil. All proportions were askew here because of the redwoods.

"Pretty, huh?" Carl said smugly. "Like a fairy tale."

"Fairy tales are not pretty," Ally said.

He smiled indulgently and she squashed her irritation. He was a good man, she reminded herself. A kind and loving man. His occasional boasting was a small matter. So what if he talked as if the entire wilderness belonged to him?

Perhaps it did. Hadn't he told her he owned a large piece of land along with the house?

They owned, she corrected herself. *They.*

She lightly touched her ring, a small modest affair, just like their wedding. But the diamond was real, and so was the marriage, and so was her status, and so was—

The car swerved sharply, its front wheels digging into the friable shoulder, scattering fir needles, hanging over the edge, the whole thing dipping, a kaleidoscope of light and dark, her strangled squeaking, as if she did not dare scream . . . and then it all stopped, and the car was back on the road, and Carl was swearing.

"Bloody deer!"

"Deer?" she whispered.

"Yes, didn't you see? A silly bugger just about jumped over us!"

Had there been a deer? Had she actually seen a pale fawn shape streak across her field of vision, suspended in the air like a monstrous butterfly? Yes, she must have seen it. She had. It must have been a deer; what else would it be?

The past was so much easier to live with when you could edit it at will.

Nightwood

The Tesla pulled into a broad driveway peppered with gravel and moss. And here it was. The house. Her new home.

It was long, and slinky, and transparent, built into the long slope that led down from the road into the wilderness of tanoaks and firs. Coiling ground fog crawled up its glass walls. It blended so well with its surroundings that it appeared inconspicuous despite its impressive size. Most of its bulk was hidden by the slope and masked by the scatter of native bushes in the unfenced front yard. Above loomed the redwoods, leaning over the house as if curious to peek into the exposed lives of its inhabitants.

Carl jumped out and trotted toward the house. He paused in the covered walkway that led to the front door, looked back at her.

"Welcome home!" he said.

Ally got out of the Tesla, her legs cramping after the long drive. She stood there, gaping at the house.

Houses are supposed to provide shelter. Houses are supposed to be where you hide away from the night, and the things that walk in the night. Houses are not supposed to be open to the woods.

"Come on!"

She walked to the glass door, tottering on her kitten heels.

At least the kitchen was brightly lit.

It was huge. On one side it blended into a dining space fronted by French windows. On the other, it was separated from the enormous living room by a bar. The top of the bar carried a motley collection of knick-knacks which got in her way while she was making dinner, no matter how careful she tried to be, but the kitchen was so crowded with mementos of other lives that Ally inadvertently knocked down a framed photograph. She restored it to its place, noting that it depicted Carl with another man and two women. Was one of them Ros?

Well, what difference did it make? These people were of no consequence anymore. People of the past.

Everything in the kitchen was big, expensive, and confusing: the green Australian-stone countertops, the large island bearing an electric range, and several ovens that stared at her haughtily with their complicated dials. The hanging lamps in red and blue glass shades provided enough illumination (and got in her way) but beyond the French window was only darkness. The ocean of green was veiled by the impenetrable night. The glow from the kitchen petered in a snarl of shadows in the huge living room. And beyond the insubstantial glass walls the redwoods nodded and whispered in the dull sky. There were no streetlights. And no sounds from the outside, except the susurrus of the rising wind.

Ally deliberately clattered pots and pans—and stopped. It sounded like a provocation.

Her nights had never been silent. Not in Mama's tiny apartment filled with traffic hum and the retching of the perpetually drunk policeman who lived next door; not when she was on her own and had to turn off the lights, so that the hammering on the door would stop and the men would go away; not even in the students' dorms in Berkeley. Malika, her roommate, liked to hang out with girls in bright headscarves whose chatter in a language she did not understand was the background to Ally's struggle with her Advanced Anthropology textbook.

The potatoes had been sliced and plunged into icy water, the meatballs oozed juices through their coating of breadcrumbs, the cucumbers and tomatoes for the salad had been chopped. All she needed was oil.

The countertop held several bottles of virgin olive oil from Spain and California, but nobody cooked with olive oil at home! She needed canola. Ally opened the enormous fridge and stared in disbelief at the supermarket-like display of sauces and condiments. Search of the freezer revealed stacks of frozen pizza and burgers.

Who kept the fridge stocked? It couldn't possibly have been in the same state since Ros' death, could it?

She closed the fridge. Carl was in his office, talking with some angel investor. Ally did not want to run to him with every paltry question like a little girl tugging on her Daddy's hand. He was her husband, not her father. And she had never had—or needed—a father.

Ally looked around and saw the door: a smooth tawny wood, flush with the wall. She pulled it but it did not bulge, so she pushed it instead. The door swung open and she saw—nothing. Inside the doorframe was a rectangle of blackness. The light from the kitchen stopped at the threshold.

Ally reached inside and felt a shy brush, as if a mass of cobwebs met her questing fingers. And then something tangible nested in her hand—a cord. Ally tugged on it and a small bulb came on, revealing steep stairs going down. A basement?

She hesitated on the first step. There was a chilly draft wafting from the depth and she heard a scratchy sound like a mouse trying to run away. How big should a mouse be to make such deliberate noise?

Ally was not superstitious: nothing supernatural could be as bad as real life. But she was unwilling to plumb the house's underbelly just now. Darkness outside and darkness inside; and the glass house a thin treacherous membrane between the two.

She began to turn when something made her look back.

Standing on the lowest step, just where the thin light dissolved into the murk, was a bottle of oil.

Ally sprinted out of the basement and slammed the door shut.

"Great potatoes!" Carl speared the last golden-brown piece on his fork. The meatballs were scattered around his plate.

Ally sipped her Mondavi pinot noir. The famous wine felt rough on her palate. The candles reflected in the window along with the red and blue lamps, making the glass wall look like an aquarium of dark water filled with luminescent jellyfish.

"You didn't like the meatballs?"

"They're a little . . . " he shrugged. "Too much bread, maybe?"

"Sorry."

"No, it's okay. I can grab some burgers tomorrow. But you need to start eating meat, honey. Just look at yourself. A gust of wind could blow you away!"

There was genuine concern in his voice and Ally patted his hand in gratitude. There was no way she would share his burgers or taste her own meatballs. Ally had been a natural vegetarian since birth. Mama told her how, as a toddler, she would cry herself blue in the face when offered a piece of boiled chicken or a slice of kielbasa. To her credit, Mama had never tried to force her, simply accepting this oddity of her daughter's and trying to find alternative means of keeping her alive, which was not easy in the penury and chaos of those ruined years. Ally would reluctantly drink kefir and swallow boiled eggs, but she adamantly refused to eat any meat. She herself did not know why. She was not a militant vegan and had no problem cooking meat for others, but the disgust that welled up when she saw a piece of flesh on her plate was as undeniable as physical pain.

She sipped more wine and felt her head fill with lightness like a helium balloon.

Carl smiled at her. The soft candlelight smoothed away a decade from his face, molded the hanging jowls back into a firm jawline, darkened the silvery hair to its original sandy color. She smiled back, giving another tiny push to her gratitude until it became affection.

"Let's go to bed," he said. "I'm pooped."

She started stacking the dishes in the sink to wash them tomorrow. He stopped her and showed her the built-in dishwasher that yawned like a hungry mouth. By the time Ally filled it, Carl was already in the master bedroom suite, which occupied a separate wing of the house.

She turned off the lights and stepped out of the kitchen to face the cavernous darkness of the living room. It felt as if she had stepped into the forest. In the dark, the glass walls were invisible. The bushes reached out for her, the furry branches of redwoods scraped at the charcoal sky, and the dense firs wove the spiky tapestry of black on black. In the clearing that was the living room, the low shapes of couches and armchairs crouched like sleeping predators. Ally grasped a supporting pillar, took a step forward. Blurry shadows danced as the wind picked up. A whitish tentacle of fog slithered along the wall, keeping pace with her, and then a sharp bang came from behind her.

Abandoning her dignity, Ally ran to the bedroom suite and closed the door behind her. She found herself in a wide hallway that opened onto a tiled room with a marble spa and a sauna. To the sides of the hallway were two bathrooms, his and hers; two dressing rooms, and the master bedroom itself, door slightly ajar. Carl's reassuring snores drifted out.

Ally peered into the spa room and quickly ducked back. The spa was glass-walled too, surrounded by gnarly shadows. Her bathroom, on the other hand, had proper solid walls and a cheerful flowery curtain. She relaxed.

Standing in front of the mirror, Ally pulled out the pins that kept her braids wound around her head. She shook her hair loose and it fell to her knees, a shiny waterfall, enveloping her slim figure like a golden cloak.

She was pretty but there were women prettier than her. She was smart but not a genius. She was tough and determined but so were millions of refugees and migrants washing up on the world's unwelcoming shores. The only thing unique about her, the only attribute that set her apart, her only true wealth, was her hair. Mama used to call it "fairy gold", and it turned out her fairy gold had an exchange rate, after all. It had bought her this fancy house, the joint bank account, and the husband to underwrite it all.

She quickly finished in the bathroom and snuck into the bedroom. Carl's snores changed in pitch as he rolled over and threw his heavy arm over her. Normally, she had to steel herself to suffer the noise but now she was glad of it. It covered up the distant bang coming from the heart of the house.

Chapter 2:
The Witch

Morning, and Ally was frying eggs.

Her messily done braid slapped her back as she scuttled between the range and the counter. She had not had the time to brush and braid her hair properly, a procedure that could take as much as an hour. Carl liked his breakfast early.

A rhythmic noise was coming from the basement gym where he was running on the treadmill. The door stood open and, in the fresh morning light, her night fears appeared ridiculous.

Carl came up, mopping his neck with a towel, his meaty shoulders straining his SLAC T-shirt. His belly, big despite his regimen of exercise, hung above the waistband of his shorts.

"Mm, smells good!"

She kissed his sweaty cheek. His kindness made up for everything, even the fact that he was her husband.

She poured coffee from the coffeemaker that she was proud to know how to operate. Carl added cream and sugar to his; she put a slice of lemon into hers.

After breakfast, Carl took a quick shower and was on his way out the door, only pausing to toss the keys to the Prius onto the counter and instruct her to have dinner ready by 7 p.m. The bright yellow Tesla roared out of the driveway and disappeared down the snaky road. Ally was alone.

It felt as if the house suddenly released a long breath. She stood still, staring into the front yard, covered by a tangle of wild strawberries and native grasses. Front yards in Berkeley were small and pretty, bordered by a picket fence and boasting perfectly mowed lawns. Ally used to wander off Shattuck Avenue to gaze at the islands of soft grass with nodding irises and kids' bicycles, trying to imagine herself in possession of such a paradise. And here she was, mistress of a place that would dwarf suburban homes ten times over!

She cautiously opened the front door. The cool air was intoxicating, spiced up with a medley of unfamiliar green smells. Everything here was a little off, even the pine scent which she remembered from her infrequent country outings with Mama before . . . well, before. But then the redwoods were not really pines, were they?

The trees were all around her, choking her field of vision with their endless shades of green: the tarnished emerald of tanoaks, the blackish viridian of firs, the hard coppery sheen of madrones, and the somber duskiness of redwoods. Carl had bragged how his house—*their* house—was situated in the open space, far from the suffocating proximity of others, but she felt hemmed in.

There were flowering bushes at the end of the driveway. Lilacs? Ally ran toward them, only to draw back in disappointment when she saw they were not lilacs at all. Not Mama's favorite flower with its heart-shaped leaves and heavy clusters of fragrant blossoms. These flowerets were meager and stiff, their smell faint. Of course: the native Californian bush *Ceanothus*.

Ally turned back to the house. And almost stepped on something that looked like a length of copper pipe that crept away on a slimy skirt. The thing was a slug as long as her hand! She shook her head, torn between wonder and revulsion.

She went to her refuge: the bathroom and the dressing room where she could draw the curtain and not see the woods. But she could not hide there forever. Ally put on some of her new clothes, bought in Westfield Mall where she spent more money in one glorious afternoon than Mama had made in a year. She proudly emerged into the main part of the house, smelling of a Jo Malone perfume and wearing Free People jeans, only to shrink under the indifferent gaze of the wilderness. The emerald light was dimmer. The clouds were coming. from below, crawling upslope like large puffy whales. The sky above the treetops was still clear, but there was a dullness in the air like a disturbed sediment in muddy water.

Ally stepped out onto the backyard deck and saw in the gaps between the redwood trunks glints of blue and white: the bay and the salt marshes around it. She was struck by the sudden longing to be down there. There were people all around the Peninsula. And cars. And stores. And coffee shops.

A sharp knock shattered the silence.

Ally jumped and scanned the treetops. Carl had warned her that dry branches could break off suddenly and fall onto the house. She could see nothing untoward.

The knock came again, and Ally realized it was coming from the front door. She went back inside and saw a dark silhouette through the glass. The visitor was getting impatient. Ally had no idea who it could be and unexpected guests always made her nervous, but she reminded herself it was California and boldly strode to the door and unlocked it.

For a moment, she and the woman stared at each other, both shocked by the other's appearance. The woman apparently had not expected Ally; Ally had not expected a witch.

"Witch" was an unkind description, but it fit. The woman was tall and shapeless, flesh falling off her in random rolls and bulges even though she was not obese. Her ensemble of an oversized t-shirt and capris did nothing to improve her appearance, and the most striking thing about her was the absence of a chin: her face sloped away into her neck, loose flesh piling up above her breasts.

"Is Mr. Morris home?" The witch inquired in a brassy voice. "I thought I saw his car last night."

Ally forced her fascinated gaze away from the woman's shaking wattles.

"He's gone to work," she replied.

"And you are . . . ?"

Ally frowned. She knew when she was being put down.

"I'm Mrs. Morris. Who are you?"

The witch's eyes opened wide.

"Of course!" she exclaimed. "We've heard about Carl's marriage! I'm so sorry, dear, we didn't expect . . . Anyway, sorry again, and let me introduce myself. I'm Pat Donegan; we are your neighbors down the road. May I come in?"

Ally reluctantly nodded.

The witch—Pat—plunked herself down at the breakfast counter, her small, sharp eyes scanning the kitchen as if taking inventory. She picked up a framed photograph—the same photograph Ally had almost broken last night—and sighed deeply.

"I'm glad it's still here!" she exclaimed. "Of course, dear, you might want to redecorate but I'd be sorry to see it go! So many memories!"

Ally studied the picture. It showed Carl—a much younger Carl, his belly a slight bulge under his tight-fitting shirt—laughing on the beach in the company of another young man and two women. Carl's arm was looped around the shoulders of one of the women.

"This is me!" Pat said. "Can you believe it? Santa Barbara, twenty years ago!" she sighed. "I wouldn't wear this swimsuit today, believe me!"

In Ally's opinion, she should not have worn it then either: even though Pat's body twenty years ago bore less resemblance to a melted candle, it was not exactly made for a bikini.

"This is my husband, Kyle," Pat prattled on, pointing to the other man whose most distinguishing characteristic was a face of bushy hair that Ally thought of as the Cossack moustache. "We've been Carl's friends and neighbors forever!"

"And who is this?" Ally asked, pointing to the woman Carl's arm was resting on.

Pat's disheveled brows rose slightly.

"Oh, didn't he tell you?"

"Tell me what?"

"It's his . . . it's Ros."

"Oh," Ally said, scanning the picture. She was sure Pat would read more into her exclamation of surprise than what was there and was trying to figure out how to amend the situation. But why should she care? Whatever mistaken conclusions this unpleasant stranger would draw about her, it was no skin off her nose. On the other hand, Pat was her neighbor and if she was to be believed, Carl's dearest friend . . .

Then why hadn't he mentioned her when describing the people living in the woods?

Conscious of Pat's scrutiny, Ally handed the picture back to her. Ros Morris had been a beautiful woman twenty years ago when Ally was in the kindergarten: dark hair, dark eyes, a dazzling smile, curvaceous body. What she had been before her death of lung cancer a year ago, Ally neither knew nor cared.

"Would you like some tea?" she asked Pat.

"Herbal, if you have any."

"We don't."

"Coffee will do, then."

Ally poured some for herself as well, defiantly adding lemon. For a moment they sipped in silence, glancing at each other over the rims of their mugs.

"I'm so sorry," Pat said, "I didn't catch your name. This accent you have . . . "

Ally's cheeks flamed and she hated herself for her fair skin that blushed so easily.

"Ally," she said, enunciating it as clearly as she could.

"Is it your real name? Pat asked. "Oh, I'm sorry, I apologize, I'm putting it so badly. What I mean is, did you change your name or something?"

Ally looked her straight in the eyes.

"It is my name," she said coldly.

"And where are you from?"

"Ukraine."

She did not elaborate, and Pat asked no more questions. She just nodded and finished her coffee.

"I have to run," she said, getting up. "It was so delightful to meet you . . . Ally. Could you please tell Carl we'd love to have you over for dinner this week? On the other hand, don't bother. I'll give him a call."

Ally watched Pat get into her car that she had parked in the driveway. Didn't she say they lived close by? But she was used to Americans driving distances that normal people would cover in a five-minute walk.

She went back into the kitchen. The hushed silence of the morning had been shattered by the intrusion and she did not know whether to feel angry or relieved. The sense she had had of being watched by the trees had dissipated; now the multihued layers of green outside had flattened out into a mere backdrop.

Without the ominousness, the magic had gone as well.

"Banana slug," Carl said.

They were lounging in the hot tub in the spa room. Outside, the velvety sky was crisscrossed by the delicate lace of branches. The sun had set but the mauve light still lingered, giving a strange otherworldly glow to the empty road. Ally had been surprised by Carl's unconcern that their naked bodies lit by the flicker of candles could be seen from the outside, but he told her nobody was likely to drive by. Indeed, their house was the last one on the road, which terminated in the perpetually locked gate, guarding the entrance to an open space preserve. Considering that their road was private, it was not clear to her how hikers were supposed to get there.

"Banana slug?" she repeated, wrinkling her nose.

Her head was buzzing again. Carl had insisted on having a glass of wine in the hot tub and she went along.

"They are harmless. But funny-looking, I agree." He laughed raucously and reached for her, stroking her cheek, then running his fingers gently down her throat. Ally sighed. She was not exactly in the mood; she also knew, from experience, that if she told Carl she wasn't, he would instantly desist. Paradoxically, the knowledge made her want to be in the mood, which was almost as good as the real thing. So, they retired into the bedroom where she turned off all the lights—not out of modesty but because then she could pretend to be surrounded by opaque walls. And eventually, pleasantly tired, she snuggled up to the snoring bulk of her husband. She poked him to make him roll over, thought of her new Alexander Wang dress, and sunk into restful sleep.

Ally woke up suddenly and completely. She seldom remembered her dreams, but she knew this one to have been unpleasant.

She lay on her back staring into the gray play of shadows on the high gabled ceiling. Carl was a still bundle under the blanket on the opposite side of the king-sized bed. The bedroom was as transparent as the rest of the house, its walls mere glass panes held together by narrow wooden frames. Even the roof had glass panels set into it. Ally turned her head and squinted into the spiky curtain of thorns interspersed with vague greyish splotches that she took for boulders, even though she did not remember any boulders on this side of the house. She sought the glimmer of stars but although she could discern where the black lace of branches ended and the gunmetal-colored sky began, it appeared overcast. She felt exposed, like a mouse with an invisible owl patrolling the sky.

What was the point of having a house like that? Ally had never asked Carl why he had built this multi-million-dollar glass box in the middle of the Santa Cruz Mountains, so far from the nearest town that getting a carton of milk necessitated an hour's drive. Seclusion? Beauty? A place for his cars?

Could she induce him to move elsewhere? But where? All of

America would be as alien to her as this place. She might just as well try to make the best of it.

She would be happy to hear Carl's snoring now but perversely, he was as quiet as a dead man. Perhaps he *was* dead, felled in the middle of the night by a quick stroke, and she was all alone here, surrounded by miles and miles of dark woods, in bed with a corpse.

Ally sat up in bed, kicking off the handmade quilt, and shivered. She was sleeping naked, and the house was unaccountably cold. She reached out for her bedside lamp but though her fingers encountered its slick stem, she could not find the switch.

Was she still dreaming? Could this be a nightmare?

Ally knew it was not. One did not get out of the life they had had by not knowing the difference between dream and reality.

She was facing the slope on the east side of the house: the grey expanse of dappled shadows, knobby branches sticking out into the turgid air. The evening wind had died down long ago and all was still. Except . . . something moved in the tangle. She strained her eyes. All she could see was some stealthy movement. A swish of bushes, a crinkle of dry leaves, a dim silhouette of . . . what?

It was nothing, she told herself. Nothing.

A door banged loudly down in the basement.

Ally slid down under the quilt and lay there very still, breathing in soft, shallow gasps, making as little noise as was consistent with being alive. The night went on and on, and eventually she slept.

Chapter 3:
Gabriela

When Carl emerged from the basement gym and gulped down a cup of coffee with enough cream and sugar to undo the calorie burning of his exercise, he told Ally that they should have a dinner party for their friends and neighbors on the mountain.

"Saturday, I think," he said. "I talked to Pat. She said she'd dropped by."

"She did," Ally said, slathering her bread with jam.

"Got the shock of her life, I bet." Carl laughed and gently tugged at Ally's braid, which was properly done this morning. "She didn't expect a beauty like you!"

Carl's friends believed he'd gotten himself a mail-order bride though Ally knew he did not think of her that way. In his eyes, theirs was a marriage of equals. He had money; she had beauty and intelligence. The twenty-five years of age difference was a bonus; or if it was more than that, he never talked about it. He could be vulgar on occasion, but he treated Ally as his sweetheart. She had a more objective view of their respective positions but whatever the underlying calculus of her marriage, it was nothing compared to what she had been forced to offer to the market forces before.

"Let's see," Carl tapped on his smartphone. "Pat and Kyle, the Websters, Susie and Mitch—you got to meet them before she's carted off, Alzheimer's coming on . . . Hmm. Ron and Don? No, that's not right. I can never tell these guys apart. They're like twins! Anyway, Ron is a doctor, Don an investor, or is it the other way around? What the hell, I'll just drop them a line. So . . . ten people, give or take?"

Ally shrugged. "Sure," she said. "Why not?"

Her mother's kitchen had occasionally seated ten people and it was about as big as her breakfast nook.

"We can get catering," Carl continued. "Or will you cook?"

Ally may not have been as finely attuned to the subtleties of the English language as she would like to be, but a man's desire was the same in any tongue. He wanted her to cook, just as he wanted her to wear her most fetching dress and to display her golden hair to its best advantage.

"No problem," she said cheerfully. "I'll cook."

After Carl left, she surveyed her domain.

The enormous living room, with big abstract sculptures and expensive Italian furniture, was as beautiful and impersonal as a home design show. The Morrises must have hired a professional to do their decorating for them. Ally had been shocked not to see bookshelves—at home, even the meanest apartment would have one. But then, she discovered the library, located between Carl's and her own offices. The library held Carl's financial reports, classic car manuals and a large case with thick hand-bound volumes and severe hardbacks. The titles intrigued her. She tried to open the case. It was locked.

Were these Ros' books? Her selection of reading material was surprising, to say the least.

This was what she had already explored but there were the two guest wings. And there was the basement, the dark underground kingdom under her feet.

Ally decided to start with one of the guest wings. She pushed the closed door and walked into the dusk. Her light-adjusted eyes blinked in surprise until she realized it was not particularly dark— just normal. The wing had solid walls and ordinary curtained windows. And it was populated by the past: worn-out cushions, old posters, scuffed tables, and bowlegged chairs. Its three bedrooms were spotlessly clean but had a hangdog appearance of being ready for a yard sale. She opened a built-in wardrobe. Empty. The bathroom had a full complement of toiletries that looked slightly used. Had they belonged to Ros?

Ally was about to go back to the main part of the house when she heard footsteps.

Her heart raced. She pressed herself to the wall and listened intently. The footsteps were heavy and unmistakably real. A bang. Then another.

There was a back door in the guest wing. If she scuttled away, crept out of the house, she could make it down the slope that led into the densest woods . . . Nobody could find her there.

Suddenly she heard Mama's voice: "*You are an officer's daughter!*" She did not know whether it was actually true, but truth was what you believed. She was an officer's daughter and officer's daughters didn't run away.

She straightened up and walked back into the kitchen where she was confronted with a thickset woman in rubber gloves busily lining up things on the countertop. The woman screamed and dropped a bottle of ketchup that spread a blood-red stain at her feet.

It took some time to sort it out in a mixture of incomprehensible Spanish and rudimentary English. The woman's name was Gabriela. She cleaned the house once a week and had already been paid a month in advance. Ally decided that eventually she would get a cleaner who spoke proper English—like many immigrants, she was a stickler for linguistic propriety—but meanwhile she was happy to let Gabriela get on with the program. The presence of another human being in the house felt good.

She briskly went through the second guest wing, which was much like the first one: stocked with odds and ends of the past and waiting in vain for the guests of the future. Gabriela clearly had been at work here and Ally noted with satisfaction that she had done a good job.

She was closing the door of the last bedroom when she saw something bright on the grey carpet. She lifted it and stared at it, not because it was strange but because it was spookily familiar.

It was a rubber bird: a duck or a swan, meant for an infant's bath-time. Since Ally was an only child—or at least, an only *actual* child—and there was no room in their tiny apartment for nostalgia, Mama had given away all her toys. But Ally remembered just such a bird with a yellow crown on its squashy head and the soft beak curving into a perpetual smile. She must have loved it to remember it so well but holding it gave her a shivery feeling. Even though the toy was clean, it felt slick, as if just now pulled out of water. And what was it doing there, anyway?

Carl and Ros had had no children. Ally asked about it during their courtship, but Carl said they had not wanted kids at the beginning and then it was too late. He showed no sign of regret; nor did he hint that perhaps it was not too late for *them*, for which she was profoundly grateful: Ally had no desire to start a family. Carl was a simple man, his passions were obvious and few: his venture capital company, expensive cars, and Ally. Having had to deal with complicatedly wretched men most of her adult life, Ally basked in his simplicity.

But then, how to explain the toy? Had Ros played with rubber ducks in her palatial bathtub?

She snorted and went back to the kitchen where Gabriela was on her knees, diligently cleaning the skirting board. Ally pulled out the garbage bin from under the sink, preparing to chuck the rubber bird on top of coffee filters and broken eggshells.

"*¿Puedo tener esto?*" Gabriela's rubber-gloved hand suddenly shot up. "Have this? Pleese? For baby?"

Ally looked at her in amazement. She had classified Gabriela as being in her late forties or early fifties, surely too late for a baby! Mama had been eighteen when Ally was born. In Ukraine, it was not uncommon for girls to have their first and only child in their teens and rely on grandmothers to help bring it up, though this was not the case with Mama whose own parents were gone and never spoken of. But perhaps Mexicans had the same arrangements. Perhaps Gabriela wanted the toy for a grandchild.

"Of course," she said, handing the bird to the cleaning woman.

She wandered out of the kitchen and stopped on top of the stairs leading down to the basement. The green radiance that permeated the house was dim here, petering out at the first landing where she had seen that bottle of canola oil. She had been too spooked to check later whether it had stayed there, and Carl had never mentioned it.

Should she go down and explore the basement?

Ally decided to work on the menu for the dinner party instead.

Chapter 4:
The Party

Two things happened the next day. One was nice. Ally could not decide about the second.

The nice thing was a chatty text from her Berkeley friend Malika inviting her for coffee on Telegraph Avenue. Ally wrote back immediately with an enthusiastic yes, surrounded by a cloud of emojis. Only after she pressed "Send" did it occur to her that it would be the first time she would be off the mountain in more than two weeks.

The other thing started with her wandering into Carl's office during the day. He never told her not to, she reasoned; and why not? Shouldn't she become more interested in her husband's business affairs? After all, it was not like she had many of her own.

The thought brought a blush of shame to her cheeks and a resolution to go back to her studies immediately. This calmed her down and she pushed the door and walked into the room which, like all the rest of them, was little more than a glass cube jutting out over the sloping forest floor. The day was grey and overcast; tree drip leaving tearful streaks on the foggy glass. The ground fog coiled below, obscuring thick stands of contorted manzanitas. The tops of the redwoods were veiled by the clouds and their bare trunks held up the roiling sky like columns in some cyclopean temple. It was cold in the room and Ally, shivering in her new Dolce and Cabana dress, looked around timidly at the several Macs scattered on a wraparound desk, an Alienware computer that Carl used for occasional gaming, and a whole lot of old-fashioned paperwork, most as incomprehensible to her as if it were written in Chinese. Some *was* actually in Chinese. She leafed through a couple of files, understanding only that her husband was probably even richer than she had known, and turned around to walk out of his boring sanctuary until something suddenly snagged her to stop and scan the empty walls one more time.

No, it was rather the absence of something. There was no artwork, which she did not find surprising. Classic cars were Carl's idea of the beautiful and the sublime. But there were no family photos either and that was vaguely troubling. Of course, she had appreciated this thoughtfulness in getting rid of the residue of his life with Ros. But no picture of his dead wife here, in the office, where he would reasonably expect to be alone? Instead, that photograph of four young people on the beach, stuck in the kitchen, her domain, where she would inevitably come across it sooner rather than later? It seemed sly and malicious, not like Carl at all.

On the other hand, how well did she know her husband?

When you are weak, you attack. Bullies don't appreciate surrender but can be stunned by audacity into exposing their soft underbelly. That was one of Mama's lessons, and surely, she knew what she was talking about! So, in the evening, when Carl was relaxing with his second glass of wine, Ally picked up the picture and put it on the table in front of Carl.

"Pat went on and on about it," she remarked. "Where was it taken?"

Carl snorted.

"That woman is going batty! All I remember about that weekend is how she got drunk and threw up in the bushes. It's Santa Barbara, honey. We should go there. We'll have a better time than I had with her and Kyle."

"Didn't Ros make up for them?" Ally asked, pointing at the pretty, dark-haired girl whose shoulders were encircled by young Carl's well-muscled arm.

"Ros? This is not Ros! Why would you think so? That was my girlfriend at the time, Carmela. We broke up after that weekend. Was pissed at the time but it was for the best. Now I have you, hon. Anyway, I'm going to give this picture to Pat and Kyle. Let them have it. I don't even know how it ended up here!"

And he nonchalantly shoved it into a drawer full of odds and ends.

Ally knew better than to continue this interrogation. She was sensitive to her husband's moods and realized he did not want to keep talking about his deceased wife. But it took her a long time to fall asleep as she listened to Carl's rhythmic snores and watched damp shadows slither outside.

One of them had to be lying. But was it Pat or her husband? Did Pat dislike her? There was something about her manner during their encounter that had struck Ally as hidden hostility, even though she had seemed polite enough. Did she disapprove of Carl's quick marriage? But why would she misidentify the girl in the picture? To make Ally jealous? She must have noticed that Carl had removed all pictures of his dead wife from the house. Was she angry about it? But why would it matter to her?

And what about Carl? Was it normal for him to have expunged all traces of his previous marriage? Did he do it for her sake or for his own?

She finally fell asleep but woke up before dawn because somebody was singing the ballad of black-eyed Oksana and her escape from the perfidious Turks. It took her a couple of heartbeats to realize that the singing had been in her dreams.

The party was a success. Almost.

Ally had set aside her own culinary preferences and consulted an American cooking site that told her how to make a beef roast with rosemary and potatoes. She had to steel herself to cut the bloody meat but after an hour in the oven, it smelled nice. Not like meat anymore. For herself, she made cherry dumplings, which were a huge hit with those of the guests she herself was a hit with. These included the gay couple Don and Ron who were actually Donald and Rafael but otherwise conformed to Carl's description of them as twins: heavyset men with lucrative careers and expensive suits. Both seemed to like Ally. So did Mike and Laura Choi. Mike, an Asian American, had more millions in the bank than years of age, thanks to his killer app for pattern recognition. Laura, his wife, was from Hong Kong and had a soft accent, which made Ally warm to her immediately.

Apart from these two couples, there were Susie and Mitch Webster. At first glance, Ally could not understand why Carl had referred to them as "ancient". Susie was slim in tight-fitting jeans and her husband wore a CAL T-shirt like undergrads in Berkeley. The second glance revealed the deeply carved canyons of age on both their faces and Susie's vacant stare. She hugged and kissed

Ally but the latter was not sure the hug was meant for her. Perhaps Susie thought she was Ros.

The Websters were followed by a tall woman whose yoga pants were covered in cat hair. Her name was Jennifer Mackenzie. She did not live on the mountain permanently but was staying with a friend. He had been the actual invitee, but Eric Greenberg could not make it as he had to fly to Paris on urgent business. Jennifer scrutinized Ally's Stella McCartney dress, accepted a glass of white wine, and lapsed into brooding silence.

This left Pat Donegan and her husband Kyle who said exactly five words during the entire evening. The rest might have gotten stuck in his luxuriant face hair that seemed to filter words like a whale's baleen filters krill. She, however, more than made up for his taciturnity. Dressed in a shiny, tight-fitting sheath that emphasized every roll of her unruly flesh, Pat hardly stopped talking. The moment she stepped over the threshold she went into raptures of fake delight over Ally's appearance, praising her rose-colored tulle dress and diamond earrings, but conspicuously disregarding the golden crown of hair that made her slender neck as graceful as a flower stem. This was a subtle barb, the meaning of which was not lost on Ally, especially since Carl could hardly contain his pride in his wife's beauty.

In truth, she had put a lot of effort into it. Before dinner, she had spent an hour making herself ready. Her hair was not a problem: nothing the best hairdresser could do would add to its glory. Her makeup nowadays tended to be understated but she still knew how to make men's heads turn with cheap lipstick and black eyeliner. *But that was then and this is now*, she reminded herself. The diamond earrings that Carl had given her as a wedding gift were indeed spectacular. But this left her décolleté unadorned, and this seemed wrong—just as wrong as combining the earrings with his other gift, a ruby-and-emerald necklace. She had looked into her jewelry box, where precious stones shone through a tangle of plastic beads. Well, there was that one thing . . . She had taken Mama's little golden cross on a thin, almost invisible chain, and put it on. It was perfect.

And now Pat, looking even more witch-like with the stain of red wine in the corner of her mouth, pointed to the cross.

"Pretty!" she murmured. "Are you a Christian, dear?"

"Of course," Ally said.

"You should come to our Church in the Woods!" Susie declared suddenly, surfacing from her glazed-eyed reverie. "It's so inspiring!"

"We have a service every Sunday!" her husband chimed in.

"Really?" Ally said doubtfully. "I go to St. Volodymyr in Santa Clara. Only for Easter."

She was met with blank stares. Ally had no particular faith, but Mama had taken her to church to eat *kulich*, the pillowy Easter cake, and exchange brightly painted eggs. Praying in the woods struck her as a pagan and even dangerous thing.

"I'm not sure I believe in God," she added, making it even worse.

"There are other things in the woods. Other than God," Pat said. "You might like them."

"What do you mean?" Ally asked.

"Well," Don said, sipping his merlot, while Ron put another cherry dumpling on his plate. "We heard all the ghost stories from the couple who sold us our house. Kara and Matt, were they?"

"Mara and Ken," Ron corrected.

"Whatever. But after we signed the papers, they told us a bunch of baloncy—not before, of course, not that it would make any difference. We don't believe in that crap."

"*You* don't," Ron winked at Ally. "We celebrated *Dia de Muertos*, my mum and I did when I was a child."

"So is your house supposed to be haunted?" Ally asked.

"No, it's not about the house. There was some story about a lost Halloween party . . . I don't remember all the details but it's all nonsense, of course."

"It's true," Pat intervened. "There was a bunch of kids trick-or-treating on our road. They passed the empty cabin, you know the one that is on the corner? The next house is yours, Laura. They never got to it. Five kids. Only one was ever found and she never said a word afterward. She would only scream."

Laura's mouth opened in a perfect "O" of shock. She had already confided in Ally that growing up in the urban bustle of Hong Kong was a poor preparation for life in the woods. Ally could only commiserate.

"This is why we now have a Halloween truck," Pat continued, smiling at the effect her words had produced. "Nobody is allowed to walk that stretch of the road after dark."

"Is this true?" Laura squealed.

"What's true, honey?" Mike, who had been showing something on his smartphone to Carl, finally emerged from cyberspace. Laura lapsed into a quick patter of Cantonese. Ally explained the situation to Carl, whose already ruddy face acquired an alarming beet-like tinge as he cast a baleful glance at Pat.

"Nonsense!" he bellowed. "This house has been here for fifteen years and nothing like this has ever happened. Ken Stockbridge made it up one evening when he was too drunk to walk back home—his usual state!"

"But wasn't there some murder in that old cabin?" Ron asked. "You might remember, Suzie," he added, addressing the old woman.

She shook her head, and it was her husband Mitch who answered:

"A very long time ago, even before we moved in. And the murderer was caught, some homeless guy."

"So, it's safe to walk in the woods after dark?" Ally asked.

"I didn't say that. Mountain lions, you know."

"We just installed a wildlife camera," Mike put in, patting his wife's hand, "and it showed two deer and a bunch of wild turkey yesterday."

"What brand?" Carl inquired eagerly, and the conversation shifted to technobabble. Ally was relieved. Ghost stories were not for telling in the glass house. But even as she passed a cheese tray around and replenished wine glasses, she was conscious of Pat's eyes on her.

Chapter 5:
Malika

Ally was sitting at the corner table in the Mokka cafe, sipping her chai latte and feeling out of place as she listened to the chatter of undergrads clustering around their Macs and swiping their phones. When she came to Berkeley on student-exchange program, she had been drunk with jubilation at her incredible luck. She had enrolled in Kyiv University out of her sober recognition that she would be dead—or worse—in a couple of years unless she dragged herself out of the pit into which she had fallen after Mama's disappearance. She did not want to remember the way she had financed her Anthropology studies.

And then—a call for applications for an American exchange program in Anthropology, with emphasis on fairytale and folklore studies. Ally's English had always been excellent. Mama had somehow come into money when Ally was little, and she used it to pay for her daughter's private tutoring. And Ally loved fairy tales. All fairy tales had been history once and, living in a history-soaked land, she had been drawn to them since she was a child.

So, she had applied to the program, been selected, come to California, and met Carl. Thanks to that mysterious windfall in the past, Ally was sitting here, the wife of a rich man. She should be as content as an oligarch's cat.

She was not.

She knew Malika had entered the café by the reaction of the male patrons. Six feet tall with ebony skin and the figure of a runway model, Malika literally turned heads everywhere she went. She and diminutive Ally were as different as human beings could possibly be; nevertheless, they were friends. For some reason, the statuesque Nigerian often deferred to Ally's judgment and even treated her as a sort of mother-figure, despite the fact that they were the same age.

They hugged and Malika ordered a Frappuccino. Ally immediately noticed that her former roommate was not in the best of moods. She waited for Malika to spill out her woes, but she only fidgeted and talked about their mutual acquaintances. So, Ally asked her outright.

"My parents arranged a marriage for me," Malika said glumly.

"Congratulations!" Ally enthused but seeing the stony expression on the black girl's face, lifted a quizzical eyebrow. "Isn't this what you wanted?"

Indeed, and that was one of the areas in which cultural differences reared their ugly head. Ally was on board with Malika's hijab, which did not prevent her from wearing skinny jeans. But she could not understand how Malika would not only accept but be positively rapturous about the fact that her parents would choose a husband for her. No matter Ally's own experience with men, deep in her heart she had a romantic corner filled with Lermontov's poetry and folk ballads about doomed lovers. Even though she knew by now that passionate love culminating in happy marriage was not in her own future, she wished it for others, especially friends. Malika, on the other hand, insisted that her parents knew her better than she knew herself; that love would come in due course after intimacy was established; and that arranged marriages, including that of her own parents, were the happiest and most stable of all. And yet now she looked as happy as a patient being told by a smiling dentist that she needed an emergency root canal.

"I wanted to get married, sure," Malika responded, studying the dregs of her coffee with painful intensity. "But not . . . not to this man!"

"What's wrong with him? Too old, too fat, a lech?"

Malika was instantly indignant at the suggestion that her parents would choose somebody with one of these qualities for their beloved daughter, and Ally had to placate her before she learned the whole story. But at the end, she was no better informed than at the beginning.

According to Malika, the man in question was a son of one of the most respectable ("richest" Ally translated to herself) families in Lagos. He was young, good-looking, had an MBA from the

London School of Economics and the reputation of high-mindedness and political connections. There was not a whiff of scandal attached to him. But on their first meeting, Malika experienced a total and instant revulsion, which, according to her, stemmed from the fact that she recognized him. And yet, she had never seen him in her entire life.

Ally actually had to yell at her for Malika to snap out of her self-pitying funk and try to explain. The explanation, however, made even less sense because, according to her, she had met the man in a dream.

Ally made a feeble joke, but Malika was dead serious. The worst thing was that she did not even remember when she had had the dream. It was not a recent one but something out of her childhood, a nightmare, which she had forgotten for a long time and which had only come back to her when she met her betrothed.

In the dream, she was a little girl, her actual age ("eight or ten," she said uncertainly) and yet she was getting married to an adult man.

"He forced me to go with him. And then we came to a city. And there, he took off his hands and gave them away. And then we came to another city. And there, he took off his legs and gave them away. And then he crawled . . . " She suddenly choked.

Ally did not know what to say. Surprisingly, the dream struck a chord with her. Had she read something like this? Was it an African fairy tale?

Perhaps this was the explanation. Perhaps Malika remembered a creepy story from her childhood and was unconsciously using it to wriggle out of the marriage she did not want. Perhaps when push came to shove, she realized she would rather marry somebody of her own choosing.

Still, there was something profoundly unsettling in seeing Malika tremble and stutter. She studied civil engineering and was as levelheaded as anybody Ally knew.

"It's just a dream!" Ally remonstrated. "Come on!"

"I know what I know," Malika responded cryptically. "I'd rather die than marry him. He is not a human being! He is an *asanbosam*, a demon!"

Ally rolled her eyes.

"OK, can't you just . . . talk to your parents? They can call it off!"

Apparently, it was impossible for reasons too convoluted for Ally to follow. Having nothing better to offer her friend, she took her out to lunch in their favorite sushi place. Many hugs later, they parted with mutual promises to keep in constant touch by Facebook and Snapchat. Driving back home on the darkened twisting road, Ally considered that perhaps her own situation was not so bad by comparison. She did not love Carl, but she respected him. Certainly, there was no taint of anything demonic attached to her prosaic husband!

Green-and-gold days followed each other in such a rapid succession that it sometimes seemed to Ally that the interval between waking and sleeping got progressively shorter, reduced to a recombination of identical elements: Carl's exercise in the basement; breakfast under the watchful eyes of the redwoods; the purr of his Tesla as he departed for work; Facebook; books; clothes; cooking dinner; a glass or two or three of wine; a movie; bed. Wine definitely helped. She was beginning to understand Mama.

Every morning, she told herself she ought to explore the Bay Area. But what could she see that was more beautiful than her own land? Muir Woods, Big Basin . . . what were those but more redwoods?

Ally would sit on the deck with a book or a cup of tea for hours, staring into the green. She had learned to identify different kinds of trees tanoaks, madrones, and hemlocks. Still, her eyes would always be drawn to redwoods the majestic *Sequoia sempervirens*, so tall that its feathery canopy housed a whole other world of insects and reptiles that had nothing to do with the dry soil underfoot. The soil was dry because the trees had sucked all nutrients out of it, carpeted it with their shadows, and killed the undergrowth, leaving behind only the tinderbox-ready covering of shed needles and leaves. The trees of her childhood had been the humble and overworked servants of the city, their green fingers scrubbing the pollution out of its air. These trees were lords and masters of their domain.

One particularly beautiful morning after Carl had left for work, Ally realized she had not had any exercise in a week. It occurred to her that she should go down into the basement and explore Carl's gym, along with whatever else was hidden in the house's dark underbelly. But the sparkling light on the *Ceanothus* in the front yard was so pure that she decided she had been cooped up far too long. Putting on a pair of Gucci jeans and Adidas sneakers, she walked out. The front door clicked shut behind her and Ally stopped, breathing in the intoxicating medley of scents: lemony, spicy, prickly, tangy . . . She searched the driveway for a flash of yellow but there were no banana slugs sitting on the flagstones like miniature dragons.

She walked toward the gate that separated their private road from the open-space preserve. The land fell away on both sides in the tangle of bushes, shrubs and small trees, desperately clawing toward the sunlight stingily doled out by the redwoods. She quickened her pace though the patch where madrones and hemlocks overhung the road, plunging it into a green dusk in which the madrone bark glowed blood-red. And then she heard a quick patter of footsteps. Startled, she reached for a dry branch, but it was as light as cork.

A tawny body flashed across the road, close enough for Ally to see the graceful curve of its neck as it whipped back its head to look at her with liquid, unfathomable eyes. And then the deer disappeared up the opposite slope, dislodging a mini avalanche of bark. Ally smiled sheepishly and threw away the branch.

The trees stepped back, and Ally found herself in an open space filled with golden light. She climbed a lion-colored hill. From there, she should be able to see the necklace of state beaches, from Pescadero to Bean Hollow, strung along the edge of the Pacific. But she could see nothing except the glittering billows of white.

Clouds; the dense impenetrable sky-ocean lapping at her feet.

Standing in the sunshine while fog and clouds blanketed the Bay felt wrong. It was as if she was not in California anymore but stranded in some other unfamiliar place with the redwoods whispering behind her back, the bright lifeless fields stretching all around her, the dry grass creeping with stealthy invisible movements.

Ally descended back to the road that led deeper into the preserve. The trees began again, walls of silvery trunks hemming her in. Grizzled beards of Spanish moss swayed slightly in the still air.

Ahead, where the road made a sharp turn, a light blur flashed in the shadows. Something walked across and disappeared into the bushes. Ally turned around and ran back to the gate.

Another deer! The woods must be infested with them.

But it had not been a deer. The color was wrong and so was the shape. As much as she wanted to deny the evidence of her own eyes, she knew what she had seen. A nude body, plunging into the thorny bushes that could tear unprotected skin to shreds. A human body.

Chapter 6:
Rapunzel

Her i**P**hone **vibrated** when she let herself back into the house. It was Carl. He was having dinner with one of his clients tonight and he asked her to join them. Apparently, the deal's negotiations were successfully concluded and now it was time for schmoozing.

"Sure," Ally said, happy at the prospect of a good meal and dense crowds. She had had all the nature she could stomach.

They agreed to meet in downtown Palo Alto. She took a quick shower, washing off the clamminess of fear, and chose a Diane von Furstenberg blue dress that deepened the color of her eyes. Discovering she had no time to plait her hair, she coiled it loosely and pinned it at the back of her head. More or less satisfied with the overall effect, Ally rushed to the garage that housed her Prius and a few of Carl's previous infatuations: a Lexus, a Forrester, and a classic Thunderbird.

She sweated out the first couple of sharp curves. The sun was setting, and the road was dappled with shadows. She passed the Murphy's pink Mediterranean palace, stuck forlornly among frowning trees, and was almost down to the intersection of the private road with the highway.

She saw the cabin as she rounded the last corner: small and humble, crouching at the curb like a homeless beggar. Surely Pat's stories were just stories! The witch had just been trying to unsettle and frighten her!

The Prius glided past the cabin, and a face glared at her from between the curtains.

She fought to regain control of the car as it fishtailed on the road, deadly metal and electric power buckling like a spooked horse. Another car swished past the mailboxes and loomed in front of her. She waited for the crash, the screech of broken steel, the pain of pulverized flesh. She expected her short life to flash in front of her eyes but there was only Mama's voice singing some forgotten song in the unforgotten language . . . And then there was silence.

Somebody was banging on her door. Ally forced her shaking hands to unbuckle her seat belt and her trembling legs to move. The two cars stood nose to nose as if kissing.

"What the fuck were you thinking?" the man yelled, and it finally penetrated Ally's shocked brain that the second car had a driver.

The man loomed over her, an angry threatening shadow. This brought her back to her senses in a snap. Car crashes were an unfamiliar danger. Angry men were not.

She looked him in the eyes. He towered over her—most men did—and like most men, he wilted under her steady gaze. He licked his lips, glanced aside.

"I'm sorry," he said in a normal voice. "It was my fault, too. I should not have come up at such speed. I apologize."

He was quite young, even though a dark stubble and heavily rimmed glasses made him look older. He had the lean rangy physique of a runner under his SETI T-shirt and rumpled jeans. Tree-shadows deepened his skin to a dusky hue.

"No," she said, "it was me. I'm not used to driving on this road yet."

She saw the familiar start of surprise when he heard her accent but then he stuck out his hand.

"Let's start from the beginning, shall we? I'm Eric."

The long fingers wrapped themselves around hers. She opened her mouth—and was surprised at what came out.

"Alyona."

He repeated it in wonderment, as if tasting an unfamiliar candy. It did not sound quite right—the soft vowel after "l" was stretched into a diphthong—but he got points for trying.

"Is it Russian?"

"Ukrainian, in my case."

He smiled.

"We have a Russian software engineer in my company, but I know better than to confuse the two. Are you . . . I mean you said you are not used to driving on this road *yet* . . . ?"

"I'm married to Carl Morris," she said and watched for the strained expression she had observed in previous encounters when her interlocutor tried hard to prevent the thought "mail-order bride" from reaching his face.

But there was nothing. He simply grinned.

"So, we are neighbors!" he exclaimed. "I'm sorry I missed your party! Carl invited me but I had to go to Paris. Last-minute financing offer—and it fell through anyway . . . "

"You friend was there," she said. "Jennifer."

"Yeah, Jenni is staying with me for a short while. She is just a good friend, and housing here costing what it does . . . "

Ally made an appropriate response, noting that he made a point of saying Jennifer was just a friend. Eric suggested they examine the cars. Amazingly, both the Prius and his Subaru were undamaged. As Ally stood up from peering under the chassis, the loosened pins in her hair chose to pop out. The heavy coil unwound and fell to her knees in a golden waterfall.

She knew the effect it had on men. Some stared lewdly; some averted their eyes with a Puritanical rectitude; some made stupid remarks out of embarrassment. Eric just looked with the wide-eyed wonder of a child on Christmas morning. And then, he laughed.

"I'm sorry," he said. "Please don't take it the wrong way. Seriously. But I've never seen hair like yours. Fairy-tale hair. You are like a princess in a Grimm brothers' story. Like Rapunzel or something."

Ally laughed.

"It's OK," she said. "I'm glad you didn't say Disney. Their stories are all wrong. And Rapunzel . . . it's rather appropriate. I was doing my thesis on it. Not hair, of course, but anthropology. Folklore. Lots of it has to do with body parts."

She blushed, realizing that she had inadvertently made a double entendre. If Eric got it, he showed no sign of embarrassment. He seemed to be about to ask something else but then her iPhone vibrated insistently, and she realized she was late for dinner with Carl and his client. She apologized and drove away, amazed at how steady her hands were on the steering wheel.

Chapter 7:
Turkeys

The dreams began stealthily, no more than a subtle darkening of her usual medley of nocturnal images, most having to do with Mama and the life she had left behind. She did not miss it. She knew that some immigrants were struck with nostalgia when the land one could not wait to leave behind suddenly reappeared as a beguiling memory. But her memories were too sharp and too recent.

Nor was it her marriage to Carl. When he had proposed, she had sworn to herself she would live up to her side of the bargain, and she found it easier than she had expected. In fact, she discovered she liked Carl better with every passing day. At the beginning, she had been afraid of finding out a hidden core of rottenness under his sunny exterior. Surely a man with so much money could not be what he seemed to be! The more time they spent together, however, the more she realized that he was exactly what he had appeared on their first date: boastful, superficial, and kind.

The dreams—of cold, dirty water; of footsteps trailing her; of the branches and brambles scoring her naked flesh as she ran through the woods—were telling her something, and she did not know what it was.

Ally decided to spend more time down on the Peninsula, overcoming her fear of driving past the cabin. It was worth it just to sit in a coffee-shop seeing people's faces, hearing their chatter, immersing herself in ordinary life, but even surrounded by the ebb and flow of everyday she felt as if she was on an island.

One day, when she came back home, the twilight was gathering, and the sky was fading to an unhealthy puce color. Days were getting shorter. Every evening, the clouds crawling upslope would come earlier and the trees would shed their beguiling beauty and become a crowd of spindly giants, whispering in the dark.

Parking off the driveway, as the garage now housed Carl's latest acquisition, a vintage Porsche d, Ally ambled toward the front door—and almost fell when her high-heeled boots snagged on something. Spitting out an expletive, she looked down and saw the tangle of cables Carl had hauled out this morning in preparation of putting up the "scary lights" for Halloween. Ally lifted the whole mass and was about to toss it to the side when something moved.

Now, she was grateful for the house's isolation; at least nobody heard her childish yelp as she confronted a ginormous banana slug caught in the coils of wiring. She had seen a couple since that first one, lying in the grass like discarded toys. This one was lively, thrashing around, the blunt, eyeless front of its body, too small to be called a head, blindly poking at the air, its slimy mantle whipping around like a rag. The creature was injured, dripping repulsive ichor onto her hands.

Ally sighed. *Today is a good deeds day*, she told herself. *I should accumulate some good karma and spend it on needling Pat Donegan.* She patiently loosened the cable, lifted the slug in her cupped hands—it was disgusting to touch, as if softly rotten— and set it in the grass. It crawled away.

She went into the dark house, remembering the stony faces of the pedestrians who passed by while her ten-year-old self tried to lift Mama's vomit-splattered body from the gutter.

She was just setting the table for dinner when Carl walked in. One look at his face told her something was awry. Ally knew her husband did not like to be quizzed, so she gave him a kiss, poured some wine, served the veal schnitzel with mashed potatoes to him, and mashed potatoes only to herself. Carl was uncharacteristically abrupt at the table, hardly talking and staring at something on his cellphone, which he had never done before. When the meal was over, he walked toward his office and Ally reconciled herself to spending the evening alone in the TV nook. Then he beckoned her to follow, which she did with some trepidation.

In the office, Carl powered up his Mac and swiveled the screen toward Ally. It was filled with an indistinct mosaic of color splotches.

"You know we have a wildlife camera?" he said abruptly. "It

streams directly to my phone and the program alerts me if there is movement around the house."

Ally nodded, trying to figure out what the camera could possibly show that would justify his smoldering anger. That she had not been home all day? She had told him in the morning that she was going down!

Carl fiddled with the mousepad and the picture sprung into clarity. It showed the slope behind the house, leading down toward the stand of redwoods. The colors were off, too bright, but the resolution was good.

Something stirred among the redwoods. Ally brought her face closer to the screen and abruptly pulled back.

A figure emerged from the redwoods. Then another. Two more. They hopped and twitched like string-pulled puppets but they were unquestionably alive. Their heads went up and down with a metronomic regularity, pecking at the dry undergrowth and then swiveling around, their flat monocular eyes, set in the opposite sides of their heads, sweeping the grounds. Their raggedy wings beat the air, as if they were nothing but big, ungainly fowls. And yet, there was also something undeniably human about them. Their beaks were soft and droopy like pouting mouths and their legs wrapped around with stringy muscles. They looked like a bunch of kids dressed up as chickens, or perhaps, Ally thought with a flash of horror, like big chickens dressed up as kids.

"What is this?" she whispered.

"I don't know," Carl said grimly. "There are wild turkeys here. They came up to the house occasionally. But this . . . "

"They do look like turkeys," Ally offered, trying to reassure him, if not herself. "Or, kids?"

"Halloween is coming up," Carl muttered, "If I find out it's the Murphy's bloody nieces and nephews . . . "

He turned to Ally and hugged her fiercely.

"Don't go out into the woods, honey!" he said. "Promise!"

This was the easiest promise Ally had made in her entire life.

The news about Susie and Mitch Webster came next morning.

Chapter 8:
Prince of Cats

Jennifer Mackenzie did not like cats.

Or at least, she did not used to. She grew up in Marin with mother, father, sister, two horses and two dogs. Unfortunately, her divorced mother was in Florida, the last news of her Dad came from Oslo, the horses were dead, and so were the dogs. That bitch Connie was apparently in Minnesota—and serves her right!—but Jennifer did not want to know of her sister's whereabouts since she had unfriended her on all the social media platforms she could think of. The house in Marin had been sold and now, as her fast-fashion digital retailer start-up was going under, this put Jennifer in the unenviable position of having to choose between living in her car and relocating to some cheap place in the Central Valley where all traces of herself would be obliterated under the onslaught of one-dollar burgers and Mariachi. Fortunately, Eric came through.

She and Eric had had a brief fling in high school but lost sight of each other until she ran into him in the Venezia café in Palo Alto. He was doing very well for himself with that weird quantum-communication idea, but then Eric had always been a little weird, his geekiness only redeemed by his amazing abs. When he offered her a temporary accommodation in the house in the woods he had bought with the proceeds of his previous start-up, she was very happy. She even considered taking up where they had left off in high school, but Eric showed no inclination to do so, and Jennifer told herself it was just as well.

He spent most days in his office down on the Peninsula while she labored at her Mac, trying to come up with a new idea for a spring collection. Unfortunately, the web was overflowing with fashion and she felt as if the flood of other people's design washed through her brain like a tsunami, flattening the tender shoots of originality she was trying to nurture. One day, floundering about, she pulled up her Facebook page and saw a cat video that had already been reposted several hundred times. Snorting, Jennifer was about to kill the page, when the cat—a beautiful fluffy white tom—lifted his head and looked straight at her.

His eyes were blue and human-shaped—the pupil not spindle but round. It pierced the digital wall that insulated Jennifer from the world inside her computer screen. She knew he was as real, as palpable, as herself. And she knew he saw her as clearly as she saw him.

Since then, he appeared every time she turned on her computer or phone. Whatever page she tried to access, he was there, smiling his sphinx-smile, gracefully upright or sensuously sprawling, looking into Jennifer's eyes, reading her soul as easily as a webpage and forgiving her failures as Mum, Dad, or Connie had never done. She could not do any design, of course. She could not even read her emails. But hell, it was worth it! One moment of wordless communion with Prince—she knew somehow that it was his name—was worth days spent on beating up her dead inspiration or cajoling skeptical investors.

When one day he turned up on Eric's doorstep, she was not even surprised. She walked out to get some fresh air and there he was, as big as a bobcat but snow-white, with not a single soil stain to mar his royal coat, his blue eyes shining like sapphires, his mouth curved in an ambiguous and seductive smile. She let him in and tried to give him food and water, but he would not eat. Nor would he let her pet him. He lay on the couch, a long, supple, seemingly boneless body, and stared at her, and she knelt by the couch and stared back at him.

Before Eric came back, Jennifer remembered he was allergic to cats. Timidly, she asked Prince to follow her to her guest room and he consented.

At night, she woke up because a sweet music filled her ears, while her body was melting in delicious warmth. Prince lay on her chest, his body vibrating with a low, gentle, relentless purr. The purr filled her bones like hollow reeds, and the touch of his abrasive tongue on her neck registered only distantly.

Next morning, she could not eat breakfast, and when Eric

remarked on the bruise under her jaw, she said she had walked into the bathroom door.

Chapter 9:
The Half-Baby

She was still reeling from what Carl told her about the Websters. He had been so upset he had drunk more than half a bottle at dinner, and she had had to help him to bed, unpleasantly reminded of Mama's bad times. But perhaps he had a reason. Ally pulled out enough news from the web to feel sick herself.

Mitch was found by his handyman Miguel hanging from a tree in their backyard that Miguel had come to cut down because it was leaning too close to the house. The noose was fashioned from Susie's torn-up clothes that Mitch had woven into a crude rope. This would require hours of labor that indicated deliberation and planning. Mitch was naked and his sagging body was shockingly lacerated by thorns and brambles as if he had rolled in the underbrush.

Inside the house were piles of smashed crockery, broken family photos and garbage deliberately strewn on the Persian carpet that the couple had brought back from their travels. Of Susie there was no sign and even now, deputy sheriffs and volunteers were scrambling through the open space preserve, looking for her. Mike and Laura had volunteered but Ally had not. First, because she had promised Carl not to go into the woods; second, because she was quite sure they would not find anything.

She was drinking her second coffee when the house phone rang. Picking it up, she was greeted with a torrent of Spanish. Then another voice barged in.

"Hello? Hello? I'm Alba, Gabriela's cousin."

Ally remembered that today was Gabriela's day.

"Is she sick?" Ally asked.

"No, no! She is coming. But her babysitter can't make it. Gabriela asks if she can bring her son with her. He's quiet."

"Sure!" Ally said. The cousin fired a rapid volley of thanks and hung up. So, the child was Gabriela's after all!

But it was good to have the woman in the house because today was the day Ally was going down into the basement. She had postponed it long enough. She could not pretend anymore to be a princess in the glass palace, living out her fairy tale happily ever after. Who better than her to know that there was always a long trail of dark history dragging behind every fairy tale? And where to look for the history of a house, if not in the basement?

She plaited her hair, remembering Eric's reaction to it. Rapunzel, indeed! Jailed and then raped and abandoned in the wilderness with two hungry babies!

It was dull and chilly outside. She put on a warm sweater and jeans, pushed open the basement door, and resolutely walked down.

Instantly, she was immersed in a different world: dark, oppressive and claustrophobic. If the glass insubstantiality of the upper floors gave her the sense of vulnerability—like being out in the open with no clothes on—the basement floors slammed down on her with the brutality of a mousetrap. Her light-adjusted eyes blinked helplessly in the murk, infested with vague crowding shapes. She groped on the wall and breathed a sigh of relief when the click of a light-switch brought the shapes into visibility.

Not that the sight that presented itself to her was in any way reassuring. She stood at the entrance to a long corridor, filled with boxes, wine-racks, and stacks of unidentifiable junk. It was overhung with exposed ducts and bundles of cables and smelled of damp cement and dust. This was where the actual business of the house was carried out, she realized, in these dark bowels filled with the gurgle of water and the hiss of electricity.

On the right side, the corridor was lined with doorways. She pushed the first door.

This was Carl's gym: a large windowless room with a treadmill, a weight-lifting machine and other pieces of equipment she could not identify. The fluorescent light, magnified by the wall mirror, gave the place a bleached-out, lifeless quality. Why would he exercise here when an entire world of green waited for him outside?

Well, maybe because he was aware of naked bodies pushing through the thorny bushes, of walkers by night, and of pale faces glaring at you from an abandoned cabin.

She peeked into the next room and was greeted with miniature Himalayas: piles of furniture covered with dust sheets. She lifted the edge of a sheet and saw a clutch of entwined chairs.

The next room was filled with taped cardboard boxes and old filing cabinets. Wondering how a childless couple could have accumulated so many unwanted possessions, Ally proceeded down the corridor, banging her shin on an empty wine rack that tipped dangerously but did not crash. A fluorescent panel flickered above her head, filling the basement with jumping shadows. From above came the whine of a vacuum cleaner—a sign that Gabriela had arrived; and it relieved her tension.

There was one last room. Ally opened the door that spilled out dense darkness. She groped on the wall, found the switch, flicked it—and stared into the past.

She had wondered how Ros' presence could have been so thoroughly expunged from the house she had inhabited for fifteen years. Pictures could have been stowed away, clothes given to charity—but not even an empty perfume bottle on a dresser, or an old Christmas card in a drawer? Now she had an answer. It was as if the dead woman's entire life had been concentrated in this one basement room. Even the air smelled of something fruity and overripe, instead of the dust and mildew of the rest of the basement.

There was a swaybacked sofa covered with a multicolored afghan and piled up with embroidered cushions in pink and red. Ros' taste had definitely run to the ultra-feminine. This was confirmed by the clothes that spilled out from a large old-fashioned wardrobe and lay in soft drifts on the flowery rugs. Ally lifted up a flouncy skirt that indicated that the first Mrs. Morris had been a couple of sizes larger than herself. A pair of high-heeled boots stood in the corner as if ready to walk. There was a large dresser crowded with perfumes, creams, lotions and other assorted beauty tools. Ally wrinkled her nose, knowing from bitter experience that cosmetics aged just like people and smelled accordingly.

The mirror above the dresser was covered with a black drape. And on top of the mirror sat a stuffed swan.

At first, she thought it was a toy of some kind because the swan was not particularly large, but as she peered at it, Ally realized it was a real bird.

Bile filled her mouth. Her vegetarianism was coupled with heightened sensitivity to physical violence, especially violence against dumb, helpless creatures. The idea that somebody had deliberately killed this bird that was not even good for eating, pulled out its bloody entrails, and stuffed its corpse with plastic foam, was abhorrent.

The swan was scrawny and molting. There were bald patches on its back. It was mounted in a strange position, with its head under its wing so its eyes could not be seen. Ally did not want to touch it but she peered at its wooden pedestal covered with a thick film of dust. There seemed to be some writing on it but she could not make it out.

She turned her attention to the mirror. She knew superstitious peasants in Ukraine covered all the mirrors in the house when somebody died, but did people also do it in America? In any case, it was until the funeral, not forever! Ally touched the drape and snatched back her hand as a bolt of icy cold traveled up her arm.

She looked at the pictures tacked haphazardly around the room. She had assumed they would be all the family photographs missing from upstairs, but it was not so. There were color-enhanced photographs of trees in fall foliage and of blooming roses; poorly executed sketches of the Golden Gate Bridge; posters for long-ago exhibitions in De Young and Legion of Honor museums in San Francisco; even a framed embroidery sampler. If these had all belonged to Ros, it was a dubious testimony to her taste in art.

There were no portraits at all.

Frowning, Ally looked around and then something incongruous among the huddle of bottles and jars on the dresser caught her attention. She looked closer.

It was a dinner plate. And lying on it was half a pear.

It was a big juicy pear with a reddish skin, neatly cut into two by a sharp knife, exposing the fibers of the core and the white seeds nesting around it. And it was fresh, still oozing clear, fragrant juice.

Ally gingerly touched the fruit with the tip of her finger and drew away from its moistness. It could not have been here for a year! Hell, it could not have been here for a day! Somebody must have placed it on the dresser, like a weird offering in front of the black-shrouded mirror, very recently. And there was no doubt who it had been. There was only two people living in the house to choose from. And since Ally had not been to this room until this very moment, this left . . .

Why? Even if Carl were secretly obsessed with the memory of Ros—an obsession Ally had seen no sign of—why would he do something so bizarre? A bouquet of fresh flowers every morning, perhaps. But a cut-up pear? Ally knew about strange mourning rites in other cultures. Chinese people placed oranges and Coke bottles on little altars in Taoist temples and burned paper money on Ching Ming, the feast of ghosts. This was irrelevant as Carl was no Taoist. He was a regular, middle-of-the-road, unimaginative American. Did he actually descend into the basement every morning, pretending to exercise and instead sharing a piece of fruit with his dead wife?

Ally supposed she should feel angry or jealous. Instead, she felt chilled—both literally and figuratively. The sweetish smell of the room was choking her. The drone of the vacuum cleaner suddenly stopped and she heard the steps overhead as Gabriela moved from the kitchen to the bedroom suite. She would be done soon.

Ally tugged on the black drape that covered the mirror.

The drape slid on the floor. Ally was fully prepared to see her own pale face in the glass. Hell, she was even prepared to encounter a ghostly image of Ros staring back at her. She was not prepared for what the mirror showed her.

She momentarily thought that perhaps she was mistaken, that it was not a mirror at all. A window, perhaps, even though it was not flush with the wall? A computer monitor? A TV?

It was none of these things. It was a mirror. And reflected in it was not Ally or the fussy furnishings of the basement room. Reflected in it was a forest.

It looked like the redwoods filtered through a fever dream. The vague orange space was slashed vertically by bare black trunks. If it was a sunset, it was one in which the inflamed sun had broken like an egg yolk and spilled all across the sky.

In the gaps between the trees grew thorny contorted bushes. The bushes were leafless, but the ground was carpeted with creeping plants whose saw-toothed leaves twitched like restless fingers. It was hard to see in the orange light. The plants seemed to be colored in random splotches of scarlet and blue like no vegetation Ally had ever seen. In the foreground was a giant black bud, obscenely sticking up from the ground cover and anchored by thick creepers that trailed through the mulch. The creepers contracted and relaxed; the bushes flailed; the ground plants shuddered and strained. The nightmare forest was in constant motion.

Ally stared at the forest for a long time. She felt no disbelief or fear. Her mind was crystal-clear. She guessed it was called acceptance. Or maybe shock.

She gently touched the slick glass. She would not be surprised to have her fingers pass through the surface of the mirror and encounter the bud, which, she somehow guessed, would be hot and throbbing.

It did not happen. Instead, the forest wavered and misted over. And then her own drawn face looked back at her against the background of the basement wall. Ally waved her hand, poked out her tongue, and the reflection obediently repeated her gestures. Everything seemed normal. She even noted that the pictures on the wall were mirror-reversed as they should be.

Had she been hallucinating?

She looked again at the half-a-pear on the plate. It still oozed juice and the brownish rust that forms on freshly cut fruit was nowhere in evidence. It was as if the pear had been cut just seconds ago.

Ally's courage gave out. She rushed out of the room, but even as she slammed the door behind her, her fingers found the light-switch and thumbed it down. Nobody should know she had been there. She remembered the Bluebeard tale only too well.

She ran up the stairs to the upper floor and burst into the kitchen. The sight of redwoods was unexpectedly welcome. They were green, not colored in weird unnatural hues. And the sky, though gloomy and overcast, was normal rainy-grey, not inflamed orange.

She poured a glass of water, gulped it down. The vacuum cleaner kicked into action again in the bedroom suite. Above it rose another sound: the wailing of a baby.

Ally started, but then remembered that Gabriela had brought her son with her.

She walked into the bedroom. Gabriela was on her knees, vacuuming under the bed. She had strapped the child into a baby seat that was rocking as the infant squirmed and let out a loud scream of protest. Ally opened her mouth to say something nice and felt the words die on her lips as she saw the baby.

How was it possible that something so incomplete could be alive? What was sitting in the baby seat was surely half a child: a single arm with a pudgy fist waving in the air, a single leg kicking indignantly, a single eye squeezed shut in crying. Its face was misshapen and asymmetrical: the left half was that of a plump, rosy-cheeked infant but on the right side there was just a thin wash of skin falling down vertically to the neck, as if somebody cut off half of its head and covered the wound with a graft. Gabriela had dressed it in a blue onesie, but Ally could see that the right side of it lay flat and empty on the seat.

Gabriela straightened up, tuned off the vacuum, and gave a start when she saw Ally.

"*Me asustaste, Señora,*" she cried. "Not heard you, sorry!"

Ally just nodded dumbly. Gabriela tenderly patted the half-child's head and inserted a pacifier into its lopsided mouth.

"What . . . what is his name?" Ally stammered.

"Juan," Gabriela replied.

"Nice name," Ally forced herself to say, keeping her eyes away from the monstrosity in the baby seat.

"Mrs. Morris, Ros . . . give it to him."

"Ros gave him this name?" Ally asked incredulously.

"Si, si! Ros told me. When I was with child. How to call him."

Chapter 10:
The dog and the cat

Ally went into her own office, which she had hardly used until now. On her way, she stopped in the library. The large bookcase, with what she now knew for certain had been Ros' books, was still locked. She used a screwdriver to force the lock. Picking up one of the largest volumes, she put it on her virgin desk, decorated only by a single picture. Mama's screaming gaze met hers, the eyes huge in the gaunt face confined by the cheap aluminum frame, which was all she had been able to afford in Kiev. Her last photo: the cropped blond hair; the unsmiling mouth; the red-and-black embroidered blouse and in the deep hollow of her neck—the tiny cross necklace. Ally touched her own unadorned neck.

"I'm sorry, *mamochka*," she whispered. "I'll be good."

She opened the volume and leafed through its pages.

The Aarne-Thompson-Uther classification and catalogue of fairy tales. It had been extensively used, with dog-eared pages and underlined paragraphs. Ally knew where she wanted to look, and the volume obediently opened there. T510. Miraculous conception.

There was another bookmark sticking from the volume. AT 402. Supernatural or enchanted spouses. Tiny letters were scribbled on the margins, and when Ally deciphered them, she leafed through to another dog-eared page.

D361.1. Swan-maiden.

Something did not add up, though. Fairy tales were modular: different motifs could be shuffled at will, several motifs coexisting in the same story, only to be pulled apart in another culture and reassembled in a different configuration. Still . . . swan-maiden? It did not fit with what she knew of Ros.

But if she was right, there was somebody who could answer her questions.

The phone numbers of all the people on the mountain were available from a neighborhood listserv. Ally picked up her iPhone and called.

The phone rang for a long time and then a woman's voice answered.

"Hello?"

"Pat?"

"Who is this?"

"Ally. Ally Morris."

A long pause; Ally could hear the other woman's breathing.

"What can I do for you?"

"I need to ask you a couple of questions. It's important."

Another pause.

"Could you come over?" Pat finally responded.

"Yes. I'll be there in fifteen minutes."

The Donegans' house was about a mile down the road from the Morriss'. Ally decided to walk. It would give her the time to clear her head

The weather was still chilly and cold but the clouds hugged the ground while the taller trees stuck out from the milky stew, their tops shuddering in the pale sky. Ally shivered in her thin jacket, and her sneakers made a crunchy sound on the gravel road. Something moved in the fog and she held her breath but then she realized it was just an optical illusion. The fog parted and she saw a tree stump cut in such a way that it looked like a headless dog standing on four splayed legs.

The Donegans' house was set back off the road and screened by a dense hedge of *Ceanothus*. It was much smaller than the Morrisses' and more conventional: a two-floor wooden structure with a peaked roof and a wrap-around porch.

Pat opened the front door the moment Ally stepped onto the driveway. Her grey curls stuck out at odd angles and her sagging face was pasty, but her eyes glittered with what looked like glee.

As she entered, a yapping bundle of white and orange fur careened into her. Ally instinctively pushed it away and the tiny dog growled, baring needle-like teeth. Pat scooped it up and crooned to it while Ally took in the suffocating abundance of the house.

Nightwood

If Carl had erred on the side of minimalism while building and furnishing his glass palace, Pat and Kyle had clearly suffered from the opposite tendency. Not only was the space inside fussily subdivided into many smallish rooms, but the rooms themselves were filled to bursting with paintings, rugs, plastic flowers, vases, small tables, figurines, and plaques. It looked like somebody had raided an antiques shop and scattered their loot at random. Following her hostess through the maze, Ally realized that many of the objects—she could not call them "decorations" as their sheer accumulation undermined whatever aesthetic effect each of them might have produced—had some fairy-tale connection. She saw a big banner with an Indian flute-player, gaudy plates with the Grimm Brothers' characters, plastic figurines of fairies and elves, and inexpert drawings of princesses and witches.

Pat offered her herbal tea, but Ally declined. She wanted nothing more than to be out of here—except that she felt even less like being back home. She realized that she had nowhere to go and it gave her courage. Ally had been raised in tight corners.

She took the framed photograph of four young people on the beach out of her pocket and put it in front of Pat.

"You told me this woman is Ros," she said without preamble. "It's not true, is it?"

The dog in Pat's arms stirred and Ally saw that its head was disproportionately large, almost half of its entire stunted body.

"Why are you asking me?" Pat said. "You can compare it with other pictures of her."

"You know perfectly well that there are no other pictures," Ally said.

Abruptly, Pat got up and disappeared into another room. While she was away, the dog kept its vigil. Ally looked right back into its button eyes, remembering that dogs could be cowed by a human gaze. She had spent hours playing alone in the courtyard of their apartment complex while Mama entertained her "guests" upstairs. The big boys of the neighborhood had been a nuisance, but their barking mutts had been worse. And then she had found out that displaying dominance by staring into a dog's eyes would send it running. It worked with big boys, too.

But this dog was an exception. It growled low in its throat and opened its mouth, the unnaturally long tongue lolling out like a pink worm.

Pat came back with an old-fashioned photo album. She opened it and pointed to a picture that seemed identical to the one Ally had brought with her. Looking closer, she realized it was not. The beach was different; and though the young people struck similar poses, the young Carl's arm was not draped around the shoulders of the woman who stood stiffly beside him.

"This is Ros," Pat said.

Ally's first reaction was astonishment. She knew that Carl had an eye for female beauty—hell, he had married her, hadn't he? So how could her predecessor have been this drab little creature? She was not exactly plain but her appearance was so understated that it was impossible to say anything definitive about her. She was neither tall nor short; neither fat nor thin, neither blonde nor brunette. She was generic.

"She was a friend," Pat said with a quiet venom in her voice. "My best friend. For twenty years. She did not have many friends besides me. Carl was her entire life. She lived and breathed for him. She died because she tried to give him what he wanted. And a week after her death, he took out every single picture of her and burned it. And a year after her death, he married . . . you!"

"You meant to say, 'he married a mail-order bride'," Ally said. "That's fine, I've been called this and worse. Only it's a lie. Carl married me because he loves me. And I'm not for sale. I clawed my way out of a hole people like you don't even know exists. So don't try to make me feel bad about my marriage. Just tell me what you mean by 'she died because she tried to give him what he wanted'. Didn't Ros die of lung cancer?"

"That's what he told you?" Pat sniffed exaggeratedly. "He's even worse than I thought if he lied about her death! No, Ros died of ectopic pregnancy!"

Even though she had suspected something like this after seeing the pear in the basement and Gabriela's baby, it still felt like a punch in the gut.

"She tried and tried," Pat continued in the same slightly theatrical tone. "They had been married for almost twenty years. She tried everything—IVF, egg donors. Carl would not hear about adoption. She was afraid he was going to divorce her and marry someone younger. She sat right here, where you are sitting, and cried and cried . . . and then she got pregnant."

"How?" Ally asked.

Pat shrugged. The dog by her side shifted and sat up in an almost human posture, with its hind legs hanging off the edge of the sofa.

"She called it a miracle," Pat said. "She hoped Carl would cherish her again . . . but instead he drew further away. I was her only support. She spent most of her time here, with me. And then, one night . . . he told us she had started bleeding and by the time he drove down to Sequoia Hospital, it was too late. That was what he told us."

"Are you saying he did not try hard enough to save his pregnant wife?" Ally asked.

Pat shuffled through the photo album and pulled out another picture.

"It was taken a week before her death," she said.

Ally looked at the photograph and shuddered. Mama's other pregnancy had happened before Ally was born and naturally there were no pictures of it, but she had seen some of her friends with jutting bellies and bloated feet. She was under no illusion that pregnancy made a woman beautiful. But what it had done to Ros was horrifying.

If in the first photograph Ros had been self-effacing, the woman in this picture was as far from inconspicuous as possible. She had ballooned into a carnival monster. Her slight body was now a bulging sack straining against her tent-like dress. Her ankles swelled so much that they overhung her shoes. Her face seemed misshapen and elongated. But despite everything, the grotesque woman on the sofa had a vitality totally missing from the lackluster girl on the beach. Her eyes blazed in her puffy face.

"She must have been really sick!" Ally said.

"She was!" Pat's voice rose. "And he didn't care! He would go on his business trips and leave her alone in the house! If it were not for me and Gabriela . . . If you think he'll treat you better, you are a fool. Sure, you're young and pretty. But if you get sick, you think he'll stick around to take care of you? He'll just trade you in for a newer model!"

"Nonsense!" Ally retorted but for once, Pat's words hit their target.

"Really? So why did he burn all Ros' pictures? It wasn't for your sake! No, Carl has a bad conscience about his wife. You want to know for sure? Give him these pictures, see how he reacts!"

Ally shrugged but she had to acknowledge that Pat had a point. The disappearance of Ros' pictures was something she had wondered about herself. And it would be an exaggeration to say that she actually knew her husband. He was her lifeline, her anchor in a new country. She should find out as much as she could about him—for her own protection.

She pocketed the pictures and got up, casting another look at the sitting dog. Was the creature actually leering at her? No, with everything that was going on she was beginning to see atrocious miracles everywhere.

Before she escaped the house, though, there was one other thing she had to ask:

"Did Ros ever share a pear with Gabriela?"

Even as she was asking it, she realized how ridiculous it sounded. Pat shrugged.

"Pear? You mean like a fruit? It is sometimes hard to understand what you are saying . . . Well, I'm sure she did. More than once. Gabriela was very good to her, keeping her company while Carl was away."

Walking back to her house, Ally ran into Jennifer Mackenzie. It was surprising to see another pedestrian here and she stopped to greet the woman. Jennifer seemed to be wearing the same outfit she had at Ally's party: yoga pants and a dark sweatshirt liberally sprinkled with cat fur. The only difference was that she had the cat with her now. On a leash.

The cat was huge, with big blue eyes peeking from the aureole of fluffy white fur. It trotted stately on, unfazed at being in the position normally reserved for dogs.

"I've never seen a cat on a leash," Ally said after they exchanged greetings.

"His name is Prince," Jennifer replied. Ally realized the woman was quite attractive, despite her shabby clothes and lack of makeup, but she seemed unwell: her face pasty and gaunt, her pupils dilated.

"People seem to keep a lot of pets here," Ally remarked. "I just saw Pat Donegan's dog!"

"That witch!" Jennifer giggled unsteadily. "Her dog is evil. Prince will have him for lunch!"

Was she stoned? Ally could not smell the telltale sweetish aroma of pot. The only stink was that of her feline companion.

"Why is he evil?" she asked.

"Did she tell you his name?" Jennifer leaned toward Ally conspiratorially. "She got him in the Bleeding Grove where no sane person goes. She is stealing letters from other people's names to make one for him. It is already so long!"

She opened her arms wide to demonstrate how long the dog's name was supposed to be. Prince meowed.

"Did she steal a letter from yours?" Ally asked.

"Worse. She stole my entire middle name. I no longer remember it. Do you have a middle name?"

"No," Ally said. "We don't have middle names. We have patronymics."

"What's yours?"

"Aleksandrivna."

The cat meowed again, this time with such a rising and falling intonation that it sounded like an articulate word in some unknown language.

"Not true!" Jennifer swayed and wagged her finger at Ally. "Princc knows!"

Ally bit her lip. She knew nothing about her father except the name, Alexander, and the fact that he was an officer. That was what Mama had told her and she believed it. She was not going to doubt her mother because of a cat!

On the other hand, a familiar and unwelcome thought stirred in her brain. There was a law inherited from the old Soviet Union that a mother could make up any man's name to put on a baby's birth certificate. This was to prevent children from being stigmatized if they were born of some chance encounter or drunken rape.

Ally put the whole issue out of her mind; she had more immediate problems to deal with. She looked back at the cat and could swear he winked at her.

"Wise cat!" she said. "Where did you get him?"

"He got me," Jennifer replied. "In Nightwood, of course. But not where the witch goes. No, no, no! Don't ever go close to the Bleeding Grove!"

"I won't," Ally said, "if you tell me where it is!"

"Here, of course!" Jennifer made an expansive gesture

encompassing the dank redwoods wreathed in the rags of clouds. "All over here! But I must go. Ciao, darling!"

And she sauntered into the creeping fog. As she disappeared from view, Ally saw the cat get up on his hind legs and walk upright, jerking the leash that still connected him to the woman. Except that Ally now realized that the leash was not held in Jennifer's hand but wrapped around her wrist and brutally tied, so tight that her fingers were swollen.

Chapter 11:
Abduction

When Carl came home, she was ready; wearing her new red dress, a new ruby gloss on her lips, a new Chloe perfume on her hair. Beauty rituals were her armor against adversity.

Carl gave her a long hug when he walked in. They talked about the weather over dinner, sipping Barbera wine in the candlelight while the milky fog lapped against the glass. She felt a strange sense of nostalgia as if the entire peaceful, prosperous evening was already in the past, something she was merely remembering rather than experiencing. She was tempted not to speak, let it go. But she knew it would not work. The curious bride was saved; the obedient ones were slaughtered.

She cleared the table and came back to the dining table where Carl was finishing his second glass and staring into the darkness outside. Ally dropped the pictures she had gotten from Pat in front of him.

He started so violently that the wine bottle tilted over and spilled a long blood-red slick onto the white tablecloth.

"Where the fuck did you get those?"

Ally was used to dealing with angry men. But she was unsettled when she realized that Carl was not angry. He was scared.

"Pat Donegan gave them to me," she said.

"That witch! I should have known . . . Why, Ally? Why?"

"What is Nightwood?" she asked.

His face, dappled by candlelight, was contorted into a grotesque mask of shock and incredulity. But she was not afraid *of* him, she suddenly realized. She was afraid *for* him.

He touched the pictures, smoothed them over with his palm. It should have been a gentle gesture. It wasn't.

Finally, he spoke, his eyes riveted to the faces of his dead wife.

"I wanted Ros to keep working. She was a programmer, a good one. But we didn't need money anymore. And she loved this house. We designed it together. Well, she did most of it. And then she resigned from her company and just holed up here. She never went down except for shopping once a week. And she . . . we were trying to have kids."

He fell silent for a long time and Ally waited.

"Why did I marry her?" Carl suddenly laughed. "You think I'm trying to make you feel better? No, not really. It's the truth. I was never in love with her. I was on the rebound. And Ros was very . . . comforting. Not like Carmela, the opposite of her."

"The girl in the first picture?"

"Yeah, right. She dumped me. I was heartbroken. And Ros . . . she had a way with her. I used to tell her she had magic. I thought it was . . . whaddaya call it . . . a meta-something . . . "

"A metaphor?"

"Yes. But now I'm not so sure . . . "

He blindly reached for his glass and seemed surprised it was empty. Ally fetched another bottle and poured him more wine. She shook her head when he offered to do the same for her.

"Drink a little more. Helps you relax."

"My mother was an alcoholic," Ally said. "She got drunk one night, walked out into the city and disappeared. Nobody knows what happened to her."

"You never told me."

"No. And you never told me about Ros."

"True," Carl swigged the wine. "We should have had this talk before the wedding, huh? But what would I tell you? That my late wife was a witch? That she was going into a place that does not exist? Looking for a baby in the woods?"

"She found it, didn't she?" Ally said pointing to the picture of pregnant Ros.

Carl made a strange gesture, as he was trying to swipe the photographs off the table but stopped with his arm in mid-air. Or was stopped.

"I never wanted it," he whispered. "I had never wanted children much, and after what I saw it was doing to Ros, I didn't want it at all. She became totally obsessed. And then there were these women here, encouraging her, bringing her stupid books . . . Pat. And

Susie. I liked Mitch a lot, he was a sensible sort. Why did he marry that crazy lady?"

Ally thought that this was becoming the leitmotif of the evening: why did he marry her, why did she marry him? At least she knew the answer for herself.

Carl was rapidly sinking into drunken self-pity and Ally realized she had to prod him if she wanted to learn more.

"Did she bring the pear from Nightwood?" she asked.

He fairly jumped.

"How do you know about the pear?"

"I read my fairy tales. And so did she. I saw her books."

Carl stared into the darkness outside.

"One day I came home," he said. "I was determined to tell her that was that. No more having sex on some doctor's schedule, no more temperature charts I was happy being childless and if she was notshe was free to go I remember driving up the road, feeling great, actually hoping she would say 'no'. There was that deer—it almost rammed the car. I think it was a deer. Anyway, when I stepped into the house, she was radiant. The table was set and there was that damn pear on a large plate in the middle, cut into two. She said: 'This is our baby. We share it and we have a baby in nine months.' I thought she was insane. I stormed out, drove down to Palo Alto, stayed in the Cardinal. I remember I slept soundly for the first time in many months. I even retained a divorce lawyer. But then she showed me the test."

"She actually did get pregnant."

"Yes. I was not sure the child was mine. But it did not matter. I was afraid of her. She was crazy. No, not really. Just herself. For the first time. Not pretending anymore to be normal. To be human."

"But you didn't eat the second half of the pear?" Ally asked. Carl shook his head.

"I know who did," Ally said. "Gabriela."

He looked at her in amazement, for the first time tearing his eyes away from the pictures of Ros.

"How do you know?"

"Because she has a baby the same age as Ros' baby would have been. A deformed child. Ros didn't understand the *geis,* the spell. She had to eat the entire fruit. So, her baby was incomplete, and she could not bring it to term."

"She was bleeding," Carl whispered. "So much blood. I drove down like crazy with her in the back seat but there were people on the road. Naked people. Strangers. There are no strangers here. Ever. She was dying. And all she could talk about, all she wanted me to promise was to keep her pictures. To keep her pictures in the house. All of them."

Ally started, realizing with horror the mistake she had made.

"In the hospital they told me the baby could have never lived. I didn't care. I just wanted it to be over. I tried to do as she had asked, to keep her pictures. But it was intolerable. I felt like I was constantly being watched."

"So you burned them."

"Yes. And now they are back."

"I'll get rid of them!" Ally cried.

Carl covered the pictures with his hand and shook his head.

"No! I will do it later. Seriously, I will. Go to bed, honey, I'll be in soon."

"I'll stay with you."

"No. I need to be alone."

Ally cast about for the words that would change his mind, but she knew that words were impotent. He seemed to be shrinking, moving away from her, and nothing she could do would reverse it. Just like Mama.

She nodded and walked to the bedroom. Carl's voice stopped her.

"You know I love you, Ally."

"Yes," she said. "I know."

He did not come to bed but somehow, she managed to drift into sleep anyway. She dreamed about deer in the woods watching her with tremulous eyes.

She woke up suddenly and completely, the echo of a crash reverberating in her ears. The bedroom was filled with bright moonlight, the lovely magical radiance silvering the tree-trunks outside. The fog had disappeared, and the sky was clear, sprinkled with stars

The bed by her side was empty and undisturbed. Carl had not come in.

Ally squinted at the bedside digital clock. Midnight.

She got up, shivering. It was unbelievably cold, as if the glass barrier between the bedroom and the woods had melted into the air. Ally actually touched the wall to reassure herself that it was still there.

She listened intently but all was silent. No, not quite. The rustle of dry leaves outside, the crack of a twig. It must have been deer but strain as she might, she could see nothing moving.

And then there were footsteps. Not outside—in the house. In the living room.

Ally relaxed and chided herself for an idiot for having succumbed to her fears. Carl was here, he was coming to bed, and everything was going to be all right. Even if Nightwood was real, even if her suspicions were correct—they could still salvage their lives. They could sell the house, move back down to the Peninsula, live surrounded by the bustle of people, the ringing of cellphones, the chatter of civilization that would silence the malevolent whisper of ancient tales.

Something moved in the moonlight outside the glass wall. A figure trudging down the slope toward the tangle of manzanitas that guarded the entrance to the redwoods. A beige smudge of something alive walking through the night.

Ally wanted to believe it was a deer, but she knew better. The figure was walking upright.

She plastered herself to the glass wall. The man paused, turned his head, and looked back at her.

It was Carl, stark naked, his sagging paunch pathetic in the unforgiving light of the moon. She could see his tormented face clearly. His mouth was opened in a black oval of pleading. But before she could as much as raise her hand in response, he turned around and sped up, jerkily, toward the thorny barrier. He was walking very fast, his legs scissoring mechanically as if he were being tugged on an invisible lead. He crashed straight through the bushes and Ally winced when she saw sharp branches bite into his defenseless flesh. And then he was gone, dissolved into the silver light and lacy shadows.

The footsteps in the living room were as loud as thunder in the sudden hush.

Ally looked around frantically for something to use as a weapon. Carl had told her there was an old shotgun in the house, but she did not know where. And would a shotgun help against such an intruder?

She grasped the bedside lamp and walked out into the living room. In the moonlight, it seemed to have expanded, grown even larger, populated by swaying shadows as restless as the trees outside. The couches and coffee tables crouched in unexpected places, threatening to trip her up.

At first, she saw nobody. But then she made out a denser shadow by the far wall close to the kitchen. It stirred and stepped into a patch of moonlight.

The creature was hunchbacked and deformed, with arms so long they trailed behind it. Its outthrust head bore a short pug muzzle and as it hissed at Ally, its small teeth glistened with ropes of saliva. But then it turned and scuttled away into the kitchen, and she saw that its back was covered with large, overlapping scales.

No, not scales. Leaves.

Shaking off her paralysis, she ran after it. She collided with a rocking chair and fell. When she picked herself up, the creature was nowhere to be seen. Ally rounded the corner of the bar and rushed into the kitchen.

It was standing by the basement door. As contorted as it was, she could not estimate its size, but it did not appear to be more massive than herself. If she could get a knife, she had a chance against it . . .

The creature hissed again, opening its maw wide. Its head was covered with fine grey hair and had no eyes or ears. The rest of the body was bare and vermicular—except for the armor of leaves on the back that made it look like a giant woodlouse. Ally started to sidle around the stove, aiming for the counter where the knives were.

The creature kicked the door open and dove into the darkness inside.

Ally's heart hammered in her chest, blue circles rotating in her field of vision. She gulped air and squatted, head down, until the faintness passed. Then she grabbed a knife and went to the open door, clicking on all the kitchen lights on the way.

She stood on the first step, like a swimmer above the dark frigid water There was a moment of hesitation when she considered turning back. Could she really do anything for Carl if he had gone into Nightwood? Did she care enough to try to save him?

It was not about Carl. It was about being able to live with herself.

Ally started down, cautiously testing each step with her bare toes as if they could suddenly dissolve into nothingness. At the bottom of the stairs, she clicked on the light switch, convinced it would not work. But it did; a soulless electric light flooded the corridor. She did not bother checking all the rooms but went straight to the last one packed with Ros' possessions. The room was empty, the woodlouse creature nowhere to be seen. The half-pear on the plate had rotted into a shriveled brown stub. Otherwise, the room appeared unchanged. The mirror was still veiled.

Ally was about to back out when she realized that something *had* changed. The stuffed swan above the mirror—the last time she had seen it, its head was tucked under its wing. Now its neck was stretched forward, the beak opened in a silent scream, the glass eyes glittering.

Ally fled upstairs.

On the dining table, Carl's glass still stood beside the now-empty bottle. But Ros' photographs were gone.

Nightwood had taken back its own.

Chapter 12:
Eric.

"**I need to** talk to Jennifer."

Ally's cold fingers could not properly grasp the phone. The house was freezing.

"Alyona?" Eric said, stretching out her name until it resembled a word in a Tolkienesque language. She smiled, despite herself.

"You can call me Ally. Yes, it's me. And sorry, but I need to talk to Jennifer. It's rather urgent."

There was silence on the other side and then Eric said, "I'm afraid Jennifer is not here."

"Do you know where I can find her?"

"No."

Another blind alley, then.

Perhaps there was still time to reconsider. She wavered. And then, Mama's throaty, raspy voice in her mind: "*You are an officer's daughter.*"

Officers don't leave comrades in captivity.

It was probably a fantasy: her father may have been an anonymous drunk, a befuddled john. But it was her story and she clung to it. People lived by stories. And here, in these woods, they died by them.

"Can I talk to you, then?" she asked.

"Of course. Would you like me to come over?"

She almost said *yes* and then reconsidered. What if it was dangerous for him? She was not afraid for herself. Apparently, Nightwood did not want her. She was not sure why; perhaps because she had unwittingly done its bidding by giving Carl Ros' photos?

She realized she had been silent for a long time and quickly said into the waiting phone, "No, no! I'll come to you."

Driving down the private road to Eric's house, Ally questioned herself again. It was so seductive—just do nothing, wait for the commotion to die down, and then . . . She was young and pretty. And she would be rich. She would be an American. Before the wedding, she had consulted a lawyer who checked the paperwork. Everything was in order. She was Carl's legal heir. Everything that belonged to him was hers now.

And wasn't this why she had married him? Beggars could not be choosers; nor could they afford the luxury of self-deception. She had not loved Carl on their wedding day. She did not love him now.

But what difference did this make? She was his wife. And she owed him. She had to prove to herself that she was not just a sale item, a mail-order bride. A *schlucha*. A whore. That she paid her debts.

The car skidded on the narrow road and Ally, swearing in Ukrainian, fought to keep it under control. Clearly, she had not mastered the art of driving yet, despite it being a necessity in the woods.

Hopefully, driving was not a survival skill in the *other* woods. In the place where she was going to find her unloved husband and bring him back.

She clumsily pulled into the driveway of Eric's house. It was smaller than hers and built into the opposite side of the mountain's slope with what must be a great view of the ocean. Right now, all she could see was the milky expanse of clouds lapping at the porch.

Eric led her into the living room, which was not as designer-perfect as hers nor as cluttered as Pat's, but rather pleasantly untidy with some eye-catching objects, including a full-size replica of a Chinese terracotta warrior. He seemed very much at home here, wearing casual jeans and an Eiffel tower sweatshirt. Ally remembered that he traveled a lot on business and felt another tug of doubt: she could go anywhere in the world now, see Paris, London, Shanghai. She squelched the thought, smiled at him, and sneezed explosively.

"Sorry!" Eric apologized. "The house is full of cat fur. I'll have to do professional cleaning."

"Prince?" Ally asked.

"Yeah . . . That cat. I'm actually glad Jennifer moved out and took him with her. He and I never got along."

"No surprise," Ally said, sitting down at the kitchen counter and sipping the bitter coffee Eric offered her. "He was probably jealous of you. A familiar often is."

"A familiar?" Eric raised one eyebrow and Ally had to look into her cup in order not to stare at him. There was something about his face that made her feel flustered. Talking to him was eating at her resolve, so she cut to the chase.

"Did Jennifer tell you where she was going?"

He shook his head.

"No. I came back home and found her gone. I tried to get in touch, but her phone is off. I called her mother and sister, but they haven't heard from her in ages. A lot of her stuff is still here."

So was he concerned about her as a friend or did he want her back? Ally put down the unworthy thought, but Eric went on as if she had spoken aloud.

"Jenni and I are good friends. We even had a fling in high school but it was ages ago. Anyway, she had nowhere to go, and I was glad to help her out, but she was getting . . . a little weird. That cat and other things."

"Did she ever talk about Nightwood?" Ally asked.

He looked away.

"Why do you need her, if you don't mind my asking?" he said. "I didn't know the two of you had even met."

"Only twice," Ally said. "And the second time I met her she talked about Nightwood. I have to go there."

Eric bit his lip.

"I want to show you something," he said. "Jenni left her computer here. I know I shouldn't have done it but I was concerned. Her phone is off. Her family . . . they don't care. And that computer, it was her entire office. I couldn't believe she would just leave it like that. So, I opened it. It was child's play to break the password, I told her. But anyway, wait here."

He went to the back of the house, giving Ally a couple of seconds to marshal her unruly thoughts and check the wreath of her plaits.

Eric came back with a Mac and turned it on.

"Jennifer is a fashion designer," he said.

"What?" Of all possible occupations for the woman, this seemed the least likely. Both times when Ally saw her, Jennifer looked as if she had pulled out her clothes at random from a donation box.

"Yeah, funny, isn't it? She has her own website. She is looking for investors and retail opportunities. Or had been looking here is nothing on the hard drive, literally nothing. She erased all her files. All her designs. And if you look at her website," he typed something into Google search, "you'll see this . . . "

The website was a black nothingness, a square of dull unrelieved darkness.

"I don't even know how she did it," Eric continued, "and I'm a software guy. Now watch this."

A tiny red dot appeared in the middle of the screen, grew larger and larger, sending tendrils of scarlet through the background Like the bloodstream of a flayed creature, the network of red flowed through the darkness, cutting it into irregular fragments. And then Ally's brain shifted gears and she realized that it was the other way round: not the red spreading through the black, but the black shadowing parts of the red. The dense tangled mass of branches, twigs and fronds silhouetted against the inflamed sky.

She stretched her hand to touch the screen but before she could do it, the entire process sped up in reverse and the website reverted to the dead screen. Eric tapped on several keys, but nothing happened.

"This crashes the computer," he said. "I'll have to reset it. And there is nothing I can recover from her files."

"This is Nightwood," Ally whispered. "This is where she is gone."

Eric looked at her strangely.

"I heard rumors," he said quietly. "I bought this house when I made a lot of money selling my first start-up. I thought . . . you know, living in nature, all that stuff. And now I think I want to sell it."

"You would be wise to do so," Ally said and got up. "Sorry. I have to go."

"Will I see you again?" Eric asked, and then blushed. "I mean . . . "

Ally smiled.

"I know what you mean. I hope so. I really hope so."

Chapter 13:
The Swan

When she staggered out of the car, shivering, the glass house shone in the dark woods like a lure and tree shadows massed around it. She must have forgotten to turn off the lights, except that she did not remember turning them on. She skirted the pool of glare spilling onto the driveway, trying to make herself invisible—and almost stepped onto a fat banana slug in the grass. Ally lurched aside but then something made her kneel down and examine the creature.

It was curled up into a fleshy loop, the pointed ends of its body touching. Inside the loop, as neatly as a potted plant, was a tiny seedling with a brave leaf unfurling on top. Ally knew that leaf: heart-shaped, dark-green. Domestic lilac! Not the Californian *Ceanothus* but the flower of her childhood, of May in Kyiv when the air was sweet with the scent of purple, pink, and wine clusters. Every May, Mama spent her last *grivny* on a bouquet to decorate their tiny apartment.

Ally felt unwanted tears prickle her eyes. She looked around for something—a stone, a branch—to kill this giant slug that would undoubtedly munch on the seedling. She picked up a rock and dropped it. She could not do it, could not batter and squash living flesh, no matter how repulsive.

At the end, she compromised by picking up the slug and putting it on the other side of the driveway, as far from the lilac as she could. The creature reared its blind head after her, but she had more pressing matters to think about.

Nightwood

She snapped off the lights in the upper level of the house. Now, Nightwood was crowding all around her, giants whispering in the dark. Nightwood—or the night wood. Was there a difference?

She braided her hair into a single thick plait that reached to the small of her back. That was the most practical way of dressing it. Then she realized she was lingering in her cozy bathroom and resolutely walked out.

In Ros' room, the scruffy stuffed swan regarded her balefully with its glass eyes, its neck outstretched, its beak gaping in a soundless hiss. Ally met its malevolent gaze.

"I know what you need," she whispered to herself.

In truth, she did not; or at least, she was not sure. But the only way to find out was to try.

Magic did not exist: so much she had learned in her anthropology studies. Or rather, it did not exist in the same way as science. There was no universal body of magical tricks one could learn. Grimoires were nonsense; incantations a waste of time. But people, places and objects had power and this power could be channeled. Means of channeling, however, were as varied as people who used them. What worked for Ros would not work for herself.

Ally grew up with plaintive folk songs, sad ballads, chronicling the bloody history of her land: the massacres, the wars, the invasions, the pogroms. She grew up with riddles and ditties. Children used simple rhymes when playing hopscotch. Adults read and wrote poetry.

She was not particularly good at it. Rhymes and rhythms did not come to her naturally. But she could try.

"Feather of swan and bird's wing,
Bells of night begin to ring!"

Nothing changed and Ally winced. This sounded stupid! She tried again.

"Bird of mourning, bringer of sorrow,
Your white dress let me borrow!"

Her entire body began tingling, a wave of heat that started at her toes and swiftly climbed up her thighs, her belly, reaching into the darkness within: the nugget of Nightwood wrapping around her organs, whispering in her blood. Her clothes curled around her as if burning in invisible fire, melding with her skin, sprouting pale shafts that quickly put out soft tremulous barbs. Ally gasped when the wave of heat reached her heart and it stilled and then began beating again but at a wild, birdlike pace.

While her lips were still her own, she shouted out the first thing that came to mind:

"*Maiden swan, tried and true,*
Open the door, let me through!"

The pain that shot through her arms was unbearable. She actually heard the crack of her bones, as they were broken and reset in seconds, and she flapped her crooked feathery limbs, trying to stop the transformation, to take it all back, but the wave was now crawling up her neck reaching her face, and then it felt as if a noose of fire encircled her neck. It did not slow down the change. Just the opposite: her face melting and hardening like ice in thaw, the fire-noose clamped down onto her windpipe, choking off her words and fixing her into the shape she did not want, did not need . . . but now it was too late!

She opened her flattened, rigid lips to take it back and only a loud honk came out. The swan on the mirror honked back and the black veil slipped off. In the mirror, she saw herself as she had become, and in horror, she tried to back off, waddling clumsily on her short legs, but then she could no longer see herself, only the black bristling trunks against the bloody sky. The swan flapped her wings; but Nightwood reached through and drew her in.

Part 2:

Little Mother

Chapter 1:
The Three Horsemen

The White Horseman was late.

Alyona was drawing water from the waterless well. The moss-covered coping was slippery under her elbows as she tugged on the rope. The inky hole seemed bottomless and if she overbalanced and fell, she would be gone without even a splash. She had lost a bucket this way. The knot unraveled and the bucket disappeared as gently and permanently as a seed sliding into the gullet of a chicken. Little Mother had not beaten her for the lost bucket. Instead, she whistled and a pair of green hands, rotten flesh falling off the clawed fingers, shot out of the well and waved.

"Next time you go down," Little Mother said in her lovely trilling voice, and Alyona nodded obediently. Nowadays, she checked the rope twice before lowering the bucket. The problem was that the light from the fence-sitters was dim, and she was never sure the knot was tight enough.

She strained to bring the bucket up. It was heavy, filled with sloshing water, even though the well was dry. Her pinned-up braid slipped from under the kerchief and flapped against her back. Alyona groaned. The heavy, useless, unmanageable hair! It was one of the things that made her so ugly, along with her calloused fingers, her insipid blue eyes, and her washed-out complexion! Several times she asked Little Mother to allow her to cut off the burdensome braid but was denied permission. Well, Little Mother knew best!

But the White Horseman was definitely late! Normally, he would gallop across the lumpy landscape by the time the bucket was lowered into the well. Now, full to the brim, the bucket was finally out, and the night was still as black as tar. The only light was provided by the ruddy glare of the fence-sitters. Their burning sockets followed Alyona as she walked back to the house, trying not to step on the jagged cracks in the path.

She had already done everything. When the Black Horseman had galloped through the farmyard, stirring her from her perch in the coop that she shared with the rest of the fowls, she had quickly waddled outside, followed by their envious stares. The fowls envied her because she was the only one of them allowed to shed her plumage. Stupid birds! They did not understand how little she wanted to go through the excruciating process of change that wrenched her feathery body into a wrong shape. And for what? To become this clumsy creature, with her rough hands and wooly hair! To be conscious every moment of how ugly she was compared to Little Mother! To be troubled by slippery thoughts, elusive feelings, almost-memories! She would be happy to remain in the wordless contentment of the coop forever, sharing warmth with the other fowls. Even their cackling and wailing did not trouble her at daytime; it was only at night that she felt there was something wrong about it. She hated the words that came back to her when she stood up on those thick legs and flexed those long fingers. Words enabled you to name thoughts and feelings—and once named, they became as pestiferous as flies.

But there was nothing to be done about it. Little Mother needed help with the farm. And Alyona—that unwanted name— was the only one to help her. Alyona should feel proud of having been chosen, not fret about it.

She had worked diligently through the night. After the Black Horseman had ridden through the farm, Alyona stretched her aching back, winced at the rough feel of homespun on her naked skin, and set about her duties. First, she rushed into the barn. The cow was standing up against the wall. Her wet brown eyes locked rebelliously with Alyona's but she made no move to scramble into the corner or lower her horns as she occasionally did. Alyona could see why: the cow's udders stuck out, swollen with milk, and she needed relief, no matter how much she resented her dependency.

She pulled out a milking stool and making the cow bend down, started milking, humming a necessary song:
Cow of gold, cow of gold
Do as you have been told!
The cow was silent as a jet of foaming milk quickly filled first

one pail and then the other. This was not hard work, like hauling water, but Alyona was glad when it was done. There was something . . . something about it . . . she lost the word.

She cleaned out the coop. The fowls were all asleep. It made the task so much easier, not to have to look into their eyes and see their . . . again, the word eluded her, and she was glad of it.

Sweep the yard, clean the kitchen, draw water from the dry well.

All was done. And now, it was the time for the White Horseman and he was late!

Suddenly, a luminescent streak parted the blackness of the sky. The clutter of hoofs broke the predawn hush. And the White Horseman was there. As usual, he emerged from the tangle of the Thorny Wood, passed through the Gate of Clasped Hands (whose fingers obediently unclasped for him), and rode through the spacious yard so quickly that Alyona had no time to take in the details of his appearance. She retained only the general impression of a swirling cloak the color of mist, wide-brimmed hat as grey as ash, and the whey-pale, featureless face. He passed through the curtained entrance to the big house that was off-limits to Alyona—she was only allowed into the kitchen annex. Not that there would be anything for her to seek inside Little Mother's quarters, of course.

The sky instantly brightened, settling into the no-color of a dusty lampshade. Alyona hurried back to the coop. The fowls had already emerged, flapping their useless wings and crying in fluting voices. She threw a handful of grain onto the ground and paused to watch them squabble in the dust. An unpleasant sensation stirred her blood and she looked away.

No time to tarry! She had little time before the appearance of the Red Horseman and still one important task to conclude. Alyona quickly made breakfast for Little Mother: a cup of milky tea and a boiled egg. Her own meal of watery porridge would have to wait until the reappearance of the Black Horseman.

She went back into the yard. The Red Horseman's time! She stopped for a second to admire his scarlet cloak, big ruby hat with a nodding plume, and ruddy face. The Red Horseman followed his white brother's route: through the Gate of Clasped Hands, across the farmyard and through the curtained entryway. But today he paused, turned around and flashed a smile to Alyona.

She felt her face contort and then a word swam up from the depth of her mind to name what she was doing. She was smiling back! Her hand rose, seemingly of its own volition, to wave at the Horseman.

The other fowls stopped their mindless clucking and stood almost upright The Red Horseman dove into the house and the red ball of the sun winked into existence in the blank sky, flooding the farm with inflamed light. The fowls dropped back into their habitual hunch, their curved backs forcing their heads to the ground, their feather-fringed arms flapping as if trying to pick grain out of the dust. They could not do it, of course: their fingers had atrophied and the only way for them to feed was to root in the dirt with their soft lopsided beaks.

Alyona was staring at the sky the color of cracked glass, expecting something more, something else and it came, though in the last moment of human lucidity, she realized it was not what she was hoping for. But she could not resist the implacable force that bent her backbone, fused her lips, wrenched her arms, and sent her scuttling into the coop, there to doze with her head under her wing until the Black Horseman rode through the yard and the sun winked out.

Chapter 2:
Eric and Malika

Eric **Greenberg swiped** his phone off and tossed it at the desk. Another potential funding had just fallen through. He felt angry, disillusioned, almost defeated. But no! He would not let himself succumb to negativity. Eric was a winner. He knew it about himself. Money would come sooner or later as it had come in the past. After all, how many thirty-year-old's owned a multi-million dollar house in an exclusive mountain preserve?

Though to be honest, recently, the neighborhood had been going to the dogs. Or the cats?

It had started with Jennifer and her stupid cat. And now Jenni was missing, and he felt responsible. He shivered, looking out into the fog-wreathed redwoods. It was always chilly here, and when he had bought the house with the proceeds of his previous startup, he had wanted this: giant trees, green silence, bracing air. But now the silence seemed to be filled with stealthy rustling; the freshness turned to paralyzing cold; and the trees, the trees were watching him.

Nightwood. Where old tales lived, and ancient nightmares preyed upon the weak and the vulnerable.

Which one was he? Weak? Eric the techie. Eric the entrepreneur. Eric who had sold his first startup at the age of twenty-five.

Or vulnerable? Eric who, from the age of five, had never doubted he was going to be successful. Son of academics, grandson of immigrants. Who had escaped the hell of war-torn Eastern Europe, made it to the US, made it big. He suddenly wished he had talked more to Nana, perhaps learned the liquid tongue she and Granddad had occasionally spoken. Now it was too late. His grandparents had been dead for more than ten years.

He drummed his fingers on the side-table. Of course, he was troubled about Jennifer. Where she could have gone, how to get her back. He tried to visualize her face, as if it would place a virtual call to a place where no calls went through, but instead another face stubbornly projected itself onto the screen of his mind. Big blue eyes and high cheekbones, a waif-like figure crowned by that incredible hair . . . Rapunzel.

No, not a fairy-tale princess. Ally Morris. Wife of Carl Morris, a venture capitalist who flatly refused Eric's tentative approach for funds. Carl whose only topic of conversation was money and what it could buy: classic cars, big houses, more money. A new wife.

Of course, she was a mail-order bride, even though Eric did not think she had actually arrived on Carl's doorstep in a Fed-ex package. But she might as well have. Bought and paid for.

And yet, she had gone into Nightwood in order to bring Carl back. Why? How could she possibly love him?

Eric picked up his iPhone and speed-dialed Ally's number. It went to voicemail as it had done at least ten times in the two days since she had showed up on his doorstep, asking for a way into Nightwood. As if it were as easy as finding a place on Google maps. Clearly, she had done something right since she seemed to have disappeared as thoroughly as Jennifer. Or as Susie who, was now officially listed as a missing person. And all he had done, so far, was dial the missing women's numbers like an agnostic muttering a prayer that he knows won't be answered.

Suddenly, Eric got profoundly angry with himself. What was wrong with him? He was a doer, a problem-solver! Not somebody to waffle and procrastinate!

Not somebody to fall in love with another man's wife.

He put the unwelcome thought out of his mind and concentrated on the practical issue at hand. So, let's assume Nightwood was real. Eric was a fantasy fan, so he felt no particular difficulty in imagining an alternative dimension or even some sort of magical realm adjacent to the real world. Indeed, the lifetime of reading about portals, dragons and rings, and playing Final Fantasy games, had made him certain he would be able to handle whatever dangers Nightwood could throw at him. The issue, however, was how to get there.

If Ally had opened some sort of portal, would it not be in her house? It was worth checking out. Eric jumped into his Subaru and drove up the twisty road. At the very least, he could ascertain whether the Morrisses were indeed missing.

The sun was low in the sky and the boles of redwoods glowed like beaten bronze in the congealing light. Shadows clogged the underbrush. Something crept through the dry madrone bark littering the slope and Eric told himself it was only a gopher.

The Morrisses' glass house looked as if it was on fire. Despite his unflattering opinion of him, Eric had to admit that Carl had a refined taste in architecture. And in women.

Eric pulled in, swerving to avoid the yellow Tesla that was parked aslant the driveway. Was somebody home, then? But then he remembered that Carl collected cars.

A circuit of the house established that two cars were parked at the lower level and probably some more in the garage. Eric knocked on the door and smiled uncertainly into the security camera. He could see through the glass wall into the empty living room where shadows swayed like underwater weeds.

He scribbled an innocuous note and with some trepidation, left it on the porch. He should not feel guilty, he told himself. He was not having an affair with Carl's wife; he was just being a considerate neighbor.

As he turned around to go back to his Subaru, a black Mercedes glided into the driveway. Eric quickly retrieved the note.

A jeans-clad high-heeled leg emerged from the door. Then another. Ally!

The driver climbed out, and Eric's mouth fell open. She looked like Ally's negative: dark where Ally was fair; tall where Ally was slight, hair covered with a headscarf where Ally's was elaborately coiffed.

"Are you Mr. Morris?" the woman asked in a musical voice. Her accent was different from Ally's.

Eric extended his hand.

"Eric Greenberg," he said. "I'm their neighbor."

He belatedly realized that he might be committing a cultural *faux pas* but the woman shook his hand with no hesitation.

"Malika Abu Hassan," she said. "I was Ally's roommate in Berkeley."

"I don't think she is at home."

"No," the woman said. "I tried to call and text but no answer. I found this place on Google Maps. I just. wanted to see where she lives."

"It's a strange place," Eric said. "I live here myself but it must seem spooky to an outsider."

"It *is* spooky," Malika said. "I'm surprised she soldiers on."

"Her husband likes it here," Eric said. Malika swept her gaze around, taking in the darkening woods and the silent house.

"Is she really here?" she asked.

"No," Eric shook his head. "And neither is Carl."

"Will she be back?"

Eric shrugged. "I don't know," he said honestly.

"I have to find her," Malika said with such unexpected passion that Eric started. "She is . . . I really need her."

"I am trying to find her too," he said.

"Do you dream of her?" she asked suddenly.

Eric hoped the twilight masked his blush.

"Dream?"

"I dream of her," Malika said. "I know we had met before I met her, if you see what I mean."

"Not really."

"I don't believe in reincarnation. It is heresy. But we met. When I was a child, I was very sick. I don't remember much of it. But I have the same dream, over and over again. Ally is in it. And that . . . man. That creature. The *asanbosam*. And now my parents want me to marry him."

Eric had no idea what an *asanbosam* was. And yet Malika's statement made a sort of sense. Like him, she was somehow being drawn into Nightwood. She needed Ally, for whatever reason. This made them, well, it made them allies.

"I'll find Ally," he said. This was a promise. He was committing himself.

Malika's smile practically lit up the black forest. It made him feel self-assured. He would find a way. He would succeed as he had always done.

They exchanged numbers and he promised to inform her immediately when he had any clue to Ally's whereabouts. Privately, Eric thought he would go into Nightwood alone to rescue her—and Jennifer, of course. He did not need a traveling companion, especially not a beautiful woman from an unfamiliar culture. Another beautiful woman . . . Anyway, it was good to know that somebody believed him—and believed *in* him.

As they were going back to their respective cars, he asked:

"What does your name mean, Malika? It's a beautiful name."
"Thank you. It means Queen."

85

Chapter 3:
The Helper

She was just in time, arranging the plates and cutlery on the scrubbed-pine table in the kitchen, when Little Mother emerged from her quarters, firmly closing the door behind her. This part of the house was off-bounds to Alyona: Little Mother had made it perfectly clear what the consequences would be if she so much as peeked through the keyhole. Not that she would do it; and not just because she was afraid of punishment. She loved Little Mother!

Of course, she did.

Her beauty alone was enough to melt her heart and to drive home how uncouth Alyona herself was. Little Mother barely came up to Alyona's shoulder and her waist was as slender as a flower stem. Her gossamer-thin hair, floating in the intangible breeze, was silver, but her face was unlined and ageless, with deep black eyes and a rose-red mouth curved in a perpetual smile that never wavered or changed.

She graciously allowed Alyona to sit down. She sipped her tea and cracked open her egg. A blood-suffused yolk spilled onto the plate in a puddle. Little Mother daintily scooped it up with a golden spoon.

"You may eat your dinner," she said to Alyona in a voice as sweet and tinkling as wind-chimes. Alyona complied, gulping down the watery gruel in her dish. She would prefer to eat alone, in tiny swallows, prolonging the experience as much as possible. There was too much work to be done before the return of the Red Horseman.

"I'm going away," Little Mother continued. "You know what to do. And remember what will happen if you try to go where you are not allowed to!"

Alyona's cheeks flushed. Was there any need to repeat the prohibition? Did Little Mother think she was stupid?

"*She is taking care of you,*" a whispery voice said in her ear, and her annoyance dissipated.

"Yes, Little Mother," she said obediently.

The cupid-bow smile that never disappeared grew a little wider.

"Come here!" Little Mother commanded, pulling out a red comb from a pocket of her dress. "I'll comb your hair before I go."

Taking off her kerchief and loosening her braid, Alyona let her hair tumble down to her knees. She let her eyes linger on the yellow tresses whose color was like nothing else on the farm.

No, not true. The golden cutlery that Little Mother used.

The thought was gone as the red comb delicately touched her scalp and then went through the heavy mass of her hair, untangling knots and smoothing frizzes. She was enveloped in a cozy warmth as mindless as the contentment of a thumb-sucking infant. And when Alyona finally emerged from that cocoon, Little Mother had floated away, taking the red comb with her. Alyona's hair lay down her back, all combed out, and she braided it, lingering a little as if fishing for an elusive memory. Tying her kerchief back in place, she heard the rattle of the Gate of Clasped Hands opening and closing. Little Mother was gone.

The rest of the night passed in drudgery. Alyona collected the eggs that the fowls had laid during the day, revolted by their warm softness. The fowls huddled on their roosts, but Alyona had the uncomfortable feeling that some of them were watching her.

She brought fodder to the barn. The cow was awake. When Alyona walked into the barn, she sat by the far wall, her horned head resting on her knees, her hooved forelimbs wrapped up around her knees. Her udders were hidden from view and in this position, she was almost, well, she almost looked like a person.

The fence-sitters glared at her when she rushed back into the yard. The fire in their hollow skulls flared up, illuminating the black spikes of the Thorny Wood on the other side of the bone palisade. The parchment-skinned fingers of the Gate of Clasped Hands, each as long as Alyona was tall, waved at her.

There was some dry bread in the larder, which Alyona washed down with water. Tomorrow there would be more—or maybe not.

When the White Horseman showed up, she was struck by a

strange desire to hide somewhere from . . . she could not find words to describe her desire for herself. And so, she waited passively for the Red Horseman and underwent the excruciating transformation. But this time she was aware that the change did not come from within herself. It was as if . . . as if. Words and thoughts abandoned her, and she slept a dreamless bird-sleep until the Black Horseman showed up. Dragging darkness in his wake—his cloak a churning hole in the landscape, his hat a patch of nothingness, his face an ink blob—he crept through the yard on his sway-backed mare and disappeared through the curtained entryway.

She stretched out, her joints creaking painfully, and peered expectantly into the dull blackness of the sky. Of course, there was nothing to see. The only lights were spreading around the perimeter of the farm as the fence-sitters stirred from their day slumbers and were slowly climbing up to take their positions on the posts.

Little Mother was away but she left instructions for Alyona. A piece of parchment leaped into her hand as she made her way to the kitchen. Written on it in a beautiful cursive were the words "Slaughter and cook a fowl".

The piece of parchment fluttered onto the ground as Alyona doubled over, dry-retching. Slaughter a fowl! No! How could she?

The familiar whispery voice wrapped her mind in thick layers of dullness. It was only a fowl; of course, they were made for being eaten; of course, this is what farmhands and kitchen-maids did; of course, she would not dream of disobeying Little Mother.

Like a sleepwalker, Alyona stumbled into the kitchen, retrieved a cleaver, and went back to the coop. The fowls were asleep, except for one. She sat up on her roost when Alyona walked in and, as if alerted by her, the rest of them woke up, filling the stifling space with their thin crying. Alyona stood at the entrance and looked at their startled melee. The fowl who had been awake looked back, her brown eyes unwavering.

Alyona turned around and walked out. On her way back to the kitchen, she tossed the cleaver into the bushes.

She took out her allotment of bread and stared at the basket of eggs in the larder. Their skin was wrinkled and tufted with sparse hair. One egg was cracked, and the bloody yolk spilled out.

Alyona ate in the yard.

It was small. She realized it with a clarity impossible to deny. Why had it seemed so big before?

Before what?

She tried to peer over the bone palisade into the Thorny Wood. The fence-sitters flexed their diminutive limbs and hissed at her.

Dispirited, she turned back to the house. She had a lot to accomplish, and the night was short.

Why couldn't she work in daytime?

The path was paved with femurs, clavicles, pelvic and humerus bones, all skillfully arranged in a mosaic of interlocking parts. Something lay on the ivory path. It took her a second to realize why the thing stood out. Everything on the farm was white, black, or red: the white of bones, and feathers, and milk; the black of Little Mother's eyes and the thorns outside; the red of the comb and the fowls' egg-laying. But the long thing on the path was yellow—as yellow as Alyona's hair. Her hand went to her head to make sure that her braid was still in place.

The thing on the path suddenly twitched and reared up. Alyona screamed and jumped back. The thing was alive!

It was like a slimy rope with wavering fronds underneath and two stubby horns at one end. Torn between fascination and revulsion, Alyona bent over it, seeking eyes or mouth. It had none.

It contorted itself into a ring and in the center of the ring was something even more astounding than the yellow of the creature. Something green.

Even though the heart-shaped leaves of the seedling looked almost black in the sullen light, she recognized the color immediately. She scooped the seedling into her palm, and the yellow creature—Alyona's mind struggling furiously with its forgetfulness as it fished for a name—crawled away.

She looked at the seedling. It needed, yes, it needed soil! But where?

"*Keep it away from the ghoul's eyes,*" a voice said in her mind.

Alyona gasped, almost dropping the seedling. It was not the whispery voice that lulled her into the dull contentment of her labor. This voice was clear and sharp, cutting through the cobwebs in her brain with a flash of pain. It was coming from outside her. She looked around for the yellow thing (*slug!*) but did not see it.

She stared at the farm with its bone palisade and tar-black sky, and it seemed as insubstantial as the landscape of a nightmare.

"*Time to wake up!*" the yellow voice said.

She hurried into the cow's barn. The cow was curled up in the corner, her patchy hide smoothed by twilight, hidden by a mass of shadows.

Without thinking, Alyona opened her mouth and recited:
Cow of gold, cow of gold,
Help me break the ghoul's hold!
A ghoul? What's a ghoul?
The cow stared at her for a long time and then nodded.

Alyona quickly went to a corner where straw was piled in an untidy heap. She cleared a patch of raw earth, made a hole, and planted the seedling. A drop of water fell onto the soil. Another and another. Alyona roughly smeared tears away from her eyes. She went back to the cow and offered to relieve the pressure in her swollen udders.

Chapter 4:
Cats, Dogs, and Horses

Eric **got up** from the desk and rubbed his eyes. They felt like sandpaper.

He had spent hours with Jennifer's computer, going through the same maddening routine over and over. He would log on to her website, watch black branches sprout on the blood-red background, and the computer would crash. Again and again. He tried the same thing with other computers—his house did not lack hardware—but Jennifer's site could not be accessed from anywhere else. Hell, it did not even seem to exist! It had been expunged from the web.

He would find a way. He knew he would. One thing Eric Greenberg had in abundance was self-confidence. And persistence. The combination had taken him where he was, and he had no intention of giving up. He would keep his promise to Malika. He would find Ally. The two women danced in his mind like a pair of chess-pieces: black and white.

He was exhausted, his brain clogged with fatigue. From the long experience of all-nighters, Eric knew the perfect remedy. He walked to the kitchen, pulled a slice of cold pizza out of the fridge and nuked it in the microwave. With a can of Red Bull, it would set him right!

As he was eating at the counter, he heard the meowing of a cat.

Eric spilled his Red Bull. Was Prince back? That hateful cat who had lured Jenni into Nightwood! Eric did not understand how he could have missed the obvious fact that the giant tom was not an ordinary stray. He used to stare at Eric with his luminescent eyes from the porch before mysteriously disappearing, leaving Jennifer confused and weak. And didn't those eyes look unsettlingly human? Well, no use regretting mistakes. If the cat was back, he would make sure the creature would point to a way into Nightwood, even if Eric had to threaten to skin him alive!

Eric rushed to the door. The porch light was supposed to come on automatically but did not. Cursing—what a time to have his system fail!—Eric ran back to the kitchen and grabbed a flashlight. By the time he came back out, the sounds in his front yard had risen to a crescendo of growling, hissing and—surprisingly—yapping. The flashlight beam picked out a tangle of furious shadows that fell apart, a lighter silhouette disappearing into the bushes. Left in the circle of light was a small dog, its muzzle scratched and bloodied.

Eric recognized the dog. It belonged to Pat Donegan but for the life of him, Eric could not remember its name.

Eric was not a dog person. For some mysterious reason, Nana had hated dogs and her dislike had rubbed onto him. Still, if faced with a choice, he would prefer a pooch to a cat—at least dogs did not make him sneeze. And the creature looked so pitiful, shivering and whining, that Eric's heart melted.

"What's wrong, buddy?" he asked, kneeling in front of the dog. "The bad cat beat you up?"

The dog licked Eric's hand. He scooped it up and carried it back into the house.

In the kitchen he washed out the scratches, which were not particularly deep. The dog wagged its tail, watching Eric with beady brown eyes. Eric smiled.

"You must be hungry, buddy," he said. "No pizza for you, huh? Let me check if we can scare up some burgers."

He turned away to rummage in the fridge and felt rather than saw some ponderous movement behind his back. Eric whipped around—and froze.

The dog was getting bigger like an inflatable balloon, swelling to twice its original size. It continued to grow, even as Eric watched, his mouth hanging open in shock. This was not the smooth, computer-generated increase of a special-effect movie. Rather, it was a bumpy process accompanied by groaning and farting. The creature was distorting, its head shedding patches of fur and bulging out. Its body elongated into a wormy tube. Its mouth split almost to its ears and new teeth, yellow and saliva-wet, sprouted in its jaws. The pink rag of a wet tongue flopped upon the floor.

Nightwood

Eric backed off until he bumped into the counter. The creature growled and started creeping toward him, its tongue leaving slimy tracks on the floor.

Eric rushed out of the kitchen and into the night. His Subaru was parked outside, the keys in the ignition.

He stopped. That was a creature of Nightwood! Shouldn't he try to wrest the secret of access from it?

The creature scurried onto the porch. It was now the size of a pony, sleekly muscled like a German shepherd. The snarling coming out of its gaping mouth rose to the pitch that threatened to burst Eric's eardrums.

A strange image flashed before Eric's eyes: a pack of growling dogs,—or maybe wolves,—tugging and pulling at the bloody rags of a small body, men standing around, smoking, laughing.

He ran, jumped into the car and drove away.

When he came to the abandoned cabin, Eric pulled to the edge and sat with his head in his hands. He wallowed in self-contempt. What was wrong with him? He had been working on gaining access to Nightwood for hours but when Nightwood came to him, he ran away. Coward!

After several minutes of self-flagellation, common sense reasserted itself. What could he have done? He had no weapons at home and the dog-creature was big enough to tear him to shreds. No, he had done the right thing.

Now was time to recoup. Eric decided he would drive down to Palo Alto and get a gun. There was a place down California Avenue that would sell him an entire arsenal. He imagined himself walking into the magic land with a Glock instead of a sword. The image brought a wan smile to his lips. It would be like a game. Like Doom or something!

He sat back and turned on the engine. His eyes were drawn to the cabin, and he remembered the stories about it. He used to laugh at them. Now he knew they were true.

The white curtains in the window were partially drawn, the gap between them showing only dull blackness. How did these curtains in an abandoned cabin always remain fresh? He did not want to do it, but something compelled him to get out of the car and approach the cabin. Its splintered siding shone in the headlights. Eric peered into the crevice between the curtains but saw nothing.

The door to the cabin that had been locked in place as long as he remembered suddenly creaked and swung open.

Eric sprinted back to the car and drove away without looking in the rearview mirror.

He forced himself to pay attention to his driving. Mountain fog lay in discrete bands between the walls of trees. The Subaru wove in and out of milky whiteness like a diver going through layers of plankton in the ocean. At this hour, there would be no bicyclists, but deer loved the night, and he did not want to hit one.

When Eric finally got to the town of Woodside, he relaxed his sweaty hands on the wheel. He realized he was drained. He should find a motel, get a good night's sleep, and start again in the morning.

Something blazed through the firs on the side of the road. Eric slowed down.

Woodside was a rich person's playground: enormous rustic homes screened by mature trees; horses' pens; no sidewalks. Eric had never paid much attention to other people's houses. But this was a mansion to end all mansions. A huge compound lit by the orange glare of sodium lamps mounted on spindly pillars. A fence, bristling with chicken wire, ran between the pillars. Indistinct forms moved beyond the fence, but the light was so harsh that Eric could not make out anything.

He pressed on the accelerator. If some Silicon Valley tycoon had a party in the middle of the night, good luck fighting off the neighbors' complaints. The lighting was like something out of a World War II movie.

The car got to the intersection where he had to turn right to make it to Palo Alto. He drove through this intersection practically every day; he could navigate it with his eyes closed. But now he braked sharply because the right turn was not there.

A pale eucalyptus loomed ahead, shedding bark like leprous skin. Here the road split into two, one branch continuing into the Valley, the other turning left and leading back to Woodside. The left branch was in place. But instead of the tarmac ribbon flowing to the right, the slope beyond the eucalyptus glimmered with the skeletal whiteness of desiccated vegetation and dissolved into darkness, unrelieved by any hint of city lights.

Was he lost? How could that be? There was simply nowhere on this road to take a wrong turn.

Nightwood

Eric remembered that there was a road sign on the intersection and shone his headlights upon it. The sign was there but he could not read it. Spidery letters in an unknown alphabet crawled on the green surface.

Cold sweat dripped into Eric's eyes and he was shivering uncontrollably. Was he hallucinating? Dreaming? He hit his hand hard on the edge of the dashboard and winced in pain. The sign remained unintelligible.

He did not want to go back and could not just stay here. He turned left.

The road ran straight. Here there were some streetlights. One of them had a black sack swaying from the post. It looked like a garbage bag but as he sped past, there was a dark puddle collecting underneath.

He was back in downtown Woodside and the familiar spire of the town church rose from the trees. The church was brightly lit, every window blazing orange. A service in the middle of the night?

He slowed and saw that the plaza surrounding the church glittered with broken glass. All the stained-glass was smashed, the door wrenched off its hinges, and the harsh light coming from the inside was periodically dimmed as hunched silhouettes crossed the gaping frame.

He brought his foot down and the car shot forward, bouncing on the speed bumps. He killed his headlights. There was no need: the entire downtown was brightly lit, each home, business, and shop blazing from every orifice. The streetlights, which he remembered as rather muted, hurt his eyes. More and more of them had large sacks suspended from the posts; some had fallen and lay in leaking heaps. Eric felt that the entire town was watching him with avid, unblinking eyes, but there were no people in the streets.

And then he heard growling. Several black shapes detached themselves from the shadows and leaped in front of the car. Dogs. Big dogs. Wolf-like dogs. He saw a scowling muzzle pressing against the windshield, and then the dog was shaken off and rolled into the gutter. Another one was clipped by the fender and thrown to the side. Shouting curses, Eric plowed through.

The Subaru wove madly as he fought to keep it under control. Fortunately, the road was empty of cars. He left the downtown and was now barreling through the area of horse pens and ranches.

Looking back, he saw the diminishing shapes of running dogs—or were they wolves?—as they failed to keep up. He passed a big ranch, its white fence luminescent. Standing close against the fence, its head thrust out, was a horse. In the gaps between its pale ribs he could see the blazing windows of the ranch-house. Another horse skeleton trotted along the fence, this one stripped of its flesh entirely.

Something splattered on the windshield. Tree drip? Rain? The sky was clear.

Another splat left a red smear on the glass.

Skeletal horses were massing along the sides of the road, watching him with empty sockets. They did not try to jump the fence and insofar as he was capable of feeling anything but the overwhelming rejection of what was happening, he was grateful for it.

The road took a turn he did not remember and ahead, looming against the rich tapestry of stars, was a dark shape. He could not understand what he was seeing. It was too small for a mountain, too large for a building. It was spiky and irregular, bristling with spires and projections. And it was as black as a hole in the sky. Not a single light shone on the huge mass.

He heard something and rolled down the window. A yapping chorus of barks and growls was deafening, and as he looked back, he could see them hurtling down the road. The dogs he had scattered in the downtown were just a small vanguard of this canine pursuit.

The Subaru gave a strangled cough and stalled. Eric juggled the key, pressed the power button. The gas tank was still half-full. But the car was dead.

The dogs were so close that he could smell their fierce stink. The horse skeletons started beating their hooves on the ground in unison, the growing lines of them stomping together, the entire landscape ringing like a bell.

He wrenched the door open, jumped out, and ran.

Chapter 5:
The Pantry

Before the arrival of the Red Horseman, Little Mother was back. Smiling her eternal smile, she nodded to Alyona and passed into her quarters, carrying a squirming bundle in her arms. Alyona shivered in sick anticipation, knowing she would have to tell Little Mother she had disobeyed her order to slaughter and cook a fowl. But the very strength of her fear backfired in anger.

Who was this creature that she should be afraid of her?

Little Mother.

No mother of mine.

A ghoul.

What is a ghoul?

Surprisingly, Little Mother did not appear to mind.

"We need more live fowls to trade," she said, "and we are running low on eggs. It is fortunate that I found a fresh fowl on the market. Take good care of her. If she dies, it'll be on your head."

Alyona bowed, lowering her face.

"I will, Little Mother," she said. "Where is the new fowl?"

Little Mother went back to her quarters and came out, her acquisition toddling along on her pudgy legs and flapping her pudgy arms, barely fringed with emerging feathers. Her mouth had been sewn shut and was just beginning the transformation into a fleshy beak-like proboscis. Alyona stared at her, paralyzed by sudden horror. This was not an egg-laying chicken! This was . . . the word escaped her, as so many did.

She picked up the struggling creature to take it to the coop. Little Mother's voice stopped her.

"Don't you want me to comb your hair? It looks untidy."

Alyona squelched the wave of longing for the soothing touch of the red comb.

"Of course, Little Mother," she said. "Let me settle the new fowl in place and bring fodder to the cow, and then I'll know I deserve your kind touch."

Little Mother's perpetually smiling face was incapable of changing expression, but after a long pause, she nodded and Alyona escaped, carrying the fowl. She set her among her cackling sisters and ran to the barn. The Red Horseman was almost due.

As she stepped over the threshold a sweet, intoxicating smell washed over her, dispelling the fug in her mind. The familiar smell of . . .

The cow had forced herself to stand upright and was staring into the corner where Alyona had planted the seedling. Even in the dim light, the luxuriant blooms shone with vivid burgundy. The heart-shaped leaves trembled.

"Lilac!" she cried, and rushed to the bush, embracing it.

The perfume enveloped her, clusters of star-shaped flowers caressed her face, and the rustling of leaves shaped itself into an echo of a voice.

"Alyonushka . . . "

"Mama!"

The lilac bush thrashed as if whipped by an intangible wind. Something dropped into Alyona's hand. A thin delicate chain with a worn golden cross.

"Mama!"

The hooves of the Red Horseman clacked on the pavement outside and Alyona's body was twisted and kneaded by an implacable force, the necklace still grasped in her feather-sprouting hand.

As the Black Horseman showed up, Alyona rose from her roost, stretching the kinks out of her numbed body. The necklace was cutting into her palm. She quickly slipped it over her head, hiding it under her homespun smock. It lay in the hollow of her neck as if it belonged there.

And then a familiar clear voice spoke in her head.

"You are an officer's daughter!"

Nightwood

"Mama!" Alyona cried, waking up the fowls who stirred on their perches. She looked at them. She looked back at her roost. It was empty. But something had to be there.

She rushed out into the darkness of the yard fitfully illuminated by the glare of the fence-sitters. The door of the barn stood open, the cow crouching in a corner. Dark bruises stood out against its mottled hide.

The lilac bush was uprooted and trampled into the ground. Desiccated blossoms littered the earthen floor.

Keening, Alyona embraced the fragile stem, but it snapped in her arms.

She stood up and addressed the cow.

"Did she do it? The ghoul?"

The cow nodded its horned head.

Alyona rushed out. Anger made her light on her feet. She ran to the kitchen, the cross necklace burning her skin with an urgent fire.

The kitchen was empty. Another parchment note jumped into her hand.

"I'll be away for two nights. Slaughter the new fowl; she is usclcss."

Alyona stood in the kitchen, clutching the note, biting her lipsline. She turned to the second door set into the inner wall that separated the kitchen from the main part of the house, secured with a big padlock. She knew where the key was. It was hanging on a chain around Little Mother's scrawny neck.

She kicked and banged on the door, trying to release her anger, but it only intensified, curdling inside her like sour milk. She stopped when her fists were bloodied, but the need to get into the house did not abate.

And then something occurred to her and she ran out. The fowls (*no, this is wrong, they are not birds, they are girls!*) clustered in the yard, pecking up scant grain with their soft proboscises, their plucked wings fluttering. The new fowl stood aside. Alyona noted that she was trying, fruitlessly, to straighten up her curved spine and hold her head high.

Alyona hesitated, and then went to the new fowl.

"You have to eat," she said in a tremulous voice, realizing that it was the first time she had addressed any of her fellow inhabitants of the coop. She offered her a handful of dusty grain. The fowl batted away her hand, scattering the grain in the dust. The other fowls fell to it in a flurry of clacking.

"You have to eat," Alyona insisted. "Keep up your strength. I . . . I'll free you. I promise."

The cross necklace twitched like a live thing around her throat.

The fowl blinked and she slowly lowered her head and took a couple of grains into her crudely sewn mouth. A jot of horror went through Alyona as a word rose to the surface of her mind—and disappeared, plunging back into forgetfulness. She pressed on the necklace until it cut into her skin.

"I'll be back," she told the new fowl who was trying to chew, even though her teeth had been pulled out. Smears of dry blood streaked her dark cheeks.

Alyona stopped in front of the curtained entryway where the three horsemen entered the house. She saw what she had not noticed before: the curtain was sewn from pelts of weasels, martins, and ferrets, their heads still attached to the splayed skins roughly stitched together. She touched the curtain; the heads stirred and hissed, snapping at her with their needle-like teeth. As if in response, the fence-sitters started a ruckus, clattering their bones. The fire in their bulbous skulls flared up.

Alyona let go of the curtain, afraid that it would somehow alert Little Mother and she would hasten back. But the three horsemen entered the house through this doorway with no impediment, didn't they?

She realized she had to wait. She crouched by the dry well, squeezing the necklace so that its points cut into her skin, the pain keeping her alert, preventing the fug of slavish forgetfulness from enveloping her. There were scratching noises coming from the well; she paid them no heed.

The night dragged on forever but finally, the slight paling of the fence-sitters' fire signaled the approach of the White Horseman. Alyona jumped to her feet, her heart fluttering like a caged bird. She knew she had very little time. The interval between the white and the Red Horseman was short, but it had to suffice.

When the emaciated white horse trotted through the Gate, Alyona flew at the rider, whose blank face showed no awareness of her presence, and grasped his stirrup. The horse paused, its hoof that could brain Alyona with a single kick hovering in the air, but then it resumed its trot. The curtain twitched aside to let the White

Horseman in, and Alyona was dragged into Little Mother's quarters.

It was dim and stuffy inside. The stirrup slipped from her sweaty hand.

She looked around. The White Horseman had disappeared. She stood in a large hall whose domed ceiling was veiled by thick shadows. The hall appeared to be bigger than the entire house seen from the outside. Tables mounded with something dark lined the walls. The air was saturated with meaty stench.

Pieces of human bodies, expertly butchered and deboned and reduced to raw steaks and briskets, lay on the tabletops. The blood drained through the troughs on the side into buckets. There could be no mistake about the identity of these cuts. The heads were placed in the corner of each table, and though scalped and flayed, they still showed their ages and genders—mostly young; mostly men. Their blood-splattered teeth gleamed in their raw faces.

Alyona doubled over, fighting back the tide of vomit that rose in her throat. She kept repeating frantically—*I have not eaten meat! I do not eat meat! I will never touch meat in my life!* The nausea receded and she blessed the dry bread that had been her sustenance since she had found herself in Little Mother's domain.

How long had it been? Hours? Days? Years?

A big key hung on a hook above the tables. She removed it and searched for the door. It took her precious minutes to locate it because it was half-hidden behind the tables. She had to push them aside to get to it. Her hands were bloodstained when she finally managed to insert the key into the keyhole and turn it.

The lintel was so low that Alyona had to duck to get through the door. And when she did, she stepped into a room that was instantly familiar.

Chapter 6:
The Rescuer

Malika was thinking about potsherds.

Even as she was driving down the misty mountain road, her mind was filled with images from her latest nightmare. A barren expanse of sunbaked ground, littered with ochre-colored fragments of broken pots. Hard to imagine anything more different from the mild green lushness of the Californian woods! And yet here it was, lodged in her brain like the bullet in a wound.

Actually, there was no great mystery about the field of potsherds. As opposed to the rest of her nightmares, filled with a melee of atrocities as enigmatic as they were excruciating, she could guess the source of this one: in Yoruba mythology, the world of potsherds was the abode of the evil dead. Malika was a good Muslim girl and had no use for pagan superstitions, but she knew that much.

She considered her options. Psychiatric drugs. Suicide. Disobeying her parents.

The last was unthinkable. Malika was the only daughter. She could not bring dishonor to her family. She did not believe in psychiatric drugs; and suicide had little appeal.

But she could not marry the man. Everything about him, including his name, was such an anathema to her that in her thoughts she called him simply "the man", and perhaps even this was too charitable.

She was sure her parents would relent if she had a reason to reject her chosen bridegroom. But there was no reason. Nothing except a cloud of fever dreams, too fantastic and too mercilessly vivid, to try to put into words. If she told her family they were trying to marry her to a monster, how would they react?

Malika snorted. They would react exactly as she would have reacted before she had come to Berkeley: with mockery, admonitions, or suspicion of mental illness. And why shouldn't they when she herself had been sure she was going insane? Sure, that is, until she had met her roommate.

She had not been happy, initially, to have a Ukrainian roommate: there had been some bad blood between Nigeria and the USSR during the civil war, and though it all had ended before Malika was born, historical memories persisted. But when she saw the petite girl with the amazing hair that made her look like a doll, Malika was struck by a powerful sense of recognition, even though she knew, simultaneously, that Ally was a perfect stranger. *Déjà vu*, she had thought and forgotten about. They got along well, after all. Ally was tough and resilient, and had none of the bubbly friendliness of Americans, which Malika found fake.

But the nightmares that had started as an occasional bad dream on her arrival in Berkeley and blossomed into a nightly ordeal by the time she met Ally, receded. No more humid forests where crouching trees watched with gleeful eyes as something unspeakable reached down for her from their crowns. No more limbless trunks creeping toward her on their bellies like worms, their faces frozen in a lewd leer. No more lithe figures flickering in the green gloom, their faces masked, and the paralyzing terror when one of the masks was lifted. After Ally had become her roommate, Malika's dreams became, once again, a usual kaleidoscope of memories and impressions.

When Ally got married, Malika was genuinely happy for her. She had learned a little about the Ukrainian's previous life and thought that if anybody deserved a good husband, it was Ally. And Carl was a good husband: rich, steady, and affectionate. But when Ally had left Berkeley and moved to the glass palace on top of the mountain, the nightmares came back, worse than before. They became so vivid that Malika's daily life paled to intervals of fearful waiting for the night. Her grades slipped. And then . . . the man!

Malika realized she was speeding and slowed down. The road had become barely more than a track overhung by leaning trees. It had not appeared to be so narrow on the way up but now the twilight distorted everything. How did Ally, who was not a great driver, manage to navigate these serpentine curves? How did she agree to live here, in this shadowy, tree-infested place?

And where was she now?

She would be concerned about her friend's whereabouts in any case. But now it became a matter of self-preservation. Because Malika had seen Ally in her dreams. And where she walked in the field of potsherds, the monsters fled.

The man she had met at the glass house had promised to find Ally. He said they were friends, but Malika was not stupid. Normally, she would be offended on behalf of Carl, the lawful husband. But now it did not matter. All that mattered was that Ally be found.

Another curve. Malika frowned. Surely she had passed that moss-infested tree already, its green tresses swaying in the thickening air. No, these alien trees choking every inch of the slope with their interlocking branches and knobby roots all looked the same.

The road was too long. She distinctly remembered that the drive up from the intersection marked by an abandoned cabin to the Morrisses' residence was no longer than a couple of miles. And she had been driving down for half an hour and still had not reached it.

She sped up, heedless of the sharp curves. Night was falling and she did not want to be here when the last sunshine would be drunk up by restless shadows. The Mercedes rounded a bend in the road and Malika breathed a sigh of relief when she saw the cabin. Here the private road joined the highway and there would be other cars, other people . . .

The door of the cabin was wide open, swinging in the breeze. But how was it possible when tree branches around the cabin were immobile?

Malika slowed down and pulled over, knowing she should not but as helpless to control her actions as a sleepwalker. The door flapped again and she saw that it was being pushed by the child who perched on top of it, using it as a swing.

The child looked at her, his eyes like baked raisins deep in sunken holes, his skull-face covered by dark leathery skin. He jumped down and walked leisurely toward her, his filthy loincloth made of a jute sack sagging above his matchstick legs. His belly was rounded and tight like a drum.

Malika did not realize she was praying until she heard her own voice, and it gave her a measure of relief—dreams were silent. But when Abiku, the hunger-child, gripped the handle with his claws and pushed it down, opening the locked car door, she knew that the distinction between being asleep and awake had now been rendered moot.

Abiku thrust his perpetually smiling face toward her, so close that she felt his fetid breath. This broke her paralysis. She pushed him aside—he was as light as a bunch of twigs—and jumped out of the car.

She should run to the highway, but it was no longer there. Instead, she found herself among trees. Tree trunks, covered by thick grey bark, swelled around her in elephantine profusion. Their gnarled branches bearded with moss tried to snarl her; arthritic roots tripped her. She fell, sobbing, onto the moist, wormy dirt, got up and ran again. She had lost her high-heeled shoes and her bare feet were encrusted with mulch that swarmed with insects and larvae. It was dark among the squat misshapen boles, even though the sky flamed with purple and scarlet. And it was hot, the temperature perversely rising when the sun disappeared.

Another shag of moss slapped her across her face, but it was more substantial, heavy. Malika looked up. The tree was as broad as it was tall and denuded of leaves. Something dark crouched on its top, outlined against the garish sunset. The long rope came back and wrapped itself around her arm. It was bristling with dry fibers but it slithered purposefully, seeking purchase. The creature on top of the tree stirred and unfolded its long pincer-tipped hands, falling off toward her. Malika screamed but the body did not hit her. It stopped short, swinging in the air like a pendulum from the back-jointed legs that hooked around a branch. Its tail—for that was what it was—squeezed harder against her. Its cauldron-shaped head dipped down but its face was reduced to a blob of shadow by the sunset. Yet somehow, she knew she would die if she saw it.

This gave her strength. She tore off the tail and ran on—colliding with trees, torn and scratched by brambles, whipped by creepers, choked by lianas—feeling no pain.

Suddenly, the rotten softness of the forest floor gave way to something hard. The abrupt transition threw Malika off her feet, and she rolled, coming to rest upon the grainy surface. She was so winded that everything swam black before her eyes and she almost welcomed oblivion.

She was jerked out of it by harsh light shining full onto her face.

A familiar screech. It took her a moment to realize what it was: the sound of an emergency brake. A car door banged, and man's voice yelled as footsteps approached.

"Are you okay?"

Malika sat up. Every muscle in her body felt strained; every movement hurt.

The man stopped at some distance from her, a black silhouette, his car's headlights blinding.

"Are you hurt?" he asked.

"No . . . yes."

She pushed herself up. This simple movement sent a flurry of spots across her vision. Her rescuer appeared to swell and deflate as blood pulsed in her temples.

"Have you been hit?" the man asked. He sounded suspicious and Malika could not blame him.

"No . . . I . . . could you take me to Berkeley, please? I am a student."

The man came a little closer, though he remained an indistinct shadow against the headlights.

"I'll take you to the hospital," he said. "Stanford Medical Center. Hop in."

His voice was low and pleasant; it sounded familiar, somehow, and Malika realized it was because he had an accent similar to her own.

"Thank you," she said and hobbled to the car.

Chapter 7:
The Swan-dress

It was her own bedroom. She did not know how long ago this had been her bedroom; nor did she remember who she had shared it with, but she knew with absolute certainty that she had slept in this huge bed under the sumptuous hand-made quilt: had read in the light of these flower-shaped bedside lamps; had kept her jewelry in this Chinese cabinet. And she had looked out of these ceiling-to-floor French windows onto . . .

Alyona looked outside and gasped. Whatever the landscape surrounding her bedroom had been, she was certain it was not this.

Until now, she had only glimpsed the Thorny Wood from inside the shelter of the bone palisade. Little Mother had told her the place was dangerous even to look at, let alone enter. She now doubted everything Little Mother had told her but in this, she seemed to have spoken the truth. Black thorns scratched the white sky. The trees that comprised the Wood were leafless and thick, their gnarly trunks fissured by deep cracks. They were so close to each other that it was impossible to see the ground through their lattice of intertwined limbs. Each branch ended in a giant thorn, the ones on major boughs crooked like a scimitar, the ones on smaller twigs straight. And impaled on the biggest thorns were animal bodies. Most had rotted down to little more than skeletons, a few were still fresh. Alyona had no names for these animals, but some looked familiar, especially a long slinky grey body with matted fur and crooked teeth in a hanging jaw.

She turned away. If she escaped Little Mother's house—*when* she escaped the house—she would have to wend her way through the impassable thicket of thorns. There was no road.

But the horsemen made their way through somehow, and so

could she. Anyway, she had to find . . . again the words deserted her, but she would know it when she saw it.

She looked at the bed again and realized there was something wrong with it. The pillows on the left side (*my side!*) were stained rusty brown. When she touched them, they were ice-cold and she snatched her hand away in disgust. There was something else, as well. Even though the bed was made, the quilt on the right side rose up in a long roll as if somebody was lying under it.

Alyona had had her fill of horrors, but she had to find out. Mama had taught her that knowledge was power. Mama had taught her to look for answers. Mama had taught her to be brave.

You are an officer's daughter!

Squeezing her necklace hard, Alyona pulled back the quilt.

Lying on his back, his eyes closed in repose, was the White Horseman. He had removed his plumed hat but still had on his snowy doublet. His face was blank and unformed like the face of a fetus but there was a blush deepening in his cheeks. Red splotches dotted his clothes, and as Alyona watched, new ones appeared, spreading like ink-stains.

She hastily put the quilt back on. The White Horseman was becoming the Red one! Did it mean there was only one of them? Then she had even less time than she had thought: redness had already claimed more than one-third of the horseman's body.

She was about to exit the bedroom—whatever she was looking for was not here—but on an impulse pulled out the drawer from the nightstand on the left side. There were three things there: a comb, a handkerchief, and a half-empty box of matches.

Alyona snatched up the comb greedily. This was what Little Mother used to tame her hair, to soothe and calm her! Ever since the word "ghoul" had popped into her head, she had wondered why the creature bothered. Well, never mind the reason; now, she did not need Little Mother's ministrations anymore. She could take care of her own hair that sat on her head in a heavy tangle. Even though time was precious, Alyona could not resist running the comb through her matted tresses.

The comb went through like a knife through butter, instantly smoothing the frizzes and unsnarling the knots. A swatch of loose hair fell onto the floor with a clang.

What the hell? Alyona lifted it and held in her palm a skein of golden wire. The weight and the shine instantly persuaded her that "golden" was not a metaphor.

So, this was why Little Mother played hairdresser to her slave! Alyona slipped the comb into the pocket of her smock and after a moment's hesitation, added the handkerchief and the matches. Whatever they were, they might prove useful.

She exited the bedroom and found herself in a short dim passage with a green-marble floor. It seemed as distantly familiar as a reflection of your own face in turbulent water. On her right was a glass-walled room. Long tongues of fog licked the glass. Alyona walked into it and saw a large pool in the center. It was filled with dark liquid. She knew what it was even before the butchery smell hit her.

She ran out, retching, imagining Little Mother's delicate body luxuriating in the spa of blood. She hit the door in the opposite end of the passage that swung open, propelling her into another huge and poorly lit room.

Alyona stopped. She had expected to find another reflection of the half-forgotten house she had lived in, but this room was strange. Shadowed by black thorns, it contained numerous articles of furniture, piles of clothes and toys. It looked like a warehouse.

Alyona picked up a blue baby onesie. The label was still attached: Baby Gap. Next to it was a carriage, loaded with even more baby clothing: tiny hats, knitted shoes, cute pajamas. Most were blue, just a smattering of white. No pink. Remembering the spa, Alyona braced herself for discovering blood stains on the clothes, but they were all clean, new, unworn. She saw a row of mobiles, a box of pacifiers, and heaps of soft toys. There were several changing tables and an unopened package of diapers. There was enough here for a nursery-full of infants.

Alyona's lips curled derisively. Her fear of Little Mother was now tempered by contempt. A ghoul waxing mawkish over baby things, longing for a child she could never have!

How far had the transformation of the White Horseman into the red one progressed? How much longer did she have? She knew her time was counted in minutes.

Alyona looked frantically around, feeling suffocated by the accumulation of sad useless trinkets. There was another door in the corner, but did she have the time to explore the rest of the house? How large was it, anyway? She had a sudden horrifying vision of wandering through endless corridors, opening endless doors . . . Or worse: flying around in a mindless bird panic, shattering her bones against glass.

The sky outside was flushed with a rosy tint. Alyona knew the horseman, now ruddy-faced and scarlet-cloaked, was rising from the ghoul's bed.

And then she saw it: a white patch against the dark heap of baby clothes. She lunged and grasped it even as it stirred of its own volition, stretching its feathered sleeves and straightening out its crumpled hem. A dress made of tatty plumage. An empty dress that was squirming in her hands like a living thing.

A tat-tat-tat of hooves and a flash of the Red Horseman's incarnadine cloak outside the window. The somber sun winked on in the faded sky. Alyona wrestled desperately with the dress that tried to pin her down and force itself upon her. She felt her bones bend and snap, tearing at her flesh. The pain sent bolts of fire through her entire body.

Fire! Alyona flung the writhing bird-dress as far away as she could, grabbed one of the changing tables and shoved it upon the winged thing that was hissing and flapping like a demented swan. With trembling hands, she pulled the box of matches out of her pocket. The first match fell out of her hand onto the floor. The second flared up and went out. The bird-dress flailed, shaking the table away.

The third match burned with a steady flame.

But instead of being confined to the head of the match, the flame ran up Alyona's arm, clothing it in a roiling sheath that clung to her fingers and palm like a glove. A moment of pure, heart-stopping panic at being burnt alive—until she realized the fire was painless. Indeed, it stopped the wrenching spasm of the transformation that had been tearing at her flesh. The fire embraced her right arm and danced at her fingertips but spread no further.

Alyona thrust the fire-glove toward the feathered dress. No longer attacking Alyona, it was retreating, crawling away. For a moment, Alyona saw an old, dying bird, caught in the snares of Nightwood and forced into an unnatural existence as a go-between; a tired bird that shed its mindless malice onto those who borrowed its plumage.

And then the bird-dress caught fire.

It burnt with a bright, merry flame that danced in the filthy gloom of the ghoul's house. For a moment, the toys and baby clothes appeared as cheerful as Christmas presents. For a moment, shadows fled, hiding in the corners. But the moment was over quickly. The toys faded; the shadows returned. A small pile of pungent ash huddled on the floor.

The fire-glove winked out, leaving Alyona's arm unmarked.

But no, the fire did not disappear altogether. Instead, it sunk into her body in a shower of golden sparks. She watched, entranced, as the sparks colonized her skin, joining together in elaborate constellations, wheeling in vortexes of fireflies. She felt no pain, but her arm itched as the flesh paled, becoming translucent, almost insubstantial, so she could see the patterns of sparks . . .

These were not sparks. These were letters.

The burning letters that set her aflame. She could see through her own skin and read the fast words, forming and falling apart in a blink of an eye. She could not make sense of what she was reading—it was too quick, too complex, words and sentences whirling around each other, snapping and devouring each other, layer upon laycr of languagc but she recognized the letters. These were the ones Mama had taught her with a dog-eared alphabet book.

And with the recognition, memory flooded back.

Ally crouched on the floor, sobbing. Her abandoned tongue, her forgotten story, her new name—they all jostled for entry at the gates of her mind, so impatient and unruly that she felt like she was passing out. She yelled at her own memories, trying to hold them back, to give her a little time to come to terms with her rediscovered identity, but they were relentless.

She did not know how long she had spent on the floor but when she looked up, the thorns outside had almost merged with the dark sky. The horseman in Little Mother's bed must be almost black now.

Her arm looked normal, and the itching had subsided.

She ran back into the bedroom. The liquid in the spa was roiling and bubbling, spreading the salty odor of freshly spilled blood. In the bedroom, the bedclothes were thrown back, the bed empty.

Ally still had the key she had used to pass from the entry hall into Little Mother's quarters. She pushed it into the keyhole with trembling hands and succeeded on the third try.

Inside the giant hall, the scalped heads grinned at her with their stained teeth. The skin curtain that hid the exit was lowering above the rump of a black horse. The transformation was complete, as the Red Horseman had become the Black One, trailing night in his wake.

Ally threw herself after the horse, just having the time to toss the key onto its hook. Miraculously, the bow got caught and the key clicked back to its place. The black horse's icy tail swished across her face, the heavy curtain fell upon her shoulders and brought her down . . . and Ally rolled under it and into the familiar yard.

She stood in the darkness, shivering. The air was cold and humid, the fence-sitters had already taken their positions. They glared at Ally. She looked back at them with new eyes, the deceptive glamor of familiarity stripped away. And now she saw them for what they were—or rather, for what they were not. The term "fence-sitter" that had made them acceptable, part of the order of things, fell apart, doubled by the two languages that now jostled for supremacy in Ally's mind. But in neither language was there a word to label accurately what she was seeing: tiny toddler skeletons, burdened by skulls as big as watermelons, with a furious fire burning in the empty braincase.

She stared around the yard where she had spent . . . she did not know how many days, months or even years. And now as the false story unraveled, she saw that the fence was made of human femurs and humeri; that the Gate of Clasped Hands was a pair of skeletal hands grown into an unnatural gigantism by the same dark magic that had transformed pitiful children's remains into malevolent sentinels; and that the fowl coop was the size of a small house.

First thing's first. She went into the barn.

The cow was napping by the wall but woke up and struggled to her feet when Ally entered. Ally looked at her and the nausea that she had managed to keep at bay so far rose again, threatening to overwhelm her.

The cow was a peasant girl, sturdy and wide-shouldered, with strong legs and capable hands. But instead of a human skin, a brindle cowhide covered every inch of her nude body. Her hair had fallen out and been replaced with a pair of small rounded horns. Her eyes were moist and brown with no whites; her mouth was sewn shut and only a small opening was left for drawing in food. Her breasts were the worst: sticking out at a right angle, swollen and tight with milk.

"I'm sorry," Ally whispered.

The cow shook her head and Ally realized she could not speak. She made a mooing sound and Ally heard the Gate of Clasping Hands opening with a hollow rattle.

Chapter 8:
Fire and Ice

Cowering behind the barn, Ally watched Little Mother go into the house. She looked fragile and dejected; her arms were empty. For a moment, a shadow of pity flitted over Ally's mind. Did the woman want to be what she had become? Did she have any memory of her identity? Or was she just an empty puppet going through the motions, following a script not of her own making?

She banished these thoughts. It did not matter.

When Little Mother disappeared inside, Ally rushed to the coop. She unlocked the latch and threw the door wide. Fowls filed out, one after another, tottering on unsteady legs.

If Little Mother had abducted a farmer's adolescent daughter to produce milk for her tea, the eggs for her omelet came from even younger children. The "fowls" were prepubescent girls whose bodies had been twisted into egg-factories. The heartbreaking stamp of their original identity was clearer on them than on the cow because their naked torsos with button-like nipples were covered by human skin. Their backbones were painfully curved. Their arms sprouted feathers along their length and their hands had atrophied. Their mouths had been sewn shut and then elongated into a parody of a chicken's beak. Their little bellies protruded obscenely. They flapped their wing-arms and milled around.

Ally addressed them:

"I'm sorry, girls," she said. "I don't know if I can unmake the enchantment. But I can punish the monster who took you away from your families, humiliated and abused you. Will you help me?"

For a moment, she was afraid their sentience had been lost.

Then the bigger ones came closer and formed a circle around her, and the smaller ones followed suit.

Little Mother burst out of the house, her perpetually-smiling mouth twisted into a jagged grimace. She brandished the key to the inner rooms that Ally had fingered. It was sticky with dark stains.

"What have you done, you bitch?" Little Mother screamed.

Ally faced the creature and recited:

Cow of gold, cow of gold,
The enemy's blood is running cold
A gown of silk and a silver round,
If you trample the enemy into the ground.

The cow came out of the barn.

The ghoul had caused her callused feet to fuse into hooves and now these hooves were put to good use as the cow kicked Little Mother in the stomach, causing her to double up. And before she could catch her breath, the fowls were all over her, stomping on her delicate white hands and slender white legs, tearing strands of hair with their beaks, cackling and dancing on her prostate form. Little Mother screamed in a reedy voice, her thin pinkish blood running down her chest. Ally did not want Little Mother to be killed before she could question her. She stepped forward to halt the onslaught when the fence-sitters attacked.

Toddling unsteadily on their twiggy legs, they advanced upon Ally. The fire in their skulls flared up, throwing a welter of dancing shadows upon the bone pavement.

Ally tried frantically to come up with a rhyme that could restore some humanity to these creatures, then realized it was useless. There was nothing left of the infants. Too young to remember, the fence-sitters were nothing but empty vessels filled with an evil enchantment by Little Mother.

One of the fence-sitters hissed, opening its mouth wide, and fire burst out of it in a long ribbon, igniting a bale of straw. The fowls retreated, cackling fearfully.

Ally picked up a hoe and tried to scatter the flaming straw but sparks flew around and fell upon the barn's roof that started smoldering. A fence-sitter spat a whip of flame that raised a red welter upon her forearm. She struck the creature with a hoe and its skull burst open like a rotten melon, liberating the inferno within that spilled onto the beaten earth in rivulets of liquid fire. Little Mother laughed.

Ally whirled around, rushed to the ghoul, still held down by a couple of bigger fowls, and put her foot onto Little Mother's chest.

"Stop!" she yelled at the advancing fence-sitters. "Stop or I'll kill her!"

The toddling skeletons hesitated.

"You won't dare!" Little Mother hissed. "*Shlucha*! Ukrainian whore!"

Ally lifted her hoe and brought it down with a smack.

The sharp edge went through the fragile body, cutting skin and muscle and severing the backbone. Little Mother gave an ululating cry, so piercing and inhuman that Ally dropped her hoe and clapped her hands to her ears. The cow screamed, tearing open her sewn mouth. Some of the fowls fell down, others blundered around, dazed. The fence-sitters halted their attack, the fire in their skulls dancing fitfully.

Ally took a long breath and looked down.

She had seen violence. She had known people who had been tortured and killed by the mafia. She had seen war refugees. She knew her country's history.

But she had never killed anybody.

Little Mother was lying at her feet, a pitiful huddle in a spreading pool of red. In the dying light, her blood was indistinguishable from human.

Ally wanted to feel disgust or horror at what she had done, but she could not. All she felt was triumph.

I am an officer's daughter . . .

Little Mother's eyes snapped open.

They were pools of darkness in a pale face but now the darkness was receding, the irises contracting, and the rims of whites reappearing. Her grinning mouth relaxed. It was a human face now, a face Ally had seen, though not in the flesh.

The mouth contorted, making indistinct sounds, and Ally bent lower, trying to make out what she was saying. The teeth snapped, almost taking off her ear. Ally caught the creature's hair, wound it around her hand, and lifted the body. It fell apart, the lower half slumping onto the ground, the upper half dangling from Ally's arm, its fringe of loose intestines writhing like worms.

"Where is my husband, Ros?" Ally asked. "Where is Carl?"

"My husband!" The creature hissed. "You stole him! Stole my house, my husband, my life!"

"It's called dissolution by death," Ally said. "You died. Except so close to Nightwood nothing quite dies, but this is of no consequence to the law. My marriage is legitimate and yours is void. So let go of Carl. You don't want him anyway. You want a child, and you'll never have one, no matter how many you steal. You had your chance, and you blew it!"

The half-woman spat at Ally, a glob of pinkish saliva just missing her.

"I'll let you go if you tell me where he is," Ally said. "We both know you can go on living like this—if you call it living."

The intestines flailed in the smoky air.

"I brought him here," the half-woman whispered. "But he wanted nothing to do with me. So I traded him."

Ally remembered the meat on the metal tables.

"You . . . butchered him?!"

"No. The Ogre wanted him. He gave me undying fire in return."

"The Ogre? Where does he live?"

"In the Castle With No Windows. In the midst of the Bleeding Grove. Beyond the three Dragon Rivers."

"How do I get there?"

The red lips, no longer smiling, twitched in a mocking grimace.

"The Ogre is everywhere," she rasped. "He will find you, no worry. And now, let me go, you whore! You promised!"

Ally smiled crookedly.

"It's true. And I'm going to break my promise. I saw your books. You studied Nightwood but so did I. I know what you have become: a *lang suir*, a child-stealing monster, a flyer-by-night who will suffocate pregnant women with your intestines and take away their babies to add to your farmyard. Forget about it!"

And she tossed the half-woman at one of the fence-sitters whose oversized skull broke like an egg and released the fire within. A quick streamlet of flame ran up the ghoul's tattered clothing and up her hair, swaddling her in a cocoon of brightness. The lower part of her body squirmed and thrashed in sympathy as the upper part burned.

It was over quickly but the fire did not die. It spread through the yard. The straw in the corner exploded into another tongue of flame. The night became alive with dancing sparks that lit up the dull sky like the stars that should have been there.

Stars . . .

But there was no time to think about it. Ally grabbed the cow's hand and pulled her to the Gate of Clasped Hands. The fowls followed, cackling in distress as burning air blew into their faces, making their eyes sting.

The Gate would not open. Ally hammered at the skeletal hands, each phalange as big as her forearm, but the bones only clasped each other tighter, their claw-tipped points leaning threateningly toward her. She abandoned the Gate and tried to climb the fence, but the bony posts were as slick as ice, offering no purchase.

The inferno reached the main house and embraced its sturdy walls. The roof smoked and crackled and then collapsed with a whoosh. The heat was unendurable. Cinders flew, setting one of the fowls on fire. Her mates tried to help but could not beat off the flames. They retreated, bunching up into a knot of fearful fluttering.

Ally remembered the well. If she could draw water out of it, throw it upon the fire, at least slow down its spread . . . But the house was between her and the well. She tried to go around by rushing through the cloud of smoke that rolled upon the grounds. As she crawled toward the well, she saw the scaly green arms that lived in it reach up to the feverish sky and with one mighty yank, bring down the coping. The well sweep that held the bucket fell into the hole, plugging it.

Was she to die here? Die like those people in the story Mama had told her about partisans locked up in a barn that was set on fire? The horror of that story cost her some sleepless nights when she was a child. Was that a premonition?

All fairy tales were history once . . .

She refused to believe it. She would not, could not, die! Nightwood was not lawless; it would listen to her if she could just find the right words . . .

But the words would not come.

She retreated as far as she could, into the last untouched corner of the yard. The cow and the surviving fowls followed her, and they crowded on the shrinking island of safety, coughing, their eyes streaming as the dense smoke coiled around them.

Frantically she pawed through her pockets. The matches . . .

but what good would they do? Fighting fire with fire? That was a metaphor, and a dubious one at that.

Her fingers snagged in a fabric finer than her homespun smock. She pulled out the handkerchief she had found in Little Mother's bedroom.

It was made of heavy linen and even had an embroidered monogram: intertwined letters AP. Her lungs gasping for air, Ally tried to fashion a primitive smoke mask for herself, but the handkerchief was too small. It slipped out of her nerveless hand and fluttered to the ground.

And where it fell, a lake of frost sprung into being, quelling the fire, burying it under a crackling shield of ice.

Chapter 9:
The Three Springs

Ally, the cow, and the four surviving fowls huddled in the one corner of the yard free of ice. The cold was unbearable and coming on the tail of the fire, it chilled them to the core.

She carefully folded the handkerchief and put it back in her pocket. It was neither charred nor cold: just a nice, old-fashioned, decorative piece of fabric that one could imagine doused with perfume and put in a lady's reticule. It looked vaguely familiar somehow. Perhaps Mama had had something like this, inherited from her own mother? No, it was impossible: after her disappearance, Mama's scant belongings had been left in the small apartment she had shared with her daughter, and Ally remembered all of them. There were no memorabilia of family history.

When Ally was small, she used to fantasize about her grandparents, imagining them to have been oligarchs or foreign aristocrats. Mama had encouraged her love of storytelling, but she had squelched this one. Her parents had been members of a collective farm, *kolkhozniks*. They died. End of story. The handkerchief was probably just a magic object, such as Nightwood would be full of. There was no logic to their use—at least, no ordinary logic; which is not to say they did not obey a much older and more obscure set of rules. It was up to Ally to figure it out if she wanted to free Carl.

Meanwhile, she had her more urgent matters to think about, like surviving until dawn and finding her way out. Her companions offered no conversation to keep her spirits up but at least they could share body heat to keep themselves from freezing. She still did not know what, if anything, could be done to turn them back into human beings. Little Mother had her last laugh, bitch! Well, she was dead, and Ally felt proud of what she had done. The new wife killing the old one —what a stereotype! But the ghoul was not really the woman who had married Carl Morris when Ally was a child. She was merely a story-wraith, a residue of jealousy, maternal longing, spite, and loneliness, crossed with an imprint of Ros' mind on the fabric of Nightwood. She might even be reborn . . . but Ally decided not to worry about it.

Eventually what they had been waiting for happened. The White Horseman slipped from the blackened doorway that gaped in the ruined skeleton of the house. Ally dragged herself to her numb feet and motioned the rest to follow.

The horseman did not use the Gate of Clasped Hands to exit. Instead, he directed his hollow-eyed mare to the opposite corner of the yard. The horse neighed, the horseman knocked his whip on the bone posts, and they obediently bent aside. Even as she led the line of shivering, miserable creatures out of the yard, Ally was wondering whether he would keep coming back, signaling times of day when there were no more eyes to see his change of costume.

They had just managed to slip through the gap when the posts came back together, crushing the remnants of a fence-sitter who had been frozen hanging skull-down. And then they were in the Thorny Wood.

The black trees stood out starkly against the colorless sky; leafless but not dead. Their swollen trunks were fissured with sap-bleeding cracks and mottled with brown and grey lichen, and their twigs were green. Though the bigger thorns were wickedly sharp, she could see no impaled animal bodies nearby. The ground was littered with desiccated thorns that cracked like pistol-shots when stepped on.

The horseman disappeared but Ally could see that walking would be easier than she had expected. The trees were spaced wide enough to allow the passage of a human body. Since she had no idea what direction to choose, she turned toward the spot where the gnarled trunks were marginally further away from each other, forming a sort of avenue. She started walking, and the cow and fowls followed.

The red sun rose above the thorns. It looked like a dying red dwarf: visibly spherical, marred with black spots, and so dim one could look straight at it. It was not the real sun; Ally had known it since she figured out the comings and goings of the Black-Red-White Horseman. Little Mother had built her farm in some fold of witching time where her own unnatural existence and that of her livestock could be stretched and compressed at will.

The temperature rose marginally, but it was still cold. Ally was light-headed with hunger and thirst. Her tongue rasped against her furry palate, and the memory of the well in the ghoul's yard appeared positively enticing.

Her retinue were lagging behind, undoubtedly as hungry and thirsty as she was. She tried to think what to do with them. She could not just abandon these pitiful half-humans, but where to take them? She had no idea how to reverse their *geis* or even if it was possible. And where did they come from in the first place? Surely if Little Mother had abducted all of them from Northern California, Ally would have heard about it! But perhaps a better question was *when* did they come from? If Little Mother manipulated time . . . Ally sighed, losing her train of thought. Hunger was not conducive to logic!

The thorn-trees fell away and they walked into a clearing. Instead of grass it was covered with a dense layer of black twigs, composting into a springy covering. An occasional skeletal bush stuck out here and there. The clearing dipped toward its center where a small but energetic spring bubbled up, surrounded by a margin of wet earth.

The fowls gobbled inarticulately as they scampered toward the spring. Ally ran after the bird-girls, her parched mouth filling with saliva. She overtook them and stopped short at the edge of the marshy ground.

One of the fowls bent down awkwardly, her pouch-like stomach in the way, and tried to cup some water in her wing-hands.

"No!" Ally yelled and dragged the wriggling creature away. The others scattered. The cow made an inarticulate sound of protest.

"Look!" Ally pointed to the indentations in the wet strip around the spring. Footprints. Crisscrossing the black earth like Chinese hieroglyphs. Clawed, spiky marks. Birds, a whole flock of birds, had drunk from this spring.

"If you drink, you'll become a bird!" Ally yelled. "Never human! Never human again!"

Even as she was saying it, her own sandpaper-dry tongue

refused to obey her, longing for just a touch of the delicious, refreshing coolness. Water, so pure, so clean . . .

She turned her back to the spring and spread her arms, barring access.

The cow looked into her eyes for what seemed like a long time and then inclined her horned head, turned and walked away from the spring. The fowls followed.

All except for one. The fowl who had been the first to rush to the water wheeled around and before Ally could stop her, she was down on her knees again, dipping her malformed head into the clear stream.

Abruptly, she stood as if jerked by an invisible hand. Her arms flapped and new feathers pushed out all along their length, quickly coating the remaining human skin with a thick layer of black. Her still-human body shrank and folded in upon itself, the round belly absorbed into the horizontal trunk. Her legs buckled and shed their human plumpness, becoming thin and taloned with a back spur. The pitiful proboscis hardened into a horny beak. The eyes migrated to the sides of the flattening head, their irises flooding the white with darkness. The big crow cawed hoarsely and, flapping its new wings, rose into the air and disappeared among the trees.

Ally looked at the cow and the remaining three fowls and shrugged. There was nothing to say. She went on and they followed.

The forest was changing. Black thorns were supplanted by ordinary trees, many of which Ally recognized: elms, beeches, maples. No redwoods. The sight of green leaves and grass cheered her up considerably. The red orb was still rolling low, but the sky's milky whiteness was faintly washed with blue and veiled with cirrus clouds.

Gradually, she discerned a sound in the stillness: a low, soothing purl. She hurried up and saw a small creek, flowing briskly over the moss-grown rocks. Her dry mouth opened of its own accord, drawing in the moistness of the air.

Ally forced herself to stop and examine the margins of the creek. Its rocky bed carried no impressions. Did that mean it was safe?

The cow surged forward but she stopped her with a wave of her hand. Something was missing? What?

And then she saw it. A creek like this should be surrounded by a cloud of skimming dragonflies. But there was no insect life around it.

A bush was leaning over the running water. From its branch dangled a clump of dark fur.

Ally turned to her companions.

"No," she said. "Drink from it and you'll become an animal."

The three bird-girls walked away dejectedly and she felt a surge of pity when she saw their hunched vulnerable backs—children's backs. Ally caught up with them quickly, telling them to be patient, just wait a little longer and they'd find something harmless to eat and drink.

She was still talking to them when she realized that the cow was not following.

She swerved around and saw her standing at the very edge of the creek, staring at her own reflection in the water.

"No!" Ally cried and ran back. As mute as the cow-girl was, Ally felt real closeness to her. Without her help, Ally would have never defeated Little Mother. And she had to make up for the humiliation she had unwittingly inflicted upon the girl by treating her like livestock.

The cow dipped her head and then knelt on the edge of the creek. From behind, with her horned head lowered, she looked like a naked woman afflicted by some patchwork skin disease. Ally slipped, careened into her, and pushed her deeper into the creek. The cow's head disappeared under the water and Ally saw her sewn-up mouth tearing apart, releasing globules of blood as she drank deeply from the cool, refreshing stream.

All scrambled back and the cow rose slowly from the water on her four sturdy legs. Her shovel-shaped head lowered, and her big horns pointed at Ally as her tail lashed against her heaving flanks.

Ally stood still, the bitterness of failure amplifying her exhaustion into resignation. If the cow attacked her, she would not run away.

But the cow did not. Instead, the animal trudged away toward a small meadow. Stopping there, it started cropping the lush grass and munching it placidly.

Ally turned to the huddling fowls.

"Come on, girls," she said.

They walked for what seemed like an eternity. The thorn-trees had disappeared, supplanted by a new growth of larch, aspen and pine. It looked like the aftermath of logging: there were some old moss-covered trunks and stumps moldering in the grass.

Ally's entire being was focused on putting one foot in front of the other. At some point, she looked down and discovered they were walking on a path. It was overgrown with shaggy brambles and so faint that she could not decide whether it was made by animals or human beings.

The land was rising gradually toward an aspen-fringed ridge. The light was curdling into a mixture of purple and gold and, Ally realized, dully, that the sun was setting; the real sun—not the red orb of Little Mother's domain. Did it mean they had left it behind? Or did her death dissolve the tiny malevolent kingdom she had carved out for herself from the shifting energies of Nightwood?

They trudged up to the ridge. The ground below spread out into a rolling grassland beyond the ragged hem of the forest. The sun lingered on the horizon. Ally thought she saw faint blinking lights in the distance, but she was so tired they may have been an oncoming migraine.

As she scanned the slope leading down to the plain, she saw that the ground dipped, forming a hollow. Among the jagged bushes something gleamed, reflecting the pink sky.

She motioned to the fowls and ran down. The hollow was filled with shadows but she could still see well enough what lay at its center. A pool, a miniature lake, as placid and smooth as glass.

Ally knew that she would drink from it, no matter what. The burning in her throat, the stabbing pain in her eyes, the buzzing in her ears, nothing could be worse than dying of thirst. The ravages of hunger were a mercy compared to it. And still, she forced herself to pause at the edge to examine the water. Behind her, the bird-girls made soft cooing sounds as they clung to each other, exhausted beyond decision or action.

The pool was deep, and dark, and so still that a scatter of leaves on its surface seemed to be painted on. Its margins were overgrown by clumps of canes and rushes but at one point, a tiny beach afforded easy access. And there was a footprint in the moist soil, a shapeless indentation.

Ally bent over it, forcing her dry eyes to focus, refusing for a moment to accept the relief that flooded her. A man's bare foot, toes splayed, pointing away from the water's margin.

"Come on!" she rasped to the fowls and dropped down to her knees, cupped water in her hands, and drank.

The coolness that flowed through her parched mouth and into her shrunken body was the most exquisite sensation she had ever experienced. She drank and drank until the water threatened to pour back up. Then she splashed water on her face and chest, oblivious of how it soaked her thin smock. Only then did she stand to look at her companions, noisily drinking on the other side of the pool.

Three naked little girls stared back at her.

They ranged between something like eight and thirteen years of age. One was black; one had a round-cheeked, freckled face; and the third, the tallest of the three, showing the first signs of pubescence in her budding breasts, looked vaguely Mediterranean.

Ally smiled encouragingly and the girls edged away from her. Of course! She had been their keeper in Little Mother's slave-coop. She had collected the bloody eggs that the ghoul had forced their immature bodies into producing. And though they had followed her out of captivity, could they really trust her now?

Well, they had to. There was nobody else.

"I'm Ally," she said. "Who are you?"

The said nothing and she realized they did not necessarily understand English. She tried Russian, then Ukrainian with the same result. Ally was getting frustrated: the dusk was deepening, and they still had no shelter for the night. Stupid girls! Surely, she was cannier at their age! Or perhaps not. With a twinge of guilt, she thought of Mama's patience in dealing with her own childhood tantrums and teenaged angst. Unconsciously, she put her hand on the necklace still nestled in the hollow of her neck and repeated the question.

This time the tall dark-haired girl answered.

"I'm Talia," she said.

"I'm Margarita," said the freckled one.

"I'm Queenie," said the black girl.

Chapter 10:
The Stolen Bride

Her breath coming out in ragged gasps, Malika put her head down. The residue of adrenaline in her blood was burning itself out, flooding her mouth with a metallic aftertaste. Her rescuer had said nothing since picking her up, smoothly driving the Audi down the mountain road that led to Woodside.

She straightened up and glanced at his silhouette. It was dark outside but she could see that he was black. His white shirt glowed in the dashboard light. A golden ring sparkled.

Malika shifted on the creaky-new leather backseat. The car looked and smelled like it had just rolled out of a dealer's.

"I'm not sure I want to go to the hospital," she said. "I'm feeling better."

And I don't want to be locked up for observation when I tell them what happened to me, she added silently.

"You were running through the forest," the man stated.

Malika smiled; the man spoke with a Nigerian accent, which, to the American ear, sounded like a harder British pronunciation. But she knew a compatriot when she heard one.

"Are you from Lagos?" she asked.

The man turned around and looked at her. Malika screamed.

She was futilely tugging on the door handle as the car sped up. The man's dentist-ad smile bisected his gaunt face. He turned his attention back to the road that unspooled as a faint grey ribbon in the stuffy darkness. Glimpses of swollen trees flickered by.

"Let me go!" Malika cried.

"Your parents have given you to me," the man responded. His name was Azeez, that was how he had been introduced to her, but she had known better even then. Creatures like him had no human names.

"My parents would kill me before giving me to a demon!"

"Don't be so proud," the creature sneered. "Don't you know what happened to Chibok girls? But I'll be better to you than the fighters were to them. I'll marry you properly and I won't even take a second wife—not immediately. But first we need to make a couple of detours. I have borrowed some stuff when I came courting you and I need to return it."

Malika collapsed on the back seat, her head in her hands. She tried to pray but words dried up in her mouth. She knew the story of the Chibok schoolgirls who were abducted by terrorists and forced into slavery, but at least the terrorists were human!

A dull resignation crept into her mind, smothering it under a leaden cloud. What use was fighting? Perhaps it was fate. She may have escaped once, but the dark forest had come after her. The demon-infested jungle, the field of potsherds. The kingdom of the dead.

The Audi slowed to a crawl and the headlights picked out something in the dark. A huddle of thatched huts.

Malika stared with dust-dry hopeless eyes. Should she try to break out and run away?

What for? She was not in California anymore.

The car stopped. Several men emerged from the huts. They were tall, rangy men, dressed in t-shirts and camouflage pants. Some had automatic weapons and machetes.

The man jumped out of the car and went over to them. A brief conversation ensued. Malika huddled in the dark, trying to make herself inconspicuous. One look at the men convinced her she would get no help here.

By the end of the conversation—Malika could not hear what was being said and was afraid to roll down the window—the man who had abducted her, the *asanbosam*, the demon, bent down and with a single twist of his arm removed his left leg. There was no blood, but the leg did not look like a prosthetic. It twitched and buckled as he handed it over to one of the guerillas who silently accepted it and melted back into the dark together with his buddies. The man hopped back to the car. He grinned even wider at Malika's expression of horror and disgust as he lowered himself into the driver's seat.

They started again on the road that was now peppered with potholes. Malika tried to think.

She had seen this in her dreams. But had it happened before? Was it a memory or premonition? And how did the dream end? When talking to Ally, she had been so overwhelmed that she had broken into tears before she could tell it. Now she deeply regretted it. Unless put into words soon after waking, even the most vivid nightmare dissolved into a cloud of disconnected images. Rake her brain as she might, all she could come up with was some vague horror.

The Audi slowed again. Another village. This one looked even poorer. The walls of the round huts were scarred and pitted with bullet holes; the roofs sagged. Several women came out and Malika's heart leaped up in hope of help. But the hope died when she saw their faces, stamped with zombie-like apathy. She tried to draw their attention, but they stared through her with glazed eyes as they mutely collected the man's second leg. He was now reduced to a crawling trunk, and she realized she had a chance: grab the steering wheel, drive out of here . . . But he was lightning-quick, leaping into the seat like a spider monkey and slapping her back. Hanging on the steering wheel with one hand, he played on the accelerator and the brake with the unnaturally elongated fingers of the other. His grin was now pushing his cheeks into folds around his ears.

The third village. Or rather the ruins of one. It looked like there had been some recent fighting here: several burnt-down huts still smoked and a couple of bodies lay around the perimeter. But it was not abandoned. A huddle of children stood in the middle. Malika did not even try to call out to them. They were child-soldiers with ashen eyes and blood-washed hands. The man threw his left arm at them without getting out of the car.

He was still able to drive with one arm, tentacles of darkness leaking out of him to control the brake. His torso was elongated, serpentine. A white band glimmered at the back of his head, and she shuddered when she realized it was teeth, his grin closing around his skull.

The hopelessness of it sapped her strength like a leech. She had nobody to turn to. Ally would not be here to save her as she had . . . she had . . . And anyway, why should she? Hadn't Malika let her down? Somewhere, somehow? An almost-memory stirred at the back of her head and slipped into shadows of despair.

The last village. An empty clearing in the black forest, sown with ashes, littered with bones. And in the midst of it: a living skeleton sitting on the ground, rocking back and forth. Abiku, the Hunger-Child.

The Audi coasted to a stop and the *asanbosam* turned to her, his face no longer even remotely human.

"You'll drive from here on," he said.

His last arm detached itself from the body and crawled out, undulating like a snake. The Hunger-Child caught it and sunk his loose teeth into the flesh.

"No!" Malika said.

"You are my wife. You have to obey me."

"Never!" Malika yelled and jumped out of the car, slamming the door behind her. The rotten stink of the clearing slapped her in the face. Abiku, still gnawing the arm, lifted his expressionless face toward her, his eyes like dried raisins in his cavernous eyeholes.

The front door of the car was closed, and she had a flash of hope—surely, he would not be able to open it with no hands—but then the front window shattered and a sinuous trunk, as thick across as the biggest jungle python, spilled out, the sausage-like torso lengthening, coiling upon the ground. The upper part swayed in the air, topped with the familiar grinning face that had paralyzed her in the dream and was now coming to claim his due in reality.

"A disobedient wife!" the *asanbosam* hissed. "A bad woman! What is to be done with her?"

Abiku tittered.

"Eat her?" he suggested.

The serpentine torso swung as if ruminating upon this proposition, and Malika tried to retreat but her rubbery legs gave way,

"No!" the *asanbosam* declared. "Eating her is quick. She is not fat enough! We will give her to the farming woman! Let her find use for her!"

"Yes!" Abiku nodded enthusiastically. "Let the farming woman have her! She'll give us more fresh meat in exchange!"

The smiling head dipped down, and before Malika blacked out, she caught a glimpse of more slithering coils spilling out of the ruined car.

Chapter 11:
The Light-smiths

Ally was rather ambivalent about having the girls around. On the one hand, she was starved for human company. The loss of the cow hit her hard, especially since she realized she would never know the woman's name or origin. But now she was saddled with the responsibility for three children.

"All right!" she said briskly after they had introduced themselves. "Now come here, let's make a camp!"

But they had nothing to make a camp with.

They would no longer die of thirst, but their situation was perilous. They had no food whatsoever and as the sun set, a chill was beginning to creep up from the ground, and the girls were stark naked. Ally could not even share her clothing, as all she had on was a sodden smock.

But in the pocket of this smock was the match-box.

Ally took it out and contemplated it dubiously. Having grown up in the city, her wilderness skills were non-existent. She was not sure she could make a fire without setting the entire forest aflame. And was it wise to advertise their presence to whatever was skulking in the dark of Nightwood?

But needs must. That was one of the lessons Mama had drummed into her early and well. Ally took out a match (noting there were few left) and struck it against the side of the box. It flared up with a golden spark that ran up Ally's arm as before, clothing it with an incandescent glove. Pleasant warmth spread up her body and the girls ooh'd and aah'd. She sent them to collect brush, and pretty quickly they had a small but respectable blaze going. They crowded around it while Ally experimented with the fire-glove. She found out that the fire obeyed her emotions rather than her explicit commands. She could not coax it into a killing conflagration as she had done in Little Mother's farmyard because she was neither angry nor afraid. She needed warmth, and this was what the matchbox gave her. It rankled her that she was not in control, but it was better than nothing.

Still, that left the problem of food. She was desperately hungry and the girls must be too, though they did not complain, conducting themselves with stoic fortitude, except for Queenie who whimpered a little, but she was the smallest.

And clothes. Blundering through the forest naked would not do. Since the girls had been restored to their human form, they had human needs, including self-respect.

Ally got up and winced: her joints felt rusty, as if she were as old as Carl. She told the girls to stay put and promised to be back soon with food and clothes.

The moon was climbing into the sky, turning the forest into a chiaroscuro of silver and black. Ally regarded the moon suspiciously, knowing its reputation in Nightwood, but it did not appear to be different from the moon back home. It was half-full, the dark half faintly outlined against the star-glittering sky. Once Ally let her eyes adjust, she could see quite well. She climbed back to the top of the ridge. She wanted to find again those distant lights on the plane below, even though she had no idea how she would be able to go down and back up again. But as she found herself panting and shivering, on the ridge, something closer caught her eye. To the left, back the way they had come, was a bluish glow emanating from a dense grove of birches whose white trunks glimmered faintly in the dark.

She trudged toward it, her arms and legs whipped by branches, feet ensnarled by bracken. Finally, Ally made it to the grove, squeezed through the closely-spaced trunks and stared in disbelief.

The entire grove shone in the soft light of garlands strung between the trees. The garlands were composed of chains of live glowworms interspersed with bigger winged fireflies. They illuminated tiny houses, about human height, built flush to the trunks, piled upon each other like towers of bricks, or suspended from boughs. The entire picture was so fairy-like, so much what most people imagined Nightwood to be, that Ally was completely taken aback. Was she to encounter a Tinker Bell in a spangled outfit emerging from one of these miniature dwellings?

Something did indeed squeeze out of the open door of one of the houses and landed with a plop on the forest floor. But it was no Tinker Bell.

At first, Ally was not sure what she was seeing. A giant insect? A tiny man? After a couple of moments, the vision resolved; it was both an insect and a man resembling a praying mantis the size of a two-year-old. But it only had four limbs: the crooked legs supporting the fat segmented body with rudimentary wings; and the double-folded serrated forearms, jutting from the vertical thorax, just like those of a mantis. Its triangular head bore a human face: a sardonic, unsmiling face with a tiny, pursed mouth and beady eyes.

"Who are you?" the creature inquired in a piercing voice. "What are you doing here?"

Apparently attracted by the commotion, more creatures emerged out of the houses. Unlike the first one, many of them carried lights, so the grove was now as brightly lit as Union Square. Looking closer, Ally realized that the lights were, in fact, part of their bodies: the last segment of each emitting a beautiful green, blue or rosy radiance. It did not take a genius to figure out that the glowworms and fireflies strung in garlands were the larval stages of the house-owners.

"I am Alyona," she declared, for some reason deciding to use her original name. Not that she knew of anything resembling these creatures in Slavic fairy tales, but she already realized that the folklore she had dedicated several years to studying was an uncertain and imprecise guide to Nightwood. It was as if the human mind needed to soften the dark reality of the source of its tales by wrapping it up in the tinsel of feel-good images.

"Alyona," the first creature repeated, unimpressed. "And what do you want from Light-smiths?"

"Food," she replied without hesitation. "Clothes. I have three little girls who need help."

The lights around her flickered, plunging the birch grove into a confetti storm of multicolored gleams. It took her a moment to realize that this was the creatures'—Light-smiths'—equivalent of laughter.

"Food. Clothes," the first Light-smith replied, counting exaggeratedly on the fingers of his tiny four-fingered hand. "And we should give it to you for free. Why?"

"Mercy for the children."

Again, the lights flared up, more strongly this time.

"Our village has been raided by wolves twice," the Light-smith rasped. "Our young carried away as living torches, discarded when they could no longer light their path. Our houses trampled, our trees uprooted. And we should have mercy on your children?"

The lights now built to a crescendo of glittering, flashing, coruscating sparks, madly revolving around Ally as some fireflies rose up into the air and flapped toward her. She could feel waves of heat on her face. The first Light-smith—who, ironically, had no light, perhaps because he was the eldest in the village, straightened up to his full height and gestured toward Ally with his scissor-like forelimbs.

"Go!"

"Wait!" Ally cried, waving her hands in the air to scare away the bright swarm. "Wait! I have something to trade! I'll pay for your goods, a fair price!"

The Light-smith gestured at his folk to back off and cocked his triangular head.

"What do you have that we might want?"

"How about gold?"

Was gold of any use to creatures like these? Probably not but it was of no actual use to humans either, and yet they would die for it.

"Gold? You have gold?"

"I do."

And reaching into her pocket, Ally drew out the red comb—the same comb Little Mother had used to keep her docile and enrich herself in the process. Unpinning her sadly neglected hair, Ally ran the comb through her rich tresses that shone buttery yellow in the light of the village. The Light-smiths watched, fascinated, as the combed-out hair fell in a small pile that tinkled faintly as it hit the ground. Another swipe of the comb, and another . . . and Ally lifted a handful of spun gold, finer than wire and yet solid and heavy, and showed it to the elder Light-smith. The creature's face remained impassive, but its eyes shone with unmistakable avarice and Ally knew that she had it hooked. In fact, looking around she could see that the tiny houses, though indifferently built, were decorated with rich filigree of silver, bronze and other metals.

"Well," the Light-smith droned, "this changes the situation

somewhat. We can give you food in exchange for this . . . this trifle. But if you want clothes, you have to add more."

Ally's first impulse was to say yes; the gold, after all, literally grew on her head. But she bit her tongue. What if the creatures decided that they were better off simply jailing her and combing out as much gold as they wanted?

"You are not only heartless but stupid as well," she said and made as if to walk away. "This is as much gold as an honest workman can make in a year. And all I'm asking for are things you have in abundance or that you don't need. That's all I have: take it or leave it."

She walked a couple of steps when the piercing voice of the Light-smith stopped her.

"All right, all right!" the creature shrilled.

A swarm of activity ensued that resulted in Ally being presented with a woven basket containing some apples, a jar of honey and, best of all, a loaf of bread. Another Light-smith, emitting a sullen red glow, dumped a pile of musty-smelling clothes at her feet. They were not in the best of shapes, but Ally realized that they were probably stolen as the creatures had no need of thcm.

Ally handed the elder the hunk of gold she had been clutching in her sweaty palm, lifted the basket and the clothes, and turned to go back. The Light-smith's voice stopped her.

"We trade fair," the creature said. "Others won't."

Chapter 12:
Snake Eyes

He **stretched.** His entire body was stiff and sore.

The dawn was finally breaking: sullen clouds dragging their bellies close to the ashy ground. He looked around, trying to remember how he had come here.

He had been running for so long that every gasping breath poured into his lungs like molten lead. And yet even as he was pushing himself, he knew he would soon give up—even if it meant a dog's stinking breath in his face or a dead horse's smashing hoof in his ribs. For the first time in his life, Eric embraced resignation.

Then something clattered under his feet. Slippery shards turned, pitched him face-down. He fell, cutting his hand. He seemed to be lying on a pile of broken crockery. The barking of dogs drifted toward him but now a howling was added to their chorus. Wolves?

He picked himself up, the ground sliding and rattling under him. The sky was overcast and no lights shone in the oppressive murk. He started picking his way cautiously, trying to imagine what terrain he was navigating. A skip? A dump? But there was no smell of garbage; only prickly dust and emptiness.

The howling kept on but did not come any closer. The shards soon gave way to what seemed to be fine sand. He could still see very little but realized he was on a flat plain. He started running again, and the barking and howling receded leaving dead silence.

A cloud of dust rose around him. He slowed down, took a couple of deep breaths, tried to clear his head. He could taste dust on his tongue and his eyes were streaming with tears. Finally, the anemic half-moon dragged itself from behind a cloud and silvered the terrain. It looked like nothing. It *was* nothing—just an endless field.

Nightwood

The moon disappeared again, and Eric hunkered down, waiting for the light. And here it was.

He rubbed the dust between his fingers. It did not feel like desert sand but then, he was no geologist.

He stood up and surveyed the surroundings. The horizon looked uncomfortably close, curtained with dust-devils. The giant black structure he had glimpsed in pseudo-Woodside was nowhere to be seen.

He realized he was in Nightwood, though nothing looked less like woods than this field of ashes. He also realized that he did not want to be here. He wanted to be back in the Silicon Valley, having a latte in Café Copa, working on his Mac, his iPhone blinking with texts from potential investors or buddies-slash-competitors. Eric thought of Jennifer, dragged around by her monstrous cat. He thought of his promise to Malika. He thought of Ally. But the more he thought about the women in the hope of shaming himself into action, the less it appealed to him.

At the end it was hunger and thirst that made him get up and plod through the dust. Whatever magic was there—if this word even applied to Nightwood—it clearly did not rescind the laws of biology. He needed water and food if he was to survive.

He stumbled on something and pitched face forward into the soft billows that brought about a new bout of sneezing. When it abated, he sat up and examined the obstacle. It was a human ribcage.

Eric jumped up and backed away. But now that he had seen, he could not un-see. Bones were everywhere: femurs and tibias like broken fence-posts; rounded hillocks of skulls; phalanges scattered like beads. Many of the bones were charred.

He retched but brought up only bile. He had been breathing the dead.

He ran again, whipped into uncontrollable panic. He slipped, fell, got to his feet and trudged on. Glancing around warily, knowing that in the field of ashes, crematoria would not be far away. And people who operated them.

Indeed, there was a black building ahead, surrounded by dunes of ash and deadfall of bones. But it did not look like a crematorium. Even blinded with fear, Eric realized that he was staring at a miniature castle.

It looked totally incongruous here, but this was what calmed him down enough to make him walk toward it. There was no end to the charnel field in sight. He could wander it until his strength gave out and he joined the dead in their soft bed. At least the castle promised something else.

It was very small, but it had everything a castle was supposed to have: a pointed roof with a nondescript pennant; castellated walls; and even a moat, though it was silted with ash. The gate stood open, and Eric staggered into the courtyard.

It was empty. There was a spate lying by the wall and some rusty gardening tools. Eric examined them: they appeared to be thoroughly modern.

With all the talk about familiars, spells and fairy tales, Eric had expected Nightwood to be like something out of the Lord of the Rings. He had expected magic swords and elven languages. He had believed he would find himself at home among its antiquated dangers. Like many techies, Eric was an avid reader of high fantasy: not just Tolkien but obscure classics like Lord Dunsany and William Morris. He now realized how much these colorful volumes of fake medieval lore had contributed to the ease with which he had volunteered to go into Nightwood after Ally. Embarrassing; but he had really visualized himself as a knight in the shining armor going to the rescue of his lady. Now he knew, with the bitterness of unwanted self-knowledge, that he would be as unprepared to handle the real Middle Ages as he was now, confronted with whatever waited inside the gaping door.

He entered because there was nothing else to do. Inside was a hall, feebly illuminated by the dirt-encrusted windows. The floor was dusty flagstones. There was a big fireplace with no fire and a scrubbed table. On the table was a plate with a loaf of bread, and a bottle.

Eric only considered whether it was safe to do so after his mouth was filled with tasteless bread and his lips wet with stale water. Both were disgusting but they did not seem to do any damage. He pulled out a stool from under the table and sat down heavily.

There was a clatter in the fireplace.

A bird? He peered into the cavernous space. A flurry of soot drifted down and something fell with a bang.

It was a human leg.

There was a scream. It was only after its echoes died down that he realized the screamer had been himself.

The leg was real: he could see the meaty layers of muscle where it had been hacked off. The corrugated nails seemed to stare at him.

More clatter. Another leg thwacked down, crossing the first one as if their owner just sat down at ease. The legs had belonged to a man: their rough skin was liberally sprinkled with black hair.

Was there a dismembered body stuck in the chimney? But shouldn't it be bleeding, then? The legs appeared to be untouched by rot but there was no blood.

Eric backed toward the open door but could not bring himself to turn and run. The sheer hopelessness of his predicament—there was nowhere to run to—made him intensely curious, as if he was observing himself through a protective shield of glass. He supposed he was in shock.

One of the legs twitched and crawled out of the fireplace, foot first, undulating like a fat white caterpillar; it was followed by the second. The two legs stood primly side-by-side.

Was there an invisible body keeping them together? Eric tried to visualize it but failed. However, he did not have to wait long. More clatter, and one after the other, a pair of sinewy arms dragged itself from out of the fireplace. And then a torso. A composite man, assembling himself on the heath in front of Eric.

Perhaps he was wrong to think of his visitor as a man. There were no genitals at the juncture of the legs. The skin was waxy and shiny. The arms appeared too long for the abbreviated trunk. Eric stared at the headless creature, and it stared back at him with the blind eyes of its nipples.

The final puff of dust and he knew, without looking, what was coming down the chimney. But when the head rolled out, coming to a halt so close to his shoes that he could have kicked it like a football, he whimpered, the protective shell of his shock shattered by this latest atrocity.

The head looked at him expectantly. Its eyes were open and surrounded by folds of wrinkles. Numbly, Eric lifted it up and put it on top of the torso.

The composite creature gave a little shrug like a woman settling into constricting clothes. It was still sexless and deformed but the lines where its parts joined had faded and it appeared whole. Its face was that of an old man, foxy, unclean, and slightly mad. He grinned at Eric with his gaping mouth.

"A game?" he asked.

Eric shook his head, but the composite man plunked himself at the table and produced out of nowhere a pair of dice.

"Craps," he said.

"I don't bet!" Eric cried. "I don't play games!"

It was a lie; he was a gamer, his favorite being *Mass Effect*. But the games he liked were played in the privacy and solitude of his office, with the computer screen filtering the brute reality of winning and losing. Somehow, he knew that here, in this sooty, stuffy hall, there would be no such filtering.

The composite man just shrugged and covered the dice with his gnarled hand.

"Snake eyes," he said. "Bet for or against."

"What's the bet?" Eric asked and cursed himself because it meant he had accepted the rules of this world of ashes.

"You stay here. Or you go home."

"I don't want to bet," he repeated but the composite man just grinned his revolting grin, exposing blackened gums, because he knew Eric had already given in.

"For or against?" he repeated.

Eric had never actually played crapshoot but he had no difficulty calculating the probability of rolling one and one. 1/36. Low.

"If I bet and win," he asked, "will you let me go?"

"Of course," the composite man said. "We play fair here. We obey the rules."

Eric thought about it. In the fantasy novels he liked, and in such fairy tales as he remembered, there were indeed strict rules. Demons and monsters were dangerous, but they could be outwitted. And who better to outwit a demon than a techie?

"I bet against," he said.

The composite man grimaced as if tasting something foul and rolled the dice. Eric, his heart in his mouth, leaned over the table, following the spinning cubes as they took their time to settle. Faces flashed by him. One. And one. And one.

The dice settled, measuring him with the hollow stare of snake eyes. He grabbed the dice, turned them over. Three, two, five . . .

"You cheated!" he yelled in futile protest.

The composite man's voice boomed: "You bet. You lost. Fair and square!"

Eric lifted his eyes toward a naked, deformed giant whose

pumpkin-sized head butted the blackened groins of the ceiling. A fist big enough to crush him descended toward him.

"No!" Eric yelled. "No, no, no!"

"Do you have a hostage?" the giant asked. "Somebody to take your place?"

Jennifer was already here, in this nightmare land! And Malika, a stranger who had volunteered to come with him. And Ally . . .

He hesitated, fighting the name that hovered on the tip of his tongue, forcing it back into silence. For some reason, the faces of his dead grandparents flashed before his eyes.

The giant's fist closed around his midriff and lifted him toward a laughing, toothless mouth.

Chapter 13:
The Wolves

Ally finally relaxed. She had changed out of her soaked smock into a pair of jeans and a t-shirt with a craft brewery logo, both part of the light-smiths' hoard. Looking through the heap she had received in exchange for the combings of her golden hair, she realized that Nightwood must be in constant contact with the history world. The clothes were no medieval doublets or embroidered gowns but what could be found in any five-dollar box in a Goodwill: torn jeans, soiled jackets, brand-advertising tees. They were too big for the girls, but they did not complain, gratefully snuggling into their warmth.

They had eaten, demolishing all the apples, half the honey and most of the loaf. The rest Ally put aside, even though her own stomach was grumbling in protest. At least they had fresh water to wash down their food, scooping it from the pool with their bare hands. Ally wondered whether its shape-shifting power would work any further transformation but they remained what they were, no matter how often they drank.

They did not talk much during the meal. Ally was still not sure that they actually spoke the same language but as long as Mama's necklace granted her the power of King Solomon's ring—understanding any tongue—they could communicate well enough. But it did not tell her what she was supposed to do with them. Bringing them back home was the obvious answer but how to do it?

She did ask Talia, the oldest, where she was from. The girl looked at her with liquid brown eyes. "The Most Serene One," she said, and Ally, not being sure whether she had understood the question, let it slide.

Nightwood

They were all bone-tired and the two younger girls, Margarita and Queenie, practically fell asleep over their food. Ally lay on the other side of the fire, closed her eyes, and thought of Eric. But she did not dream of him. Instead, the dream was of standing in her kitchen in the glass house, making coffee, morning light painting stripes on the countertop, the thump of Carl's weight-lifting machine downstairs. She felt happy and secure because she was home. And then a cup slipped out of her hand, broke with a sharp crack, and she was instantly awake.

It was still dark, no hint of dawn, and the moon had fallen behind the black canopy of the forest. The fire, though still burning, was little more than an ash-blanketed scatter of embers. Something was moving in the bushes, something big.

It emerged into the hollow and though the light was poor, she knew instantly what it was. The low-slung shape, the soft canine tread, the sniffing muzzle close to the ground, the plume of the swishing tail. The enemy, the Big Bad One.

A wolf.

Ally had grown up with tales of wolves, the winter menace that pursued her peasant forebears through the frozen Slavic steppes. She had actually seen a wolf only once, in a zoo, and it had been a pitiful, mangy creature. But in Nightwood, tales of the past were dangers of the present.

She grasped a dry branch but did not move. It might just go away. She had read somewhere that predators did not like human smell and would not attack unless they were provoked or desperately hungry. She did not know whether this dubious bit of natural history applied in Nightwood, but she prayed it did.

The wolf padded down to the pool and, thrusting its muzzle into the dark water, began to lap noisily. Ally relaxed for a second, letting the sweaty fingers unclench around the branch. And then the implications of what she was seeing hit home, and she looked frantically at the girls, praying they would not wake.

The dark huddle of bodies stirred, and a head popped up. Ally pressed her finger to her lips.

The wolf was still drinking. And then another shadow pushed through the undergrowth and joined it at the pool, and another—four, no five, wolves of differing sizes circled the pool, all drinking in unison. The night was loud with their lapping and slurping.

One of the wolves stepped away from the pool and paused on

the grassy slope. Moonlight broke through a gap in the clouds, silvering the scene.

It was not the dramatic performance of a werewolf movie. There was no howling, no writhing, no shedding of fur. Instead, a sleek wave of darkness rolled over the animal, starting from the tip of its nose and sheathing it as neatly as cling film. For a moment it looked like a two-dimensional silhouette of a wolf painted black upon black. Then it folded in upon itself in a shapeless heap, trembled slightly, and rose up—a two-legged cutout. The darkness rolled off as quickly and completely as it came on and a naked man stood in the middle of the clearing, his legs splayed and his arms akimbo.

Ally caught only a glimpse of his face in the uncertain light, but her heart sank. She had hoped that a wolf-turned-human would be less of a danger than a raw animal. She should have known better! No four-legged meat-eater was a match to the predators of the streets. And this man was such a predator, she knew it immediately, as she saw the heaviness of his jaw, his bulbous nose, his slack stomach and dangling penis. She had never seen him before, but she had seen men like him her entire life: beating on Mama's door with meaty fists, bellowing filthy words; trailing her when she walked back home from school with a lewd wink and a quick grab; accosting her on the street during that time in her life she had made herself forget . . .

The other wolves were stepping off the pool as well, lifting their muzzles to the sky in eerie silence, undergoing the same quick transformation. In no time there was a group of five naked men— all men—standing in the middle of the clearing.

No, it was not a group. It was a gang.

They did not exchange a single word, which was uncharacteristic of pack behavior, and Ally allowed herself to hope, desperately, that perhaps they were under some kind of *geis*, that perhaps they would just go away and leave them alone. But of course, this was a vain hope. They must have known she and the girls were there all along. The first one to transform strode with a heavy rolling gait toward them, stepping on brambles and twigs as if it was a pavement.

"Hey, bro!" He yelled. "Look what we got here!"

Ally was on her feet instantly. She could outrun them, lose herself in the forest . . .

But she could not abandon the girls. Talia and Queenie were just stirring awake from their exhausted slumber.

"Run, girls!" she yelled. "Run!"

But it was too late. The Big Nose already had Margarita, who squirmed desperately in his arms trying to get free. He cuffed her on the head.

Another wolf—Ally could not think of them as anything else—grabbed Queenie, who flailed and cried out until a large hand clamped upon her mouth. A smaller wolf with a bent scoliotic back took hold of Talia and then snatched back his hand with a curse.

"She bit me, little bitch!" he wheezed indignantly.

A ripple of laughter, another higher pitched but commanding voice:

"You don't know how to handle bitches, Mikhailo!"

"That's why your litter is so small!"

"What litter! Poor old Mikhailo could never get it up even with a coyote!"

"A dog!"

"A poodle!"

"Cut it out, bros!" again the high-pitched voice. "Little morsels! But there is something else here, isn't there?"

A wolf stepped closer to the dying fire and its fitful gleams illuminated his stunted physique: sharp features, receding hair and the narrow pigeon-chest. Ally's heart sank even more. She knew brutishness and its dangers. But she also knew that there is no limit to the viciousness of an underdog. And the man before here was a perpetual underdog even though this pack had chosen him as its leader. He would never be satisfied with any leadership position because he would always aim for more and nurse a grudge when his ambitions were thwarted. If he had the whole world, he would still snivel that he was being denied his fair share.

"Lookee at this!" he sneered. "Not much meat on them bones either!"

Ally's hand snaked down to her pocket. She finally remembered that she had potent weapons: the matchbox and the ice-handkerchief. She could burn the gang to cinders or she could literally freeze their butts off. She allowed herself a moment of triumph, considering her choices, and then the realization hit her like a fist in the face. Both the matchbox and the handkerchief were in the pocket of her smock, which she had draped over the bushes to dry! She had forgotten to take them out!

She cursed herself even as she started sidling toward the smock, but a rough hand grasped her arm and twisted it behind her back, throwing her down to her knees.

"Where are you going, lovey?" the leader tittered. "Boys here are hungry, aren't you, bros?"

"She is too thin," another wolf growled.

"The hunt was bad!"

"Damned deer!"

"Better than nothing!"

"Small ones are tender!"

"We should take them to the Ogre," the hunchbacked wolf they called Mikhailo suddenly declared. "That was the new order. Stephan, you know that. They all go the Castle!"

There was dead silence as the wolves exchanged dubious glances. Ally's heart leaped.

Stephan did not take kindly to any challenges to his leadership. He snarled at Mikhailo. "Who made you alpha, you dog? Want to fight it out?"

The other wolf hesitated and then sulkily went down on his knees and turned his head, exposing his stubbly throat to Stephan, who gloated for a second and then thrust his face at Ally and she saw, with a shudder of revulsion, that his eyes retained their animal shape with no whites showing. His breath smelled of stale beer.

"Nah," he declared. "The Blood Man is getting too big for his britches. We are no pooches of his! We take no orders herein our own woods! Eat them! And I'll take care of this bitch!"

The wolves moved toward her. The ones who were holding the girls threw their charges on the ground and dragged them toward the fire. Ally pushed Stephan away and kneed him in the groin. But the kick went astray and only enraged the shapeshifter, who growled and dealt her an open-palm blow that made her head ring. Her braid, which she had wound around her head and tied with a kerchief, fell out, glowing in the firelight.

There was silence. The wolves stopped. Stephan tugged roughly at her braid, brought it to his nose and sniffed at it.

"She goes to the Ogre," he said, turning away. "The little ones are dinner."

And that was when the deer came.

Part 3:

The Three Dragon Rivers

Chapter 1:
Ivan and Alyona

The yurt was made of soft skins draped on poles and tied together in the shape of a cone. They looked like deerskin and Ally found it rather shocking. But the shaggy pelts she was reclining upon were of some other animal: a bear, perhaps.

She was staring dreamily at the blue sky through the circular opening at the top of the yurt. It was warm and sunny; the dry wind flapped the skins and brought in a soothing, soughing sound. The Great Steppe where the deer-folk lived was like the plains of central Russia: an enormous expanse of flat land covered with silver billows of plumed grass and hummocks of sagebrush.

Children's laughter drifted in from the outside and Ally tried to distinguish her girls' voices. Talia and Margarita loved being in the settlement; Queenie was timid and withdrawn. But at least they had food to eat and safe water to drink. The *geis* that had reshaped them into farm birds could not reach them here.

She reached for a wooden plate filled with berries and baked potatoes Ivan had left for her. Her body was still aching after the encounter with the wolves, and she decided she deserved a little self-pampering.

As Stephan the wolf had grabbed her hair and wound it around his hand, snapping her head back, she had tried to pivot but the pull was too strong. Her legs scissored impotently as he dragged her toward the bushes.

And then there was a thundering sound of many hooves beating on the hard ground and an avalanche of tawny bodies burst into the clearing.

Wolves prey on deer. Men with guns prey on wolves. But naked men, their feeble defenseless flesh exposing them for the inadequate animals they are, are prey to all. Had Stephan and his gang stayed in their wolf form a little longer, they could have turned the tables on their attackers. As it was, they did not stand a chance against the herd.

As the pull on her hair slackened, Ally rolled away, scrambled to her feet and gathered the girls to her. Huddling behind a tree, they watched the slaughter.

There were more deer than men. The males had branching antlers; the females did not; but all had large hooves, which they put to good use. The men-wolves were buffeted, gored and trampled. Even when the wolves were down, the deer did not stop their assault, reducing them to bloody rags in the churned-up soil. Ally knew she should feel pity, or at least disgust, but she was filled with fierce jubilation. It kept her in place instead of creeping away, which would be the prudent thing to do.

Just as suddenly as it started, the assault stopped, and the deer lined up in the clearing and turned their large liquid eyes upon her. It was dawning now, the sky lit up with pale pink, and she realized she had missed her chance to escape.

But they did not attack. Instead, one by one, they went to the pool and drank. The transformation was not dissimilar to that of the wolves: a brief shudder; a blackness crawling up the four-legged silhouette and crumpling it up like a piece of paper; and a human body reconstituting itself from the heap of darkness. But here the similarity ended. Each deer, whether male or female, did not remain nude. Instead, they filed in an orderly procession toward the far side of the clearing where Ally now saw a well-disguised lean-to which she had missed last evening. They pulled out clothes and dressed with the same unhurried dignity that characterized all their movements: men in long homespun shirts and leggings, women in bleached shifts and beaded sashes. And then, they melted into the forest.

Only one deer remained in the clearing: a large male with luxurious, many-branched antlers. He never took his eyes off Ally, and she was compelled to return his gaze, perturbed by some dim sense of recognition.

After everybody else had drunk, he put his muzzle down into the pool. And then he stood up as a man: a big-boned blond fellow, young and fit. Ally followed his every movement.

When he was dressed, he turned to her.

"Alyonushka," he said. "Sister!"

 Nightwood

Ally still could not wrap her head around it.

She was an only child; it was as much her identity as being a Ukrainian, being an immigrant, being a woman. It had always been her and Mama. Her grandparents died in one of the disasters that periodically struck her native land; Mama had never talked much about them, and Ally had not been interested until it was too late to ask questions. As for her unknown father, the mythical image of a tall, handsome officer killed in Afghanistan sufficed, especially in contrast to the men whom she found sitting in her mother's kitchen, drinking vodka, smoking smelly cigarettes, and following her with lewd eyes.

She had known, of course, that her mother had had an abortion when she was seventeen, two years before she carried the pregnancy that became Ally to term. Mama told it to her as a cautionary tale and she took it to heart, never allowing her contraception to lapse. Other than that, the image of a brother who had never existed was just a vague fantasy.

And here he was. Ivan. Her unborn brother was the leader of a deer tribe in Nightwood.

Ivan seemed to be genuinely happy to have his sister around and displayed no resentment at the fact that she was living a life that, by rights, should have been his own. On the other hand, he *was* alive in Nightwood and as challenging as the deer people's existence was, what with constant wolf attacks and other dangers that she did not quite understand, on the balance it was better than what would have awaited him in Ukraine. He was strong but neither cunning nor ruthless; in fact, he appeared to Ally to be a little simple, as her peasant forebears might have put it. The ruined land of his non-birth devoured men like him.

She could not figure out how the deer-people lived until he explained it to her. The tribe numbered around fifty. At any given time, about half of them were in human shape, while the others were deer. Only males had antlers and these antlers were periodically shed, which was very fortunate since the deer people were excellent craftsmen and made the discarded antlers into scraping knives, spoons, necklaces, and a variety of other implements that they used themselves or traded to other tribes of the Great Steppe: the snake people, the coyote people, and the chipmunk people. The relationship with the coyote tribe was strained, Ivan said, but it did not preclude an occasional potlatch or a trading get-together. The only people with whom the deer exchanged nothing but blows were the wolves.

"It was a bit of luck that you came to the pool when they did," Ally had said.

Ivan shook his head.

"No luck. We guard the pool. But they sneak in anyway."

There were many change pools scattered around the forest that covered the plateau above the Great Steppe, he said, but most of them held bird or animal water. The pool that Ally and the girls had stumbled upon was the only one in the vicinity big enough to support the deer tribe—and therefore big enough to support their predators.

At first, she could not understand why they needed human change-water at all. Wouldn't it be easier to remain human and only shift into animal shapes when needed by drinking from one of the many animal springs? Her question was answered as she watched a woman cook potatoes on a small fire in front of her yurt. The deer woman was about to pull the roasting stick out of the fire when a shudder went through her slender frame. She dropped onto the ground. Alarmed, Ally rushed to her side, only to witness the same process she had seen by the change pool but in reverse: a quick wash of darkness spreading over the woman's exposed flesh, her collapse into a shapeless mount; and then a graceful doe bounded away, panicked by the fire, leaving the empty cotton shift lying on the ground. Ally rescued the burnt potatoes and the shift and presented them to Ivan when he came back from whatever mysterious errand he had embarked upon. He clicked his tongue disapprovingly.

"Maria has always been a lazybones! The sun was up, it was her time!"

And he explained. Unless the deer people drank from the human change pool once in twenty-four hours, they would remain what they were—deer. The deer shape was their natural, default form. Humanity was something they had to sustain by daily effort, battling their enemies for the source of transforming magic.

All the tribes of the Great Steppe were shapeshifters but in the opposite direction from what Ally had assumed at first: animals shifting into human shapes rather than the other way around. So her brother was actually a buck deer! Well, it was no stranger than the fact that he existed at all.

But what about all the deerskin they used for yurts and other articles? Surely, they did not hunt their own! Ivan was shocked when she asked about it. Of course not. Skins were the gift the dead bequeathed to the tribe! The bodies were handled with reverence and affection: skin, antlers and hooves were removed, and the rest ceremoniously buried. The deer people were strict vegetarians, and so the question of eating the flesh of the other Steppe tribes never arose for them. The same could not be said about the wolves.

The wolves were not even a proper tribe: they had no territory of their own, no recognized leaders, and estimates of their numbers varied wildly. They were bands of marauders and killers who had been trickling into the Steppe from elsewhere, harassing and murdering its peoples, taking over swathes of territory and then melting away when attacked by the regular tribes. Ivan's usually beaming face took on a hard cast when he talked about the wolves. Ally had no doubts that he would exterminate them in a blink of an eye if he could. But the problem was that their balance of power depended on the precise timing of shapeshifting. In their animal form, wolves were no match for the deer people armed with spears, bows, and arrows. In their human form, they could be easily dispatched by a herd of rampaging deer, as Ally had witnessed. For a reason nobody understood, wolves never used any weapons and seldom wore clothing, which all the other tribes did religiously when in their human forms. But as animal predators, they would hunt down and devour fawns, does, or any weakened or solitary deer, inflicting terrible casualties upon the tribe. And as humans, they were skilled and ruthless killers, capable of taking down any tribe warrior with their bare hands and sneaking upon the encampment to kill its children and rape its women.

In order to beat them off, the deer people had to keep off-phase: animals when the wolves were human, humans when they were animals. And it was becoming harder and harder, as bands of wolves multiplied across the Steppe, staging unexpected raids or drinking of the change pools when nobody was watching. There were also rumors that some other shapeshifters, similar to the wolves but also different in strange ways, had been spotted, talking to the coyote tribe and even reaching out to the secretive bear and wolverine tribes of the forest.

"Where do they come from?" Ally asked.

Ivan shrugged. Ally tried again:

"Someone sending them?"

Ivan turned away and muttered something inaudible.

"What did you say?"

"The Ogre," Ivan said and spat on the ground.

Chapter 2:
The Steppe

Ivan's long legs devoured the distance. In his human form, he was as indefatigable as any ruminant. Ally secretly hoped that he would shift into the deer-form tomorrow and carry her. He had the change-water in a big flask, so he could choose what form to take.

He seemed to know where they were going, and she wondered how he oriented himself. There were no visible landmarks on this broad, featureless plain. They were aiming east but this was as much as she could tell from the position of the sun.

She did not like the Steppe. Its emptiness hurt her brain. It stretched out before them in an endless expanse of hummocky ground, sepia-toned like an old photograph, and denuded of any vegetation taller than a bush. It was boring and faintly ominous. She realized, with a jolt, that she missed the Californian redwoods.

Was it what they meant when they talked about immigrants becoming natives: when the balance of belonging and estrangement shifted, and what used to be one's own became somebody else's? Wasn't it as magical a transformation as drinking from a change-pool?

"How about a rest?" she suggested to Ivan.

"We'll make camp when the sun sets," he said. "Maybe we can get to the chipmunk tribe's territory. We trade with them: they'll give us shelter."

The chipmunk tribe sounded jolly, she decided. But how would they fit into the tiny mammals' burrows? No, that was silly, of course chipmunks (or *sousliks*, as Ivan called them) would be human-sized in Nightwood . . . at least in their human form. Ally tried to figure out the ratio of mass change in the transition from animal to human and gave it up. The laws of Nightwood were different from the laws of Newton.

A bird shadow slid over her. Ally squinted into the colorless sky. Wings like knife-strokes against the bleached cumulus . . . but she could not make out what kind of bird it was. A raptor, perhaps? She rubbed her arms which erupted in goosebumps. The feathered dress that had stifled her in its moth-eaten embrace, crunching her bones and darkening her mind . . . was it still out there? Ally had thought it was destroyed in the conflagration in Little Mother's farmyard but, did anything truly die in Nightwood? What if it was still flying around, searching for her?

Ivan had explained this as well. Ally was human; and for her to assume an animal or a bird form, an animal or bird skin was a must. It melded with her body and even when removed, left an imprint that could be activated by the drinking of an appropriate kind of change-water. This is why the cow-girl from Little Mother's farmyard had become a cow when drinking from the animal spring. This is why for the three girls who had been remade into fowls by Little Mother's malevolent magic, any kind of bird change-water was dangerous.

"What if I drank from your water?" Ally asked.

He shrugged and advised against experimenting.

To distract herself from the monotony of walking, Ally addressed her brother:

"How do we cross the three Dragon Rivers?"

"There are bridges," he said. "They are guarded, but I don't know what the guardians are. Don't worry, sister, we'll find a way."

I hope, she thought but did not say aloud. Of all the miraculous things she had encountered in Nightwood, Ivan's presence was the greatest miracle of all. For the first time since Mama's disappearance, Ally had a real family.

When Ally had finally figured out the dynamics of the deer-tribe's existence, a simple solution to their plight occurred to her.

"Why don't you collect water from both the human and animal springs and keep it at hand?" She had asked Ivan. "This way if the wolves come as animals, your people can dispatch them with spears or arrows; but if they come as humans, your warriors can quickly metamorphose back into the deer form and gore or stomp them to death."

Ivan's large blue eyes grew even larger as he contemplated Ally's proposal. His mouth formed a perfect "O" of surprise and admiration.

"Marvel of a sister!" he cried. "Alyona the Wise! Not one of our people is half as wise as you are! We will gather our council and let them hear what you said!"

He rushed out of the yurt leaving Ally with the mixed feelings of satisfaction and unease. It was nice to be called Alyona the Wise; but what did it say about the mental capacities of her brother's tribe that such a simple solution did not occur to them? It was perhaps unfair to expect military genius from gentle animals, even in a human form, but how would they fare when the wolves came up with another trick? And come up they would; wolves were smart, even outside of Nightwood, and if Stephan's gang was any indication, the wolves here combined the worst of human cruelty and animal persistence. And then there were these other predators sent by the Ogre . . .

Ally sat outside the yurt, staring into the featureless distance veiled by a thin white mist. The Steppe lay all around her, vast and indifferent. Now, having escaped the farmyard serfdom, she could finally take stock of who she was and what she had to do.

There were three paths before her. She could stay with Ivan. She could try to escape Nightwood and go back to California. And she could continue on her quixotic quest to find and free her husband.

Ally rejected the first one immediately. She loved her brother with a simple sibling affection that had been denied to her in her lonely childhood. But there was no place for her among animals, even if half the time they pretended to be human.

Going back to California? She was not sure how she could find a way out. Even if the swan-dress had not been destroyed, Ally would never trust herself to that malevolent helper again. She shivered, remembering the stinking, suffocating bird-being that had enveloped her when the swan-dress had forced itself upon her.

There would be other gates, of course. Nightwood was nowhere and everywhere, whispering in dreams and nightmares, spreading its roots through old tales, growing in the rich soil of history. She could find a way.

Except she did not want to.

Ally stood up and stretched. Her rough smock scratched her skin but her heavy plait, newly washed and braided, smoothly slid down her back, giving her a feeling of comfort. She patted her pocket where lay her three treasures: the gold-producing comb; the fire-making matches; and the cold-generating handkerchief. She was as well-equipped to brave the dangers of Nightwood as anybody.

And she could not do otherwise. Not if she wanted to keep any self-respect. Not if she had any hope of molding a coherent personality out of the mess of evasions, compromises and self-lies that had been her life so far. She had sold herself for a living. So had her mother. *Shlucha*. A whore, daughter of a whore. An unwanted immigrant. A stranger in a strange land.

But now she had the chance to change all of this. To free her husband. To transform a business deal into a marriage. To be a hero, like her father.

You are an officer's daughter.

It was not a hard choice.

So when Ivan came back from his council, flushed with success and eager to put her plan into action, Ally was ready. She had packed s deerskin pouch with such meager provisions as the tribe could spare, rolled up a couple of blankets, found a pair of moccasins that, stuffed with dry grass, could fit her small feet. She was ready to be on her way but first she had to explain herself to Ivan. She had dreaded the explanation, but it turned out the easiest one she had ever done.

"Your husband has been abducted by the Ogre," Ivan said slowly, nodding his handsome blond head.

"Yes."

"And you are going to free him."

"Yes."

"We are setting out in the morning," he declared.

Ally thought she had misheard.

"We?"

Ivan looked at her reproachfully.

"Sister Alyona," he said, "you are my flesh and blood. Your husband is my brother. I never had the honor of meeting our mother, but I know what she would expect me to do. How could you even suspect that I would let you go alone to confront the Ogre?"

Ally's eyes blurred with tears as she hugged Ivan, her arms not quite reaching around his broad back. He was as solid and reliable as an oak tree, all of a piece, living in a simple world of right and wrong, black and white, truth and lie. She loved him and envied his simplicity because she could never be like him.

She remembered the lilac seed that had grown into a shadowy semblance of Mama. But it had been destroyed by Little Mother, who had taken away Ivan's only chance of seeing the face of the woman who had refused to let him live. And Ally realized that this was the ultimate proof of Mama's love for her unborn son: that she would not allow him to be broken by the world. Perhaps she, Ally, was the less-loved.

She took off Mama's golden cross necklace and put it around her brother's neck.

"It was Mama's," she said. "You are the eldest son; it is yours by right."

And at that moment, Talia barged in.

Ally groaned. She had all but forgotten about the three little girls, or rather she made herself forget. They were an unwanted burden, an unnecessary complication. She had no idea what to do with them. Like her, they were immigrants from the world of history. Or perhaps, they were, like Carl, victims of kidnapping. But in either case, she had no idea how to bring them back where they belonged.

Talia babbled something that Ally could not understand. At first, she thought it was because the girl spoke too fast; then she realized it was actually in a foreign language. Italian, maybe? Of course; she no longer had the necklace that, like Solomon's ring, had given her the ability to understand every tongue. She contemplated the uncomfortable option of asking Ivan to give it back, but her brother, putting his head to one side, listened intently and then responded in Ukrainian.

"Yes, I think she would agree,"

Talia giggled, planted a wet kiss on his cheek, and ran out of the yurt.

"They want to stay here, with my people," Ivan explained. "They promise to drink of a bird spring occasionally, so they can be useful as scouts. They don't want to go back to where the farming woman snatched them from."

Ally smiled. Everything was working out!

And now their day trek on the faceless plain was winding down as the sun dipped toward the horizon, painting the empty sky in the pastel hues of washed-out pink and pale yellow. A scatter of tiny birds peppered the vast firmament. Ally watched them suspiciously, but they appeared to be ordinary starlings.

Something loomed ahead in the smear of shadows. Ivan squinted and waved his hands.

"The *sousliks'* camp!" he cried. "We can rest here!"

Ally sighed in relief and breathed in the scents of sage and dust. And of smoke.

Chapter 3:
Sun, Moon, and Talia

The *rii were* choked with dead bodies.

The canals smelled worse than they did in the height of summer when dead fish and household slops combined into a gooey mess under the steamy sun of La Serenissima. But it was early spring now, the water cold and grey, the dome of San Marco tracing a fading outline against the cloudy sky. And yet the Most Serene One, the Queen of the Adriatic, the Republic of Venice, stunk like a charnel house.

Talia staggered out onto the embankment. There was a swollen bulk bobbing by one of the wooden posts gondoliers used for navigation. A large gull was lethargically pecking at its head. It did not move when Talia clapped her hands and she let it go. It was easier to see corpses when they were balloons of anonymous flesh, half-eaten bird meals. Then it meant you did not have to think of them as people. It was fresh bodies that were unbearable because they looked as if they would wake up and smile or talk to you. The bloated buds of buboes that the Black Death scattered over the flesh of its victims were mercy, really, because they marked the final separation between the living and the dead. Once they bloomed on you, you were carrion. Meat.

Talia sat on the wet coping, oblivious of the fact that her skirt was soaked through. She was constantly cold anyway; even when there was still wood to burn, the small fire could not counteract the chill of starvation. And she needed the respite from the constant feeble crying that she seemed to hear even now, emanating from the house, though the blinds were tightly closed as were the blinds of every house along the canal.

A rat skittered on the rubbish-covered pavement, dragging a rag of flesh. Talia followed it with dull eyes. There had been many more rats after the council ordered cats and dogs killed on the suspicion that they were spreading the pestilence. The Black Death only picked up after that: the dancing skeleton whose footsteps Talia heard in the depth of night when the wailing finally stopped but she still could not fall asleep, as if the unusual silence screamed in her ears. She was skeptical of the idea that domestic animals were to blame, anyway. The rumor that the Jews living in the ghetto had cast some malevolent spell over the city seemed more reasonable to her.

The rat, though . . . it was sleek and well-fed, as were all the scavengers of La Serenissima: rodents and birds alike. Thinking of it, Talia felt saliva flood her dry mouth.

The babies were finally silent, and Talia let herself hope . . . and recoiled from the hope with a flash of shame. They were her charge now. She had sworn on an image of Santa Maria delle Salute to take care of them.

But was it fair?

A splash of water in the dead silence of the dying city. Talia lifted her head wearily and stared at the canal. Her mouth fell open in surprise.

Rounding the bend in the *rio* was a fancy gondola, its six-pronged bow-piece smoothly cutting the steel-grey water. And standing in the bow was a tall figure swathed in a voluminous black cloak. Under its wide hat, its face was beaked and bone-white like the skull of an enormous raptor.

Il Medico della Peste! The plague doctor! At the beginning of the pestilence, there had been many such on the streets of La Serenissima, walking around in full costume, confident that the aromatic herbs in the curving beak of their mask protected them from the foul vapors. There had been fewer and fewer as the Black Death strode over the Laguna of Venice; and once Talia saw a flock of pigeons pecking on a black-cloaked body, she had lost faith in their curative power. Still, her ingrained deference to the authorities reasserted itself as she curtseyed deeply before the imposing figure. The gondola slowed down, the plague doctor moored it at the post and stepped out. Talia shivered under the glassy stare of his blank, round eyes and had to remind herself these were spectacles. A plague doctor covered up every orifice through which the Black Death could enter a body. Except that the dancing skeleton apparently had its own secret entryways.

"Who are you, maid?" the plague doctor asked in a high, squeaky voice that reminded her of squalling birds.

"My name is Talia Barbarigo, Signore."

"And is your house marked, Talia?"

Talia licked her chapped lips.

"I lived with my elder sister, Signore," she whispered. "She died a fortnight ago and her body was removed. Our parents are long dead."

"And are you healthy?"

"I am untouched by the pestilence," Talia exclaimed eagerly. "Look!"

She uncovered her neck and shoulders. Her wasted flesh was as dull as parchment and as wrinkled as if she had been thrice her age of thirteen summers. But it was clean of buboes and lesions.

"Very well," the doctor said. "Our glorious Council of Ten that prays daily for La Serenissima has sent me to deliver provisions to those whom the divine mercy has spared. It has also authorized me to remove those showing signs of sickness to the plague island of Lazaretto Vecchio where they can die in peace. Are you alone in your household, maid?"

He hefted a sack from the bottom of the gondola, balancing it in one gloved hand, and Talia saw the rounded shape of a loaf underneath the burlap. She licked her lips again.

"Yes," she said. "I am alone."

And a baby's shrill cry came from the house, echoed by a second one. The doctor lowered the sack back into the boat and cocked his head, his curving beak pointing at Talia.

"These are my sister's bastards!" she cried. "She left them in my charge but I have no more food to give them. Mercy, Signore!"

"Bring them out," the doctor said.

Talia rushed back into the house and brought out two swaddled bundles which she put on the pavement. The boy's face was red with crying, but the girl's big black eyes opened wide as she stared at the *Medico* in fascination, reaching out with a twig-like hand.

"What ages are they?" the doctor asked.

"They are twins, one year old. My sister, God forgive her, conceived them in sin, though she always denied it. She called them Sun and Moon instead of giving them Christian names because she claimed they were born of light."

"Remove their swaddling," the doctor said, and Talia complied.

The blank eyes studied the small bodies, so thin that each frail bone stood out in sharp relief under the transparent skin.

"I see signs of sickness upon them," the doctor said. "They are inconclusive but the council charged me with power of judgment. They have to go to Lazaretto Vecchio."

"Those are but flea bites!" Talia cried. "The children are healthy. When their mother died, they stayed by the corpse and yet showed no contagion!"

"The judgment is mine," the doctor repeated. "They have to go to Lazaretto. However, since they are babes incapable of reason, their caretaker has to accompany them. Gather your belongings, maid, you are going to the plague island."

Talia prostrated herself at the doctor's feet, sobbing and kissing his embroidered shoes. Under the rich brocade, a sharp bony hardness seemed to repel her entreaties.

"It is sad, indeed," the doctor said meditatively. "You are healthy and when the pestilence leaves La Serenissima, as it has always done, you would have been spared. The babes, on the other hand, will die—whether from disease or hunger. Too bad you have to accompany them to the Lazaretto since no one comes back from the island of the dead."

Talia's sobs petered out and she stood up. The plague doctor towered above her, his bird-face looming against the dusky sky.

She glanced at Sun and Moon. They did not cry. The boy's blue eyes stared blankly at nothing; his sister's black lashes were lowered, as if she were asleep—or faint.

The babes will die anyway . . .

"Signore," Talia asked, "if these unhallowed children were dead, as are so many of our upstanding citizens of La Serenissima, would you give me food and let me stay in my parents' house?"

"Yes, indeed," the plague doctor said. "It would be better for all if they were dead."

With one swift movement, Talia swept the children off the slippery embankment, pushing them into the thick water of the canal. They sank like stones.

The plague doctor's beak dipped toward Talia and his cloak swooshed, spreading out, as an enormous bird silhouette blanked out the dregs of daylight. A clacking, chittering sound came from behind the mask—except Talia suddenly realized that the mask was not attached by ties to the head. It *was* the head.

The beak opened up, disclosing not a cavity filled with aromatic herbs but a wet, scarlet gullet. A stink of rot washed over her, and Talia felt her bones crunch and her flesh shrink as a pall of verminous feathers fell over her.

Chapter 4:
The Sousliks' Village

Ally bumped into Ivan's back when he stopped abruptly, lifting his hand to enjoin silence. She squinted into the tangle of shadows ahead. Used to the bright lights of the city, she found the nights on the Steppe creepily dark.

But the smell was unmistakable now: the bitter stench of burning that brought tears to her eyes.

"Something's wrong," Ivan whispered. He dropped to his belly and crawled forward. After some hesitation, Ally did the same. As they came closer to the encampment and her eyes adjusted, she could make out squat silhouettes of dugouts surrounded by plumes of tall silvery grass. Of course; it made sense that the chipmunk tribe would live in burrows rather than tents! But where were the guards? Ally knew that every tribe on the Steppe posted guards around their settlements to ward off predators' incursion and to protect their change-springs from poachers. So where was everybody? The settlement was quiet and dark, the crouching dugouts like wary animals against the bruised sky. But nothing stirred.

Ally had a bad feeling about it. She touched Ivan's shoulder to indicate that perhaps they should retreat. And then a hard, lean body slammed into her, knocking the breath out of her and rolling her over onto her back, her neck open to its teeth.

It was totally silent: no snarling or growling; and it made the attack all the more shocking. Its meaty rotten stench wafted over her.

Ivan kicked the creature and it turned to him, its wet teeth gleaming in the dark, its eyes sparkling ruby-red. Ally scrambled to her feet and grasped the stick tipped with a deer antler Ivan had insisted she take. Swinging it awkwardly, she hit the creature on its low-slung head, and it finally gave a sound: a thin, human-like moan. It snapped at her, tearing the sleeve of her smock. But Ivan was upon it in a second, kicking it in the throat and then pounding it on its head with his own, heavier stick. The creature collapsed. The moon, finally climbing above the horizon, shed uncertain light upon its twitching hide. It looked like a large dog or a small wolf but Ally saw, with a shudder of revulsion, that its legs ended in splayed human hands.

"Watch out!" Ivan cried as a wave of lean grey bodies poured out from the nearest dugout.

The next minutes were lost in a scramble of fending off snapping teeth and slavering jaws. Ally's stick was slippery in her sweaty hands; the creatures' stench clogged her nostrils and pounded in her head. Without Ivan, she would have been the wolves' meal in no time. But even with the two of them fighting together, they were in serious danger. Ivan's bow was useless at such close quarters and the eerily silent grey shadows seemed to multiply; just as one fell under a well-placed blow, another one slunk forward to take its place.

Ally's braid unraveled and she felt teeth tangling in, and tearing at, her hair. Filled with disgust, she lunged away from the creature and suddenly remembered what she had in her smock's pocket. Frantically, she pawed through her treasures, afraid of dropping and losing one of them. Ivan, as if aware of what she was doing, positioned himself between her and the line of attackers. His muscled arm rose and fell with a regularity of a metronome and each blow felled a snarling wolf. But then a bigger one jumped at him from the side, closing its teeth in the flesh of his arm.

Ally finally extracted a match from the matchbox. One try, two . . . the match refused to light. Ivan's grunt of pain was shocking against the silence of their attackers.

A bright tongue of fire sprung in Ally's cupped hands and ran up her arm, clothing it in a gauntlet of flame. The wolves retreated immediately, crouching low to the ground, their ruby eyes wary. She advanced upon them, holding her burning arm aloft like a torch and thrust it at them, remembering how it had burnt the swan-dress.

Now in the bright light she saw that the creatures had an appalling mixture of human and canine features. Some of them had bare hands instead of paws; some stood on hind legs; and the one in front had a fat pink face crookedly sitting between the furry ears of a wolf. But they all had enough of an animal in them to be afraid of fire. They retreated; Ally pressed forward, swinging her flame-cloaked arm. Her fingers grazed a clump of dry pampas grass and it caught fire. Silvery plumes went off with a whoosh. A feverish orange glow danced on the glowering creatures who kept backing off, still in the same unnatural silence interrupted only by the crackling of the flames.

Something zinged past Ally. Using her as a cover, Ivan had unshouldered his bow and loosed arrows at the dog-wolves. One of them—the one with a pink human face—convulsed on the ground, a feathered shaft sticking from his neck. Another one loped away and was felled by an arrow. The rest turned tail and ran, melting away into the dark.

"We need to put out the fire!" Ivan yelled. Tearing off his shirt, he started slapping the spreading flames with no visible success. Ally was jolted out of her paralysis. They had some water, but it was precious: without it, her brother would be a deer forever. But better that than to burn! The flame gauntlet blinked out as she reached for the flask in her backpack—and then she remembered.

She pulled out the linen handkerchief she had taken from Little Mother's bedside table and tossed it onto the ground. It made a white patch, painted pink by the flames. And then the rosy tint faded out as the whiteness spread in concentric circles, covering the ashy ground. The fire dipped low and went out. The smoky air bit with frosty chill.

Ally and Ivan stood together shivering in the sudden darkness. A streamlet of blood crawled down his arm from the wolf's bite, and he staunched it with his charred shirt.

"Let me," Ally said. "No, wait, we need to wash it out!"

"The *sousliks'* spring is here," Ivan said grimly, pointing toward the clearing in the middle of the settlement. "But I don't think it'll be of much use."

Indeed. When they came to the lip of the tiny natural pool, they saw it choked with rubbish. At first, Ally thought it was just dry branches and leaves but realized that the compacted mass fouling the change-water was composed of odd pieces of clothing, bits of paper, even broken jewelry mixed with unidentifiable organic matter. It gave her the creeps and she turned away. At the end, they used some of their own precious water to clean Ivan's wound. Fortunately, it was shallow.

After it was done, Ivan dove into one of the dugouts and came out quickly, his thinning lips like a gash in his pale face. When Ally poked her head inside, she could see the scattered bodies on the earthen floor. She could also see that, like their attackers, the tribe people were a mixture of human and animal features as if they had been caught in the middle of a transformation. Some of them had fully human bodies but adorned with a striped tail; some had delicate chipmunk paws clutching the hands of their tiny babies; for some, a muzzle was poking through the strands of their disheveled hair. But no matter how human or animal, they were all dead. And they did not die easily. Their throats were torn out; their flesh hung in tatters; blood soaked their meager possessions. When she saw a small, bushy-tailed child, his body opened like a can, guts spilling out, Ally ran out and threw up into the bushes.

Ivan's face was grim as he completed his circuit of the *sousliks'* settlements.

"The wolves came when the tribe was in their human form," he said. "Sousliks are no great warriors; they prefer to changeover and scatter into their underground lairs where wolves can never reach them. But the wolves had fouled the spring and the water lost its potency, so the sousliks were stuck in-between, unable to defend themselves, and the entire settlement was slaughtered. This has never happened before."

"But the wolves also looked in-between," Ally said. "Why?"

Ivan shrugged and went to examine wolf carcasses. He beckoned Ally and when she came over, he pointed to the open mouth of the wolf killed with an arrow.

The tongue was missing; there was only an inflamed stump inside.

"This is why they did not howl," he said. "Somebody cut out their tongues."

They decided to make camp in the clearing of the settlement. Ally was initially against it; the despoiled place filled with corpses was horrifying. But Ivan, always practical, pointed out that stumbling around in the dark where the wolves could easily attack was a foolhardy thing to do. The clearing was easy to defend and perhaps some sousliks who had survived the massacre would return to their homes and offer them hospitality.

They made a small fire in the middle of the clearing. Though Ivan had a fireboard, Ally volunteered to use her matchbox; rubbing a spindle in the notch of the board was labor and time-intensive and she was tired and cold to the bone. Only after they had a cheerful flame going did it occur to her that her supply of matches was limited.

No use brooding about it, she thought, and turned her attention to the bread Ivan was toasting over the fire. It was then she heard footsteps in the dark.

Ivan was up immediately, peering into the twitching shadows. Ally jumped up, nervously clutching her stick. The steps were light but it seemed that there were several pairs of feet.

Ivan hefted his stick just as a small figure barreled into the circle of light and launched itself at him.

"Talia!" Ally exclaimed as Ivan was hugging the distraught girl who clung to him, sobbing.

Margarita and Queenie stepped into the clearing.

"The wolves came," Queenie said in English.

Chapter 5:
Hansel and Gretel

The ravens crowed in the colorless sky, flapping their black wings above the ruins. The bombs had fallen through the nights but at the dawn, the planes had flown back, and the dust had settled on what once had been houses and gardens.

Margarita stood by the shelter. Its door was open and an earthy smell wafted from the dark interior. Her mother came out of the house, carrying an armful of broken china, which she dumped onto the ground. Once upon a time, their neatly painted house surrounded by the meticulously tended garden had been the envy of the neighborhood. It still was but for a different reason. Choked by rubbish, its windows crisscrossed by masking tape, it was still standing. Not many others were.

"Gretel!" her mother called. "What are you doing here?"

Margarita turned slowly to her, taking in every detail of that unloved face: defeated wrinkles, an anxiously pursed mouth, and shifty eyes. Her hand compulsively clutched her pocket where the official letter with the black letterhead rested. The eagle on the letterhead had seemed so reassuring when she had impatiently torn the grey wartime paper and before she had read the few lines. She had almost believed that it was an announcement that Hans was coming home.

A raven landed on the churned earth close to her and Margarita had a momentary vision of the eagle rising from her pocket and scattering the cackling birds of ill omen, together with all the rest of the enemies: traitors, spies, whiners, and complainers. Perhaps it would then float majestically into the sky and spread its wings over the neighborhood, protecting it from the death-dealing American planes.

"What's that?" her mother insisted. "Come on, girl, move! I need your help. I have to get our rations and with those crazy lines, we will never have bread and milk! Yesterday I spent three hours queuing and what did I get? A couple of rotten potatoes! "

"We *will* have enough food!" Gretel spat at her. "Stop grousing, Mother! If everybody talks like you, how shall we win the war?"

Mother muttered something under her breath and turned away. Margarita felt a righteous anger rise in her chest.

"What did you say?"

"I said, they drove you nuts in that *Bund Deutscher Mädel*," her mother yelled back, her stooped back suddenly straight and her faded eyes sparking. "What victory? Look around you, girl! Here, we're grubbing in the dirt like animals under American bombs! Your brother is in the army that has been retreating for a year! They should surrender now before it's too late!"

"Traitor!" Margarita hissed. "Shut up! Neighbors will hear!"

"How dare you talk to me like this?" her mother lashed back. "I have had enough of you! Your father, God rest his soul, bought that party garbage hook, line and sinker. I should have said something earlier, before they took my son and poisoned my daughter's mind! But I won't be silent anymore. The war is lost. This "thousand-year Reich" nonsense is over, and not a moment too soon. Now all we have to do is to survive the bombings and wait until Hans comes back home."

"Home?" Margarita sneered. "My brother is a hero of the people. He would be ashamed to hear his mother spout enemy propaganda! Maybe it's better that he . . . "

She stopped.

"That he what?" her mother insisted.

Silently, Margarita took the letter out of her pocket and handed it to her mother. The words "missing in action" flashed at her from the crumpled page crowned by the black eagle clutching a swastika shield in its talons.

"I wanted to protect you, but you don't deserve it. You don't deserve a son like Hans!"

Her mother's gnarled hands smoothed out the letter. She looked at it briefly and handed it back to Margarita who stared at her uncomprehendingly. She expected a flood of tears, a hysterical fit, and derived a bitter satisfaction from the pain of loss her mother would endure. But instead she saw . . . could it be a smile?

"More lies," her mother said placidly. "Throw it in the trash, Gretel."

"What? How dare you . . . ?"

Her mother grasped her hand and drew her close. Her onion-stinking breath touched Margarita's ear. "It's not true," she whispered. "Hans is alive. He has been taken prisoner by the British. They treat our soldiers well, not like the Russkies. He will wait out the war and come back home to us."

"How do you know?" Margarita wrenched herself free and took a step back. "How could you possibly know?"

Her mother did not answer but her eyes went back to the house. Through the open door, Margarita could see the ancient radio set in the kitchen.

"You did?" she gasped. "No! You listened?"

Her mother shrugged. :

"Yeah, I listened. To BBC. They read out lists of prisoners every night. They tell the truth about this war. And if your bigmouths in the League of German Maidens call it treason, screw them. I don't care."

She walked out of the yard, carrying her ration-book and a net-bag that would be too big for the pitiful loaf she would bring back. Margarita stared at her retreating black-clad back, feeling hatred well up in her throat. Witch!

More ravens landed in the ruined yard, pecking at the mounds of rubbish. Their beady eyes stabbed at Margarita as she collapsed on the ground, sobbing. But her tears soon dried out. Ramrod-straight, she marched out into the street. There was a public phone booth on the corner and miraculously, it had survived the bombing. Or maybe not so miraculously: the repair-crews knew that nothing was more important than keeping up morale. And they knew why an anonymous phone-line with the connection to the security service was crucial in maintaining it.

When Margarita came back from the brief conversation she had had, the ravens had left. She sat on the stoop, still clutching the army letter. It seemed ridiculous that she had hesitated giving it to the witch, afraid to upset her. As if she would care! People like her had no human feelings. Traitors! Enemy stooges! Listening to the enemy's lies while her son was battling them in the air! Well, never mind, she would get her comeuppance pretty soon!

The punishment for listening to enemy transmissions was death.

Margarita bit her lips until they bled. She did the right thing. The witch was no mother of hers. Hans would come back home, and they would live happily ever after, he and she together. She would tell him what she had done for the Fatherland, and he would be proud of her.

Wouldn't he?

A dark shadow slid over her. Margarita jumped to her feet. A plane? But there had been no siren! And the shadow advanced silently and unhurriedly, gliding over the yard with the majestic slowness of a rain cloud. She craned her head up and saw the black wings swallow up the sun. It was just like her momentary fantasy: an eagle the size of the world hovering above her, blotting out death from the sky, embracing her with its protective might.

The eagle dipped its head and she saw the mindless crimson eye and smelled the charnel stink of rotting flesh. Its beak gaped wide as it banked down, suffocating Margarita in the stench of death.

Chapter 6:

The Walker in the Marsh

They huddled together through the night. The girls finally fell asleep but Ally could not. She watched Ivan as he sat with his head down, his big hands folded between his knees, staring into the flames. She wanted to console him, but she did not know how. Nobody had consoled her when Mama had disappeared. She had just learned to hide her grief away from the prying eyes, to smile and say that everything was all right. Stoicism was her only defense, but it could not be shared with others.

Or maybe it could. Ivan was her brother, after all, and he seemed to react just as she would: with quiet dignity rather than unrestrained mourning. But his loss was even worse than hers had been. Losing your parent was expected in her country. Losing your entire community . . . well, such things had happened in her country's history as well, but she had hoped she had left it all behind when she came to California. Apparently, she had not.

Queenie told them that the entire deer tribe had been slaughtered. Perhaps she was mistaken. Perhaps some people had survived. But the wolves had been thorough this time. Well-organized, they stole into the camp in the middle of the night in their human guise, killing an unsuspecting guard. The other one alerted the settlement and, as had been agreed upon, instantly drank the deer change-water to turn himself into a powerful quadruped. So did the rest of the tribe, ready to rush out and trample the intruders with their stone-hard hooves.

Unfortunately, the intruders did the same.

The wolves had come with their own change-water, and as the tribe people metamorphosed into animals, so did they. A pack of hungry wolves against a disoriented deer herd. The deer did not stand a chance.

Some tried to shift back into humanity, but intelligence waned when the tribes of the Steppe were in their original animal forms; and by the time the deer-folk figured what to do, it was too late. The yurts were upended and torn, the clearing littered with animal, human, and half-human bodies, and the wolves . . . the wolves feasted. Some shifted back into a human shape, just so they could enjoy it more.

When Queenie had finished her recitation, Ally just sat there frozen, her hand clapped to her mouth to stem the tide of nausea rising in her guts. Had she done it? Was it her fault? She did not mean it to turn out like this, but she knew perfectly well how little good intentions mattered. She had offered advice. They had taken it. They were all dead. Whatever contortions she forced her conscience into, she could not escape this simple equation.

Talia and Margarita spoke little, sitting together, staring at the fire. Margarita made some remarks, which Ally, bereft of her necklace, did not understand, though she noted the girl spoke German. So, the fowls—she hated to think of them like this, but this was what they had been in Little Mother's farmyard—had been abducted from different places. And from different times, she surmised. There was something about Talia's graceful movements and Margarita's stern demeanor that spoke of the past—or rather, pasts. Queenie, on the other hand, appeared thoroughly modern. Her English—which Ivan, of course, heard as his mother tongue— sounded a lot like Malika's and had Ally not been so devastated by her tale, she would have asked her what country in Africa she was from.

Finally, the girls dozed off, worn by their precipitous flight through the Steppe. They had managed to escape thanks to Queenie's vigilance. The black girl had not trusted the deer, for whatever reason, and slept uneasily, listening to noises outside. She had awakened Talia and Margarita and the three of them slipped out of the yurt in the middle of the massacre. They had followed Ally and Ivan on the path that led to the sousliks' encampment, almost turning back when they saw wolf-tracks but pressing on because they had nowhere else to go.

And here they were: Ally's burden, Ally's responsibility. Another mistake to make, in addition to all those that seemed to buzz around her like a retinue of bloodsucking flies. Carl, the cow-girl, the deer-folk . . . and Mama. Had Ally been a better daughter, her mother would not have dissolved into the night, gone without a trace.

Ivan stirred and Ally looked at her handsome brother whose life she had stolen.

"We need to rest, sister," he said. "Tomorrow is a long day. Tomorrow we cross the first Dragon River."

"Are you still coming with me?" Ally blurted out.

Ivan shrugged and turned away from her, checking the contents of his pack and tightening the string on his bow.

"The Ogre has sent the wolves," he said.

The lay of the land was changing. the ground sloping down toward the horizon wreathed in humid fog. The sun floated above their heads as a dull, pewter disc behind the veil of yellow clouds. The ground squelched under their feet, soaked with stagnant water.

Ally could not see the path, but Ivan seemed to know where he was going, and she followed mutely, burdened by guilt heavier than her backpack.

The girls followed as well. What else could they do? Ally had given up puzzling over their fate. They were human. They were alive . . . so far. It was better than laying eggs in Little Mother's hellish farmyard or being raped and slaughtered by wolves. There was nothing she could do except take them wherever she was going. They seemed to understand this. Talia and Margarita plowed on Occasionally, Talia would wait for Queenie, who lagged behind, being the smallest and weakest of the three. Ally had already noted that Talia had taken on a quasi-maternal role with regard to the African girl, while Margarita kept her distance. Queenie seemed to be afraid of her. To be frank, Ally did not like Margarita either: there was something about the girl's pale, stony face that revolted her, and remembering her speak German, Ally thought she knew why. The histories of Germany and Ukraine were tied together into a blood-slicked knot that she had no desire to untangle.

Without the cross necklace, she could not talk to Talia. But Queenie spoke English. Ally dropped back and walked by the girl's side.

"Are you all right?" she asked.

Queenie nodded. Her skin was an unhealthy ashen color and she shivered in her thin shift, even though it was not cold.

"Do you remember how you came to be . . . here?" Ally asked, unsure how to approach the sensitive subject of Little Mother's coop.

"I . . . " the girl swallowed, her eyes sliding off Ally's face as if she could not bear to look at it. "I think . . . it's all wrong! I am not supposed to be . . . this!"

"Of course not," Ally hoped she sounded reassuring but in truth, she did not know how to talk to a small and undoubtedly severely traumatized child. She had had a very limited experience interacting with kids. "You are supposed to be at home with mom and dad. Do you remember where home is?"

"I wasn't at home!" Queenie cried with unexpected energy. "I . . . I'm not a child!"

Ally had read somewhere that traumatized kids grew up very quickly and often thought of themselves as adults. Still, Queenie was the youngest of the three girls, no older than seven. She was casting about for something child-friendly to say when Ivan, who was leading, stopped suddenly and lifted his hand, enjoining silence.

They stood in the middle of a marshland, dull green and bronze under the glowering sky. A tracery of inky runnels stitched together the mosaic of moss and horsetails. Swollen plants, their succulent leaves dappled with maroon, fringed the path. The silence was profound; not the slightest breeze ruffled the thick water of pools and ponds.

And then she heard it: a distant mournful howling.

Talia and Queenie held hands and even stoic Margarita edged closer to them. Ivan unshouldered his bow.

"They haven't been mutilated," Ally told him. "They still have their tongues. Maybe the Ogre hasn't gotten to them yet."

Ivan pointed toward the curtain of vapors that shivered over the thin fingers of water to the right.

"We need to go deeper into the marshland," he said. "Wolves don't like it here. There is something in the bog they are afraid of."

Ally nodded and followed suit as Ivan veered off the trail and jumped from hummock to hummock, balancing on the slick grass and trying not to land in the black mud in between. The mud smelled of rot, and the pond water was the color of rust and old blood. Ally tried not to imagine worms and maggots breeding in its stagnant depth. And were they really better off confronting something that wolves were afraid of?

Queenie slipped and landed with a splash in a pool. The water was shallow, only coming to her waist, but she cried out in distress. Talia helped her up but cried out when she saw a slimy black tube attached to Queenie's leg. Ally, who was not fond of leeches, was steeling herself to pull it off when Margarita reached out and with one efficient jerk dislodged the bloodsucking creature and threw it back into the marsh. Just as efficiently, she wiped a thin trickle of blood off Queenie's leg. Still, Ally noted that she never once looked in the other girl's eyes or smiled at her.

Ivan pointed to a small grove of stunted birches whose ghostly white trunks shone through the fog.

"We'll make camp there," he said. "The first Dragon River is just ahead. No more than an hour walk. But we should not go in the dark."

Ally was happy to comply. Her thigh muscles were on fire from leaping and balancing on the hillocky ground and the pewter sun had slid toward the horizon, mottling the sky with a feverish scatter of red clouds like the rash of a celestial smallpox.

The grove was spooky. Most of the birches were dead but their low-lying trunks were twisted and contorted. The ground was covered with black branches and gray, hair-like grass. But at least it was relatively dry.

They decided to risk a fire again. They were wet and cold, and if wolves wanted to hunt them down, they could do it by smell just as well as by vision. Of course, natural wolves were afraid of fire but not the wolves of Nightwood. This time, however, Ally let Ivan use his fireboard. She kept checking obsessively that the three magic objects stolen from Little Mother's house were still safe in her pocket. The matchbox, the comb, and the handkerchief were their best chances for survival. It was very fortunate that Ally had not had the time to ransack the house, looking for more magic. Three was the number of success; anything more or less could be useless or harmful. That was how Nightwood worked.

Their backpacks were still full but now, with the three girls added to their party, they had to be careful. Ally toasted some bread and made tea with boiled pond water. She was reluctant to do it, despite Ivan's assurances that once boiled, the water was safe. It still smelled sick. But they could not use up their own precious supply.

As they huddled around a tiny fire that Ivan fed with twigs and dry leaves, a sound broke the marsh's uneasy silence. A series of squelching, sucking noises as if something big and shapeless blundered in the mud. Ally had a sudden sickening vision of the leech pulled off Queenie, swollen to human size and grown human legs, trying to make its way back to its underwater lair. Then there was a rustling as if of enormous wings, a shrill hoot, and silence again. A wind rose. It smelled of the putrid deposits on the sides of a latrine.

Chapter 7:
The First Dragon River

Next morning found them emerging from the grove like timid animals from a hideout. They were stiff, cold, and sore. Ally's joints ached as if she were twice her age; the girls drooped; and even Ivan looked somehow faded. But they were alive, and nothing had molested them in the night.

On the edge of the grove, the land dipped again and Ally thought at first she was looking at the continuation of the marsh, only more watery, the land diluted and dissolving. And then she realized she was actually looking at a river.

The first Dragon River was a broad ribbon of algae-covered shallow water, sluggishly crawling between the slimy banks. Indeed, the banks were so boggy and so piled up with refuse and rot that it was hard to discern where they ended and the river began. A sharp stench wafted from the coffee-colored surface dotted with tufts of brown cattails and swamp grass.

Ally turned away in disgust, and the girls, huddling behind her, made soft noises of distress like a trio of doves. Ivan found a path leading down to the river and started on it. They followed.

Closer still, the stench was almost unendurable. The green rotting water was studded with shapeless bulks. Ally could not tell whether these were animal corpses or clumps of dead vegetation. The entire place exuded a palpable aura of sickness. The few trees sticking out from the marsh were grey leafless skeletons. Rafts of dead insects floated in dank puddles. A puffed-up beaver corpse lay across the path.

"Do we have to go here?" Ally asked.

Ivan nodded. Lifting the hem of his shirt, he wrapped it around his nose and mouth and bid Ally and the girls to do the same. They complied; but Ally noticed that Talia had gone greenish-pale and swayed as if she were about to faint.

They walked in a single file, following Ivan along the edge of the river, or rather along the uncertain boundary between more and less firm soil. A couple of times, Ally's foot went through the sodden mat of vegetation, releasing puffs of sulfurous gas. Fortunately, her moccasins were waterproof; she remembered, with a lurch in her stomach, that they were made of the hides of her brother's tribe mates. A gift of the dead.

The walk seemed to go on forever, as if time itself had fallen into a sluggish fever. Fog slithered across the marshland. Yellow clouds veiled the sky and a fine rain started falling. Instead of refreshing the air, it emphasized every variety of stench.

"Here is the bridge!" Ivan said suddenly, bringing Ally out of her miserable stupor.

The bridge was just a couple of planks thrown across the river which, at this point, narrowed down to little more than a creek and was so shallow that the shaggy growth of weeds on the bottom cleared the surface. The planks were slippery with algae and black with moss.

"That's it?" Ally was incredulous. "And if we cross, how are we better off?"

Indeed, the opposite bank was no different from the one they stood upon. In fact, it was exactly like the one they stood upon.

Ally looked to her left where a scabrous willow trunk poked out of the mud. Across the river, a scabrous willow trunk loomed in the yellow vapors. Was it some weird atmospheric phenomenon, projecting their reflections upon the screen of the fog? But no, she could not see any human figures on the other side.

Ivan gingerly stepped onto the bridge and Ally moved to join him.

There was a deafening noise of cackling and flapping in the air, and a wave of reek so overpowering that it burned Ally's sinuses and blinded her with tears. She squinted as a ragged silhouette suddenly loomed on the bridge, swathed with dirty bandages of fog. She could not understand what she was seeing. A bird the size of a man? A man so crippled he looked like a bird?

Ivan backpedaled, barely able to keep himself from falling off the slimy planks into the polluted water. Behind Ally, one of the girls cried out.

Ally caught Ivan's arm and dragged him off the bridge as its guardian advanced upon them.

It was visibly growing, swelling like a boil, and towering into the sky. Its beaked head dipped threateningly toward them. It was dressed in black rags, stiff with old blood and pus. Its flat head was crowned with a crest of mangy feathers. Round eyes, sunken into the bony skull-face, gleamed with the glassy sheen of spectacles. Its fleshless, taloned hands groped toward Ivan and Ally. Its arms were rudimentary wings but most of the feathers had fallen out, leaving behind suppurating lesions. Somehow, Ally knew that the real danger came from these lesions rather than from the sharp, wicked-looking talons.

Ivan fumbled for his antler-tipped spear, while Ally reached for her matchbox. Her hands shook and one precious match rolled out of the box and disappeared into the liquid mud. The creature cackled. The interior of its beak was scarlet-red, puffy and dripping.

Somebody rushed past Ally, pushed her aside, and almost sent her sprawling into the bog. Ivan caught and steadied her. She saw that a girl stood on the bridge between her and the birdlike abomination.

Talia!

"Il Medico della Peste!" the Italian girl said. She was speaking in her native tongue but Ally, clinging to her brother, shared the magic of the cross necklace and understood her perfectly. "Signore Doctor! I repent me of my bargain. I repent me of my cruelty toward my sister's children. Give Sun and Moon back to me, and I shall willingly go to *Lazaretto Vecchio,* the Isle of the Dead. And let these people pass. I offer myself to you in their stead."

The creature gaped at her, growing bigger and bigger, swelling until its diseased darkness seemed to swallow up the dregs of the grey daylight.

Sun, Moon, and Talia! The most famous of Italian fairy tales!

No happy ending, though. Not when she ended up in Little Mother's farmyard. And not for Sun and Moon, clearly.

Il Medico della Peste. The Doctor of the Black Death.

All fairy tales were history once.

Ally shook off her unruly thoughts, tensing for action, grappling again for her box, her hands clumsy, fettered by the fear of losing more of her irreplaceable matches.

The bloated monstrosity shook like a water-skin, diffusing waves of stink, then popped, showering them with a rain of liquid rot. Ally gagged, falling to her knees, her stomach in knots.

The creature was dissolving into cancerous flesh and curdled blood, slopping off the bridge. But something was left behind after its fall, like a smear of darkness on the fading daylight, like a doorway hung with whipping curtains of black gauze.

Through the tears running down her face, Ally saw two small figures emerge out of the pile of filth left on the bridge and totter toward Talia. Two toddlers, a boy and a girl, their small faces set in infant frowns.

Talia reached out to them, and they took her hands and led her toward a black hole in the world left behind by the fall of *Il Medico*. Guiding—dragging?—her they stepped through and were gone.

The heavy clouds above the bridge suddenly parted and through the shining rent, Ally saw the brassy disk of the setting sun and the pale new moon in the clear sky.

Chapter 8:
The Second Dragon River

The forest closed around them like a prison's walls. Thick trees plunged the ground into perpetual gloom.

After crossing the first Dragon River, they had abruptly found themselves in a very different terrain. Having tiptoed across the slimy planks of the bridge, they stepped not into the viscous marsh as expected but onto a dry, shrub-overgrown bank that rose steeply toward a line of trees. And so here they were, in this ominously dark forest.

Ally, Ivan, Margarita, and Queenie followed an almost invisible path through the woods. Ivan said it had been made by animals, but he was not sure what kind. Not deer, at any rate. They found no droppings and no hoof-prints.

The forest was very different from the redwoods. With a sudden spasm of nostalgia, Ally remembered her first incredulous sight of California's giants. How lost she had felt; how much a stranger in a strange land! And yet, now the memory of that sunlit greenery, with feathery tops nodding high in the crystal sky, felt like a call from home.

But of course, *this* was home, not California. Having spent her entire adult life in a big city, Ally had a rather vague image of the European countryside but nevertheless, she realized that these dense broadleaf trees, so low compared to the towering redwoods, were what her ancestors had immortalized in mournful ballads and magic tales. Larch, birch, rowan . . . she could tell a story for each of them. But they felt alien and hostile, like a crowd of malevolent dwarves, whispering behind her back.

The path ahead was blocked by a thicket of bushes with luxuriant dark-green foliage, their branches laden with clusters of brown pods.

"Hazelnuts!" Ivan exclaimed, stretching his long arm toward a particularly generous cluster. Ally licked her lips. Her previous acquaintance with hazelnuts had been in a chocolate box, but she was hungry and tired of the bland diet of thin soups and dried vegetables.

"Nein!" Margarita yelled, running forward and striking Ivan's arm, deflecting it from the bush that trembled and rustled its leaves, though there was no wind in the close woods. Ivan looked at her with perplexity. Margarita cautiously pulled off one nut in its fibrous casing, picked up a rock, and smashed the tough shell. Inside was a white kernel but as Ally watched, it stirred and crawled out of the shell, unfolding its plump pale body as it did so. A large worm slithered through the undergrowth and was gone.

They squeezed through the hazelnut thicket that suddenly came alive. The bushes flailed their many-fingered limbs in the still air, whipping and scratching them. A gnarled, fissured trunk strained to pull itself out of the ground as they passed, its roots popping out. The nuts showered the ground but fortunately, only few cracked open, releasing their verminous tenants. Margarita stamped on them with a cold, dispassionate efficiency. Queenie cried and cowered away from the worms until Ivan picked her up and carried her through the bushes.

Beyond, the ground rose in a gorse-covered wave toward a ledge furred with evergreens. The sun was already below the horizon, and they stumbled through the treacherous twilight toward the higher ground, risking pitfalls and hidden rocks. Ally was about to suggest they camp out here when Margarita said something that only Ivan understood. He scrambled toward the girl who was pointing at the indistinct pool of shadows at her feet. Ally joined them.

The ground was broken by a deep ditch. Ally realized that this was the first ordinary manmade feature she had seen in Nightwood. Unlike Little Mother's witchy farm or the Steppe tribes' encampments, there was nothing magical about this pit. It could have been dug by a repairs crew in the world she had left behind. But what lay at the bottom of the pit was not pipes or cables. The gleam of exposed bone, the smear of desiccated skin, the ragged edge of rotten clothing . . . There were bodies at the bottom of the ditch: old bodies, hardly more than skeletons, which explained why the fetor of rot mingling with the green aroma of the forest was so faint. But once she smelled it, it was inescapable.

The pit looked like a mass grave: an unfinished one, as if whoever had tried to bury the bodies had just lost interest or gone away.

Or perhaps had joined the others in the ditch.

Ally and Ivan exchanged glances; he shrugged. They went on.

On top of the rise was a grove of black pine trees, their arcing branches dipping low to the ground, their scaly trunks covered with splotches of lichen. It was so dark in the grove that the decision to pitch a camp on the edge was taken spontaneously, even though Ally would prefer to be further away from the grave.

She cleared away the fallen needles the best she could. They were as gray and brittle as an old man's hair and gave off the smell of dust. Ivan made a small fire with his fireboard and boiled some herbal tea. Their supply of ordinary water was running low again, even though they had replenished it by the first Dragon River.

Margarita, wrapped up in her blanket, fell asleep—or at least, she lay on the other side of the fire with her eyes closed. Ally was relieved that she did not have to talk to her. Her spirits were low and if her intuitions about the German girl's provenance were correct, she did not want to revisit her grim story.

All fairy tales were history once.

Ivan was subdued and silent; still mourning the extermination of his tribe, Ally surmised. What could she tell him that would make it better? She had taken his place in the other world, and here in Nightwood, she had only brought devastation to his people.

Queenie huddled in the shadow of the pines, and Ally forced herself to get up and go over to the girl. She liked her but felt at a loss talking to her. She could not figure out her background. African folklore was not her strongest point; in her studies she had paid more attention to Eurasia.

Ally touched Queenie's hand and the girl lifted her head. Her face was drawn; eyes red as if she had been crying.

"Don't be sad," Ally said awkwardly. "We'll find our way. We'll get you home."

"I'm not sad," Queenie said tonelessly. "I'm frightened."

You and me both, Ally thought but did not say. She was an adult talking to a child, she reminded herself. She had to project strength.

"Frightened of what?"

"*Asanbosam.*"

Now they were getting somewhere! The *asanbosam* was a creature from West African folklore; Ally could not quite remember what it did except that it was something unpleasant.

"It's not here," she said with more certainty than she felt. "See, we are in a different forest. Trees of the North. *Asanbosam* does not live here."

Even as she was saying it, she realized it was wrong: Nightwood was the source of human storytelling; and wasn't it the case that all fairy tales had the same origin? North or south, monsters of the dark lurked in the forest of the human mind, which had its r own geography.

Queenie shook her head.

"It's following me," she whispered. "It wants me."

"Why?"

"To marry me."

Ally recoiled. That was the one thing that filled her with complete and utter disgust; that even in her former life she had found beyond the pale. No man who liked underage girls had ever been allowed to come near her. Mama would have clawed their eyes out.

"You are a child!" she exclaimed. "Nobody can marry you!"

"They do," the girl said sadly. "They steal girls and marry them. Or turn them into slaves. Or both."

Ally knew about the stolen Nigerian girls. Apparently, so did Queenie. Did it mean they were contemporaries?

"I won't let them," she said, patting Queenie's small hand. "I won't let the *asanbosam* get you."

The girl looked away.

"So I thought," she said. "I thought you'd protect me. But you did not."

The guilt that had been hanging over Ally's head the whole day came crashing down. Queenie was right. She had not protected the girls in Little Mother's farmyard. Worse, she had helped the ghoul exploit their mutilated bodies! How was she better than a collaborator? A failure at best; a traitor at worst!

You are an officer's daughter.

The familiar refrain sounded like a hollow mockery in her head.

Nightwood

With nothing to say, no way to defend herself, she mutely put another blanket around Queenie's thin shoulders and went back to her own place, staring into the fire, listening to the noises of the forest throughout that interminable night. At some point, she dozed off but was awakened by a hoarse cawing, as if of a giant raven, deep among the pines.

Next morning dawned bloodless and grey. The clouds were not the humid vapors of the first Dragon River but rather a high cumulus of the northern skies, neither threatening rain nor promising sunshine, and it was perceptively colder than yesterday. Ally shivered in her thin smock and counted the matches in the magic matchbox. She was shocked to realize that only three were left.

"Do you know where the second River is?" she asked Ivan.

He nodded.

"I've never been here but I talked to people from the wolverine tribe who came to trade with us. They said it was beyond the Black Pines."

"Do wolverine people live here?" Ally asked. Wolverines were hardly her favorite animals, but their company would be preferable to the chilly emptiness of the pine grove.

"They used to. I don't see any sign of them. The wolves must have been through."

Ally shuddered and listened for a distant howling, but the only sound was the mournful soughing of wind in the pines.

They slugged on, and the further they went, the more depressed Ally felt. It was as if the chilliness of this dark forest insinuated itself into her bloodstream, squeezing her heart in the slavish penury of fear. Hope was gone, and so was defiance. In the perpetual dusk of the pine grove, her companions looked as insubstantial as a group of fading ghosts.

No! She looked to her brother, seeking support from his strength. She was not alone here, she reminded herself. She had a family. She would find Carl, and the love that had always eluded her would finally bloom, making their marriage real. Ivan would have a loving sister and brother-in-law to make up for what he had lost.

And they lived happily ever after.

Yes, she muttered to herself. *Yes, fairy tales do come true.*

I made it to California, didn't I?

Lost in her thoughts, Ally failed to notice that the serrated ranks of pines were thinning out, colorless light diluting the gloom. Plump cushions of emerald moss dotted the ground.

Margarita, who had been walking steadily behind Ally, increased her speed until she was running ahead of them. Ivan yelled at her to stop, but she rounded a sprawling pine and disappeared from view. Ally took off after her.

Ally's running spooked a couple of blackbirds that rose from a dead, mistletoe-infested tree. This was the first sign of life in the pines, but Ally could do without it. Birds of any kind seemed to be bad news.

She broke through the tree line to find Margarita standing on a grassy verge. Ally braked just in time. Her sprint could have easily sent her over the lip of the gorge. She peered down where the steely ribbon of a river wound through the narrow valley. A massive stone bridge spanned the river, guarded on both sides by squat watchtowers. On the other side, a small castle huddled in the shadow of the gorge's wall. It appeared to be ruined.

"Are we going there?" Ally asked, forgetting that without the necklace Margarita would not understand her. "Is this the witch's house?"

Margarita shook her head and started down toward the river, the rest of them following her lead as if unconsciously recognizing her mastery of the terrain. The gorge was badly eroded which made their descent relatively easy. It was an old land.

The banks of the river were encased in stone: blocks of granite as grey as the sky above their heads where a whole flock of birds wheeled and dipped, strangely silent, as if awaiting a signal. Blackbirds, ravens, crows . . . black letters spelling some untranslatable doom.

Margarita climbed the short stairs leading to the bridge. Ally saw that the deck and the parapets were pitted with round indentations. She touched one, her fingers lingering on the roughed surface, refusing to believe what they were.

She grasped Ivan's hand, pointed to the necklace, which he quickly removed and gave her. Putting it on, she hurried after the girl.

"Margarita!" she cried. "Gretel! Be careful! The witch is waiting for you!"

The girl turned her hatchet-like face to her.

"The witch is here," she said in German, which was as comprehensible to Ally as it was hostile. "I am the witch."

A figure emerged from the ruined castle on the other shore. Only it was not a castle. The fairy-tale blinkers misled her into seeing the safe medieval past instead of what was really there.

A bunker.

The figure walked with slow halting steps toward them. When it crossed half of the bridge, Ally could see that it was a stocky woman in shapeless, washed-out clothes. Her lined face drooped with fatigue; her hair stuck out in the artificial curls Ally had only seen in old wartime movies.

"Gretel!" the woman said gently. "Sweetie!"

The girl stood as still as a wooden figure. Finally, she spoke.

"Mother," she said. "Where is Hans? Where is my brother?"

"Your brother is dead," the woman said.

A wail broke from Margarita's lips, and she fell to her knees, rocking back and forth in a paroxysm of grief. Ally stepped forward and addressed the woman:

"How did she betray you?" she asked.

The woman smiled sadly.

"IIow do you know shc did?"

"Because of the time you come from. The time of betrayal. All fairy tales were history once; and yours is the history I know. These are bullet holes, aren't they? Not a cavalry of knights but Panzer tanks and heavy artillery. Your soldiers killed my great-grandfather. Whatever she did to you, you deserve it!"

"She is my daughter," the woman said. "They brainwashed her, filled her head with lies. But she meant well."

Margarita lifted her head, her face distorted with rage. The cloud of black birds dipped lower, forming a funnel above her head. She spread her arms wide.

The birds alighted on her shoulders, arms, and head; clung to her clothes; sunk their talons into her hair. She tottered on the bridge: a human-shaped murder of ravens.

Ally reached for her matchbox. This witch was not to be bought by gold or frozen by ice. This witch had to burn.

The woman stepped forward and embraced the seething maelstrom of black feathers. The birds roiled and cawed, rising up in a cloud of wings and beaks and settling again over the two indistinct lumps of humanity. A scream was lost in their squawking.

A spray of red erupted from the melee, splattering the stones. Ally rushed forward, swinging her stick. One crow cocked a malevolent orange eye at her and flapped its raggedy wings. Ally's blow brought it down.

As if receiving a signal, the birds rose off in a black flock, peppering the three remaining humans with feathers and dung. They spiraled into the clouds and were gone. Ally lifted something from the mess: a torn piece of paper with spiky gothic letters and an eagle-crowned logo.

The cross necklace would translate it for her, but she did not want to read it. The history these letters spelled was too recent, too painful. In her homeland, that war had never ended.

She gave the necklace back to Ivan and silently, they crossed the second Dragon River.

Chapter 9:
The Third Dragon River

This was not what Ally had expected.

When they stepped on the opposite bank of the grey river, whose swiftly running water smelled of cold and gun-smoke, she had unconsciously prepared herself for another kind of forest: perhaps a tropical jungle or something closer to the redwoods. She had spent so much time recently in various natural environments, from the blankness of the Steppe to the closeness of the Black Pines, that her urban self had gone to sleep; memories of asphalt pavements and crowds of shoppers surfacing only in dreams. But it was apparently the time for the city girl to awaken.

The city sprawled around them, empty and hushed. A shantytown, a slum. There were taller buildings in the distance, looming above the maze of crooked huts, peeling walls, bristling roofs, and dirty curtains, the urban glitz hidden under the detritus of poverty. Garbage choked the gutters. Broken windows squinted from under sagging eaves. Jerry-built constructions grew upon each other, jostling for space like mushrooms on a log. Perhaps this *was* a jungle of sorts, after all.

Looking around, Ally realized two things. First, this was no medieval township or even a World War II besieged city. The shantytown was modern: she could barely see the humid sky through a cat's cradle of crisscrossing and interweaving cables. Second, the inhabitants were not simply having breakfast indoors. The place was deserted. The silence was so thick you could cut it with a knife.

Ivan sidled close to her, his mouth hanging open, his eyes round. Of course, for a deer this was as alien an environment as the surface of Mars. Ally patted his hand reassuringly, but she was far from being at ease. She knew all too well that city predators could give wild beasts a run for their money.

She looked at Queenie. The girl stood still with a strange expression on her face: half-incredulity, half-fear.

"Do you know where we are?" she asked her.

Queenie shook her head.

"I have never been here before," she mumbled. "But I know there is a river in the city."

Ally cast about for a way to go but she could see no obvious direction in this urban chaos. There were no streets to speak of, just a labyrinth of trashy alleyways. But her brother relied on her! Just as he had been their guide in the natural environment of Nightwood, it was clear that now this role devolved upon her. She did not want it but could not escape the responsibility.

You are an officer's daughter!

"This way," she said, pointing to one alley that was marginally wider than the rest and seemed to slope ever so slightly downwards. Perhaps it was leading to the river.

After a hundred yards or so it became clear that this was no way to go. The alley took a sharp turn to the left, skirting a steaming garbage pile crawling with fat black flies. Disturbed by their approach, the flies rose up in a buzzing cloud. Ally, covering her face, rushed forward but had to stop when the alley doglegged around a pockmarked wall and petered out in a tangle of rusting wires hung incongruously with brightly colored clothes.

Queenie picked up an elaborately folded headscarf patterned in red and blue. Ally hissed to put it back: she did not want to raise her voice for fear of attracting unwanted attention, but touching anything in this place seemed dangerous. Instead, Queenie put it on.

Ally gasped.

Queenie was growing.

Growing like a stop-motion recording of a child's maturation into a woman. But there was nothing smooth about the process. It was clear how painful it was; how every growth spurt forcibly pulled the muscles and wrenched the bones; how cruelly it reshaped the flesh as if it were a lump of Play-Doh. Ally almost expected to see indentations left by invisible fingers on the girl's kneaded skin.

Tainted by the bird-shape she had been forced to endure, Queenie was becoming human again and paying the price in pain.

But did it mean that her little-girl form was not her real self either?

The question was answered for her when she saw what Queenie had become.

Where a child had been now stood a tall, grown-up woman looking around in confusion, her athletic body barely covered by the tatters of a ripped smock.

"Malika!" Ally cried.

She rushed to embrace her friend. Malika passively submitted to a hug, but she seemed to be in shock, barely aware of her surroundings. Questions tumbled off Ally's tongue and remained unanswered.

And then Ivan yelled: "Look out!"

Ally whirled around and saw that the alley was no longer empty. Several men emerged from behind a ruined warehouse. Ally knew they were in trouble.

There was nothing exotic about the men. They were perfectly familiar. And this was precisely why she would rather face the Red-White-Black horseman of Little Mother, the flaming fence-sitters, or the avian Doctor of the Plague. Hell, she would rather face the Ogre's wolves! No monster could be as dangerous as these dead-eyed men in faded camouflage, toting assault rifles. Whatever you called them—guerrillas, terrorists, freedom fighters—they were killers.

"Run!" she shouted to Ivan. He took off with an easy animal grace, picking his way unerringly through mounds of rubbish and across the cracked pavement. He rounded a corner and disappeared from sight. Ally also sprinted back the way they came. But Malika stood paralyzed, trembling, as the men advanced with mocking smiles on their scarred faces. One of them said something in a language Ally did not understand and the rest laughed.

Ally grasped Malika's hand and dragged her forward. One of the men lifted his gun and loosed a volley of shots that rained wooden chips and slivers of glass. He had deliberately aimed above their heads, but the meaning was clear.

Malika dropped into a crouch, her hand sliding bonelessly out of Ally's, who also stopped, facing their attackers, one of whom yelled "*Zeru!*" and pointed at Ally's hair.

She fumbled in her pocket, drew out Little Mother's linen handkerchief and threw it on the ground in front of the gunmen.

The ice crust spread quickly over the pavement like skim on milk, plugging potholes and hiding a scatter of garbage under its slick surface. It ran up the gunmen's boots, covering them in elaborate rime patterns and freezing them in place. The men cried out in shock and surprise as the ice squeezed their feet and crawled up their legs, encasing their torsos in a shining armor.

But the air was thick with heat and moisture and Little Mother's ice-magic—who knows where it had come from, what Arctic region of the storied universe she had looted to get it?—could not compete with the laws of physics. No sooner did the ice crust form than it started melting, dripping down the men's bodies in rivulets of spring water. Their shock was wearing off as they struggled in their ice fetters, cursing and smashing them with the butts of their rifles. One of them, his arms freed, lifted his rifle and pulled the trigger.

Ally and Malika ran away, dodging bullets. They ducked into another dim alley that echoed with gunfire as the men shot blindly through flimsy walls and broken windows.

Ally tried to put as much distance between them as possible but she practically had to drag Malika, who moved with maddening slowness as if wading through molasses. Ally screamed at her, trying to get her to snap out of whatever PTSD held her in its grip, but it did not help. Her own mind was brimming with questions.

How and why had Malika been hiding in the body of a little girl? Or was it her own little-girl's body? Had Malika been caught in some sort of time-loop like a rabbit in a snare? Had the Queenie who followed Ally out of Little Mother's farmyard known who she was? Belatedly, Ally remembered the meaning of Malika's name: queen.

They ran blindly through more of those maddening mazes that defied the ordinary distinction between indoors and outdoors: winding back alleys; covered arcades, their walls bearing a thick crop of graffiti; mean courtyards piled up with splintered furniture and bald tires. If there were actual streets here, Ally saw no sign of them.

The noise of gunfire faded but this was the only positive aspect of their situation. Ally had no idea where the river was. And more worryingly, she also had no idea where Ivan had disappeared to.

Had her brother been captured by the gunmen? He would stand no chance against them! Would she now have to live with his death on her conscience? After Mama, after Carl . . . how many more?

The guilt threatened to overwhelm her, and she tamped it down, focusing on the here and now: the sun beating down on her head; the pain in her bruised ankle—and the silence.

Ally slowed down and let go of Malika's hand. They were in a medium-sized courtyard surrounded by blind walls whose pink stucco was dappled with water stains. The only open entrance was the one they had rushed through: an arched entryway leading back to the alley. But there was also a door in front of them. It appeared to be locked.

Ally peeked into the alley. It was deserted. They had somehow shaken the gunmen off—or perhaps the ice magic had deterred them, after all. That was good news. The bad news was that one of the three magic objects she had pilfered from Little Mother was lost to her.

Nothing to be done about it! Ally turned her attention to Malika who was huddling by the wall, her head in her hands. She looked like the wreck of the proud, confident woman Ally had known in Berkeley. Kneeling by her side, Ally lifted her chin. Malika's eyes were dull and unfocused.

"Hey!" Ally whispered with false cheerfulness. "A Greens dinner on me when we get back!"

The name of her favorite San Francisco restaurant failed to move Malika, who showed no sign of having heard what Ally said.

"We need to go, sister!" Ally insisted. "We can't stay here."

Malika muttered something. Ally leaned closer.

"What did you say?"

"Not dreams . . . " Malika repeated. "Memories."

"You remembered that I saved you? So, you remembered the future?"

"Not the future," Malika whispered. "A future."

What did it mean? Ally had figured out that Malika was caught in a time-loop. But when they had last seen each other in California, neither of them knew about Nightwood. So sometime after Ally had been snared by the feathered dress, Malika must have been pulled into the story world. But why? What had she done to be punished even more severely than Talia and Margarita, forced back into her childhood body and mutilated into a monstrous fowl?

And "a future"? A possibility, then; not certainty. But how could one remember not only what had not happened but what may have happened?

These speculations gave her a headache that, coupled with thirst, fatigue and the burning residue of adrenaline high, made her faint. She pulled out her water flask, drank some and forced Malika to do the same.

They had to escape the shantytown. They had to find Ivan. They had to go to the third Dragon River and confront whatever dragon lay in wait for them. Like soldiers, they had to do what needed to be done. Like her officer father. He would be proud of his daughter if he could see her now!

"Come on!" Ally tried to pull Malika up, staggering like an ant trying to pick up a beetle. The effort had a psychological effect if not a physical one: Malika climbed to her feet under her own steam and followed Ally back to the archway.

And then the locked door into the courtyard was flung open and a woman stepped out.

A woman! Ally was momentarily relieved. Until she saw what the newcomer was.

The woman was swaddled from head to toe in a thick black *abaya*: an outer garb that was supposed to leave only the eyes uncovered. But there were no eyes. The opening showed unrelieved darkness, as if an empty garment lurched and staggered toward them. And then another and another. A host of walking cloaks billowing with protrusions that could belong to no human body spilled into the courtyard from the house.

Behind her, Malika whimpered.

Ally turned around to flee but the archway was clogged with more flapping black figures like a murder of scrawny ravens or an army of scarecrows. Not a glimpse of human flesh showed anywhere. Only a void stared from beyond the mesh of eye-openings. The unclean fabric rippled and folded as if trying to give shape to what was shapeless—but alive and seething with malevolent energy.

The wraiths' *abayas* were worn, dusty and much mended. They looked as poor as everything else in the shantytown.

Ally pulled the comb out of her pocket.

"Ladies," she said in an unsteady voice, wondering whether they would even understand her. "Lovely as you are, think of the golden necklaces and bejeweled earrings that could enhance your beauty. Think of all the wonderful things you could buy for yourself in exchange for what I am offering you. I will give you all the gold you want if you let us pass."

And she ran the comb through her loosened hair.

Hunks of golden filigree fell, clinking, onto the pavement. Ally lifted one and tentatively proffered it to the nearest black figure. The *abaya* waved toward her. An invisible hand snatched greedily and the gold disappeared into the darkness inside. The edge of the garment brushed her arm, and a painful jolt traveled up to her shoulder as if she had touched a live wire. Her hand went numb. Ally dropped the comb.

The cloaks rushed toward them, scrambling for the gold on the ground. They pushed and shoved like birds fighting for crumbs but in total silence, broken only by the swishing of the fabric and the whisper of hot wind. Another wraith touched Ally. An electric shock convulsed her entire left side and she staggered back from the melee and bumped into Malika who was edging toward the exit.

Ally looked at the heaving mound of empty garments, bristling with invisible discharges. It would be suicide to dive into it, trying to retrieve her comb.

She took Malika's hand and they tiptoed back into the alley.

The sun was dipping toward the horizon and blinding with its dazzle. Thick shadows massed on the ground. But the sunset brought a rising of the wind that roamed through the stagnant labyrinth of the shantytown. And the wind carried a faint but unmistakable smell of water. Malika suddenly perked up.

"The river!" Malika took off and Ally followed.

The meandering passage broadened into an almost-thoroughfare—the jumble of houses on both sides fell back—and ahead of them an oily expanse of water glistened in the feverish glow of the sunset. They shot out onto the cobble-paved embankment and down below, leisurely licking the shingled beach, was the third Dragon River. And the bridge: surprisingly modern and intact: a wide concrete ribbon with a sidewalk and car lanes, though empty of both cars and pedestrians.

Malika made straight for the bridge. Ally hung back.

"Come on, girl!" Malika's foot was poised above the steps leading up to the bridge. She had shaken off her lethargy: her face shone with purpose, and she stood proud and erect, just as she used to do in Berkeley.

Ally shook her head.

"Ivan," she said. "My brother. I can't leave him here!"

"We can come back!" Malika insisted. "We'll find help. But we have to go now! The *asanbosam* is after us. He can't cross running water."

Ally hesitated. The shantytown filled her with greater horror than the grave-dotted forest or the polluted bog. Something in this modern city that called to the detritus of pain and humiliation she had buried deep in her memory; and now the ghosts of her rejected past stirred and rose from their graves. It would be so easy to follow Malika across the river. Wherever they found themselves after that, it could not be as bad as this.

And then she thought of Mama. And how she could be watching from . . . wherever she was. Seeing her daughter betray her son.

"No," she said. "I can't. But you go, Malika. Please. This is what is meant to be. What you saw in your dreams . . . You'll go and be safe. Be back in California. This is not your story. It's wrong for you to be here."

"No!" a male voice said behind her back. "It is not *your* story. You just blunder in where you are not wanted. Your people always do. Destroying our culture, defying our traditions. Coming between husband and wife!"

Ally slowly turned around but not before she saw Malika tremble and almost collapse.

The man stood behind her, loose-limbed, smartly dressed and confident. There was nothing strange or frightening about him. Against the background of the ruined city, he exuded the comfort of civilization. His bespoke suit and shiny Italian shoes put to shame the detritus of poverty and war around him.

Ally knew his kind: oligarchs and sharp dealers; men who bought and sold hopes of millions; who broke lives as easily and elegantly as wineglasses. She used to hate them with the silent fury born of impotence. But her sojourn in the Silicon Valley had given her a new perspective on the one percent. Having been one of them, albeit provisionally, she knew that they were no more than people.

"She is not your wife!" she said contemptuously. "What do you think, you can buy her like you buy your whores? Malika is not for sale. Leave us alone! There are empty dresses for you to play with!"

The man laughed and now she saw, with a shudder of revulsion, that he was not quite as ordinary as he had appeared. His curving mouth grew and grew until it looked like a gash in his face; blindingly white teeth multiplying like the teeth of a shark.

"Look who is talking of whores!" he exclaimed mockingly. "You have the guts, *shlucha*! Her parents have given her to me. She is mine, to do with as I please!"

"*Asanbosam!*" Malika wailed.

"Go!" Ally yelled at her. "Cross the bridge! I'll keep him off!"

And she lit up a match.

A bright golden flame ran up her arm, clothing it in a fiery gauntlet. She lifted it up and stepped in front of the *asanbosam*, who flinched away. Buoyed by her power, Ally managed to put out of her mind that only two more matches rattled loosely in the box.

And yet Malika hesitated, as if hypnotized by the *asanbosam's* stare. She even moved imperceptibly closer, coming away from the bridge steps.

"Go!" Ally bellowed, waving her flaming arm.

There was movement behind them on the bridge and Ally saw, her heart sinking, that the *asanbosam's* shark-like smile grew even wider, the corners of his mouth curving behind his ears.

She looked back.

A group of small figures walked toward them.

Children!

But even in the dimming light of the sunset, she could see these were not ordinary children. Boys, aged from eight to twelve, wearing fatigues and carrying machine guns. Their eyes were empty and flat. Their hands dripped with red paint.

Except it was not paint.

She threatened them with her flame and they paused, but then began advancing again.

"I'll burn you!" she screamed. "Back off!"

Could she really burn children? Yes, she could. She knew what they were: child soldiers, combining the amorality of childhood with the cynicism of seasoned killers, their hands washed with blood as part of their initiation. Twice as ruthless as adults. Yes, she would set them on fire if this was what it took to cross the bridge.

But Malika . . . Malika swayed like a tree in the breeze, shrinking away from the advancing boys. Caught between them and the *asanbosam*, she could see no way out.

The *asanbosam* reached out to her. His face settled, once again, into an ordinary human mold, the laughing grimace gone. He looked like a strong, protective man.

And Malika folded into his embrace.

Ally turned away in disgust and thrust her flame at the boys, who were now so close that she could see the fresh scars on their faces, the sharp cheekbones protruding from under the thin skin. They were so gaunt they looked like mummies. They looked emaciated. Hungry.

Their uniforms caught fire and in a moment, a line of golden torches blossomed in the twilight, uncannily beautiful. Ally expected screams, flailing, and the stench of burning flesh. But while their uniforms burned, the bodies within remained impervious. And as the clothes were quickly reduced to ash and floated away in grey puffs, they came closer: a gaggle of bony, skeletal children, their sharp-toothed mouths smiling widely.

Her fire had gone out.

Ally lit another match and swiped a whip of flame across their hollow chests. This time the flesh did catch fire, and they burned with a thick, oily smoke that choked her so badly she was down on her knees, coughing and retching and wiping her streaming eyes. When she got up, they surrounded her.

A fence of hollow bones and empty skulls, a posse of skeletons. Their flesh burned off but their bones were still animated with the same unquenchable hatred that had taken away their childhood.

Her fire had gone out.

Through the gaps between the skeletons, she could see the *asanbosam* and Malika, locked in an embrace, her head hidden on his chest. He watched Ally with a malicious smirk but it gave her courage to see that the embrace was not voluntary: he was actually holding Malika down, the muscles on his arms standing out as he strove to prevent her from breaking free.

Ally lit up her last match.

It flared with a crimson flame unlike any she had seen before. She smelled cinnamon and sulfur, a mixture of home-cooking and hellfire. The child skeletons rattled and pulled away. But the flame reached out to them, clothed them in garments of splendor, and consumed them in bursts of golden sparks like oversized Roman candles.

Ally was free. And she had no more magic weapons.

She turned to the *asanbosam*. Except he was no longer there.

Or rather *something* was there—something so strange that it took her overloaded brain a couple of precious seconds to figure out what she was seeing, and then it was too late. It was upon her.

The *asanbosam's* body had fallen apart, disassembled into a collection of independently moving segments. The two arms wound around Malika like pythons, binding her in coils of living rope, the splayed hand of one gagging her mouth. The two legs weaved in a grotesque dance. And the impossibly long, sinuous torso crawled toward Ally, the head smiling widely, the facial features disappearing into folds of skin as its toothy maw gaped.

Ally could no longer run, her entire body feeling like an open wound. She stumbled away but the torso was impossibly fast. It tripped her, and as she fell down heavily, striking her hip on the stone of the bridge. It coiled around her, squeezing her chest. She felt her ribs crack.

And then a thunder of hooves as a graceful form of a deer bounded upon the bridge, his antlered head held high. The deer kicked the *asanbosam's* torso, stomped on it, grinding it into the pavement. The head hissed and spat.

Malika broke away from the arms and was running toward them when the dancing legs suddenly joined together at the crotch and the arms jumped on top, unfolding into a pair of pale membranous wings. A cruciform headless dragon sprung into the air, picked up Malika with its clawed feet and bore her into the clouds.

The deer had almost succeeded in pushing the thrashing torso off the bridge. Ally crawled toward him on her hands and knees, too battered to stand upright.

The deer turned its liquid eyes upon her.

And then the torso jumped up, uncoiling like a worm, and sunk its teeth into the deer's throat.

Ally's scream echoed around the silent shantytown as she ground her fingers into the creature's eyes and pummeled its head against the sturdy parapet. It flailed around, striking her with its sinuous length, but she felt no pain. It gave a last convulsive shudder and lay still.

Ally cradled her brother's dying body. Her smock was drenched with his blood. The light was failing as the sun set but she hoped to see Ivan's face one more time as she whispered half-remembered Ukrainian lullabies, dredging up memories of the childhood they had never shared. But it did not happen. His eyes dimmed, and his body shuddered and deflated like an empty sack as he died. But those were still the mute eyes of a deer, and a deer's furred carcass rested on the bridge.

The night fell; the city was dark; no lights came on; and Ally stayed with her brother's corpse above the silently flowing third Dragon River.

Part 4:

An Officer's Daughter

Chapter 1:
The Night Mare

The road stretched into the distance Weeds were whipping her legs as she walked on the shoulder. She did not want to walk on the tarmac for fear of being hit by a car coming unexpectedly from around a bend.

Cars. People. California.

Nightwood had tossed her out.

She had failed in everything. She had not saved Carl. She had let Malika down. And worst of all, she was responsible for her brother's death. The fact that he had never actually lived in her world was irrelevant. Mama had protected her unborn son from the cruelty that was his heritage. She, his sister, had dragged him on her own vain quest, exposed him to the horrors bred of history, and eventually killed him. Not with her own hands but out of weakness and vanity. Just as she had killed Mama. Had she been a better daughter, Mama would not have drunk herself into a stupor. She would not have gone wandering in the dark. She would not have disappeared without a trace.

She wanted a soft life, an easy life. But it was not for people like her. It could only be bought by suffering: if not hers, then somebody else's. She thought she had hit a jackpot when she married Carl. She had. Now she would have all the money she had ever wanted, and all the company she had ever deserved: the company of ghosts.

When she had finally cried herself out of tears on the bridge, cradling Ivan's body, she lifted her head and discovered that night had fallen. The sky was peppered with brilliant stars but there was no moon. Nor was there a single light in the shantytown. The broken houses and rubbish-choked alleys stretched into the gloom all around her. All she heard was the asthmatic splashing of the thick water under the bridge. And a distant howling.

It was the howling that made her act. She felt so empty that she almost considered staying on the bridge, waiting for the wolves to attack. She had no more stolen magic to defend herself with; no more friends or allies. She would be at peace. But she knew the wolves would savage her brother's body, whether they came in their human or animal form.

She looked down into the treacly gleam of the river. The water was dirty, polluted. But it *was* flowing. She remembered what Malika had said: the demons of this particular corner of Nightwood could not abide running water. Water cleanses. Eventually.

It took her almost an hour to shift the deer carcass to the edge of the bridge deck. She closed his big, eyelash-fringed eyes and whispered a prayer. Only later did it occur to Ally that the prayer was the one the Orthodox Church used at baptism, not funeral. She caressed her brother's proud antlers and the wound in his throat that had finally stopped bleeding. Her fingers touched the delicate chain of the cross necklace. Ally hesitated for a moment. It was the only thing she had from Mama, and it did have some magic . . .

She snatched her hand away as if burned.

With one final spurt of strength, she pushed the body over the edge of the bridge and listened to the splash. And when the river resumed its slow purl and the howling came so close that were it daylight, she could probably see the wolves massing on the shore, she got up and, with halting steps, crossed the Third Dragon River.

She found herself in an empty room, the walls peeling and water-stained, the single window covered by a white curtain. There were two doors: one leading into a sad-looking bathroom, the other opening to the outside. The night had stayed behind. A familiar sunshine streamed through the worn curtain. Ally unlatched the door and stepped into the green hush.

Here was the intersection where she had almost collided with Eric's car. Here were the banks of mailboxes, one of them bulging with some just-delivered Amazon package. Behind her was the haunted cabin that had given her nightmares.

The cabin stood open and empty, its only occupants a couple of geriatric spiders. The nightmares were over. She was home.

She repeated the word "home" to herself until it dissolved into a meaningless, mocking sound.

Nightwood

Trudging up the slope, Ally tried to imagine that when she finally reached the glass house, it would be just as it had been in the early days of her marriage. Carl obsessing about a new car; Gabriela polishing kitchen counters. Couldn't Nightwood throw her one of its time-loops like a life preserver?

Why would it do so? The story world was not simply dangerous. It was malicious. Its animating power delighted in pain and suffering. Why? Ally had no idea. Folklore had not prepared her for anything like the Three Dragon Rivers. Old stories were often dark, yes; but this was beyond darkness. Raw history seeping in and contaminating the universe of timeless tales.

Disjointed thoughts circled in her head. She was too tired to follow any of them. She just wanted a place to take off her blood-stained clothes, to lie down, to rest. The image of a hot shower floated before her like an enticing mirage. The sun beat on her head as it climbed up in the flawless sky.

Where was everybody? No cars on the road. Well, people who had jobs on the Peninsula must have driven down already. People like Eric.

What would he think of her, coming back with her tail between her legs? Coming back alone, without her husband.

If there was a car, she would ask for a ride. Yes, even if the driver was Pat Donegan. The witch. Compared to Little Mother, ordinary witches were as harmless as Halloween dummies.

A sound broke the hush. Ally perked up and subsided with a groan. Not the purr of a car's engine but the clip-clop of a horse's hooves on the tarmac. Bloody Woodside riders! They had their own trails and pastures; what were they doing on the private road into the preserve? Well, at least the rider could spare some water. She was parched.

The horse emerged from around the bend. And Ally dove into the bushes on the mountain side of the road, plowed through and fell. She went rolling down the slope, lacerated by sharp twigs, whipped by pliant branches, collecting dry needles under her shift, which ripped as it caught on the side of a manzanita. It slowed down her roll and eventually the slope terminated in a shallow bowl. She came to rest there, out of breath and bleeding from innumerable tiny scratches and cuts. The pain was nothing compared to the overwhelming fear that he would hear the rustle of the undergrowth as the horse made his way down, following her.

Reason kept telling her that the thing was too heavy to descend this steep slope. But it was silenced by the discordant voices in her head as dread and relief clamored for supremacy.

There had been no rider. What would ride on such a steed? The elongated skull, gleaming in the sunlight; the square yellow teeth in the lipless maw; the tarmac showing through the gaps between the ribs. But not a skeleton, no! There was still hide on those moving bones. Patches of worn skin and rough hair stuck to the funnel-shaped chest and something scarlet and wet pulsated in the hollow abdomen. Naked tendons clung to the polished femurs; a discolored tail swished along the moth-eaten flanks. And there were eyes in bony sockets: mad and staring, all white and no pupil. Ally remembered a painting by Fuseli she had seen once called "Nightmare". Night-mare. This was what was on the road above her, mercifully veiled from her sight by the curtain of manzanitas and Ceanothus.

It was terrifying. But it meant she was still in Nightwood.

She had not failed.

Chapter 2:
Ashes

Eric knew he was going to be dead in five days.

He calculated it precisely. It took him some time to learn the rhythm of this place where light and darkness came randomly if at all; where the most common time of day seemed to be a sort of sluggish twilight that dragged on and on until one of the three Horsemen showed up with his cargo of new recruits. The recruits were first told to remove the bodies of those who had recently died in the ash-mine and then sent to grub in the grey hillocks, smoking with clouds of fine dust. The dust would get into their lungs, and they would start coughing and spitting within hours, the liquid oozing from their mouths ink-black. They would try to stretch out their meager water rations. They would stop washing. Their faces would be quickly covered by a thick crust that adhered even to the corpses, so that the living wore their own death masks.

The corpses stacked beyond the fence blended with the grey dunes so well that it was impossible to count them or to differentiate between mummified human remains and bleached wood or splintered animal bone.

Not that it mattered. The inmates were here to die, though not until they had fulfilled their quota of mining. The average lifespan, as far as Eric could tell, was about two weeks, most of which he had already used up.

He dug in the compacted cinders with a large pottery shard shaped like a convex rectangle. They had not been given any tools, such as spades or pickaxes. Not that those would be necessarily useful for scooping up the fine ash that flowed like heavy water. He had found the shard himself.

When he had had been brought here, he cried and squirmed

like a baby in the grasp of the thing that had bested him in the game of snake-eyes. He had been shoved into the corner of the ash-field where layers of broken pottery rose up in uneven hillocks and sharp-edged shelves. There he had seen the Horseman.

That was the moment of choice. He could have demanded his rights, yelled at the impassive blank-faced figure in the clothes the color of whey that he did not belong here, that he was an entrepreneur, a techie, a rich man . . .

And then he would be dead.

Instead, some ancestral memory kicked in and he did what Nana must have done in the period of her life she had never talked about. He kept his head down and did as he was told. He found a tool for his own slave labor. And he had gained two weeks of life.

The potsherds were strange: some very big, seemingly of vessels large enough to contain gallons of oil or wine; some as tiny as his fingernail. Some were so old that they crumbled at the slightest touch; some new, brick-red, ribbed, or smooth. He was lucky to find that big shard that was so useful in cutting through the layers of compressed ash and cinders and scooping up handfuls of just the right size. Other inmates were not so fortunate. The man next to him had to sift through the acidic dust with his bare hands that were bleeding badly, the skin worn through. The blood mixed with ash into lumps of gluey material that weighed him down, making his scrabbling pitifully ineffective. Despite this, his haul, laid out on the scrap of burlap that each of them had been outfitted with, was bigger than Eric's.

Eric did not know the man's name. At the beginning, when such things seemed to matter, he had tried to talk to other inmates. No one had responded except for one who gabbled excitedly, black saliva running down his chin. Eric could not tell whether the man spoke an unfamiliar language or was insane. It did not matter as next morning his contorted body was thrown beyond the fence.

Something gleamed in the handful of viscous stuff that he had lifted from his shallow excavation. His fingers closed around a slick curved cylinder with the consistency of soap. By now he knew better than to hold his find for longer than it took to deposit it on the burlap, but the thing seemed to nestle into his palm like a kitten and he had a glimpse of what it was. He reflexively tossed it away, shaking his hand as if to dislodge a cockroach, and it sunk back into the ash. Eric went scrabbling for it. The food rations were proportionate to the amount of haul. Even if one fulfilled the quota, they were barely sufficient to keep one alive. Not for the first time, Eric wondered whether it would not be easier just to lie down in the soft embrace of ash. Even if the things they were digging for were indeed alive; even if they homed in on him as they might be homing on the blood of his teammate—so what? Grey dust would soon clog his airways and bring him the solace of oblivion. What were minutes or hours of nightmares compared to the eternity of nothingness?

And yet, he would not do it. Some kernel of stubbornness inside rebelled against the idea of giving in and giving up. And so, he dug to fill his quota; and averted his gaze from the Horsemen and their retinue; and ate the wormy soup and hard bread; and washed his face in stinking puddles. And survived.

He plunged his shard deeper into the compacted layers of cinders. It hit an air bubble, slipped out of his fingers, and disappeared. Eric groaned. Lying on the billows of ash, his eyes watering, he groped through the powdery material.

When his shoulder threatened to dislocate, his fingers finally touched something. It was inert. So it was not another mining find. But neither did it feel hard like his lost potsherd.

Eric pulled it out and stared at it uncomprehendingly. It was an old bath-toy: a squishy rubber bird so filthy that its original color was impossible to determine. Its beak curved in a clownish smile.

The things they were mining for came in a multitude of shapes. He had not seen anything as creepily familiar as the bird, but it did not mean that was impossible. Still, the finds he had to hand to the Horseman at the close of each work period had one thing in common: they gave you nightmares.

That was what they were for. Eric had realized, with the useless benefit of hindsight, that the so-called magic of Nightwood had nothing in common with the swords, spells or talismans of his favorite games. The magic came from histories fused into horrors, from the mass of suffering, pain, and betrayal that humanity left in its wake as it plowed forward through time. All fairy tales had been history once.

The rubber bird felt strange in his hand. It did not give him flashes of ragged women running away from soldiers as the slick cylinder had done. It projected no other atrocious images. nor did it send pulses of fear and nausea through his body. It was as inactive as if it were indeed a mere old toy.

But there was something about it, some distant sense of familiarity intertwined with non-recognition. It was not a memento of his own childhood. He was sure of it. But it had some connection to himself: an ambiguous and perhaps dangerous connection . . . but not altogether hostile. In the hell of ashes, potsherds, and bones, even that was a gift.

Eric shoved the rubber duck into the pocket of his jeans. His captors had left him his clothes. They did not care for the carceral pageantry of prison uniforms. Anyway, the emaciated figures grubbing in the endless field of ashes all looked the same regardless of whether they had originally been wearing business suits, homespun tunics, or something more exotic. They looked like grey staggering ghosts.

Some movement in the dull haze drew Eric's attention, and at the same time, he heard a distant howling. His neighbor crouched in the ash, trembling and hiding his face in his hands. Some recruits were unreasonably afraid of the wolves. Eric was not among them. He found it difficult to take the shape-shifting guards seriously: they were too much like something out of a bad horror movie. He was much more wary of the Horsemen.

His neighbor keened, rocking back and forth. Eric's eyes were drawn to his haul laid out on a piece of filthy fabric: six random objects, from a rusted spoon to a black pebble, all giving off a palpable sense of wrongness. Six finds meant a double soup portion. If he took one the inmate would not even notice; he was too far gone . . .

Eric snatched his hand away. The one unbreakable rule of camp-life: you don't steal from other inmates. He did not know how he knew it, but it was as clear to him as if it had been written in letters of iron over the gate to this place. Except, of course, there was no gate.

He turned his attention back to the indistinct shapes in the murk. Several wolves loped toward him, their red hanging tongues the only splashes of color in the field of ashes. No, not the only ones. Behind them, a larger shape emerged from the swirling dust: a cloaked rider on the richly caparisoned horse. The horse pranced as lightly on the ash-dunes as if it were flying. The rider's clothes and the horse's harness and saddle were of a rich scarlet, as obscene in this place as a goblet of wine in a leper's hands.

"The Red Horseman!" Eric shouted to his neighbor, hoping to shake him out of his funk. The appearance of one of the Horsemen signified passage of time, which meant they could be fed. Or allowed to sleep. Or killed.

All over the grey wasteland men stirred and stood up, following the passage of the scarlet figure with hungry, frightened, mad eyes. Only men; there were no women in this place.

The horse passed Eric by, so slowly that he finally got a good look at the rider's face. It was round-cheeked and ruddy, with a fixed grin and tiny, gimlet-like unmoving eyes. In his wake, the sky changed. Its flat flinty vault flushed with pink. A fan of febrile light unfolded above the ash-field and a tiny red sun blinked into existence somewhere close to the zenith. The position of the sun made no sense astronomically, but Eric had long ago realized that this was not the real Sol. Before his abduction by the thing in the castle, the sky of Nightwood had seemed identical to that of his world but on this darkened plane both time and space distorted out of recognition.

The Red Horseman stopped at a point that seemed no different from any other in the field. The wolves surrounded him in a ring, panting, still in their canine form. Eric preferred them this way.

The crimson gauntlet rose into the dusty air, beckoning, and the inmates staggered through the ash toward the Horseman, carrying their scraps of burlap jealously wrapped around their haul of nightmares. Eric's burlap was empty. He stood unmoving.

Another beckoning gesture of the red hand, and one of the wolves swiveled its head toward him, a low growl beginning in its throat. It rose off its haunches. Eric started toward the Horseman, slowly pulling his feet out of the compacted mass of ashes. It was like walking through quicksand. The wolf growled again, and he forced his cramping muscles into action. He had seen a bottle hanging on a lanyard around the animal's neck and he knew that whatever was in it could transform a vicious canine into a doubly vicious human. In one way at least, the horror movies were wrong: to shape-shift, one needed a physical agent, like the liquid in that bottle. He had seen the wolves lap awkwardly at it and then stand up as naked men. The first time it had happened he almost laughed: none of these guys would pass a muster in a gym! This had been before he saw what a gang of them did to an inmate whose haul was deemed insufficient by the Horseman. Now he would rather be savaged by animal teeth.

Each inmate opened his package and displayed his finds to the Horseman, whose unblinking eyes were focused on the invisible horizon. Nevertheless, he would motion the inmate either right or left with a wave of his red gauntlet. On the right, one of the wolves in his human form—a rat-faced hunchback—would shove into the inmate's hands a bowl of soup, a hunk of dry bread and a bottle of water. On the left, a group of wolves lay together like a pack of guard dogs, their muzzles down.

A man whom Eric had seen grubbing in the hillocks near the potsherds dump, hobbled toward the Horseman and unwrapped his roll with trembling hands. Only three random objects were inside.

The Horseman motioned to the left.

The man stood still. The wolves growled deep in their throats and rose to their feet. The man backpedaled, and then turned around and tried to run, raising plumes of dust in his painful slogging. He did not get far.

Eric turned away but he could not block out the high-pitched screaming and the liquid tearing and lapping. The screaming was mercifully brief; the liquid sounds went on.

The line of grey figures slowly shambled forward. Eric was the last. His hands were empty.

More people were motioned to the left where the sodden ash spread in a scarlet patch. The wolves yawned. One of them nosed a pile of stained clothing aside. With a detached interest, Eric noted that there was a medieval-looking doublet there. Clearly, Nightwood spread as wide in time as in space.

So that was it. Death. Well, one owed death to the world, and this was his time to discharge his debt. Eric tried to remember the Hebrew prayer "Shma" that Nana had taught him but could only dredge up a couple of words. Never mind. She was here, with him. She had faced the same . . .

. . . and survived.

Eric's hand touched the squishy rubber duck in his pocket. Should he offer it to the Horseman in a pathetic attempt to buy one more bowl of soup, one more sleep? Wasn't it more dignified to die . . .

. . . torn apart by slavering canines? No! Survival is dignity.

He squeezed the duck. It wouldn't help, he knew. Even if the Horseman accepted it in lieu of a real nightmare, it was only one. Some of the people sent to the left had had three or four.

His fingers caressed the worn rubber. It felt warm under his fingers. The ash-field was either stiflingly hot or icy cold. That was the warmth of living flesh like a touch of Nana's fingers on his feverish forehead when he was a child.

How did this prayer go? *"Oh, that I had the wings of a dove! I would fly away and be at rest. I would hurry to my place of shelter."* No, that was not right. It was not the last prayer, maybe one of the psalms.

The line moved forward. One man between Eric and the Red Horseman. One man between him and a pack of bloodstained wolves licking their chops.

"Oh, that I had the wings of a dove."

The toy bird moved.

And a spasm went through Eric's body, bolts of heat and cold shooting through him, his bones crackling like ice and his blood boiling like water, his face scrunching, drawing in upon itself, reshaping into a feathered mask, his mouth gaping in a scream but only a loud honk coming out.

The Red Horseman drew in the reins and his horse neighed loudly. The wolves milled around in confusion, growling and snapping at each other, their muzzles raised to the flinty sky where a big swan was flapping his wings awkwardly, disappearing into the crimson-tinged, ash-laden clouds.

Chapter 3:
Prince

Ally crept cautiously through the undergrowth. The realization that she was in Nightwood did not change her plans: she still needed food, clothes, shelter. And hopefully, some magic objects to replace the ones she had lost on the Three Dragon Rivers. If this part of Nightwood corresponded to Northern California, the best place to find those would be in what was the fairy-tale equivalent of her own home. Or was her own home already a fairy-tale locale? A glass palace on a tall mountain. A princess with golden hair locked in it. A witch. How could she be so blind as not to realize what it amounted to? A raw edge of reality where history and story rubbed against each other.

But of course, it was not her own story, or at least, not only hers. If the world boundaries became so porous on the mountain that fairy tales bled into, and contaminated, ordinary lives, why would she be the only one trailing a dark plume of ancient wonders?

Ally now realized that the confusion of Nightwood stemmed from the fact that anybody drawn into it would find their own history bloom into a thousand tales, all intertwined with, and influencing, each other. Ros went looking for a baby and found herself transformed into a ghoul who had become tangled up with bird maidens, animal shapeshifters, and the golden-haired Rapunzel. Malika brought in the stark tales of women sold to monstrous bridegrooms. Talia and Margarita, "Sun, Moon, and Talia" and "Hansel and Gretel", stamped with the horrors of their origins in pestilence and war. All fairy tales had been history once.

But if just being on the mountain drew you into Nightwood, what about Carl? Where was the spoor of his story? Ally could not escape the thought that perhaps there was none because she had been late. Despite what Little Mother had said, Carl was dead.

No, she would not believe it! Finding her husband was supposed to be her redemption, and she would not give up until she did—or until she knew for sure that he was gone.

And what about her own story? So much of what Ally had experienced had been echoes of the familiar Slavic tales of her own childhood: sister and brother lost in the woods; crossing three dragon-guarded rivers; the bird maiden laboring under the enchantment of her feathered shape. But they did not come together into any plot she could recognize and disentangle, follow to its happy conclusion. For it had to have a happy ending: all fairy tales did!

Except she knew it was not true. Happy endings were a Disney invention, obscuring the grim reality of the ancient stories distilled from humanity's struggle with itself. But if she could at least know what her story was, it would give her something to hang on to. Because now she was back to square one. Going back to the glass house and starting from the beginning.

Sunlight filtered through the green feathery boughs, dappled the moss with golden coins. The fact that the giant redwoods did not allow lesser vegetation to flourish in their shadow made going easier. She came to a familiar place. Beyond the barrier of manzanitas, she could see the ribbon of the road, with huge boulders standing sentinel on the slope above.

Something moved ahead in the lacy confusion of sun and shadow, something big and tawny. Ally's heart gave a leap. A deer?

Before she knew it, she was running on the road, crying out her brother's name. A mini-avalanche of dry earth slid onto the road as the creature vaulted the slope and disappeared among the redwoods. She could not even get a good look at it.

Disappointed, Ally took a deep breath and trudged on, rounding the protruding, moss-draped boulder that loomed over the road. Something made her look up. Her heart skipped a beat.

Sitting on top of the boulder and basking in the sunshine was a mountain lion.

Mountain lions were a frequent topic of discussion in the community, with Carl and Mike having endless chats about the latest sighting caught on wildlife cameras. Ally found those discussions boring and the blurry videos of big cats slinking through the dark unconvincing. Rationally, she knew they were real; emotionally, she could not muster any fear-response to them. As opposed to wolves, who had been the fairy-tale nightmare of her urban childhood, mountain lions looked just like familiar street cats rooting in garbage bins, only bigger.

But now, seeing the slinky feline creature above her, its tail swinging like a metronome, Ally realized how wrong she had been. This was not a scruffy city scavenger. This was a predator.

She backed off slowly, remembering Carl's admonition that running away was the worst thing to do when confronted with a mountain lion. If you did, they would treat you as prey. If she could convince the creature she was inedible . . .

In one fluid motion, the predator jumped off the boulder and onto the surface of the road. It stood just a couple of yards away from Ally, in a patch of sunlight that made its fur scintillate like ice crystals. And Ally saw it was not a mountain lion, after all. Even her scant zoological knowledge told her there were no mountain lions with a fluffy white coat, a flat face and large blue eyes. The creature advancing toward her with graceful fluid steps was just a big housecat. A *very* big housecat.

"Prince!" she exclaimed with a mixture of relief and apprehension. She had last seen Jennifer's pet when Jennifer had told her about Nightwood and warned her against Pat. And there was something else she had said, some place she had told her to stay away from. The grove? The Bleeding Grove?

In any case, since then, Prince had grown significantly. When Jennifer had had him on a leash, he could pass for an unusually large Siamese. Not anymore.

Or had *he* had Jennifer on a leash?

A pink tongue delicately licked Prince's nose and he yawned, disclosing sharp teeth. Ally took another step back. Wasn't it an Internet meme that if your cat could eat you, it would? This cat certainly could.

"Prince?" she said again. "You must remember me. I'm Jennifer's neighbor."

Prince meowed with a rising and falling intonation, but Ally could not understand what he had said, if anything. Once again, she regretted the loss of the cross necklace—and once again, she forbade herself to think about it. She had done the right thing by leaving it with Ivan's body.

Prince turned around and walked on the road. After a couple of steps, he turned around and looked back at Ally. His meaning was unmistakable. He wanted her to go with him.

Ally hesitated. She did not trust the big cat. Eric had said something about him seducing Jennifer. And in any case, Ally had already learned the hard way that most animals in Nightwood were bad news.

But what could she do? Forge on with no knowledge of what lay ahead, no plan, no helpers, and no magic objects? This was not home (and when had she started thinking of California as home?). This was Nightwood.

The cat meowed again.

"I'm coming!" Ally yelled and followed him.

She expected the cat would take her to some secret palace in the woods, but he trotted unhurriedly ahead of her on the road. Ally noted that the road seemed exactly like the one Carl had driven his Ukrainian bride on to their glass house. This was not particularly surprising: if Nightwood could contain Third World slums and bullet-scarred bridges, why not tarmac? Even though the road was in poor shape, with visible potholes and eroded shoulders, it did not materially differ from Ally's memory of its Californian counterpart.

Prince sauntered to the entrance to a driveway and Ally caught her breath. This was Eric's house! She remembered very well how she had driven here on the morning after Carl's abduction. Jennifer and her feline familiar lived here. Eric told her that his friend disappeared together with the cat and showed her an image of Nightwood on Jennifer's computer.

So was Jennifer here now? And where was Eric?

Ally lingered, questions and apprehensions buzzing in her head like a cloud of gnats. Prince glanced at her over his shoulder. Ally took a deep breath and followed.

The house, previously masked by a row of Ceanothus, came into view. It was exactly the same as she remembered it: a modernist cube built into the slope of the mountain, its wide deck facing the ocean. There was even a wildlife camera over the entrance.

Prince gracefully leaped onto the porch and pushed the front door. It swung open. He held it for Ally with his paw. She walked in.

The living room was also the same: a life-size copy of a Chinese terracotta warrior in the corner, some framed prints of London and Paris, a scatter of books and computer hardware in the sunken pit in front of the fireplace, a multicolored lump of Murano glass on the kitchen table. It looked as if the owner of the house had just stepped out. The illusion of reality was so strong that Ally was about to call out Eric's name. It was as if she was back in her own life and everything that had happened was some weird dream, as insubstantial as the memories of her birthplace.

And then she blinked and saw a white cat the size of a mountain lion lounging on the sofa.

Ally walked over to the armchair and lowered herself onto the soft leather. Every bone, every muscle in her body ached. Her bloodied clothes chafed her skin. Her feet throbbed. She was nothing but a bundle of discomfort.

"So, where is Eric?" she addressed the cat. "Where is Jennifer?"

Prince purred.

Ally shook her head.

"We won't get very far like that," she said. "I don't have the necklace anymore. I don't understand what you are saying."

Prince jumped down and slunk into the kitchen. Ally followed.

He nosed the door of the fridge and looked at her expectantly. She smiled.

"Not easy to open a fridge with no hands, huh? Is this why you brought me here? To fill your bowl?"

Prince blinked his beautiful blue eyes. Ally opened the fridge and stared into its cavernous emptiness. So much for lunch! She was ravenous.

Prince butted her hip. Ally looked back and saw that the fridge was not totally empty. There was a bottle in the door.

Ally took it out and looked at it dubiously. It was glass like a wine bottle but without any label; the liquid inside perfectly transparent. She pulled out the cork and sniffed it. There was no smell at all.

Prince meowed.

"You want to drink?" Ally asked. "Tap water's not good enough for you? Spoiled rotten, that's what you are. Americans! Do you want ice in your water too?"

Prince's claws lightly brushed her forearm.

"All right, all right!" Ally found a bowl and filled it with the water from the bottle. "Here you are! But after you drink, I'm going to fix myself some lunch. Sorry, kitty, but I'm starving!"

Prince snorted in indignation. When Ally put the bowl down on the floor, he lowered his head and lapped at it delicately.

She should have expected this. But when a nude man with blond hair and blue eyes stretched luxuriously and smiled at her, she screamed.

Chapter 4:
Among the Empties

Malika had expected the worst. And she knew what the worst would be.

But it did not happen. She remained unmolested. She was, in fact, simply unnoticed by the malevolent figures with painted faces and blood-dripping hands who laughed and caroused outside the compound. She heard the voices but could not understand a word they were saying. It was neither English nor Yoruba or Hausa. Smoke occasionally wafted in from their cigarettes or cooking fires and she would cough and hear them fall silent, as if surprised that somebody alive was inside, even though the compound was crowded. But the others did not cough—or speak. If Malika was making too much noise, one of them would drag her away from the window with its soft, shapeless paw, the cloth curling around her forearm. For empty cloaks, they were amazingly strong.

For this was what the other inhabitants of the compound were— empties, billowing piles of scratchy dark fabric that stank of old sweat. There were no eyes behind the mesh insert. There was no body under the covering of the *abaya*. And still, they moved with a restless, swirling motion, clogging the narrow corridors and filling the tiny rooms, suffocating her inside her already suffocating jail.

When the *asanbosam* had deposited her in the courtyard and she had found herself surrounded by those packed figures, she felt a tiny stir of relief: at least she was she was with other women! But very quickly she realized that she had all the disadvantages of shared misery and none of the advantages. She could find no help or commiseration from the brainless empties. But neither would she ever be alone to grieve or plan her escape.

Escape? The shame of what she had done—or rather, *not* done—kept nagging at her and at first, she had tried to find a corner to herself to have a good cry or to pray. But that was impossible. The empties flocked around her like a murder of mute ravens. They would not leave her to herself even in the bathroom and though they were female garments, it made her uncomfortable. Remonstrating with them, though, was as effective as talking to clothes in the closet.

Malika eventually learned to disregard the whisper of fabric on the floor as the empties eddied around her in mindless perambulations. She sought refuge in her thoughts. She could figure out, disentangle the hopelessly knotted strands of her life. She had been studying to be an engineer and considered herself a clear-headed, rational person. This could not be taken away from her. Even if everything else had been.

When she awoke in that terrible coop, her body distorted into a chicken parody of herself, her mind occluded, she had accepted it with dumb resignation. She had known Little Mother's farmyard her entire life. Together with her abduction by the *asanbosam* it had been a persistent nightmare so intricately woven into the texture of her experience that it blurred into a shapeless blob of fear, a lurking darkness at the edge of her memory. She had been sure it was the result of scary tales she heard from her nanny—and so had been her parents, who admonished the woman for filling their baby daughter's head with nonsense. Now Malika realized that those were indeed memories, but not of a distant childhood. Somehow she had grown up remembering what would happen to her adult self in California. The little girl turned into a bird; the little girl running away from the monster who wanted to marry her—these were neither fairy-tale-inspired fantasies nor childhood nightmares. They were flashbacks of a trauma that had not yet happened.

Released from Little Mother by Ally, Malika found herself floating in a weird in-between limbo of shock. Her child body did not fit her adult mind; her memory was bifurcated by two incompatible timelines; and the past and the future chased each other around like demented snakes, swallowing each other's tales. But one thing stood firm in that mental quicksand: Ally would save her. The first time she had set her eyes on the diminutive Ukrainian girl in Berkeley, she had known it. Malika was not superstitious, but she believed that the future was fixed, determined by God's design. Ally was part of this design, and she was glad of it because she genuinely liked her roommate.

But now she realized that the design, if there was one, was incomparably more complex than a human mind could encompass, a multidimensional carpet of branching and looping timelines. There were infinite futures depending on the choices one made. And the choice she had made landed her in this hell, killed Ally's brother, and perhaps Ally herself. And that was such an insignificant moment, razor-thin, just a couple of heartbeats when she had hesitated on the Third Dragon River's bridge. How fair was it to balance her entire life on such a shaky pivot?

Well, fairness did not really come into it.

The empties rustled past her through the narrow passage separated from the cubicle she was in by a threadbare curtain. There were no inner doors in the compound. The tiled floor was spotlessly clean, swept by the hems of the moving cloaks, but the whitewashed walls were stained by dirty slicks where the empties rubbed against them. Another stain was already forming where Malika's head rested against the wall. There was very little furniture in the compound. Malika sat on the floor, slept on a piece of rug she had found in a corner, washed herself from a pitcher over a hole in the floor, and ate dry flatbread and overripe fruit that occasionally appeared in the room she thought of as a kitchen, even though it had neither a stove nor any cooking implements. The men from outside the compound must be bringing the food in but she never saw it happening.

The thought of these men made her shiver as the sound of their rough voices drifted in through the tiny shuttered window. If they ever set foot into the compound, she did not want to be around. At least here she was protected.

No! Malika jumped to her feet, bumping her head against the low ceiling. That was the kind of thinking that had landed her where she was. Protected? Yes, like a chicken in a coop!

She leaned against the wall and peered through the window, seeing nothing but the white sunlight on the white wall. The men were close, but her angle of vision was too limited to make out where. She could not understand a word of their rapid banter.

One of them passed so close to the window that Malika shrank away involuntarily, even though he could not possibly see her through the slats of the blind. But she got a good look at him. To her surprise, he was a white man, dressed in some sort of nondescript fatigues. He whistled as he went by, and then tipped back his shaved head as he drank from a plastic bottle. His shadow on the wall flickered and contorted.

Wolves! Her mind went back to the horror of that moment when Ally and the three girls were caught in the woods. She remembered the feeling of helplessness and confusion. And she remembered how Ally protected the three of them.

Malika thought of her fellow prisoners in Little Mother's farmyard. Talia had been nice to Malika but having no common language, they could not talk to each other. And Margarita had not even bothered to hide her disdain for the black girl. But eventually, both Talia and Margarita made the right choice, confronted their dragons, and let Ally pass. And she, Malika, did not.

Malika shook off the familiar stifling cloak of guilt and helplessness and leaned closer to the window, trying to see what was happening. She was rewarded by a glimpse of a slinky canine shape.

So, it was change-water in those bottles. If she could get some . . .

She shuddered, remembering the wrenching pain of her transformations. She did not want to be a fowl again. But what if she could become a swift animal and escape the compound? It was not much of a plan as she had no plausible means of laying her hands on a bottle, but just thinking of escape cheered her up.

Suddenly, there was a commotion outside and the Brownian motion of the empties in the corridor shifted as they all flowed in one direction. Malika jumped to her feet, rushed out and pushed through the clog of dusty cloaks. They felt like pressurized balloons. But she used her strong arms and long legs, encouraged by what she could see above their cloth-covered pates.

There was a shaft of sunlight at the end of the corridor.

She had been shoved through that door by the relentless pressure of the milling empties when the *asanbosam* brought her in and then the lock had clicked shut behind her. She had not seen the door open since that day, which must have been at least a week ago.

She popped into the courtyard like the cork out of a bottle, blinking in the dazzle of the bright sunshine. The glare solidified into a clot of shiny white in the middle of the open space. Malika rubbed her eyes. And then she realized that the whiteness was indeed solid.

A wedding gown, lavishly decorated with knots and embroidery, stood stiff on the worn cobblestones, topped with an elaborate white headdress made of feathers. There was no frame inside the dress to keep it up, but Malika knew it was not necessary. The dress was filled by longing. Her own and others like her. To be a bride, to experience that fairy-tale pinnacle of beauty and power that makes every woman a princess for a day.

She approached the dress, touched the delicate layers of beaded chiffon. Diamonds were worked into the applique. This was no cheap imitation. A real thing. Such as her parents would wish for their daughter on her wedding day.

She squinted into the brightness. The men stood in parallel rows, their gazes modestly averted, their guns on the ready to fire the wedding salute. They wore traditional robes, even though many of them were white. The bridegroom would walk through their serried ranks to greet the bride.

Malika looked back to where the black-clad empties crowded the compound, their blind eye-slits greedily turned toward her, eager to be filled with her glory.

She approached the gown that gracefully dipped toward her, unfolding like a flower.

Malika opened up her arms and the gown flew toward her, swan-like, embracing her body, flowing down her legs in a cascade of glitter. The feathered headdress planted itself snugly on Malika's short hair.

But before the dress fully settled in, Malika lunged forward and snatched a water bottle from the belt-pack of the nearest man standing at attention to greet the bride. The man was so enchanted by the wedding dress that he leaned slightly in, his face flushed with sickly adoration. It took him a couple of heartbeats to process what happened and by then, it was too late. Malika had drained half of the bottle in a single gulp, change-water flowing recklessly down her chest and staining the dress.

And just as the courtyard erupted in shouts and curses, just as the bridegroom—resplendent in his traditional robe and stolen human body—rushed toward the commotion, just as the empties fell down in concentric circles of fabric like pricked balloons, a large black swan rose majestically into the hot sky.

Chapter 5:
The Trickster

"Just put on** some clothes, will you?" Ally said in disgust. Not that Prince could show her anything she had not seen before but his total shamelessness in parading around the house in his birthday suit unnerved her. It was either insolence or innocence, and either of these qualities in her host was bad news.

He grinned but complied, disappearing upstairs and returning in a pair of jeans and a nondescript t-shirt. Both fit perfectly, which seemed to indicate that this was his house and that its resemblance to Eric's domicile in California was some sort of *geis*. Why? She had no idea. Nightwood was not lawless or illogical but both its laws and logic were beyond common sense.

"Would you like a bite to eat?" he purred.

"I thought you'd never ask," she responded testily.

He grinned again, as if imitating his famous literary predecessor, the Cheshire Cat. There was still something faintly feline about his broad face, his slanted eyes, and his shock of reddish-blond hair. With the flourish of a circus magician, he opened the door of the empty fridge, and Ally gasped.

The fridge was positively crammed now. There were bottles and containers; there were pizza boxes and salad bags; there were ready-made meals and packaged cheeses and salami. Just looking at this unexpected cornucopia made Ally's mouth water. She reached for a loaf of sliced bread still in its plastic wrapping but then snatched her hand back, remembering the solitary bottle of change-water residing in the fridge just minutes ago. She glanced at Prince suspiciously.

"No ashes," he assured her. "No silly midnight transformations. Good nutritious food."

Ally set to it and in a short while the kitchen table bore a plate loaded with cheese sandwiches and a bowl of salad. She left salami alone—her Nightwood adventures had not diminished her instinctive revulsion from meat—but she hesitated thinking of her host. Cats are carnivorous but was Prince a cat in a human body or a man in a feline form?

Oh, to hell with it! She gestured to the table, and he joined her willingly enough. He even produced a bottle of Californian merlot and poured a full glass for each of them. Definitely a man!

"So," she asked after a pleasant warmth spread from her stomach to her head, "why didn't you leave some change-water outside?"

"I like it cold," Prince responded. He had a high-pitched baritone and spoke with a vague British accent.

"But if needs must. There should be a spring in the vicinity, right?"

"There is. But it's . . . let's just say it's inaccessible right now."

"Guard-dogs? Or rather, guard-wolves?"

"Pah! They are spreading all over the place. Pests!"

So, Prince did not like the Ogre's minions. Well, that was understandable.

Ally sipped more merlot, remembering the last dinner she had with Carl. The slim tops of redwoods outside swayed in the clear mauve sky.

"Do you know where my husband is?" she asked.

Prince smiled over the rim of his glass. There was something unnerving about his smile. His eyes remained remote as his lips moved. Ally realized that his pupils were still spindle-shaped like a cat's.

"Where he has always been," he said.

"The Bleeding Grove," Ally said.

"Yes. The Bleeding Grove."

They were silent for a moment. The evening light curdled into dusk by imperceptible degree.

"I'll be honest with you, Alyona," Prince said. "I can help you but there will be a price to pay. Here nothing is given for free. Not even gifts. Particularly gifts."

"I did not expect anything else," Ally said. "As long as the exchange is fair. And my name is Ally."

Prince shook his handsome head.

"No," he said. "Your real name is Alyona, and it will never change. In Nightwood, things are known by their true names. But don't fret. Your name has power."

"So does yours. If it's really Prince."

"It is. What did you think it was, Marquis de Karabas? That was a silly tale made up by a bewigged Frenchman for entertainment of his mistresses. No, I'm no Puss-in-Boots. I am Prince. But . . . "

"A prince is not a king," Ally said.

"Yes. And this is why I need your help."

The hot shower was pure bliss.

She stood under the powerful jet for half-an-hour, lathering her hair with actual shampoo, rinsing it out and lathering again. When she was done, her hair, so long neglected, shone like gold.

Wrapped up in several towels, Ally flopped onto the bed in the guestroom. The bed was made with Egyptian cotton, smooth and silky and cool. Her body, used to the fairy-tale discomforts of bug-infested sleep-rolls or hard earth, was rediscovering the pleasures of civilization muscle by sore muscle.

The guestroom could have been in any of her neighbors' houses in California. There was electricity. There was no TV but many of the more progressive crowd had tossed those out anyway, relying on iPads and smartphones.

Ally examined the furniture and the knickknacks but found nothing exceptional. Some of the dolls on the dresser seemed to follow her with their beady eyes but then again, she was exhausted to the point of hallucination. And too wound-up to sleep.

Prince's offer was logical and rational, and this was why she distrusted it. She quickly realized what the man-cat was: a trickster, the most ancient of Nightwood's many ancient archetypes. Tricksters were unreliable and often malicious, like Loki, the Scandinavian god-demon, and they were creepily powerful, like the Coyote, the Navajo creator deity. But Prince was a faded echo of these primordial figures. He had been around the human world too much: rubbing against people's legs, lying in his mistresses' laps, stealing their toys and their hearts. Could he really take on the Ogre?

He refused to tell her what archetype the Ogre was, and Ally found this troubling. Her knowledge of folklore was her only weapon in Nightwood. But Prince had said she did not need any weapons.

"You are strong," he had said. "You killed Little Mother. Now her power is yours."

"Much good did it do on the Three Dragon Rivers!" she objected, bitterly.

He shrugged.

"You are alive."

Yes, she wanted to say, *and my brother is dead!*

But she had to admit that he had a point. She had survived. She had vanquished the three Dragons—the *Dottore il Peste*, the feathered Plague Doctor; the murder of ravens hiding in the body of a little girl; and the *asanbosam*. She had done it with the help of allies and magic objects, but this was how Nightwood worked. The idea of a lone hero vanquishing enemies all by himself was nonsense. And of course, the *asanbosam* still lived . . . and had killed her brother . . . but was it really her fault? If Malika had not hesitated on the bridge, wouldn't Ivan still be alive? Ally was aware that she was swinging between emotional extremes, ready to upbraid herself for failure one moment, fully justify her actions the next, but she was so tired, sinking into sleep and yet fighting to keep awake in order to think Prince's offer through.

He had a good reason to help her. The more she thought about it, the more she believed him. Nothing was as strong a motivator as ambition and desire for power. The history of her country had taught her this lesson well.

And he was no monster like Little Mother, composed of archaic longings and raw resentments. He would be a suave and politically-minded ruler of Nightwood, working to unify its many tribes and quell its many wars. He would not stop Nightwood's incursions into the world of history, but so what? History shed tales like a bird shed feathers; and without them, what people called "reality" would be intolerable. No, as long as these incursions were discreet and did not involve abductions, Ally was in favor of them.

He had promised her that if she killed the Ogre, she would come back home with Carl. And he had insisted that she was capable of it.

"He is weak," Prince had said. "Weak and old. Just like her."

Little Mother. Remembering the charred smell of cooking flesh in the farmyard gave her an almost sensuous satisfaction. It also gave her a pause. Really? She puked when she saw a raw steak but did not blink when a woman burned to death?

Well, Little Mother was not a woman! And she deserved it. The fowls in the coop, the feathered dress.

She would do it again in a heartbeat! And if she could inflict similar punishment upon the wolves who had butchered her brother's tribe, upon the *asanbosam* who had abducted Malika and torn out her brother's throat, shouldn't she at least try?

The Ogre must be . . . well, an ogre, some uncouth monster hulking in a rot-smelling cave. She could take him on. Not with a sword like some epic fantasy heroine—Ally had a very sober awareness of her own physical limitations—but with guile and knowledge. This was what she had planned all along. This was why she had come to Nightwood. What reason did she have to reject the trickster's help?

She would take Prince's offer. He would help her defeat the Ogre; she would help him take over the Castle With No Windows, the seat of the Ogre's power.

Having come to this conclusion, Ally yawned. Her eyelids drooped. She listened for Prince, but the house was silent. Anyway, she had locked the door—not that she thought Prince had any but pragmatic interest in her, but one never knew with tomcats—so unless he could pass through walls, she could sleep undisturbed.

She turned off the bedside lamp and looked out the second-floor window into the tangle of wind-tossed redwood branches against the starry sky. Something whitish moved through the night but she could not discern whether it was a streak of fog or a sleek feline body.

She woke up with a chorus of chirping and whistling. The birds sounded like Californian jays and when she peered outside, blue wings crossed her field of vision, flying into the mist-shrouded canopy.

Ally opened the closet that she had been too tired to explore last night. A sumptuous array of clothes practically spilled onto the carpet. She fingered them dubiously. They were not medieval gowns, but neither were they of any obvious practical utility. They were fancy designer dresses: flounced, lacy, sharply cut and boldly sewn in a variety of bright colors. In her capacity of Mrs. Morris, Ally would have loved each one of them. Now she was disappointed not to find something more appropriate for a trail.

She checked out the labels. All the clothes had a tag with "Jennifer J." on them. Ally frowned, remembering what Eric had told her about Jennifer's unsuccessful fashion business.

Eric . . . Even thinking his name tugged at her. She squelched the feeling. He was undoubtedly back home in California where she would soon be too. Together with her husband. And Eric would be their neighbor, nothing more.

She put the clothes back and dressed in her own scruffy outfit. To her delight, she found flat ballerina shoes that felt as soft as gloves on her chafed feet.

Dressed and with her hair properly braided, Ally went downstairs. The house was deserted. But when she entered the kitchen, there was a flurry of movement as the coffeemaker turned on, a skillet jumped onto the suddenly lit stove, eggs broke into a bowl, and the enticing aroma of toasted bread make her mouth water.

Ally smiled, remembering Beauty and the Beast. Prince clearly had his own unseen domestic retinue. Was there a beauty languishing in the house somewhere? She did not count: she was on the trail of a different story altogether.

She was ravenously hungry—the starvation diet in Little Mother's farmyard and on the trek through the Three Rivers country had melted away whatever scant deposits of fat she had had on her bones. Having finished the breakfast, she politely thanked the invisible servitors and went back upstairs. There were still rooms to explore.

The master bedroom was empty, the king-size bed untouched. Clearly Prince had not slept here. Was he roaming Nightwood in his feline form, spying on the Ogre? She could only hope so. She was still dubious about his help but tried to convince herself it was rational to count on it. The only way you trusted people was when they had their own interest in helping you. That was the lesson Mama had taught her. Only family would assist you for nothing. And she had no family left: father, mother, brother, all dead. Until she brought Carl back, she could only rely on herself.

But was Carl really family?

Ally tossed back her braid, delighting in its silky heaviness, and resolutely set her mind to more immediate concerns. Yes, Prince would help her, precisely because he wanted something in return. And not an insignificant something: taking over the Ogre's vacant throne was a very big deal.

Still, it made sense to snoop around and see if she could discover something else to hold over him.

Ally opened another door and was confronted with a woman staring back at her. She yelped and chided herself for an idiot. A full-length mirror, that's all!

But when she looked again, she realized that the reflection was taller than it should be.

Ally squinted into the dimness of the small room. The woman in the mirror was herself: the worn smock, the stained leggings, and the golden gleam of the braid. But even as she unconsciously smoothed down her smock, the reflection refused to repeat her actions. Instead, the woman in the mirror bent forward, pressing her face to the glass separating them as if the mirror was a windowpane. Her features squashed and distorted, swelling into a jellyfish blob. The yellow hair darkened, the braid crawling up and spreading into an untidy bob. Her mouth worked energetically but no sound emerged as she beat on the glass with her fists. And her eyes, pleading with Ally, narrowed and shifted through the spectrum, settling on green. The face was that of a stranger now. Or no, not a stranger . . . familiar like a distant Californian dream . . .

"Jennifer!" Ally gasped.

She heard footsteps downstairs and turned to listen. When she looked back into the mirror, she met her own startled gaze.

Chapter 6:

The Helper, the Guide, and the Gifts

"Here they are!" Prince said proudly, laying them out on the kitchen counter.

Ally looked at his gifts dubiously. A large rusty key, a stoppered glass vial and a small Victorinox knife. She brushed the key with her fingertips: old, tired metal that stained her skin with rust.

"The key to open the door, the potion to put him to sleep, the knife to cut off his head," Prince said.

The objects looked like worthless junk, giving off the sad aura of an impoverished yard sale. But hadn't her own weapons, stolen from Little Mother and lost on the Third Dragon River, been the same? Had she found the red plastic comb in a dime store instead of the enchanted farmhouse, would she have given it a second glance?

"Cut off his head," she repeated with a grimace.

Prince snickered.

"That's what we do here," he said.

Ally gave him a disdainful stare. He was definitely getting on her nerves, a two-bit crook that he was! Either she had gotten used to his smirking face or his feline aura had worn off. He now looked like an ordinary man: a smooth-talking wheeler-dealer, a schemer, or what Russians called a *kombinator*. She had met many of his kind in the period of her life she had worked hard to forget. She was not afraid of them. If you did not succumb to their oily charm, they would eventually learn to respect you. It would be different if one such turned into your pimp or your pusher but Ally had never touched drugs of any kind, not even cigarettes, though Mama had smoked, and she had never let herself be bought and sold by others. Sometimes she wondered where that iron resolve came from and imagined her unknown officer father had bequeathed it to her.

In any case, she knew how to handle Prince's kind. Wolves, whether in canine or human shape, terrified her much more: their irrational violence; their psychotic unpredictability. And then there was yet another sort of evil that she had encountered only infrequently and would be glad not to have known at all: a pursed-lipped, cold, calculating malevolence, totally convinced of its own rectitude. Oligarchs were of that kind, and before them, generations of true believers that had devastated her motherland.

"How am I supposed to come close enough to saw through his neck?" she asked testily.

Prince giggled.

"A pretty lady such as yourself, why do you even ask?"

Ally rolled her eyes and started packing the knife, the key and the vial into her new backpack that was also Prince's gift. He had come home laden with a bunch of plastic bags as if he had been shopping in Walmart. He asked her whether she had been exploring but, mindful of the story of Bluebeard's wife, Ally just shrugged. He did not insist.

She fingered a too-big pair of jeans, a generic hoodie, and some energy bars. Her sojourn in Nightwood had given Ally a healthy appreciation for the comforts of modern civilization. She would be happy to shed the rough smock and homespun leggings. Still, there was something jarring about these things with their "Made in China" labels and nutritional information on the energy bars. Clearly the trickster had been raiding the history world! What else had he been meddling in? She thought again of Jennifer's face in the mirror and her clothes in the closet.

But if she wanted to confront the Ogre, she could see no other way except following Prince's lead. She did not know where the Castle With No Windows was and her acquaintance with the geography of Nightwood made her realize that "where" was a relative term. The space of the story world did not obey the rules of distance and proximity. You followed your guide and, if he was the right kind of guide, he would eventually bring you where you needed to go. She could only hope that Prince was the right kind of guide.

But if he had been in the history world, why had he not brought a more modern weapon? Ally would be happier to have a gun than a small knife.

A gun? Where did this come from? Ally had kept away from the criminal bottom where the ooze of arms trade sucked in ruined lives. She had never fired a gun in her entire life.

Would I be able to do it?

Of course. My father must have.

Prince handed her a bottle of Evian water.

"I don't want to be a bird again," she said.

"Nobody's asking you. Change-water is expensive anyway. This is for drinking on the trail."

"A trail? You make it sound like hiking! Should I wear a Fitbit too?"

Prince smirked.

"Didn't get one this time but they are cool! I don't know how much hiking is involved. But our guide does."

"I thought *you* were my guide."

"I'm your helper. I'm coming with you, but we need somebody who knows the route. This is how things work out here."

"I know," Ally said irritably. "Where is this guide?"

Prince threw open the front door with a theatrical gesture. Basking in the late-morning sunshine, the yard appeared to be perfectly empty.

"Are you making fun of me?" Ally bristled.

"Whoa, easy! Look, they are waiting for us."

Prince pointed to the ground. And there it was: a fat golden sausage lying placidly across the driveway.

A banana slug had helped her in Little Mother's farmyard, bringing the seed that had grown into Mama's eidolon and given the cross necklace back to her. But was it the same one? Ally had no idea how to tell one slug from another.

"Does he speak?" she asked.

"Not English," Prince smiled toothily. "But in their own way, yes. Their name is Slugfest."

"Their?"

"It's both a boy and a girl. Their kind is funny that way."

True enough, slugs were hermaphrodites. Ally shouldered her backpack. The slug's gender identity bothered her less than his—their—means of locomotion. Banana slugs crawled at a pace that made tortoises look like sprint champions. Would she and Prince have to mince their way in tiny steps to fit the creature's leisurely progress?

It turned out she needn't have to worry.

The slug reared up like a miniature cobra, its mantle a-flutter. And then it practically shot through the driveway and into the road. It did not crawl but slid a couple of inches above the ground as if resting on an air cushion. Ally and Prince hurried after it—them, she reminded herself.

For a while, the surroundings looked vaguely familiar: the narrow-paved road; the green tangle of bushes on the sides; the red bark of tall trees swaying high above their heads. But everywhere Ally looked, something new and strange was peering through. The redwoods were festooned with gross burls shaped like headless torsos. The bright green of madrones was fading to dusty brown, their contorted trunks tying themselves up in knots and loops. The glossy leaves of tanoaks sprouted a fringe of black needles like wasps' stingers. Trees appeared that Ally did not recognize: squat boles wrapped around by air-roots that bulged like distended veins.

The road itself narrowed down to a dirt track. The light was failing, getting dimmer and dirtier, as if a muddy sediment was being stirred into the air. A damp chill rose from the sodden ground cover, making Ally shiver.

Slugfest suddenly stopped in mid-air and then dropped down onto the soft mulch.

The sojourn in Nightwood had made Ally sensitive to the atmosphere of a place, and this place gave off very bad vibes. The winding path of moist black earth was hemmed in by unfamiliar trees, gnarly and fissured with squat trunks and small, ungenerous leaves. Giant ferns grew in rank profusion, reaching for her with their green paws. She realized that there were no wildflowers anywhere. The bright splotches of color—yellow, purple, scarlet— were creeping lichens. There was a faint smell of rot in the air.

"What's up?" She asked Prince. He bent over Slugfest as if listening. Ally heard absolutely nothing and was about to tell him to cut the crap when she realized that the slug's mantle was vibrating energetically in short, structured bursts.

"They tell us we need to wait," Prince declared and plunked himself down on a tree stump.

"Why?" Ally asked.

"Danger. Wolves ahead."

Ally sighed and sat down on a bulging root as far from Prince as she could. She had no reason not to believe him—but she did not.

Suddenly it hit her. The cat-man was nervous! He was fidgeting as they waited, listening to the slow breathing of trees. Cats were not supposed to be nervous. Ally was not a cat person (and after her close acquaintance with wolves, she decided she was not a dog person either) but she knew one reason people were so attached to their pets was their calming effect. Calming! Prince was about as calm . . . well, as a cat on a tin roof!

Perhaps he could smell the wolves? Ally sniffed but could smell nothing except a faint stink of decaying leaves and stagnant water. She glanced at Slugfest and saw that they still vibrated energetically, whipping around on the lush moss. Were they trying to say something?

"Can't we go around them?" she whispered. Prince shook his head.

"We wait," he said.

He was lying! He spoke in a normal voice and wolves had very acute hearing. If Prince believed they were close, he would be whispering back.

She looked at Slugfest who reared up, their blunt front end turned to her.

She got up.

"I'm going on," she said.

"No!" Prince jumped up. "You'll kill both of us! Just wait and they'll go away!"

"You are really afraid of dogs, aren't you?" she asked mockingly. "And you are afraid of their master. You are afraid of the Ogre. How are you going to depose him?"

Prince's blue eyes narrowed into cold slits.

"Yes," he said, "I'm afraid of the Ogre. Everybody in Nightwood is. You should be too if you want to defeat him. Heroism and stupidity are not the same."

"But why? You defeated him already in so many stories. Isn't it a sign that you will again?"

She could not read the expression on his face. It was as if some sly animal feeling tried to break through his human features.

"Nightwood is eternal," he said. "We are not. We die, and some of us are reborn in a different form, but without memory and identity, what good is it? And some of us are new. You people are good at hatching monsters."

"Is the Ogre new?" Ally had the feeling that she had made some terrible mistake.

Prince did not answer. His eyes focused on something behind her shoulder.

She turned around.

The Red Horseman did not bend his head to look down at her, as if she were too small and insignificant to risk dislodging his plumed hat for. He sat as a straight as a ramrod on the giant roan stallion, his magnificent cloak lying in heavy folds around him. His ruddy face was bloated and impassive, the tiny eyes almost drowned in apoplectic cheeks.

Chapter 7:
The Bald Women

She ran, following the golden streak in the blurry air. Smoke burned her sinuses as if she were running through a battlefield. Large coils of multicolored vapors wound around her: red like blood; white like a corpse's skin; and black like the wings of the ravens feasting on dead flesh. Behind her, the soft, jungle padding of a predator's feet.

Ally coughed; her face wet with tears streaming from her blinded eyes. The scream of the gale swallowed up the clip-clopping of hooves and whisper of feline feet.

When she turned back to Prince, outraged by the betrayal, the blue eyes that looked back at her were set in a cat's flat face and there was nothing in them except animal cunning. The cat lifted its front paw. Its claws smoothly slid from the toe pads—long and wicked.

The banana slug had risen into the air like a miniature golden dragon, had flown through the confusion of swirling colors, and Ally had followed. She had to trust somebody; and only strangers were left.

She ran. And ran. And ran.

The light was weakening to somber maroon dusk. The cold winds plummeted her, coming, impossibly, from all directions at once. Ally smeared the tears off her face and squinted into the murk. The woods warped and shimmered in black and red, inflamed fog crawling up tree-trunks that were becoming sparser and squatter, hugging the fat soil like needle cushions. A hot metallic stink fouled the smoky air.

The golden streak dropped to the ground.

Ally looked back, into the tangle of black thorns. She could not understand how she had passed through without cutting herself to ribbons. Her pursuers had, apparently, not been so lucky. She could see no sign of either Prince or the Red Horseman.

She turned around and gasped. Slugfest had not abandoned her. But perhaps they had abandoned themselves, tired of their invertebrate unity. Standing before her, in the clotted pre-thunderstorm light, were two figures. Both golden, shimmering with liquid fire, as delicate as porcelain dolls with small pretty faces and tiny ineffectual wings. No clothes on their perfect little bodies, so she could see their sexes.

"I am Slug," said the girl.

"I am Fest," said the boy.

Their voices were tinny, as if produced by an old-fashioned speaker.

"Thank you," Ally said.

"We pay our dues," the boy said.

"We paid our dues," the girl corrected. "We helped you once. If it were not for him," jabbing the boy in the ribs with a sharp little finger, "we would stay out of it. The cat is bad."

"The man is worse," the boy piped in. "Maybe you can kill him."

"Or maybe you can be killed," the girl said, "and he will leave us alone."

"He'll never leave us alone," the boy said, turning his identical face to hers. "He'll feed the Bleeding Grove till nothing else is left."

"We hide," the girl said.

"We can't hide," the boy objected.

"Wait!" Ally interrupted this dialogue—or was it a monologue? "Who is the man? The Ogre?"

Slug and Fest nodded together.

"I want to find him," Ally said. "Will you lead me?"

The boy seemed to hesitate, but the girl shook her head.

"We are just a banana slug," she said. "It is not our fight. But you don't need a guide. Follow the black path," she gestured to the ribbon of bare earth snaking through the thicket of thorns. "If the bald women let you through; if you survive the Bleeding Grove; if you escape the wolves and the horsemen, you will see the Castle With No Windows. There is no ingress but maybe the door will open for you."

And with that mysterious injunction, the two of them—or was it only one?—rose into the dark air and fluttered away on their impossible wings.

Ally stepped onto the rich black soil that gave underfoot with a squelching sound as if it was soaked, even though the thicket was dry. She listened; not a sound. She looked up but the sky was obscured by lowering clouds the color of scarlet fever. She hoisted her backpack and started walking.

Now she was truly alone.

She walked for what seemed like hours, but there was no sun and no change in the roiling red twilight. The path was bordered by gnarly naked bushes, their arthritic roots nuzzling Ally's feet. She tried to peer through their intertwined limbs, but could see only the deadly lace of their dagger-like thorns fading into the brown murk. The bushes twitched and rustled when she came too close.

The scarlet sky settled down, like a lid on a mousetrap. She was the mouse.

There was nothing to do besides walking. *You made your bed, you sleep in it*. Mama's saying.

But what had Mama's final bed been like? Her body was never found. After the encounter with the lilac bush, Ally had no doubt her mother was dead. Only the dead spoke from trees and flowers in Nightwood.

She pulled the water-bottle out of her backpack and contemplated it dubiously. Nightwood had taught her the dangers of ordinary actions: getting a drink, eating a fruit, looking into a mirror. At any moment, your world could swivel on its axis and dump you into a vortex of nightmares.

But she was parched.

Ally sipped from the bottle. Nothing happened except that her thirst momentarily receded.

But something *was* changing. Not the light: it was as bad as ever. It reminded her of the red orb rolling above Little Mother's farmyard. The Red Horseman was still after her. The thorny hedge on both sides of the path was growing even thicker, the black contorted limbs thrusting at her. Their skeletal nakedness veiled with a faint green as tiny leaves sprouted from the tips of their branches. Ally looked closer and recoiled: the leaves were actually green caterpillars, wriggling out of the wood.

She could hear it better now: a hoarse phlegmy noise like many asthmatic patients breathing in unison, forcing air through their locked throats.

The path opened out into a clearing of moist black soil that looked like it should feed lush grass but was as bare as a tombstone. And here they were: the bald women.

The human chain barred the clearing, cutting through it like a fence. A fence of withered grey flesh, sags and wrinkles, ashen hopelessness, and parchment skulls. The women were embedded in the soil, planted like hedge bushes. Some as deep as their waists, some only up to their hips.

Ally backed off. The women stared at her, their eyes so deeply sunken into their emaciated faces that they all seemed to have identical black gazes. Old women, bald women . . . No, not old. Prematurely aged. As Ally's eyes traveled along the line of skull-like faces, she realized that some of them—perhaps all of them—had been young. Before hunger shriveled them into death's-head parodies of themselves. And bald . . . No, not bald. Shorn. Their bumpy skulls were crisscrossed with lurid scratches where the hair had been shaved or pulled off. A forgotten tuft stuck out here and there.

The clearing was surrounded by the dense mass of thorny bushes that would not let even a mouse through.

Ally took a step forward. One of the women whose arms were buried in the soil up to her elbows stirred and pulled them out, shedding clumps of dirt. Her yellow skeletal fingers were tipped off with crooked claws as sharp and deadly as the talons of an eagle. Ally took another step. The woman hissed, opening a black mouth. Her tongue had been cut out.

Ally looked to the sides. No way could she push through the thicket of thorns. There were only two directions she could go: back or forward. Back to where the Red Horseman and the treacherous man-cat were hot on her heels. Or forward, though the barrier of claws.

She remembered how she had implored the cow in Little Mother's farmyard.

Dear ladies, fair and true
Open a way, let me through.

They gave no sign that they even heard, let alone were willing to oblige. Some of them were pulling themselves out of their soil beds, shaking off like dogs. They were frightfully thin, with xylophone ribs and sunken bellies. But their claws clicked and twitched, hungry for prey.

There was a flash of red at the end of the path.

She took the Victorinox knife out of her backpack. It lay in her hand like the toy that it was. How stupid had she been to believe that the trickster's gifts were anything but mockery?

One of the bald women staggered toward Ally, her taloned fingers reaching for her.

"Wait!" Ally tugged at her braid, pulled it free, let it slide down like a golden rope.

"Wait! Your hair has been stolen. I'll give you mine!"

And clicking open the knife, she hacked off the braid close to the nape of her head. Unwinding it, she tossed hunks of yellow hair toward the bald women.

The hags, forgetting about her, fought over the hair, clawing each other, tearing their desiccated bodies, splattering the thirsty soil with thick reluctant blood. They could not cry or scream but they hissed at each other with their empty cavernous maws.

A passage opened up in their disordered ranks and Ally sprinted through. A claw grazed her cheek, drawing blood, but she was already on the other side of the clearing, running on the path that led deeper into the darkening grove. She heard a horse's neighing and risking a glance back, saw the Red Horseman pulling short at the barrier of frantic bodies. Prince was nowhere to be seen, but Ally could not think about it as she ran and ran, the wind cold on her suddenly light head, tears in her eyes.

Chapter 8:
Birches and Oaks

At some point, she realized she needed to rest.

The black path led her to another part of the forest, this one composed of trees that Ally, though no botanist, found familiar. They were slender white-barked birches with sere, autumn-yellow leaves. Ally knew that birches were immortalized in many a song and tale of Northern Europe, but she did not like them. Their thin, peeling bark was unpleasantly reminiscent of human skin and their perpetual trembling, even though there was no wind, made it look like they were affected by palsy.

There was nothing around her but the black path, the red sky, and the white trees. But Ally felt hostile and amused eyes on her. She stopped and listened. The trees merged into a background of vertical strokes like an abstract painting, but nothing moved in its stippled depth. Ally touched a fissured trunk. The configuration of dark cracks made it look like a human face with a gaping mouth and only one eye. A withered leaf floated down, resting on her shorn head as if in mockery.

The light changed. Suddenly and with no warning, the thick, reddish clouds above her turned the color of spoiled milk. In the white dusk, the white birch-trunks faded into the background. Only the black path and the black markings on the trees stood out like threatening hieroglyphs scribbled on a dull parchment.

The White Horseman! Or rather, the one and only Horseman undergoing his periodic metamorphosis! At least it meant he was subject to some law, some *geis,* that he could not violate without violating his nature. So he would become the Black Horseman soon and that meant that darkness would descend, hiding Ally from pursuit. And giving her time to rest.

She would prefer to be out of the birch-grove by the time it happened but no matter how she hurried, the leprous trees still surrounded her. She only had the time to find a hollow by the side of the path as the darkness fell, so thick that Ally felt blinded. . There was not a glimmer of light in the dull sky. Of course: the Horseman blocked off the sun and moon and stars. They had never shone above Little Mother's farmyard. But there the fiery fence-sitters had provided illumination. Here, Ally had to wait until the Horseman took on his white persona.

She lay down but could not find a good position to rest. The humid soil stank: a meaty, salty smell. Ally could not stand it, and so she sat up again, leaning against a birch trunk. It vibrated with a rhythmic beat. Ally tried to tell herself it was her own heartbeat.

She had no appetite, but she knew she had to keep up her strength. She groped inside her backpack, dug out the water-bottle and an energy bar, unwrapped the bar and cautiously bit into it. The bar tasted like cardboard, which, presumably, meant it was untainted by anything more dangerous than GMOs. It would sustain her for a while. She tried to force herself to fall asleep but could not.

She smoothed down the ragged ends of her now-short hair. And then tears came again, so powerful that she doubled over, pressed her hand to her mouth to gag the sobs that something might hear in the dark.

The hair would grow back, she kept telling herself. It would grow back.

But what am I without it?

No looks. No mother, no brother, no country. No husband.

I will bring him back.

And live happily ever after?

There was nothing to do but patiently endure the mockery of her own thoughts circling in her head like a flock of cackling crows. Eventually, she grew so weary that she fell asleep. And woke up to the redness in the sky.

Ally drank a little more water, ate another energy bar, and started walking. White birches still surrounded her, their black-tipped bare branches tracing unreadable scribbles on the inflamed clouds. But there was a change, albeit so gradual that she only noticed it when the imperceptible accumulation of small things tipped over into an abrupt shift in the landscape.

Nightwood

Ally stopped and stared at the close trunks fencing in the path. What had been just an impression yesterday—or before the Black Horseman, at any rate—was an indisputable fact now.

The trees had faces.

Poking out from the gnarly boles like cancerous growths, swathed in rags of filmy bark, wooden faces, their mouths—black gaping holes, their eyes—bulging nodes or tiny slits, open wide or screwed shut in paroxysms of pain. Burl faces like bas-reliefs. Old and young. But women, all women.

Faces of mute, dumb, patient suffering.

Trembling, Ally touched the nearest one, expecting to encounter the softness of flesh. Her fingers brushed the silky smoothness of birch bark. But the face—it was of an older woman, fissured by the cracks of wrinkles—twitched slightly like a cat dreaming. Ally backed off and collided with another human-faced tree on the opposite side of the path. The birch trembled, showering her with twigs, and an almost-human voice groaned. Ally whirled around and saw the peeling visage of a young woman strain on the bole, its mouth working. It was trying to open its eyes but they were covered by moss. And throughout this seemingly endless grove of corpse-white trees, wooden faces were awakening, twitching and crying out in thin inarticulate voices, branches whipping around in the still air as a storm of torment blasted through the grove.

Ally ran.

She slowed when her peripheral vision registered an alteration in the sullen ambient light. Breathing heavily, she sat down to get over the stitch in her side.

She was still surrounded by trees, the black path still unwound in front of her in an endless ribbon, but the forest had changed once again. Squat, knotty trees, their charcoal-grey bark deeply scoured with cracks and fissures, crowded along the path, their sturdy branches overhanging it and filtering away most of the already dim light. In the scarlet gloom, their many-fingered leaves looked black. Ally recognized the characteristic oak shape. The ground was broken by grotesquely eroded boulders and littered with giant acorns.

Ally peered fearfully at the closest oak but there was no human face formed by its tough bark. She listened, but the silence of the forest was so deep that she could hear the hum of blood in her own veins.

Had the Red Horseman given up on his pursuit? And where was Prince now? She strained her eyes, trying to discern a stealthy feline shape moving in the gloom, but there was nothing.

What had Slug and Fest said? She would have to pass through the bald-women barrier. Well, she had done so. Ally's hand automatically went to her shorn head, but she forced it down.

Why had the bald women been there in the first place? Ally racked her brain but could not remember any such folkloric motif. Instead, she had an unwelcome recollection of having read some book describing concentration camps and piles of cut hair being used for knitting socks.

All fairy tales had been history once.

Well, what else was she to expect? Slug and Fest had mentioned wolves. She listened but heard nothing, not even the soughing of the wind.

The *sousliks'* encampment. Tiny bodies, caught in the midst of transformation and ripped apart. Her brother's tribe, slaughtered. The lewd faces of the men in the forest, stupidity blended with cruelty.

"You'll pay for this!" she whispered to the Ogre in her mind.

She drunk from the water bottle, noting that her supply was running low. Perhaps she would run across a creek or a spring—preferably with no animal or bird markings around.

The ground was flat, and the oppressive crowding of the trees made Ally feel as if she were locked up in a small room. She swore to herself that when Carl was back, she would make him sell the house in the woods. They could move into a mansion on the Peninsula or into a townhouse in San Francisco. She tried to visualize their life together, surrounded by all the comforts of civilization—and could not. Nothing was real except this: the red sky, the black forest, the sick dread in her bones.

Ally forced herself to walk on. She stepped on something slick, lost her footing and was pitched forward, just avoiding being impaled on a protruding oak branch.

What the hell? She looked down: one of those bloody acorns! They littered the naked soil so thickly that there were whole piles of them under each tree. Were it a normal forest, there would be animals all over the place munching on this bounty. Didn't wild boars love acorns? And bears too. These babies were so fat that just a couple of them would provide a decent meal for any omnivore.

Nightwood

Wait a second! Ally peered at the brown-yellow oval nut cradled in a spiky cupule. It was as big as her hand—no, bigger! Weren't acorns supposed to be small?

She pushed it with the tip of her shoe. The acorn rolled over, wobbling, and disclosed its underside. Ally's hand flew to her mouth.

There was a face on the other side of the acorn: a miniature face, like that of a doll, only nobody would make a doll with the rugged, heavy features of a boxer, his nose smashed, his brow split. And even if they did—what doll would have its toothless mouth working so desperately, trying to get a word out?

Ally bit off a scream. She knew that making a loud sound here, in this grove of silent trees laden with a crop of angry faces was a very bad idea.

The huge acorns were all around her, scattered among the stumpy trees like billiard balls, covering the black ground in puddles of sickly yellow and dull brown. Some of them were rotting, settling into the mulch, but even they had faces that tried to move their disintegrating lips and open their missing eyes. The grove was big and every tree was fruitful with pain. Even as she watched, another acorn fell off a near oak and rolled onto the path, its face scrounged up in the grimace of impotent rage, its small mouth torn by the inaudible scream. It was a man's face too; and as Ally looked around, not wanting to yet unable to un-see what she had already seen, she realized all acorns were male. Faces glared at her from the gloom, twisted with rage and impotent lust. And now she could smell it: what she had taken for the reek of rotting oak leaves at first but now knew for the salty stink of unwashed masculinity.

Ally fell to her knees on the path, images she had worked so hard to forget flooding her brain.

A man's rough hand on her breast.

The acrid stench of smoke.

Pretty girl!

Hair like Rapunzel.

Shlucha!

Mama! Where is my mama?

"No!" she said loudly, no longer afraid of breaking the silence. "No!"

A rustling of leaves, a clatter of falling acorns.

Ally got up, shouldered her backpack, and with one kick, sent an acorn off the path and into the dimness under the trees.

"Fuck you!" she said. "Go and rot! I am Ally Morris now!"

And she went on, smiling to herself because she had said it in English.

Chapter 9:
Sleeping Dogs

The oak grove ended quite abruptly. Ally saw the fever light seeping through the opening at the end of the tree-lined tunnel. So, she was still in the domain of the Red Horseman! Well, there was nothing she could do about it. But she would be glad to be out of the tangle of oaks hung with enraged male faces and stinking of old sweat. Acorns mouthed obscenities at her; those still attached to their branches trembled violently as if trying to shake themselves loose. Some succeeded in detaching themselves from their stems and flying through the air. But once away from the tree, they were subject to the law of gravity and plummeted straight down, harmlessly embedding themselves in the soil and covering the forest floor with their comically-cupped heads. There was nothing comical, though, about their demented expressions that would undoubtedly find an outlet in a flood of foul language—if they could make a sound. Where oak branches overhung the path, some acorns managed to aim themselves at Ally. Her head, no longer protected by the wreath of braids, got hit a couple of times. Another acorn snapped its tiny teeth at her as it dropped on the ground. Ally gave it the finger. The acorns on the ground tried to roll into her way but she kicked them away, deriving enormous satisfaction from the way they flew helplessly through the air. She would like to smash their wooden skulls, grind their angry faces into the dirt, but something stopped her.

She reached the edge of the oak grove and peered out cautiously, still keeping to the shadow of the trees and disregarding the squirming of acorn-heads above.

There was another clearing ahead. Beyond it, the woods began again, though they were quite different from the somber tangle of the oaks. Even in the uncertain light, they seemed airier and more open. But Ally could not focus on them. Her gaze was riveted to what was in the clearing.

Covering the trampled soil like a shaggy carpet was a large pack of wolves.

They lay in untidy heaps of large paws, scruffy gray coats, and twitching tails. A cloud of gnats and flies hovered in the air above the furry bodies. Occasionally, an ear would perk up like an antenna and then subside. Their hot carnivorous stink wafted toward Ally.

She pulled back into the oaks, angrily swiping away at a falling acorn that dealt her a glancing blow on the cheek. She had no desire to stay among the crop of psychotic faces, but neither was she ready to brave the wolves. Her horror of the human-canine predators came back in full force. Last time she had confronted them she had had Ivan at her side and her magic weapons to wage battle with. Now Ivan was dead, and she had no weapons.

No, not quite true. She had the things Prince had given her: the knife, the stoppered vial, and the key. She had already used the knife, though not for the purpose Prince said it was intended: to cut off the Ogre's head. Well, she was not fool enough to trust a trickster's gifts! But what was she to do now?

Ally watched the wolves. They were indeed asleep: she could see the rhythmic rise and fall or their lice-infested chests. Their eyes were closed. But surely predators sleep lightly! She counted the wolves: ten. Far too many to try to fight with a Victorinox knife. And if they shifted into their human form. Ally shuddered and squinted into the bloody murk. Yes, there was a glint of glass among the supine forms. Some—perhaps all—of them had bottles on lanyards around their necks.

Perhaps she could just go around the clearing. The black path continued through the lighter woods on the other side.

Ally started sidling off into the oaks that grew so closely together that even her slight body could hardly fit into the gaps between the squat boles. Still, it seemed she could make it.

Smack!

A hard ball hit her head. And then another and another. Acorns showered her like a hailstorm. Here, away from the path, with the oak branches tangled above her head in a near-impenetrable canopy, it was not just an occasional hit. She was pummeled by an avalanche of acorns that were getting bigger and bigger the farther she deviated from the path. Some of them were almost big enough to brain her. And these were not inanimate objects, obeying the impersonal law of gravity. There was malice in their blows, a deliberate desire to humiliate and hurt. Their rotting mouths gaped in derisive laughter.

An acorn as big as an ostrich egg whistled past her, the shredded lips squirming. It hit a boulder and split apart, bloody jelly oozing out. Ally rushed back to the path.

The bombardment slowed but did not cease. The wolves were getting restive. One of them opened a bloodshot eye, blinked a couple of times, and closed it again, subsiding into slumber. But how long before they woke up? Even if she ran back the way she had come, they would come in pursuit, following her spoor.

Think, Alyona!

Yes, Alyona. These were the monsters of her childhood, the creatures of her native nightmares.

Your real name is Alyona, Prince had said. *It'll never change. Your name has power.*

What an idiot she had been to listen to a trickster, a traitor!

But even traitors had their uses.

Ally opened her backpack. She had used the knife for the opposite purpose than its intended one: to cut off her own head, metaphorically speaking, rather than her enemy's.

Her hand touched the slick glass of the vial.

The sleeping potion.

The wolves were already asleep.

Ally pulled out the stopper and drank the content of the vial in a single gulp.

It tasted like nothing: a single swallow of cold nothingness that entered her body and dissipated before she could become properly afraid.

She stepped into the clearing.

The wolves twitched and groaned in their sleep as she passed between and over them, as light-footed as a dream. They panted, their wet scarlet tongues hanging out of their stinky maws. But they did not smell her. If they saw her at all, it was in their mind's eye, as a prey to hunt, to bring down and tear to pieces—not before having some fun with her in their human form. But dreams are dreams. A brain, whether human or canine, knows the difference and sends a signal to the muscles to relax, not to pursue a phantom. And they did not.

Ally passed through the ranks of sleeping wolves and sped on the black path. Toward the Castle With No Windows.

Chapter 10:
The Bleeding Grove

Beyond the wolves' clearing, the woods changed drastically. Airy and sparse, the trees fell away from the path that stood out against the green forest floor covered with ferns and moss. Tangled aromatic shrubs grew here and there but otherwise the woods were spacious and quiet. No grimacing acorns, no burly faces.

Ally examined the nearest trees. They were familiar but not like the birch and the oak—the uncanny familiarity of a childhood fairy-tale-induced nightmare. Those trees belonged to a much more recent stage of her life. Though she did not know all of their names, they seemed to smile at her like old friends. Madrone, bay laurel, manzanita, larch; trees of California. The bloody light was clotting into near-dusk, as the Red Horseman was getting ready for his next metamorphosis, but she could see graceful towering silhouettes against the scarlet sky. Redwoods.

So here she was, back in California, or rather back in Nightwood's version of California. She should not trust it any more than the Nightwood versions of the Slavic steppe or of the German Black Forest, but she was happy to see the bushes and trees of her mountain home. An immigrant's happiness. She touched a redwood's fissured bark. It did not twitch, did not try to speak, did not bite back. As far as she could see, these were just ordinary trees.

It was still here with the silence of deep woods, filled with almost imperceptible but soothing noises: the crack of a falling branch; the rustling of leaves in a small gust of wind; a whisper of ferns, and the gentle pitter-patter of tree drip.

Ally almost ran on the path. She had a strong feeling the Red

Horseman was about to turn black and she wanted to make as much progress as she could before it got dark.

Here they were: redwoods. The giants that had so spooked her on her first drive into the mountains. Ally stopped and threw back her head, looking up into the gently swaying furry branches against the darkening sky. A drop fell onto her face, and she swiped it away. Rain? The sky was so uniformly scarlet that it was impossible to say if there were clouds or not. But Ally did not want to be in the open if the capricious weather of Nightwood decided to unleash a thunderstorm. Redwoods' attenuated canopy provided no shelter.

The light changed.

It did not grow dark; just the opposite. The Red Horseman became the White One.

With a blinding speed, the color of the sky changed to that of a dusty lampshade: dirty-white with streaks of beige. The illumination was lifeless, leaching colors from the woods. The green of the undergrowth became grey; the tracery of branches— black. But the columns of redwoods stood out in wet scarlet against the dull background.

Ally touched her face, looked at the red stain on her fingertips.

The tree-drip intensified; now the entire grove reverberated with the plinking sound of falling drops. Ally remembered her mornings in the glass house. Coastal fog, blanketing the redwoods in moisture. Puddles on the forest floor.

The puddles were red. Every twig, every branch, every bough leaked a slow but unending stream of thick, clotted liquid that gathered in reluctant streams, crawled through the undergrowth, pooled in scarlet ponds. The bark glistened with seeping sores.

The redwoods were bleeding.

And now the smell hit her, and Ally fell to her knees, retching, her stomach trying to turn itself inside out. She vomited until there was nothing left inside her, and yet even this was not enough. She wanted to empty herself out. Like the little girl who threw up when her mother put a meatball onto her plate; the little girl who suddenly realized that she was asked to eat the corpse of a living creature. The little girl named Alyona.

Had she known about the Bleeding Grove? Had she dreamed of it?

Get up. One foot forward. Then another.

Mama's voice.

Walk.

This is how we survive.

What cannot be cured must be endured.

Ally walked through the serried ranks of bleeding trees, the blood drip falling onto her shorn head.

The White Horseman did not change, keeping to his light incarnation through the interminable time it took her to traverse the Bleeding Grove. Did he expect her to be shattered by the sight? If so, he had miscalculated. Atrocities have a way of becoming ordinary.

Nothing changed for miles. Flayed redwoods; gore-soaked ground; a drip of blood.

Boring.

And then it loomed ahead. The Castle With No Windows.

Her house.

Chapter 11:
The Castle With No Windows

The glass walls looked opaque, glistening like a snake's scales. The bleeding redwoods surrounded it like sentries, their tops hidden by coils of fog. The fog also wreathed the top of the building, obscuring its true dimensions. But it was, unmistakably, the same house Carl had brought his Ukrainian bride to.

Of course.

There were no windows because the entire house was one giant window.

Ally stood at the entrance to the driveway. Was she to walk like a beggar to her own house, knock on the door, and plead to be let in?

But was it really her house? Had it ever been?

Legally, yes. But had it ever been a home?

What was home? The tiny apartment she had grown up in with Mama? The apartment soaked in the smells of tobacco, booze, and humiliation? The apartment she had been so happy to sell before leaving for the US: like a snake shedding her skin, becoming something else, something new?

Was it possible for people to change their identity? Was it ever possible for an Alyona to become an Ally?

She went down the driveway and stopped.

Slouching by the front door was Prince.

He was in his human form, wearing the same nondescript jeans and t-shirt he had had on when he was about to deliver Ally to the Red Horseman. The expression on his face, when he finally looked up at Ally, was dejected, but his eyes were still those of a cat: remote and inscrutable.

"So, you made it here," he said. "Congratulations."

Nightwood

"No thanks to you," Ally spat at him. "Traitor! Double-dealer! You tried to sell me to the Horseman, didn't you? 'Prince who wanted to be King'. Ha! More like a scruffy cat licking his master's hand!"

"My master is your master too," Prince responded.

"What's that supposed to mean?"

"Do you really think you could have escaped from the farmyard, crossed the three Dragon Rivers and outwitted the wolves all on your own? Do you believe you could just stroll through the Bleeding Grove, if its owner did not tell its guardians to go easy on you? Do you think Nightwood is some stupid Disneyland where the heroine slays all monsters with a wink and a song? Don't be an idiot, Alyona. He wanted you here from the very beginning. And here you are. I was just a helper. There are requests you cannot refuse if you want to live."

Ally's knees went weak.

"Why would the Ogre want me here?"

"You'd have to ask him," Prince said.

She shrugged and put her hand on the familiar door handle.

"So, I will."

Prince bent closer, his hot breath tickling her ear.

"Don't do it!" he whispered. "If you cross this threshold, you'll never come back. I'm just a cat but there are things that are too bad even for me. If you turn around, I can delay him. You can get back to California. Slugfest will help. And then just run away as far as you can and keep running."

She looked into his inscrutable animal eyes.

The glittering glass wall above them seemed to be visibly growing, elongating, and piercing the lowering sky so it loomed above them like a crystal cliff.

The lesson of fairy tales. Never open the door into the bloody chamber. Never eat the forbidden fruit. Never ask questions that are better left unanswered.

"Who is the Ogre?" she asked.

Prince shook his head.

"I cannot tell you."

"So, I'll find out myself," Ally said. "Out of my way!"

She pushed the doorhandle.

And stepped into a vertiginously strange space.

And saw a man striding toward her.

"Hello, Alyonushka," he said.

Chapter 12:
The Ogre

She had subconsciously expected the interior of the Castle to be like her house. But it was not.

She stood in a chilly stone hall, its granite walls weeping moisture, the floor under her feet flagged and worn. The glass of the outside was just a decoy. The hall had no windows and was illuminated by spluttering torches set into iron brackets. The ceiling was lost in gloom, arching high above the railed gallery. It was vaguely medieval: more like the popular concept of a fairytale castle than anything she had seen in Nightwood so far.

There were some obscure banners hanging from the walls and a grand staircase spiraled down from the gallery. A man was walking down, smiling, his hand outstretched.

Ally gulped. The horror of her premonition dissipated so quickly that she did not know how to react.

When Prince told her that the Ogre wanted her here it was as if a bright light went on in her head, illuminating the shadowy landscape of her memories, so that it made a perfectly terrible sense.

She had gone into Nightwood to find Carl because she believed he had been drawn into the bloody tangle of old tales by his dead wife's *geis*. But how well had she really known her husband? She had never loved him; she had gone on this quest out of the sense of obligation and the need to create a new identity for herself. What if the entire thing had been some elaborate and malicious setup? What if Carl Morris had been in league with the dead wife of his youth, with his witchy neighbors and with his own enchanted house?

What if Carl *was* the Ogre?

For the duration of several heartbeats that felt as long as hours, Ally had been sure that the master of the Castle who would step out to welcome her into his lair would be her own husband. And so, the sight of the man who was walking down the staircase toward her hit her like a blow because he was a stranger.

He was a trim, slender, middle-aged man, not exactly attractive, but there was something arresting about his angular face, his small thin mouth that stretched into a smile, and his deep-set eyes under heavy brows. He was going bald. His remaining hair was salt-and-pepper; but his light step and muscular body seemed to belong to a much younger man. He wore a uniform of some kind, but Ally was so focused on his face that the details of his attire blurred together.

She had never seen him in her entire life, she was sure of that. And yet, and yet . . .

"Hello, Alyona," he repeated.

"Hello," she said, her voice croaky. "Who are you?"

"I am your father," he said.

Ally stood in front of a large mirror, admiring herself. She had been dirty, scruffy, wearing torn travel clothes for so long that she had almost forgotten how beautiful she was.

The long dress with a bell-shaped crinoline skirt cinched tightly at the waist, making Ally's slender figure look as fragile and shapely as a flower. The dress shimmered in layers of dark and light gold decorated with stiff golden lace. The square décolleté, revealing just as much of Ally's modest bust as to create the impression that there was more, was trimmed in gold braid. Bronze-colored satin shoes peeped from under the froth of apricot petticoats. She shone like the sun in the soothing dimness of her opulent bedroom.

She closed the clasp of her necklace. The stones were pink diamonds set in the elaborate golden filigree. The matching earrings dangled from her earlobes. She had done the best she could with her short hair, sweeping it off her face and dressing it with a black velvet band embroidered with golden sunbursts. Her father had been disappointed when he saw her shorn head, but he was a true gentleman about it, saying only that the hair would grow back in no time.

An officer and a gentleman . . .
You are an officer's daughter.
"Call me Alexander," he had said.
"Is it really your name? Is my patronymic true?"
"It is true."
The room was like the princess's room in the Cinderella illustrated book she had devoured as a child: sumptuous and baroque, glittering with lavish embroidery, gilt and precious stones. She realized why she had never felt at home in Carl's glass mansion. No matter how expensive the furnishings, it was too modern, too streamlined, too soulless. Deep inside, she was a simple Ukrainian girl whose idea of luxury came from stately 19th century homes.

The Castle had all the splendor and none of its discomforts. A fairytale magic took care of everyday conveniences. There was no electricity but, apart from the entry hall, there were no guttering candles or smelly torches. An even glow permeated every corner, coming from nowhere in particular; Ally's face bathed in its peachy warmth.

She pivoted gracefully and walked toward the door, the silk of her dress and the chiffon of her petticoats billowing gently around her, carrying her on soft waves.

Her father waited outside. He offered her his arm and they descended the main staircase into the dining room. The illumination was a fraction brighter than in her bedroom but just as warm and diffuse. There were no windows, of course, but heavy wine-colored draperies masked the stone walls. The long table was set with an array of dishes that made her mouth water. She was starving but it was unladylike to show too much eagerness.

He led her to her seat and only sat after she did. He poured some ruby-red wine into a crystal goblet.

"Is this really gold?" she asked with childlike wonder, twirling a salad fork between her fingers.

"Of course. Nothing is too good for my daughter."

She smiled at him. They clinked the goblets and she sipped the wine. *Merlot,* she thought, and then her Californian experience of the wine country kicked in. *No, not really. A little too sweet.*

She studied her father's face from under her modestly lowered lashes, trying to see a family resemblance. It was there, actually. The more she looked, the more she saw: the delicate but firm jawline, the straight nose. His eyes, once you looked deeply into them, were almost the same color as hers: blue-grey.

They always said I looked like Mama.

She squashed the thought.

The invisible servitors started bringing in the dishes: golden trays whose covers they removed with a flourish, revealing jewel-colored salads and steamed vegetables. A loaf of freshly baked bread and a dish of freshly churned butter, sunflower-yellow.

Her father piled her plate with food.

"You are too thin" he said. "Put some meat on those beautiful bones."

She smiled gratefully. It had been a long time since anybody was worried about her wellbeing.

Her father had a good appetite as well, though his neat figure belied any suspicion of gluttony. He was still dressed in the same uniform he had greeted her in. She tried to figure out what, if any, country or army it belonged to but could not. It looked vaguely old-fashioned with gold braids and epaulettes, but her knowledge of military history was minimal. She decided not to worry about it.

"You look so beautiful, Alyona," he said. "I waited for so long to see how my little girl has turned out. But it was worth the wait."

She smiled again, feeling a blush spread over her neck and cheeks. It did not bother her: she knew it suited her fair complexion.

"Thank you, Daddy," she said, reveling in this word she had not said in her entire life. He smiled back and lifted his goblet to his lips.

"You may call me Alexander," he said. "But Daddy will do too."

It felt wrong to call your father by his given name. Disrespectful. Mama had been very strict about it. She had always been Mama, never Oksana. But Daddy did not sound right either. She rolled it on her tongue silently and realized what was off.

They were speaking in English.

Or was it her necklace making it sound like this? She lifted her hand to her neck, touched the intricate whorls of gold filigree. Of course, the cross necklace had plummeted to the bottom of the Third Dragon River with her brother's corpse. But was this one magic as well?

The wine buzz in her head receded. She gulped down some water.

"Alexander," she said, stumbling a little over that name, suddenly familiar in a strange, elusive, and faintly unpleasant way. "Are you . . . from here? I mean . . . California? The US?"

He laughed uproariously, as if she had made a hilarious joke.

"Not really," he said, switching to flawless Ukrainian. "I just wanted to see how my investment had paid off."

"Your investment?"

"How do you think your mother could afford private English tutoring for you?"

Ally stared at him, cold-sober all of a sudden.

"You paid for my English?"

"Yes. And it was money well spent, Alyonushka. You would have never made it to Berkeley otherwise. And as for your academic interests—this was fortuitous. A pretty woman does not need a PhD but it smoothed things over."

"But why? Why did you want me here?"

He lifted his hand.

"Enough for now," he said, and there was steel in his voice. Ally almost flinched as some invisible whip lashed—not quite at her but close enough to feel a cold breeze on her cheek. "No more questions. Let's celebrate our reunion."

He made a beckoning gesture, and the invisible servants came back into the dining room, bearing another course. It looked like serving plates and tureens simply floated in, but Ally knew that they were borne in by actual hands, though whether human or not, she was not sure. She wondered whether her father's domestic staff was larger than Prince's and decided it must be. She had already realized that her father did not like competition.

The trays and tureens were deposited on the snow-white tablecloth and the covers removed with a flourish. Aromatic steam rose into the air and Ally gagged.

One course was roast beef. Another—medium-rare steaks with all the trimmings. Still another tray held what looked suspiciously like venison.

"To your good health!" her father toasted, refilling her goblet. "Try all of it—it's delicious!"

Ally scraped a dollop of mashed potatoes off the side of the roast beef, avoiding the gravy.

"It does look delicious," she said. "But I am a vegetarian."

Alexander's thick brows met over his nose as he frowned.

"Forget this nonsense!" he commanded. "This is just what stupid girls do. I expected better from my daughter! What are you, anorexic?"

"I am not," Ally replied mildly, lifting a forkful of potatoes to her mouth. "But I don't eat meat. I never have."

"Not here!" he thundered. "You are in your father's house! You'll do what I tell you to do!"

"I know, Daddy," she replied. "It is your house and your rules. But I don't eat meat. And I won't start now."

They stared at each other for what seemed to Ally like a very long time. Again, the faint sense of familiarity touched her, now stronger than before.

Her father's lips twitched, and he lowered his head, staring into his plate. Then he got up, almost overturning his chair, and thundered out of the room.

She lay in her princess bed, the cool satiny sheets caressing her body. The light in her bedroom had sunk into a pleasant ambient luminescence when she had walked in. She was glad: she did not want to be in the dark. She could just imagine how the Castle With No Windows would be if all the lights had gone out; as black as the grave.

Ally's gaze flickered to the door. She had latched it but there was no lock.

She had nothing to be afraid of, she told herself. What was safer than your father's house?

How do you know he is really your father?

"*I do*," she answered her acerbic inner voice. "*He is my father. He looks like me.*"

He did, actually, far more so than Ivan. She had accepted Ivan's claim of their kinship with no doubt. Was it because Ivan had been such a guileless, open, and sunny person?

And now he was dead.

Ivan had said they had the same mother, but he had said nothing about their father—or fathers. Ally tried to remember whether this question had ever arisen in their conversations and could not. Probably, she conceded bitterly, because she assumed that Ivan's father had been some nameless one-night-stand. Mama aborted her son, after all; but had birthed, educated and taken care of her daughter.

You are an officer's daughter.

An officer of what army?

He paid money for my education.

Ally had started her private tutoring at the age of five. The tutor—a dour university professor forced to supplement her meager governmental salary with private lessons—kept up their biweekly meetings until Ally was eleven. Six years. And then one day, Mama got a phone call and took Ally aside to tell her that Olga Vasylievna had a heart attack and was not coming back. Ally was upset because the teacher had been an important part of her life for so long. She genuinely enjoyed their English conversations, which often culminated in Olga pulling a collection of fairy tales from her bookshelves and reading out a story of Three Oranges or Jack the Giant Killer. Sometimes she would loan the book to Ally with strict warnings not to read it at the dinner table, which Ally routinely ignored. But then she was growing up, seeing her future options narrowing down into following in Mama's footsteps—and where those footsteps led. So, the tutor was quickly forgotten.

It came to her in a flash of belated revelation that Mama must have had enough money to pay for six years of private lessons—at the time when her only legitimate jobs were of a cashier-cum-cleaner variety, while her illegitimate occupation, as Ally learned later from bitter personal experience, would cover cigarettes, vodka and bread-and-butter at most. Had the money come from Alexander? Hadn't Mama told her that her father had been killed in Afghanistan, in the war that ended with the collapse of the USSR?

What the hell was she thinking? Ally sat up in bed, tossing away the padded-silk coverlet. What was wrong with her? What Afghanistan? What USSR? She was in bloody Nightwood, the land of timeless stories. And her father was alive. And he was no Soviet Army officer. He was, he was . . .

She refused to think the name.

She swung her legs over the side of the bed. The mattress was so soft that she had practically sunk into it. It felt like sleeping on the clouds of paradise after innumerable nights spent in the rough. Now she was beginning to be disgusted by it and the long lacy nightgown that clung to her like exploring hands, gently constraining her movements.

Nightwood

The princess and the pea.

She padded into the bathroom that was thoroughly modern, with a flush toilet and a clawed-foot giant tub. An array of cosmetics lined the marble counters. She picked up a shampoo bottle from a well-known French company, the same brand she used to buy in Westfield Mall.

Nightwood was not separated from the world of history.

All stories were history once.

Ally perched on the side of the tub and forced herself to remember.

The butchered bodies in Little Mother's house. The company of men-wolves making obscene jokes about three frightened little girls. The slaughter in the *sousliks'* camp. The *asanbosam* carrying Malika away. Ivan's blood on her hands. The bleeding trees. Prince's shifty, frightened gaze.

The Ogre had taken possession of Nightwood and was perverting its nature, gathering and amplifying its darkness, stomping out the sparks of hope and courage that always shone through the gloom of even the oldest and most barbaric tales. No longer content to be the repository of dreams, Nightwood under his rule was becoming the breeding-ground of nightmares.

And it was no longer safely insulated from the physical world. As she had discovered in California, Nightwood was spreading, sending its tendrils into the houses and minds of the rich and powerful. Instead of stories arising out of the residue of history, stories were *becoming* history.

The history of bloodshed.

And her father was at the center of it. In the Castle With No Windows that was swollen with darkness like a fat tick gorged with blood.

Ally jumped off the tub, fired by the irresistible impulse to do *something*, to demand an explanation, to confront the man who had sired her. If he was, or had been, a man . . .

And then the lights in her suite went out.

Chapter 13.
On Being a Bird

Eric discovered that being a swan was a terrible way to live.

His body ached all the time. His wings throbbed with dull fatigue after each flight. Every night when he tried to find a marginally comfortable position to sleep by tucking his head under his wing, the vertebrae in his long neck cracked like the joints of an old man. The ticks crawling in his plumage drove him to distraction. Water-lilies gave him indigestion and once when he swallowed a frisky frog, the riot in his stomach made him wish for death, or at least a bottle of Tums.

He had never given much thought to animals, being a techie through and through, but if asked, he would have probably responded with the usual platitudes of the Californian eco-culture about natural harmony and peaceful co-existence of all living things. Now he discovered that struggle for existence was no metaphor. Every day was a struggle; and it was one he was not winning.

The thing he was most afraid of was losing his mind. How long could a human mind fit comfortably into a bird's brain? Fairy tales never discussed the neuropsychology of human-animal transformation but for Eric it had become a matter of life and death. He would rather die than be deprived of his intellect. So he tried to make sure that he retained his edge by running lines of code in his head, or replaying his best sessions of Warhammer, or trying to remember as many digits of pi as he could. He thought he was doing pretty well but how was he to know?

Fortunately, his bird body knew the basics of survival, or he would have undoubtedly smashed himself to bits during his escape from the mine of ashes. His mind went into a total blackout as his powerful wings beat the dusty air, carrying him away from that ghastly place. If his eyes provided any visual input, he was too far gone into shock to process it.

He finally came to—more or less—when the field of ashes was far behind, suspended above a checked expanse of light and dark green. Suspended? No. He was actually being carried by a flying thing . . . and then he realized the flying thing was himself.

He did not think of the bird body as his own. It was a contraption, an organic machine, and he was imprisoned in it. He likened his situation to his favorite anime: *The Ghost in the Shell*. It gave him a measure of comfort.

His sensations were incredibly weird. At the beginning, the flapping of his wings felt as if he was energetically pumping his arms up and down. Instinctively, he tried to increase the tempo, as if he were in a gym, only to discover that it made him list and keel over. So, he let the wings do their work.

When fatigue finally made him realize he would drop out of the sky if he kept on flying, he folded his wings—and then he was indeed dropping like a stone, his beak gaping in a silent scream.

Finally, he landed with a bone-shattering jolt and tried to take a step, only to find out that he had to move two stunted clownish appendages if he wanted to walk on land. Eric had been proud of his speed as a runner. Looking down at those leathery splayed feet filled him with revulsion.

And food. He had had no idea what swans ate. He would not be surprised to find out he had to subsist on a diet of worms. But when he saw the succulent water plants dotting the placid surface of the lake, his mouth filled with saliva—birds do have saliva, he discovered—and before he could make a rational decision, he was gobbling up crunchy stems that tasted of nutmeg and plump roots. He tried to avoid crawling insects and amphibians, but one or two frogs found a way into his stomach. At least he did not have to chew their slimy bodies.

The lake was beautiful. Surrounded by mountains, it was shaped like an elongated comma, with the narrow end petering out into a cane-dotted marsh. On the wide sire, emerald-leafed larches, parasol-shaped pines and berry-laden bushes came down to the water margin like a spillover from the curly green mantle of the mountains. The shallows were overgrown with pink and mauve waterlilies whose floury roots provided the mainstay of Eric's diet. Still, he was not so far gone into the survival mode as not to appreciate their beauty. Their colors seemed unearthly vibrant to him and he remembered reading something about the sharpness of bird eyes. Or could he now see in ultraviolet?

After a couple of days, with the first shock of his transformation wearing off, Eric was confronted with the question of what to do next. He had escaped certain death. That much was clear. But living out his life as a big ungainly water-bird was out of the question. He had to regain his humanity. But how?

The worst thing was that there was no magic in Nightwood or at least none that corresponded to his ideas derived from fat fantasy volumes and video games. There were no spells, talismans or rings of power. How had he become a bird? Had it been the fervency of his desire to escape? Or the squashed rubber bird he had found in the field of ashes? Or the words of the psalm running through his head as he confronted the Red Horseman? Well, his desire to regain his humanity was apparently not strong enough to shed as much as a single feather in his wings. The rubber toy was lost; and though he repeated the few Biblical lines he remembered from his bar-mitzvah in his head, they had no effect whatsoever.

Eric realized he would have to fly away from his lake sanctuary and seek out—what? He did not know. He had come to Nightwood with the ridiculously chivalric idea of saving Ally. Now he needed to save himself.

And still he lingered at the lake, telling himself he needed to build up his strength and to learn how to live in his alien body if he were to undertake a long journey. But the truth was that he was afraid. What he had witnessed in Nightwood seared itself into his consciousness. The wasteland of bones; the field of ashes; the casual cruelty of human wolves; the impenetrable blankness of the Red Horseman as he sent people to their deaths. The horror was not of strangeness but of familiarity. He had read about such things in books about the two world wars and heard about them from his grandparents. Was there no refuge from history even in fairy tales?

Apparently not; and he had to learn how to survive in this junkyard of nightmares. Eric had almost psyched himself into taking a long flight, reconnoitering his surroundings, when a troop of female swans landed at the narrow end of his lake.

He hid himself behind a stand of horsetails, observing them

suspiciously. He did not know how he knew they were female—they were roughly the same size as himself and the human metrics of breasts and hips were, of course, irrelevant—but he had no doubt. He even felt a slight stirring in his nether regions and was horrified, not least because, birds and bees notwithstanding, the mechanics of avian sex were a total mystery to him.

The pens—as Eric remembered female swans are called—were five in number and a mix of white and dappled. One of them was pure black with a coral beak. Eric's plumage was white, but he had always admired Australian black swans and this one was uncommonly graceful, the sleek feathers on her long neck glistening like obsidian. He kept looking at her, even as the rest of the pens dipped their heads into the sunset-rose water, dragging out tangles of vegetation.

Having eaten their dinner, the pens got out of the water and waddled toward the marsh. He barely restrained himself from running after them. The loneliness of his situation was intolerable; and here was company! But could he even talk to them? Was there a swan language? Were these magnificent creatures dumb birds or intelligent beings like himself?

The last question, at least, was soon answered.

There was a tiny bubbling spring in the marsh, surrounded by deposits of ochre mud. The pens approached it in a single file and the first one lowered her snake-like neck, drinking from the spring. Eric had just one second of astonishment—he had assumed waterbirds did not need special water-sources—when a violent shudder went through the pen's body. She dropped to the ground, writhing, as the rest watched. Her body contorted, her wings beating a rapid tattoo upon the ground, her neck whipping around, and then her outline blurred in the honey sunset light, the feathers sloughing off . . . and a woman stood up, nude. On the ground at her feet was the flat feathered cutout of a swan like an emptied skin or a carnival garment. She lifted it up and stepped aside. And then another pen underwent the same metamorphosis, which now, as the first shock had worn off, reminded Eric of the ungainly transformation of Pat's dog that had heralded Nightwood's intrusion into his house and life. There was something equally heavy and painful about these swans shedding their bird-skins and becoming human. But even if it hurt like hell, he was barely restraining himself from jumping out of his hiding and rushing to drink from the spring.

Two women, three. They were of all ages and all shapes. One was a comfortably padded grandmother, another a girl barely into her tweens. Finally, only the black swan lowered her head and stood up proudly, even as the pangs of transformation racked her body that grew and unfolded like a flower, towering into the dim air. When it was over, a statuesque black woman lifted her discarded black plumage, hanging it over her arm as if it were a raincoat. A bar of late sunlight illuminated her features.

Eric waddled toward the spring, in such a hurry that he had to flap his wings clumsily to speed up his progress. The other swan-maidens had by now drifted back toward the lake but the black woman stayed, watching him. He drank.

The pain went through his body like a red-hot poker, scrambling his guts and reverberating in every nerve and muscle. He intended to stand tall and proud like the black swan but, when it was over, he found himself splayed on the ground and his discarded swan-garment balled up under his bare back, poking him with sharp feathers.

Eric stood up. The black woman regarded him thoughtfully, apparently unfazed either by his less-than-stellar performance or by the fact that they were both stark naked.

"Hello, Eric," she said.

"Hello, Malika."

"So you did make it to Nightwood."

"And so did you."

"I was abducted."

"So was I."

"But you escaped."

"So did I."

"How long have you been a swan?"

"Not very long. You?"

"Probably longer than you, but time in Nightwood is a funny thing. I was lucky to find this flock. Are you alone?"

"Yes. And I did not know about this spring. I thought I'd have to be a bird forever."

"You'd die if you were trapped in an animal form without changing periodically back into human. Or worse: human and animal would fuse, making you into a monster. This is what these ladies told me. We are constantly on lookout for change-water to maintain our humanity."

"Can you get rid of your swan-skin?"

"Yes, it can be burned. But it has to be a special fire."

"We can find this fire!" Eric exclaimed, his natural optimism reasserting itself as he was comfortable again in his skin—literally so. "We can burn the bird-shirts and find a way out of Nightwood!"

Malika shook her head.

"Not so fast," she said. "We will need the wings of a bird when we are looking for her. We have to find her. She is in trouble."

"She?"

"Ally."

Chapter 14:
The Key

Ally pressed her back to the wall. The darkness was absolute. Had the Castle taken away her sight? She ground the heel of her hand into her eyes and saw blue stars.

She tried to move and collided with the edge of the tub. The pain made her double over and when she straightened up again, there was a change in the quality of darkness. It was not that it got lighter: just the opposite. Even though it seemed impossible, there was a clotting and thickening of the gloom, a black-on-black granular shift that made the uniformity of nothingness churn with some imperceptible movement. There was a sound, too: a barely audible rustle. It was so low that Ally could not figure out whether it was close or far.

She hunkered down by the edge of the tub, listening. A swish, a light crackle, a footstep. Somebody was here. Searching for her. Hunting.

She barely dared to breathe. What kind of creature could move around in this total darkness without running into walls or furniture? And if it could somehow see without light, why didn't it see her?

A wisp of smell wafted in her face: a hot animal stink. It came again, in a wave so pungent she squeezed back a cough rising in her throat. Her useless eyes watered.

A wolf? No, the smell was different, though related. The reek of a carnivore: old blood rotting in its fur, its yellow fangs encrusted with filth. A cat? Cats were fastidious creatures: Prince did not stink like this.

A bear.

Ally had never been close to a bear except in a zoo but she recognized it from the dim accumulations of ancestral memories:

her peasant forebears cowering in their flimsy huts as the shaggy death stomped through the snow, tearing out the throats of their livestock. Bears and wolves together, digging through a pile of naked corpses, a tidy bullet-hole in each forehead. A bear carrying away a screaming infant.

Instead of battering her into paralysis, these images whipped her into action. She had seen worse in Nightwood—and survived. Her ancestors had faced the terrors of darkness—and survived. She was here, wasn't she? A living testimony to their survival.

Ally grasped the slick edge of the tub and vaulted over it, crouching in the bottom. She groped for the flexible tube of the hand-held shower and breathed out her relief when she touched the taps. She took a shower before her dinner date with her father and knew that whatever *geis* was responsible for the plumbing in the Castle With No Windows, it did not stint on hot water. An almost-boiling jet would deter any predator.

She walked her fingers to the chrome knob. As she touched it, the light came on.

And illuminated her father, still in his uniform, towering above her.

Ally climbed to her feet, feeling like an idiot. At the same time, she was getting angry. No man walked uninvited into her bathroom, father or no father!

"Were you frightened?" Alexander smiled, patted her hand. "Sorry, Alyonushka!"

"What was it?" she asked gruffly, sidling past him to survey the bedroom. The mussed-up bed was as she had left it. There was no bear.

But a faint animal smell still hung in the air, mixing with her perfume and body lotion.

"A power outage," Alexander said; and before she could protest that a *geis* is not supplied by a utility company, he landed a kiss on her forehead, wished her good night and was gone.

Ally considered the question of how to secure the bedroom door. Finally, she compromised on barricading it with a chair. It would not stop a her father, but it would give her a warning if he tried to come back.

She lay back in bed, determined to get some sleep. She needed her strength for tomorrow.

Her princess dream was over.

She woke up in the light of morning. And then remembered that there was no morning light here, in the Castle With No Windows. How big was it?

How big had her house been?

She remembered her first timid explorations of Carl's glass mansion. The inside of the Castle was like its negative: stone instead of glass; old-fashioned baroque luxury instead of modern streamlined simplicity; presided over by her father instead of her husband. But in some sense, it was the same: she was the ward of a powerful man.

Ally got up and pulled off her silk nightgown. There were scars on her forearms and scratches on her shins. A bruise bloomed just below her collarbone. Mementoes of Nightwood; the price demanded and paid. Honestly and in full. Her hand went up to her shorn head. Wouldn't Carl be disappointed that his bride no longer had her fairytale hair?

Ally snorted and went into the bathroom where she took a long shower. Carl first needed to be found. And if he did not like her new hairstyle, he could go to hell!

Now for some clothes. The idea of putting on the same frippery as yesterday filled her with revulsion. But her own pants and shirt stank of blood, peppered as they were with the drip from the Bleeding Grove. Suddenly she had an inspiration:

Maid unseen, honest and true,
Garments of blood wash in dew!

What a doggerel! Ally winced in embarrassment, but it worked. Invisible hands whisked away her filthy clothes and returned them five minutes later, clean and smelling of fabric softener. Ally considered the money she could make if she could find a way to import such a *geis* into the history world. A magic start-up! Perhaps there could be positives to Nightwood's incursions into California.

Her backpack was thrown into a corner. Ally rooted through it and pulled out Prince's three gifts: the knife, the now empty bottle, and the large rusty key. Had the trickster sold her out? Undoubtedly. There had been a conspiracy to draw her into Nightwood. Alexander had said as much. He wanted his daughter with him. His princess.

But how far back had the conspiracy gone? Was Carl's abduction part of it?

She looked at the gifts again. They had worked after a fashion, though not exactly as promised. The knife cut off her hair to allow her passage through the barrier of bald women. The potion in the bottle made her invisible to the wolves.

A trickster always had a trick or two up his sleeve. Prince betrayed her. But who was to say that he was not betraying the Ogre as well?

Ally tucked the key into her pocket and exited the bedroom, cautiously pulling the chair away from the door.

The owner of the Castle was not at home. Somehow, she knew it even as she found herself in the stone-flagged corridor illuminated by torches set into the iron brackets on the walls. Thought her father was not around, the invisible servants were. In the dining room a hot breakfast waited for her on the snow-white tablecloth. The servants would obey her. Up to a point.

Don't keep me locked inside this mount
Open the door, let me out!

Nothing happened, and Ally was not surprised. Her father clearly did not want his little girl to wander back into the Bleeding Grove, where the evidence of his tastes would rudely wake her from princess dreams. She ate a piece of toast with jam, exited the dining room and went exploring. It reminded her of snooping through Prince's house. She had considered herself to be in some version of the Bluebeard tale, but she had been mistaken, of course. Prince had plenty of secrets but not of the Bluebeard kind. He did not keep dead women in a locked room. Ally was sure he preferred them lively and varied.

He had drawn Jennifer into Nightwood but was it under orders from the Ogre? In the mirror in Prince's house, Jennifer had tried to warn her against trusting the cat-man. Just as the actual Jennifer had warned her against the Bleeding Grove. In both cases, Prince had allowed it to happen. This was not the behavior of a Bluebeard avatar.

But what *was* her tale now? Ally pondered as she padded through a maze of stone passages. If not Bluebeard, then what?

The passages were monotonous, chilly and boring. While the décor of the Castle was much more in accordance with most people's vaguely medieval ideas of the fairytale world, Ally knew it for a fake. The burning torches were just a distraction from the actual lighting that came from nowhere and as she had discovered last night, could be turned off at any moment if the owner of the Castle so desired. The thought of finding herself in the dark again made her hurry. Until her father came back, she was determined to find out more about who or what he was. *Knowledge is power*.

There were locked doors in the passages—sturdy ironbound oaken doors, with appropriately large and ornate keyholes. Ally tried her key on each one of them. None fit.

Fear and premonition drove her on. The more she thought about what happened last night, the more unsettled she became.

The passages seemed endless. They unspooled in front of her like the stone intestines of a giant dragon that had swallowed her up without noticing. The doors multiplied. If she tried her key in each of them, it would take hours. Hours she did not have.

Ally stopped and studied the nearest door. The ironwork around the keyhole was not just abstract curlicues: it was a very elaborate monogram, composed of several overlapping letters. She walked to the next door. The same, only the letters were different.

She followed the endless line of doors, peering at the ornament on each. Even if the monograms indicated what key to use, how would it help her? Her key was plain, with no lettering or other signs.

The corridor came to an intersection. Three identical passages led away from it. Ally stopped. Which one to choose? There were no indicators, just the soul-crushing monotony of cold gray walls, sputtering torches, and locked doors.

She chose to go left.

More doors, their ironwork containing not just letters but other motifs: birds, flowers, griffons, skulls. All significant, all meaningful in the universe of stories. None meaningful to her.

She suddenly stopped. One door bore an elaborate design of a crown surmounting intertwined letters A and R. A was the first letter of her name but R? Her maiden name had been Shevchenko, like the famous Ukrainian poet.

Still, something niggled at her. And then she remembered.

The handkerchief she had stolen from Little Mother; the magic handkerchief that she had lost on the Third Dragon River. It was embroidered with the letters that she had read as A and P. But in the Cyrillic alphabet P is read as the Latin R.

And what does R mean? It could be Rex or Regina. Or it could be . . .

Ally pushed the key into the keyhole and turned it. The door opened.

Chapter 15:
The Conservatory of Flowers

The light blinded her. When she blinked away the tears, she realized it was not exceptionally bright, just unexpected. She was standing in daylight. Not the unnatural red or white of the Horseman but the honest-to-goodness sunshine, filtered through, and concentrated by, the glass ceiling.

A conservatory! She was in a conservatory. Plants in large tubs were arranged in neat rows. There was a padded bench along one wall.

Ally looked around. The plants were mostly flowering bushes of different kinds. There were also individual flowers in smaller pots. Mingled odors of rose, jasmine, iris and carnation perfumed the air.

Ally looked back at the door that had clicked shut behind her. The over-sweet aroma made her feel nauseated. She did not want to explore this place. Its lush beauty horrified her more than the starkness of the stone passages.

But neither could she turn back.

Mama's soft voice in her mind:

You are an officer's daughter.

A lie. A lie that had given her the courage to fight against the overwhelming odds and win.

But now was the time for the truth.

There was a large Ceanothus bush in a wooden tub. She had grown to like the native Californian lilac: its pale-blue clusters of flowerets, its delicate aroma. She inhaled and coughed violently. The flowerets exuded an overpowering stink of rotten water and overripe fruit. Their milky blueness was the color of a drowned woman's skin.

She went down a row of planters and stopped before a large rose bush covered in blowzy blooms. Each of them framed a face. All faces were identical: a woman's, round and fresh, pink-cheeked and pouty-lipped, pretty in a rather insipid way. The rose bush looked like a rose dragon, heavy with many heads. Or was it only one head, multiplied many times?

The blossom-faces' eyes were closed. They looked asleep. But when Ally approached, they eyes opened, and the roses turned on their stems to stare at Ally. Their blue eyes glowed with poisonous hatred.

Ally jerked back. A chorus of overlapping voices rose from the bush, or rather one voice, multiplied and repeating the same word:

"Whore!"

Ally rushed to the next planter. And the next. Each bush, each flower carried a woman's face. And all the faces were animated with distaste, jealousy or animosity. A large dahlia looked daggers at Ally with sultry black eyes. Under the tight curls of a hyacinth, a young girl stuck out her tongue at her. From the sweet-smelling clusters of jasmine, identical exotic beauties glared at her with contempt. A stand of tulips pivoted away from her, gabbling indignantly.

She ran away from the angry flowers and saw a small tree in a square of soil. It looked like a Canadian maple. She and Carl had a Canadian maple in their front yard, which he ordered their gardener to surround with a wire fence to protect it from deer. This was also surrounded by a barbed-wire fencing, but the spikes of the wire were turned inwards, toward the tree. Ally came closer. The tree shuddered and stretched its branches to her. Its disheveled canopy dipped and trembled, and a face peered from under the mop of twigs.

Ally recognized it. It looked back at her from a mirror not long ago.

"Hello, Jennifer," she said.

The tree-face worked but no sound escaped the cracked lips. Jennifer was still recognizably herself. Her skin was dry and filthy, but it was human. The tree bark only began halfway down her chest. She writhed violently, as if trying to escape the transformation that was inexorably claiming her.

Ally came closer.

"Can you talk?" she asked.

Jennifer opened her mouth. The inflamed stub beat uselessly against the palate. Like the wolves that had attacked the *sousliks'* camp, she had her tongue cut out.

"I'm sorry," Ally whispered, uselessly. "Why is he doing it? Why is he taking language away?"

The maple Jennifer shook violently. Ally touched her cheek, brushing the dry skin with her fingertips.

"I'm sorry," she said again. "You tried to warn me. Thank you."

Tears rolled down Jennifer's cheeks as she tried to mouth inaudible words.

"I won't let him get away with it," Ally whispered.

Jennifer's eyes moved. Ally turned, following her line of sight. Behind a decorative wall of creeping ivy, clusters of purple flowers rose toward the glass ceiling.

She went there. A luxuriant lilac bush—no, a lilac tree—bloomed in a carved planter. Not a modest Ceanothus but the sweet, lush, overpowering bloom of her childhood. The flower of May, of spring celebration and renewal. Mama's favorite flower. The lilac trembled, showering the ground with star-shaped flowerets. From the interplay of light and shadow in its dappled depth, a face came together like an old-fashioned photograph developing. Thin lips smiled, hollow eyes blinked.

"Alyonushka."

"Mama."

"You should not have come here, darling! I tried to warn you. Gave you the necklace, to lead you out. Back to safety. To your home."

"It's not my home, Mama. I did nothing to earn it."

"Beggars cannot be choosers, daughter."

"I'm not a beggar!" Ally flared. "And neither are you!"

"I tried to do my best for you," the lilac tree whispered. "Took his tainted money, so you could get education and get out of the bloodlands!"

"Is he really my father?"

"Yes. He has had many lovers. But not many children. He kills his sons."

"What is he, Mama?"

"He is the creature of the bloodlands. He has sprung from the corpse-rich soil. He is as old as murder and as young as genocide. He wants to rule the world."

"Story world? History world?"

"Both."

Ally knelt in front of the lilac tree and put her arms around it. The sweet smell enveloped her just as it had on those long-ago evenings when they walked in the Botanical Gardens through the lilac-shadowed alleys. The heart-shaped leaves caressed her cheeks and the flower clusters gently landed on her head.

"Did he abduct you?"

"Yes. Like all the others. Keeping us here, neither dead nor alive. Neither human beings capable of action nor plants freed of memories. He is the gardener of death. He tends corpses and grows them into hatreds. He will not rest until the Bleeding Grove covers all of Nightwood and the wellspring of stories is poisoned."

"What can I do, Mama?"

"Run away. It's not too late. The cat-man will help you. Run away to your Golden State and never look back!"

Ally jerked back.

"No!"

The lilac tree rustled, and a shadow fell over the conservatory. Ally looked up and saw the sun wink out and a scarlet orb roll low in the colorless sky.

"Then kill him! Avenge our country! Avenge your grandparents! Avenge me!"

"How?"

The lilac whispered, its leaves whipping back and forth, and she bent closer, listening.

The rest of the flower-women trembled and shed leaves in distress, and heavy footsteps sounded in the passage outside.

Chapter 16:
Allerleirauh

Another dinner.
There was meat on the table again, medium-rare steaks swam in blood when the Ogre cut them with a sharp serrated knife. But he did not insist Ally partake and let her eat her vegetables in peace. He seemed to be in a good mood.

He had brought her another dress, even fancier than the one she wore last time: a full silver-colored brocade skirt covered in a crystal-beaded net that sparkled like the starry sky; a velvet bodice embroidered in silver and gold; and a white-gold necklace. He insisted she wear the outfit and she complied.

She was still coming down from her adrenaline high. When he had entered the conservatory, she hid behind the lilac bush like a child playing hide-and-seek. She was ready to be discovered, only regretting she had not thought of filching a knife from the dining-room. Not that golden cutlery would make a good weapon but it would give her something to bolster her confidence when she confronted her father.

At the end, there was no need. He just paused at the threshold and surveyed his flower harem. Ally caught a glimpse of his self-satisfied smirk. Just for a moment, it seemed that yellow tusks jutted from his lower jaw but then his face settled again in his bland, handsome mold. Ally wished she could un-see their family resemblance, but it seemed to be even stronger than before.

He did ask her what she had done the whole day and when she said she looked around the Castle, figuring he would know it anyway, he voiced no objections. In fact, he benevolently told her to ask him for keys to select rooms next time.

"I have to keep the doors locked," he said. "We don't have your fancy bank vaults here."

"Are you afraid of thieves?" Ally asked.

He shrugged.

"Thieves, assassins. We have many enemies."

She lifted an eyebrow.

"We?"

The Ogre grinned at her.

"You are my daughter," he said.

She studied his face surreptitiously. He still looked like an ordinary man: a youngish, well-turned-out, well-spoken middle-aged man with a military-straight back and commanding air. He had his uniform on but no matter how Ally racked her brain, trying to dredge up some knowledge of national insignia, she could not pinpoint what army he belonged to.

She had waited in the conservatory until the footsteps in the passage receded and then sneaked and rushed back to her suite. She had hidden the key in the wardrobe under a pile of frothy underwear but did not think she would need it again. She had learned all she could from the lilac bush. She would like to talk to Mama again but rationally she knew it was not much different from gazing at a picture of a dead loved one or listening to a recording of their voice. The lilac tree was a shadow of Mama, her reflection in the story mirror of Nightwood. Her mother was dead.

But her father was alive.

"The world has become chaotic," he said. "Crime, terrorism, gangs. Petty nations that have no right to exist yapping at great powers like rabid dogs. It's all falling apart."

Ally sipped white wine from her silver goblet. She had asked for white, pointing at her moon-colored dress, but the truth was she no longer trusted her father's reds, even though they were probably just excellent merlots and cabernets.

"It's true in our world too," she said cautiously.

"There is no difference," her father said. "Our world, your world—it's all the same. This is another truth people have forgotten and have to be reminded of. Soon."

"Are you the one to remind them?" Ally asked. She knew she was taking a risk, but she needed to hear it from him. He *was* her father.

I am an officer's daughter.

Mama had not lied, after all. An officer. A gentleman. A killer.

He smiled at her and there was such a sunny charm in his smile that she felt the muscles of her face respond without her conscious volition.

"Yes!" He drank more wine—red for him. "But not I alone. We—"

"What do you mean?"

He bent toward her conspiratorially.

"You are my daughter, Alyonushka. My only child. I had other children but they . . . they died. And they were not like you. Weak. But you—you are strong. I saw you battle your way through Nightwood. You took on Little Mother. That whiny hag! I was getting tired of her, and the way you coped with her . . . it was magnificent!"

Ally winced, remembering the meaty thwack of the cleaver through the frail body.

"Did you track me through Nightwood?" she asked.

"Most of the time. I lost you a couple of times. I'm telling you, the place is becoming ungovernable, but we will change all of it! I wanted to protect you, of course, but I also hoped you'd show yourself worthy of my protection. And you did! You really did!"

"Did you bring my husband in so I would follow?" Ally asked.

"That brainless American leech! Yes, I did. But he is no husband of yours, Alyona. Forget about him. You are here, finally, where you belong. With me. And now our great work can begin. Unifying the two worlds, restoring order, bringing back glory and might! There will be nothing but Nightwood, the way it was meant to be. And when our realm is whole, we will sit on its throne, you and I together. King and Queen!"

Ally's blood ran cold.

She finally knew what her story was.

"Daddy," she said, forcing her reluctant lips to move.

"Call me Alexander!"

"Alexander . . . will you bring me a gift? A special gift to celebrate."

"Anything!" he laughed raucously, and she saw he was getting drunk—on power and wine. That was dangerous. She remembered Mama pushing out her drunken gentlemen friends when their yelling in the kitchen disturbed her little girl in her safely locked bedroom. Mama had taken good care of her. Except when she had chosen her father. If she had had a choice.

She forced herself to touch his hand lightly.

"That's a beautiful dress."

"Only the best for you, my dear!"

"I know. You brought me a dress the color of the sun. You brought me a dress the color of the moon. For tomorrow night, the third night, will you bring me a dress the color of a bird's wing? A swan-dress, so I may rule the sky—together with you!"

He squinted and her heart plummeted. He was the ruler of Nightwood—or at least a pretender—surely, he knew what she was asking!

But being *in* a story, how would you know how it ends?

"A white dress … " he said meditatively. "The color of a swan's wing. Yes, it is appropriate. Indeed. I'll bring it to you, Alyonushka. For the third night, the final night."

He smiled lewdly at her but she saw with a shudder of revulsion that his eyes were flat and dead like buttons. There was nothing in him, not even desire, however perverted. Just death.

She got up.

"I need to go, Alexander," she said. "To rest, to get a good night's sleep."

She was afraid he would try to detain her, but he only landed another perfunctory kiss on her forehead and waved her off. It was done; his decision made; his intentions revealed. Now he had other things to attend to.

She went up to her room and barricaded the door again, though she knew it was useless. And then she sat on her bed and cried.

Her own story.

"Allerleirauh." Also known as "Donkeyskin". Also known as "The King Who Wanted to Marry His Daughter".

Once upon a time, there was a mighty king who had a beautiful wife. When she lay dying, she asked him to marry only a woman as beautiful as she was. And he looked around and realized that the only woman who fit this description was his own daughter.

The princess escaped and wore a cloak of many furs and feathers to disguise herself and avoid her father's pursuit. She became a creeping beast and a timid bird. She lived in the dark forest, hiding herself in their shadow.

The tale continued and at the end, the evil father got his just comeuppance, and the princess married a prince. But this was Nightwood, and stories lived here, intertwining and mutating, birthing new versions and shedding old ones, feeding on blood, sweat and tears.

All fairy tales were history once.

And will be again.

Ally got up and wiped her eyes. She had lived her entire life without a father and had done pretty well. She had a loving mother, a faithful brother, a good husband . . .

All dead.

Well then, she was an orphan and that was not a bad way to be. But first, she had to make sure that she was indeed an orphan.

If she could.

Ally went to bed but could not sleep, running the story of Allerleirauh in her head. She had never liked it. It had seemed so archaic, so cruel, and so remote. The poor princess abasing herself by wearing animal skins in order to escape her incestuous father. She wondered whether there was a part missing. Was it the princess' bid for power? A daughter's desperate revenge on generations of bad fathers? Better to be an animal than to live in your world.

He is the creature of the bloodlands.

And then she was asleep.

In the "morning", when she went down to get breakfast prepared for her by the invisible servants, she found the door to the kitchen wide open. Was the Ogre slyly indicating that she should get ready for her housewifely duties? Ally methodically finished her toast and marmalade and drank two cups of coffee. She had to keep up her strength.

Then she walked into the kitchen.

It was very big and very modern: in fact, it strongly resembled her own kitchen in Carl's house. An electric range on the large green-marble island in the middle; a breakfast nook; gleaming appliances. It even had a microwave! Ally peeked into the larder that was dutifully stocked with dry goods and condiments. She smiled sadly at a large bottle of canola oil as she remembered the first night in the mountain house.

Poor Carl! She used to wonder, half-guiltily, whether she had married a man so much older than herself because she had subconsciously been looking for a father figure. Well, she wondered no more. There was less in common between Carl and her father than between a lamb and a bear.

But something was missing. Ally looked around and realized there was no fridge. That was puzzling. At the end of the kitchen, where a window should have been but was not, was a stainless-steel door. Ally walked over and pushed it.

A cloud of cold air wafted in her face. It was an industrial-size walk-in freezer.

Inside, hanging on butcher hooks, were her father's food supplies.

A corpulent man, skinned like a rabbit. Another man, younger, his well-muscled thighs hacked down to the bone. A woman, her breasts missing. Ally observed it all, dry-eyed, but retched when she saw several frozen babies, tied together like a brace of grouse.

Puddles of frozen blood collected below the hanging bodies.

As she went up to her room to wait for dinner, she wondered whether some benevolent fairy had whispered into the infant ear of the Ogre's daughter never to eat meat. Who knows how early her father might have tried to convert his child to his tastes?

Chapter 17:
The Swan-dress

He knocked on the bedroom door.

At least he did not just walk in. Not yet.

Ally opened. She wore a simple silk shift she had found in the closet.

Her father smiled at her: a confident smile, a proprietary smile. The smile of an owner.

She had seen such smiles on men who accosted her in smoky cafes on Khreschatyk. She had gone with one of them. Once.

He had changed. His chest was covered with rows and rows of shiny medals on multicolored ribbons. Profiles of men she had seen in history books: leaders and generals; great warriors and greater dictators. Creators of the bloodlands.

His uniform shimmered with black and gold and green and khaki, shifting color every time she looked at it. He owed allegiance to no particular flag. He needed all of them.

His face had changed too, though in no specific way that she could pinpoint. There were no obvious deformities. But it was the face of a monster.

He tried to plant a wet kiss on her cheek, but she stepped back.

"My dress?" she said.

He laughed raucously. It felt like he would spit out a mouthful of broken glass.

"A little princess, aren't we? Won't play until Daddy got her a gift? All right, Daddy's good tonight. He will oblige. For now."

He clapped his hands and the invisible servants glided into the room, bearing the dress.

Ally recoiled. Was this what she had hoped for? Would it work? Only one way to find out.

She stepped toward the magnificent creation held upright as if already molding the body inside. It was nothing like the scruffy, molting feathered garment Little Mother had used to enslave her. This was a dress fit for a queen.

The snowy outer gown was gathered at the waist with a satin ribbon studded with pearls. The pearl design was mirrored at the low-cut bodice and the wide turned-off cuffs. The bodice, made of white quilted silk, was cut in the front to reveal the matching under-gown, patterned with a design of feathers. The over-skirt, looped above the tulle petticoats, was embroidered with silhouettes of royal swans, picked out in seed pearls and glittering crystals. The entire ensemble shimmered in hues of white: the sparkle of fresh ice; the meditative blankness of lilies; the ivory of piano keys. And above all, the multilayered lustrous white of a swan's proud plumage.

"A wedding gown!" her father laughed again, and she saw tiny blood bubbles froth on his lips. "Or as good as!"

She touched the warm silk, and it nuzzled her hand like a living thing.

"I want to change," she said. He nodded, and she realized he was not going to step out.

The dress fit her perfectly: the corset snugly embracing her narrow waist, the sleeves sliding softly over her arms, the heavy skirt flowing over her hips. She turned to face her father.

"You are beautiful!" the Ogre whispered, enchanted. He stepped toward her, and she held up her hand.

"Daddy," she asked, "what does AR mean? It's your name, isn't it?"

"Alexander Rex," he said. "Alexander the King."

"No," Ally said. "R stands for *Reznik*. The Butcher."

And as she said it, she started to change.

The white dress dissolved in a cloud of living light, surrounding Ally's slight body, expanding and coruscating, layers of skin flowing around her, sprouting feathers, fusing with her flesh and bone, clothing her in a garment of power. The pain pierced her like the pangs of birthing or dying, burning away everything that made her human: hesitations and doubts; second thoughts and uncertainties; fears and regrets.

A giant swan, as big as an extinct Pteranodon, flapped her wings, sweeping away the draperies and rungs, shattering the mirrors and ornaments. Her red beak opened wide, hissing and honking. Her serpentine neck swelled and undulated like a cobra. She stepped toward her adversary.

The bear swiped at the bird with his clawed paw. He was as big as a grizzly but had the proportions of a brown bear. His shaggy coat was matted with filth; his low-slung head thrust forward, opening a yellow-toothed maw. He roared and breathed out a cloud of fetor.

The swan flapped to the ceiling and with a lightning-quick strike, lashed out at the bear's muzzle and pecked out one of his eyes. The enraged beast roared thunderously and swiped at the swan again. This time the paw connected and a flurry of feathers drifted to the floor.

The swan hissed. She was faster than the enemy and she had the advantage of attacking from above. But the bedroom was too small to enable the bird to fly high enough to evade the bear's enraged blows. The swan glided out through the door and the bear, half-blinded, his muzzle covered in blood and maddened by pain, stumbled after it. He lost his footing on the grand staircase and slid down, bumping his head on the stone steps. The light flared up and down as if in sympathy, flickering through all the shades of the spectrum and settling upon somber red. The bear landed at the foot of the staircase and lay there in a furry pile.

The swan floated close to the ceiling, regarding the enemy with a quizzical sidewise stare. Seeing that the bear was immobile, she alighted close to the body.

The bear's paw shot out and grabbed the swan by her long neck.

Now the animal had the advantage of brute force over the bird. His dagger-like claws pierced the protective plumage and the swan's white coat ran with blood. She flapped her wings desperately but with her neck held fast by the bear, she could not use her sharp beak. The bear forced the neck down, pinning the swan to the flagged floor, disregarding the convulsive flutter of her wings. The swan's eyes dimmed. The bear, balancing on his three legs, bent over the prostrate bird, his lolling tongue dripping saliva.

The Castle With No Windows suddenly flared with sunshine as its stone walls dissolved into panes of glass. No sooner did the blank walls become transparent windows than the glass shuttered, showering the bear and the swan with crystal shards. Two swans flew in through the cloud of glass and sunshine: a white cob and a black pen.

They pecked the bear with their razor-sharp beaks, beat it about the head with their powerful wings. Roaring, the beast stood up, but in doing so, he let go of the other swan who rose unsteadily to her feet. She joined the fray but by this point, the bear was already outnumbered and outsmarted. Reduced to the blind ferocity of an animal, he snarled and swiped at the trio of birds who were attacking him in concert, following the instinctual strategy of their avian kind that they used in defending their nests against predators.

The bear retreated toward the rear end of the hall, the three swans following, pecking and jabbing, never letting up. Their honking rose to a deafening pitch.

The first swan found an opening through the bear's windmilling paws and quickly struck at his foaming muzzle. The animal roared in pain. The roar dwindled into a human scream as the swan lifted the bloody orb of the bear's second eye in her red beak. The bear fell on the floor, convulsing, his fur falling out in hunks, his bloodied flesh contracting. The three swans surrounded the dying bear and observed his end with unblinking and pitiless birds' gazes.

And then it was done. A man's slashed body sprawled on the floor, his eyeless face streaked with blood.

The three swans looked at each other.

Chapter 18:
Sleeping Beauty

Ally paused at the entrance to the basement. The cluttered passage was overgrown with shadowy vegetation. Leaves and vines twined around gurgling pipes. Mushrooms clustered on piles of boxes. Wine racks bore a harvest of grapes. Thorny bushes grew out of the walls.

Once the Ogre was dead, the Castle With No Windows reverted to its form of the Morrises' house. But this form was insubstantial and flaky. The walls cycled from stone to glass and back again; the grand staircase dissolved into a modern living room that suddenly mutated into a medieval keep; the kitchen blinked in and out of existence. There was a whisper of many voices on the empty porch as the invisible servitors debated their allegiances. Through the waves of chaos, only four things remained stable: the mutilated body of Ally's father and the three naked people staring at each other in shock over the drift of feathers at their feet.

Ally was the first to break the stalemate when she threw her arms around Malika's neck and the two women hugged each other in silence for a long time. When she turned to Eric, she found that he had improvised a loincloth out of a kitchen towel and brought an armful of the same for the women to cover up. Malika quickly snatched up a couple, but Ally just looked at Eric and he looked back.

"Why did you come into Nightwood?" she finally asked.

He shrugged.

"I was looking for . . . you. And her," he nodded at Malika. "And then that thing . . . in the castle . . . and I was in an ash-mine . . . and then . . . "

"Hello, sister," Malika interrupted, "we came here to save your hide and you are sounding like the KGB! Stop interrogating and say 'thank you' like a good girl!"

Eric laughed but Ally did not even smile. She lowered her head.

"Thank you," she said.

Malika made a face at the corpse on the floor.

"So, this is the Ogre?" she said. "Not much!"

Ally turned away.

"Not much," she said. "Not anymore. But the bloodlands are still there."

"Where?" Eric asked.

She shrugged.

"Wherever people make them. Eastern Europe, Africa, Middle East. Maybe the US one day. All fairy tales were history once, and history never stops."

"I don't know about you," Malika interrupted, "but I don't like it here. This house is structurally unsound. Let's just go back home."

"How?" Eric asked.

"Nightwood has lost its master, so it'll be obedient for a while," Ally said. "Tame. It'll let us go. Just walk out and you'll find yourselves back in California."

"What about you?"

"There is something I have to do first."

The basement wavered as she walked, leaves and branches snagging on her clothes, trying to hold her back. She pushed them aside. Something fluttered from the murk above and landed on her head like a soft, boneless bat. Ally brushed it away.

And here it was: Ros' room. She stood on the threshold, flabbergasted. She had had a very clear idea of what she would find, and she was taken aback to see that the room had not changed at all. The same piles of worn clothes, the same bad paintings on the walls, the same chaos of old cosmetics on the dresser. No, something was different. The stuffed swan was missing, and the veiled mirror leaned to the side. Ally lifted the cover and was confronted with jagged remnants of mirror-glass in the frame. The mirror was broken.

But where was . . . ? Suddenly, she realized her mistake and was back out, running through the corridor toward the door that led to the underground garage. Leaves rustled under her feet as they fell off the walls in autumn-like flurries. Thorny branches broke off as she pushed through.

Ally threw open the garage door. Carl's babies nested side by side: a classic Thunderbird and a bright-yellow Tesla. She went over to the Thunderbird.

Inside, his head resting on the steering wheel and his snores reverberating in the confined space, was Carl.

Ally shook his shoulder; he slumped on the seat and the snores increased to a deafening volume. Ally bent down and planted a firm kiss on his lips.

Carl blinked, opened his eyes, and sat up. He was naked, and his thighs and backside bore the pale tracery of scars, inflicted by the thorns of Nightwood.

"Hon!" he exclaimed. "Is it time for dinner? Sorry, was catching forty winks!"

"We'll have to eat out tonight," Ally said. "I was busy, didn't have time to cook."

"No problem," Carl responded gallantly. "I wanted to try that new Burmese restaurant anyway. Hey, what happened to your hair?"

"I cut it," Ally said curtly.

Carl swallowed his next remark in the interest of domestic peace.

"It'll grow out, I'm sure," he finally managed his best diplomatic response. "What the hell, where are my pants?"

"In your closet," Ally said. And hand in hand, husband and wife went back home.

Chapter 19:
Happily Ever After

Eric saw the bald woman as he was driving down Telegraph Avenue. He slowed down but the angry honks from behind forced him to move on and when he finally found a parking spot, she was nowhere to be seen. Desperate, he ran up and down the colorful street filled with second-hand bookstores and juice emporiums, cutting through knots of cellphone-wielding students.

And then he saw her. She was rooting through a box of one-dollar books on the pavement.

"Hello, Ally," he said.

She straightened up and looked at him. Her naked skull made her small face stark, emphasizing the hollow eyes and high cheekbones. She looked almost emaciated, even though her loose clothes—a black long-sleeved t-shirt, cargo pants, and heavy Dr. Martens—made it impossible to determine whether she had actually lost weight.

"Hello, Eric," she said.

There was a moment of silence. Then he grabbed her hand.

"I'm buying you lunch."

"At 4 pm?"

"Dinner, then. I've been trying to get hold of you for the last three months. No Facebook, your phone is off. I even tried to talk to Carl to find out where you were!"

Eric winced remembering the conversation that did not go well.

"I have a new phone," she said. "Anyway, early dinner is fine. That Indian place on the corner."

That Indian place was quiet: just a couple of stragglers circling the buffet. Eric and Ally found a table in the corner.

"It suits you," he said awkwardly after a dreamy-looking waiter took their orders.

She ran a hand over her shaved head but said nothing.

"Are you living in Berkeley now?"

"Studying. Finishing my Masters."

"PhD next?"

"Probably. But maybe not here."

"So you and Carl . . . ?"

She shrugged.

"The divorce proceedings are still going on," she said. "Funny that it takes so long, even though there is no contest."

"How could he, after what you did?"

The fierce blue fire of her gaze felt almost like a physical slap.

"I filed for divorce," she said. "Not he. Carl did not want to let me go. I had to . . . convince him. But Malika helped."

"Malika? Where is she? I lost touch with her as well."

"Home. But she is coming back. She and Carl are speaking on Skype every day. But of course, they will not move forward until he is divorced. It would not be proper."

Eric tried to visualize Carl and Malika together and decided they'd make the world's most mismatched couple. On the other hand, hadn't he felt that way about Carl and Ally as well?

Their Vegetable Pakoda and Aloo Tikka made their appearance on the table, but Eric could hardly swallow a single bite. Was it the taste of ashes in his mouth?

Ally also barely touched her food.

"Have you heard from Jennifer?" she asked abruptly.

He shook his head.

"No."

Their eyes met.

"She was there, wasn't she?" Eric whispered.

"Yes."

"And she is not coming back?"

Ally pushed her plate away.

"I don't think so," she said.

Eric waved to the waiter and ordered two glasses of red wine. Ally finally smiled.

"The wine here is not the best," she said. "There is a wine bar down the street . . . But this will do."

The wine gave them something to look at besides avoiding

looking at each other. Eric gulped down too much and started coughing. Ally just sipped.

"Did you see Pat Donegan recently?" she asked.

"No. Their house is for sale. So is mine."

"Where are you moving?"

"I wanted San Francisco but the prices are impossible. Maybe here, around Oakland. Close to the Peninsula, at any rate."

"Your start-up?"

"That fell through, but I have another idea."

Ally nodded and got up, her food and wine barely touched.

"Have to go," she said. "It was good to see you, Eric."

He watched her walk to the door and was on his feet just as she slipped outside.

"Wait!"

Ally turned around: a scarecrow figure in loose unbecoming clothes.

"I want your phone number," Eric said.

There was a moment of hesitation and then Ally smiled slightly, pulled out her iPhone and exchanged numbers with Eric before disappearing into the crowds outside.

Ally liked hanging out in clubs and coffee shops until the closing time (which in some of these places came in the morning). She did not dance and drank only as much as was consistent with not being thrown out. But she needed to be surrounded by people. Her rented apartment was on the first floor of a seedy building on Shattuck and the landlord warned her about the traffic and the homeless camping out under her windows. She had not told him it was the place's main attraction. She could only fall asleep with the soothing hiss of passing cars and drifting sounds of loud conversations. Even the noise of broken glass and drunken shouting was better than silence because in silence she could hear the trees.

College town Berkeley was hemmed in by the woods, spilling over from the heights of Tilden. Even the downtown was not free from green, tremulous branches, sturdy trunks, and prickly needles. Everywhere she went, trees followed. Sometimes she dreamed of living in a city of concrete and steel where sidewalks were free of all but human life. But did such cities even exist? She had been enchanted by pictures of Hong Kong skyscrapers until she learned that much of the Hong Kong Island was covered by tropical forests.

Tonight, Ally decided to skip clubbing. She felt tired and in low spirits. The deafening house music of her favorite club held no lure. She went into a tiny co-op and bought some almond milk, quinoa salad and fresh fruit. Since moving out of Carl's house, she had become almost strictly vegan, even though she indulged in an occasional cheese sandwich. But she never bought milk and eggs in their original, unprocessed state. They looked too familiar.

The twilight deepening, Ally trudged back home. She did not actually think of that small but prohibitively expensive walk-in as home: it was a lair, a place to hide. Carl had been very generous, all things considered, and she could probably afford a down payment on a place of her own, but with tuition and uncertain job prospects she preferred to economize as much as possible.

She shifted her cloth bag from one hand to the other. She had lost more weight and muscle mass. She knew it did not suit her, making her look like a concentration camp inmate.

The bald women.

Never mind. There was nobody she needed to impress anymore.

He asked for my phone number.

She decided there was no reason for them to meet again. That had been the right decision then and it still was now.

Lost in her thoughts, Ally almost collided with a child who was running down the street. She stopped and so did the child, a sturdy blond boy about five or six years old. Ally muttered something and tried to move on—children made her uncomfortable, but instead of continuing on his way, the child planted himself in the middle of the sidewalk, blocking her way and regarding her quizzically.

She looked at his round, serious face under the fringe of hair so blond it looked white. His large eyes were blue. He looked familiar.

"Vanya!" A woman rushed toward the boy, grabbed his hand. "Come on, honey! Sorry," she apologized to Ally. "I don't know what came over him."

The last sentence was spoken in English.

"Alyona?" the boy said uncertainly.

Ally dropped to her knees and peered at what was around the boy's neck: a small gold cross on a delicate chain.

"That's fine," she said, getting up and addressing the boy's mother in Ukrainian. "We know each other. Didn't I see you in St. Volodymyr's?"

The woman smiled broadly, hearing her mother tongue.

"Haven't been there for a while," she said, "but we'll sure come for Easter. Do you live here?"

"I'm a student at Berkeley," Ally said. "Glad to see your son is doing well."

The woman bent closer to Ally.

"He is adopted," she whispered in her ear. "They found him in Tilden woods two years ago. Not a stitch on him but that cross necklace. He refuses to take it off but that's fine. My husband says it brings luck. He is a good boy."

"I'm sure he is," Ally said. "Well, it was good to meet you. See you at Easter!"

She waved at the boy who let his mother lead him away, looking back at Ally over his shoulder.

Two years ago. Another of Nightwood's time-bending games.

Her brother was safe.

The darkness had fallen, and the ecology-minded Berkeley never had enough streetlights for Ally's taste. She picked her way carefully along the sidewalk littered with trash and remnants of homeless encampments. An indistinct white shape darted out from a doorway and disappeared in the gloom.

Just a street cat, she told herself.

A very large street cat.

Her phone rang. Eric's number flashed on the screen.

Her thumb hovered over Decline.

She did not need him. She did not need anybody. She had her story, and it was enough.

But what is a story without a sequel?

In Nightwood, stories never ended. They changed, and shifted, and crossed with each other, and went on. Lovers separated, and reunited, and separated again. Children searching for their parents and finding a new life. Parents searching for their children and discovering adventure. Monster-slayers becoming monsters. Cowards dying as heroes; heroes surviving as suburban retirees. All fairy tales were history once; and history never stops.

The Ogre would be reborn. Perhaps his daughter would have to fight him again. Or perhaps a new tale was awaiting her. And in that tale, she did not want to be the only character.

Happily ever after was a lie. But pursuit of happiness was not.

She touched Accept.

LittlE SisteR

**Enjoy this excerpt from
Elana Gomel's *Little Sister***

THE LOST NOTEBOOK

THE DAY HER father was arrested, Svetlana lost her notebook.

The notebook was important because all the latest definitions were there, written down in her careful round script. She searched for it everywhere: under the roll-up top of her desk, where balls of blotting paper nested like spider eggs; at the bottom of her satchel where she discovered an ink-stained white ribbon; on the floor of the classroom, crawling between the rows of desks until she was chased away by old Aunt Sonya, the cleaner.

She could not find the notebook and went home downcast. She could always ask her best friend Tattie. But Tattie lived five streets away and the winter day was drawing to a close—the sky was like a dusty bowl filling with darkness. It was at night when the oborotni came out and prowled the streets. Though the Patrols of Light were there to protect the workers coming home from late shifts, children were strongly discouraged from venturing outside after dark. Even if, like Svetlana, they no longer considered themselves children.

A snowball hit her between the shoulder-blades and cold wetness trickled down through a rent in her old coat. The boy had dived into the gaping mouth of a house but she had seen enough of his face to know him for Misha, one of her classmates, rather than something more sinister. Lazy, stupid, good-for-nothing! Well, if anybody was destined to be caught by an oboroten, it was him! Svetlana defiantly stuck out her tongue and hurried on. A heavy hand landed on her shoulder.

"Little sister," said a hoarse voice, and a cloud of warm tobacco smell enveloped her, "where is the nearest dorm?"

She looked up. The day had curdled into a purple twilight. Sparse snowflakes shivering in the frigid air landed on the soldier's

307

shabby greatcoat. His face, under stubble and dirt, was haggard and thin. He looked barely older than her.

"You mean a Visitor's House?" she asked.

"Whatever you call it here. A place to kip."

"Over there," she pointed toward the city center where the dark windows of granite-clad towers frowned at the wide boulevards lined with bare black trees. Many of the towers were abandoned, infested by the Enemy who wove its cocoons in the stuffy dark. There they were hatching new generations of shape-shifting oborotni, of brutal kulaki or Fists, named so because their faces were giant clenched fists, of wily kosmopolity or Kosmops, whose beguiling squeaks grew louder as their stature diminished in their successive generations—the latest brood were the size of rats—and worst of all, krovososy, the crawling vampires whose human bodies had degenerated into a fat wormlike tube, tipped with a toothy snout.

Or perhaps these scary images were yesterday's news. Wasn't there something about a new menace: former people, the living dead? Svetlana once again bitterly regretted her inattention in class. She had written down today's definitions in a daze of fatigue, their meaning sliding off her mind like water off a duck's back. Of course, she was tired but this was no justification for slacking. She was not the only one to have spent the night glued to the dining-room mirror and listening to the Voice.

She had been mesmerized by the Voice's rich cadences, but most of all she had been entranced by the everyday miracle of His words materializing into tiny flame soldiers who marched off into the darkness to do battle with the Enemy. She loved watching this happen. How unfortunate that one paid for sleepless nights with drooping eyelids and a foggy head the next morning. Her parents had fallen asleep on the couch, still sitting upright, as if she would not notice.

Now, her notebook was lost and she was unprotected against the Enemy's inexhaustible wiles. What was it the teacher had said? In addition to the former people, mertvetzy, there seemed to be a new variety of the krovosos that walked upright and had a human face with a coiled proboscis hidden in its mouth, like the stinger of a bee. Or was it a new oboroten?

Svetlana realized that the soldier was looking at her expectantly. She blushed. So much for her good manners.

"I'm sorry," she said. "It's a ten-minute walk. I'm going in that direction. Would you like to come with me?"

"Sure."

As the soldier fell in step by her side, Svetlana became aware of the profound stillness of the city. The shuffling of pedestrians, the screech of streetcars, the smart marching of the Patrols, all had been hushed by the snowfall. The only sound was a soft rustle coming from the soldier's feet that were wrapped in layers of newspaper inside his scuffled military boots. The snow was now collecting on the ground, giving off a pale ghostly light.

"Are you on home leave?" she asked.

The soldier mumbled something.

"What?"

"I'm not . . . I don't . . . Shellshock, you know. Not very clear in the head."

Svetlana did not know what shellshock was but she nodded, afraid of appearing ignorant. Obviously, it was some new trick of the Enemy. It was hard to keep up with them. At unpredictable intervals, the Voice would issue from a mirror, illuminating the Enemy-infested darkness with his flaming words. Most of what he said was incomprehensible, though sometimes an occasional sentence or even a whole batch of them would sound quite ordinary, and she would tremble, suffused with love and gratitude for His guidance. But even if the entire speech were spoken in no human language, it did not matter, for His word was made light, and life, and battle. Then, there would be classes for schoolchildren and emergency meetings for adults, where the Voice's pronouncements were painstakingly translated into new definitions and instructions for rooting the Enemy out.

Svetlana wrenched her thoughts away from her lost notebook, glanced at the soldier again. What if he was a Word incarnated? Often, as she watched flame soldiers disappear into the darkness, she tried to imagine them swell up to human size, clothe themselves with flesh, acquire names, faces, eyebrows, birthmarks, zits . . . Nobody knew whether it actually happened, but she liked to believe it did.

"What's your name?" she asked.

"Andrei. And yours?"

"Svetlana," she said a little reluctantly. Normally she was very proud of her name, which meant 'light', but she liked the way he called her 'Little sister'. This is how nurses were addressed, and Svetlana had decided long ago that she was going to be a nurse when she grew up, healing the devastation wrought by the Enemy on the human bodies and souls. Not everybody had to be a warrior, she told her classmates, and though some boys curled their lips in contempt, the teacher agreed.

"Svetlana? Sveta? I had a sister named Sveta."

"Really?" she smiled at him. "So, you can still call me 'little sister'."

The bent pin holding her hair under the kerchief chose this moment to break, and her plait tumbled down.

He gently tugged the thick fair rope of hair braided with a threadbare ribbon.

"My sister was a pest. I bet you're a good girl."

"I bet you pulled her hair all the time and this is why she was angry with you," Svetlana giggled.

A black shadow detached itself from the ruined building at the corner, ran screaming toward them, its ragged coat of loose skin flapping over its shapeless body, a piercing shriek coming from the hole in its fist-face, the thick head-fingers stretching toward them.

"Run," Svetlana screamed but the soldier stood petrified. The sour stench of the creature washed over her, old blood and rancid fat, and despite the waning light, she could see with painful clarity the juddering sack of its belly, filled to bursting with the larvae of its young coiling under the pale membrane.

She tried to drag him away, but the soldier stood staring at the Enemy, his mouth hanging open.

He was a soldier; she was a schoolgirl, dispensable. There was really no choice. She stepped in front of him, shielding him from the ravening creature.

Then, a powerful side-blow sent her sprawling into the snow and a deafening noise exploded in her ear.

Svetlana scrambled upright. The soldier was bending over the creature that lay on its back in a pool of black blood, its belly-sack split and the larvae squirming feebly, trying to crawl out. In one hand Andrei clutched a curved stick. A thin smoke was coming from its end.

"Don't," she screamed when she saw how close he was to the kulak and its offspring. "Back off! They'll jump on you!"

He turned around; his face was the color of the steely-gray sky.

"What . . . ? What is this?"

"It's a kulak. A Fist. A big one. They're getting uppity, and the weather is good for them too. So cold."

"A kulak?" he repeated uncomprehendingly. "What do you mean? There was a kulak in our village, Uncle Vassily, but he was exiled . . . Anyway, this is not a man!"

"Of course not. It's a kulak!"

The larvae were now spilling out of the rent in the creature's stomach like a clutch of bleached earthworms. It was really terrible how their shapes approximated humanity. Wrinkling her nose in disgust, Svetlana stomped on them.

"What the hell are you doing?" the soldier dragged her away. "Those are babies!"

"Babies? What are you, daft?"

Suddenly a horrible suspicion blossomed in her mind and she backed away from him.

"Who are you?" she whispered.

He saw the change in her face and lifted his hand.

"Little sister . . . "

"Don't call me this," she screamed. "Patrol!"

But there were no Patrols and no passers-by. The city lay empty around them: ice, iron, and broken concrete.

"Listen, Sveta," he said slowly, "I don't know what's happening, and where I am, and who the hell this monster is . . . I was fighting, okay? Kurskaya Duga. The Battle of Kursk. The fritzes were coming at us like bats out of hell and we were hunkering down in the trenches and the Commissar was giving his pep talk and then . . . I don't remember. I thought I had a concussion and was given some R&R. I heard from mates that it happens—your memory is wiped clean, like, and then it comes back . . . But sure as I am my mother's son, I could not have forgotten something like that!"

Half of what he said made no sense but despite this, she was curiously reassured that he was no Enemy. He seemed too human, too lost. The bewildered blinking of his eyes telegraphed his honesty to her.

"Who are the fritzes?" she asked. "A new kind of Enemy?"

"New kind? They are the enemy! German fascists. Lackeys of imperialism. Bloody vampires."

She nodded.

"I thought so," she said. "I knew you were fighting them, but where is your torch?"

"My what?"

"How did you . . . ?" her words petered out.

She had seen no flash of light, such as given off by the sacred electric torches of the Patrols. They were the only infallible weapon against the Enemy. Ordinary fire did not work so well—even assuming that there was something to burn, which increasingly, was not the case.

"How did you kill it?"

"With my Nagant, how else? You were just in line of fire . . . Why the fuck did you step in front of me?"

The question stung badly. Svetlana turned around and walked into the rising wind that cut her cheeks like broken glass and justified her tears.

Andrei caught up with her and grasped her arm.

"I'm sorry," he said. "I've to watch my tongue, I know, but this is what you pick up in the trenches . . . You're a nice girl. But I just . . . I just don't understand. Am I dead?"

"No," she answered sulkily, "you would know if you were, and former people don't talk."

He sighed.

"All right. Is there anybody around who can explain the situation to me?"

She was going to direct him to the Speak-House but they had already passed the street where the turn-off was, and darkness was gathering behind them, a frigid wall of livid purple and black enlivened with fleeting shadows.

"Well . . . " she said uncertainly. "My Dad. He knows everything."

"Please!" Andrei grasped her hand. "Take me home. I know it's hard for civilians now, but I still have my ration. Tobacco, even some chocolate . . . I'll share!"

She was not doing it for food but she did not argue. They hurried through the inky dusk, hearing the mournful cry of a krovosos from a courtyard.

"A vampire," she explained. "You must be used to this if you're fighting them all the time."

"Germans are pigs but they don't squeal like this," he muttered.

Svetlana's parents were already home. She hid her face in her mother's warm bosom, for once not being ashamed of behaving like a baby. Andrei was standing patiently at the door while she tried to explain to her parents who he was. Her mother frowned but her father invited him in.

While they were drinking tea with the promised chocolate—crumbly, and chalky, and tasting like heaven—Andrei looked curiously at the smoky homemade candles that sent legions of dancing shadows into the corners.

"I only saw those when I was a child," he said, "I thought all cities have electricity now."

"We do," Svetlana's father replied. "All the Patrols are armed with electric torches."

"Despite the blackout?"

"What do you mean, blackout?" Svetlana's mother asked sharply. "How could we fight the enemy if there was a blackout?"

"But the raids . . . " Andrei started.

From the standing mirror on the dresser came the Voice. The paper flowers in a glazed ceramic vase, poppies and carnations that Svetlana had made in her crafts class, instantly burst into flame. A stream of power poured into the tiny apartment, filling it with a cataract of sound, echoing from the peeling walls and shabby furniture, sweeping over the four people like a mighty river. Svetlana stole a glance at her parents' bowed heads, but the moment was really too private to share with anybody, even them. Trembling, she watched the feeble candle-flames shatter into seeds of fire that sunk into the already pitted and scarred floorboards. From these black holes, miniature flame figurines crawled out and rushed toward the window, galloping over the four people in their eagerness, leaving scorched streaks on Svetlana's arms and shoulders. She felt no pain.

The Words joined with the other flaming hordes rising from the lit windows of human families—too few, in the city encroached upon by the Enemy, but still enough to fill the frozen air with the maelstrom of dancing stars. Then, the host or Words shaped itself into a whirlpool of fire, rose, and disappeared beyond the clouds.

"What was that?" asked the soldier hoarsely.

He was huddling at the table, his hands sliding off his ears where he had clamped them, wearing a pained expression on his face.

"I thought it was a broadcast . . . sounded like, you know who . . . But no, of course not, I couldn't make out a single word. How can you stand this bloody noise?"

"Who did you bring into our home?" screamed Svetlana's mother.

The door burst open.

Dark helmet-wearing figures crowded the doorway, their torches stabbing the dusty air. Svetlana backed away from Andrei, torn between the horror of having been taken in by the Enemy and the gratitude to the Patrol for having arrived in the nick of time.

"Comrades . . . " Andrei took a hesitant step forward.

Svetlana thought, dazed: This cannot be. He should shrivel and crawl into the corner confronted with the Light, shed his deceptive human masquerade, reveal himself for . . .

But she could not finish the thought because the Patrol, a bunch of tired, callow youths, their leather coats torn and filthy, paid him no attention. Their leader, whose red star-crowned helmet sat askew on his shaven head, shoved him aside and marched toward Svetlana's father. Before she could process what was happening, before she could take in her mother's thin wail, he kicked the man to the floor and the Patrol crowded around him, their torches trained upon the huddled mass.

Svetlana threw herself at them, cannoned into their tobacco-smelling wall, pushed them aside, rushed forward to lift her father—and was caught by rough hands, pinned between two swearing, angry, tired young men.

But she did not even struggle. She looked.

Looked as her father, the kindest, wisest of men, rolled himself into a ball like a hedgehog, his arms covering his face tightly, but not so tightly that she could not see the transformation taking place.

The familiar face was sloughing off, washed away by a thin stream of evil-smelling liquid, and another face was unfolding like a poisonous flower. The hooked snout with needle-sharp teeth, the tiny ruby-colored eyes set so close to each other that they looked like a single raw wound below the bulging bony forehead, the forked black tongue, ceaselessly licking bleeding lips . . . His hands were fleshless claws now, and his stooped back arched into an animal spine . . . An oboroten? Her father: a shape-shifter, a werewolf!

Everything went black before her eyes and from far away she heard voices, distant and unimportant.

"Where are you taking him, Comrades?"

"Where else?"

"Stay with the girl."

"Calm down, Mother. We're doing you a favor."

"They never see it until it's too late . . ."

She understood each word but they made no sense. Nothing did.

Buy a copy of *Little Sister* at https://geni.us/LittleSister

The End?

**Not if you want to dive into more of Crystal Lake
Publishing's Tales from the Darkest Depths!**

Check out our amazing website and online store
or download our latest catalog here.

We always have great new projects and content on the website to
dive into, as well as a newsletter, behind the scenes options,
social media platforms, our own dark fiction shared-world series
and our very own webstore. If you use the IGotMyCLPBook!
coupon code in the store (at the checkout), you'll get a one-time-
only 50% discount on your first eBook purchase!

Our webstore even has categories specifically for KU books, non-
fiction, anthologies, and of course more novels and novellas.

About the Author

Born in Ukraine and currently residing in California, Elana Gomel is an academic with a long list of books and articles, an award-winning writer, and a professional nomad. She has taught in Israel, Italy, and the US, and is known in the academy for her (purely theoretical) interest in serial killers, alien invasions, and rebellious AIs. Her upcoming academic publication is the Palgrave Handbook of Global Fantasy. She is the author of more than a hundred stories, several novellas, and five novels of dark fantasy and dark science fiction. Several of her stories appeared in Best of the Year anthologies. Her most recent collection is *My Lady of Plagues and Other Gothic Fairy Tales*. She is a member of HWA and can be found at https://www.citiesoflightanddarkness.com/ and on social media

Readers . . .

Thank you for reading *Nightwood*. We hope you enjoyed this novel

If you have a moment, please review *Nightwood* at the store where you bought it.

Help other readers by telling them why you enjoyed this book. No need to write an in-depth discussion. Even a single sentence will be greatly appreciated. Reviews go a long way to helping a book sell, and is great for an author's career. It'll also help us to continue publishing quality books. You can also share a photo of yourself holding this book with the hashtag #IGotMyCLPBook!

Thank you again for taking the time to journey with Crystal Lake Publishing.

Visit our Linktree page for a list of our social media platforms.
https://linktr.ee/CrystalLakePublishing

Our Mission Statement:

Since its founding in August 2012, Crystal Lake Publishing has quickly become one of the world's leading publishers of Dark Fiction and Horror books in print, eBook, and audio formats.

While we strive to present only the highest quality fiction and entertainment, we also endeavour to support authors along their writing journey. We offer our time and experience in non-fiction projects, as well as author mentoring and services, at competitive prices.

With several Bram Stoker Award wins and many other wins and nominations (including the HWA's Specialty Press Award), Crystal Lake Publishing puts integrity, honor, and respect at the forefront of our publishing operations.

We strive for each book and outreach program we spearhead to not only entertain and touch or comment on issues that affect our readers, but also to strengthen and support the Dark Fiction field and its authors.

Not only do we find and publish authors we believe are destined for greatness, but we strive to work with men and woman who endeavour to be decent human beings who care more for others than themselves, while still being hard working, driven, and passionate artists and storytellers.

Crystal Lake Publishing is and will always be a beacon of what passion and dedication, combined with overwhelming teamwork and respect, can accomplish. We endeavour to know each and every one of our readers, while building personal relationships with our authors, reviewers, bloggers, podcasters, bookstores, and libraries.

We will be as trustworthy, forthright, and transparent as any business can be, while also keeping most of the headaches away from our authors, since it's our job to solve the problems so they can stay in a creative mind. Which of course also means paying our authors.

We do not just publish books, we present to you worlds within your world, doors within your mind, from talented authors who sacrifice so much for a moment of your time.

There are some amazing small presses out there, and through collaboration and open forums we will continue to support other presses in the goal of helping authors and showing the world what quality small presses are capable of accomplishing. No one wins when a small press goes down, so we will always be there to support hardworking, legitimate presses and their authors. We don't see Crystal Lake as the best press out there, but we will always strive to be the best, strive to be the most interactive and grateful, and even blessed press around. No matter what happens over time, we will also take our mission very seriously while appreciating where we are and enjoying the journey.

What do we offer our authors that they can't do for themselves through self-publishing?

We are big supporters of self-publishing (especially hybrid publishing), if done with care, patience, and planning. However, not every author has the time or inclination to do market research, advertise, and set up book launch strategies. Although a lot of authors are successful in doing it all, strong small presses will always be there for the authors who just want to do what they do best: write.

What we offer is experience, industry knowledge, contacts and trust built up over years. And due to our strong brand and trusting fanbase, every Crystal Lake Publishing book comes with weight of respect. In time our fans begin to trust our judgment and will try a new author purely based on our support of said author.

With each launch we strive to fine-tune our approach, learn from our mistakes, and increase our reach. We continue to assure our authors that we're here for them and that we'll carry the weight of the launch and dealing with third parties while they focus on their strengths—be it writing, interviews, blogs, signings, etc.

We also offer several mentoring packages to authors that include knowledge and skills they can use in both traditional and self-publishing endeavours.

We look forward to launching many new careers.

This is what we believe in. What we stand for. This will be our legacy.

Welcome to Crystal Lake Publishing—
Tales from the Darkest Depths.

www.ingramcontent.com/pod-product-compliance
Lightning Source LLC
Chambersburg PA
CBHW060858210726
48293CB00006B/1857